GW01090456

Four St

Vier Erzählungen

E. T. A. HOFFMANN

A Dual-Language Book

Edited and Translated by
STANLEY APPELBAUM

DOVER PUBLICATIONS, INC.
Mineola, New York

Copyright

Bibliographical Note

This Dover edition, first published in 2003, includes unabridged German texts of four stories by E. T. A. Hoffmann, reprinted from standard editions (see Introduction for details on the earliest publications). The German texts are accompanied by new English translations of all four works by Stanley Appelbaum, who also wrote the Introduction and provided explanatory footnotes in English.

Library of Congress Cataloging-in-Publication Data

Hoffmann, E. T. A. (Ernst Theodor Amadeus), 1776–1822.
   [Short stories. English. Selections]
   Four stories = Vier Erzählungen / E.T.A. Hoffmann ; edited and translated by Stanley Appelbaum.
       p. cm.
   "A dual-language book."
   Contents: Rat Krespel—Die Bergwerke zu Falun—Das Fräulein von Scuderi—Des Vetters Eckfenster.
   ISBN 0-486-42696-3 (pbk.)
   I. Title: Vier Erzählungen. II. Appelbaum, Stanley. III. Title.

PT2361.E4A14 2003
833'.6—dc21

                                                                    2003043779

Manufactured in the United States of America
Dover Publications, Inc., 31 East 2nd Street, Mineola, N.Y. 11501

INTRODUCTION

Hoffmann's Life and Literary Works

Hoffmann was a man of many talents. As a writer of opera, ballet, incidental music to plays, songs, and chamber works, he has been called the first Romantic composer (though his music was more old-fashioned than that of, say, Carl Maria von Weber, his junior by ten years). As a music critic, Hoffmann was decidedly ahead of his time, always appreciating and encouraging the best work (in 1820 Beethoven thanked him for his many years of moral support). As an artist, Hoffmann painted stage scenery and portraits, and was an exceptional cartoonist and illustrator. But this Introduction will concentrate on his most special legacy to mankind: his fiction, often imitated and extremely influential on writers, composers, and visual artists all over the world. He is, of course, particularly esteemed as a master of the eerie and uncanny.

Hoffmann was born in Königsberg, East Prussia,[1] in 1776, the son of a prominent lawyer, and baptized Ernst Theodor Wilhelm; he changed Wilhelm to Amadeus in 1804 out of reverence for Mozart. When his parents divorced in 1778, he was left in his mother's care (his father died in 1797). From 1781 or 1782 to 1792 he attended elementary school; his musical talent was in evidence by at least 1787. In 1792 he was matriculated as a law student at the University of Königsberg,[2] and by 1795, at least, he was utilizing all his varied talents (his juvenile novels are lost).

In 1796 his mother died, and a messy romantic involvement led to his move to Glogau in Lower Silesia (since 1945, Głogów in Poland), where he became engaged to a cousin in 1798. (After moving to Glogau, he made only occasional trips to his native city, the last of which was in 1804.) Also in 1798, he traveled to Berlin as a candidate for a judgeship; he was assigned as an assistant judge to the city of

---

1. East Prussia, on the Baltic, formerly the easternmost German province, was punitively partitioned after World War II. The area including Königsberg was annexed to Russia, and the city was renamed Kaliningrad. 2. He was not particularly interested in the lectures of the university's most famous professor, Immanuel Kant (1724–1804), also a native of Königsberg.

iii

Posen (Poznań) in 1800. (Poland had been partitioned, and a large portion of it was under Prussian administration.) Caricatures of his superiors, which they found unfunny, caused his rustication to the tedious little town of Plock,[3] about fifty miles northwest of Warsaw. There he broke off his engagement and married a local woman, unintellectual and self-effacing but a true helpmate through thick and thin (financial and psychological) ever afterward.

In 1803, a piece by Hoffmann was first published, in a Berlin periodical. In 1804 he was transferred to the much jollier and more congenial Warsaw, where he conducted an amateur orchestra. His only child, Cäcilia, was born there in 1805, but lived only two years. In 1806 Napoleon invaded the German lands, abolishing the thousand-year-old Holy Roman Empire and replacing local rulers with his own puppets. Hoffmann refused to work for the French, and was out of a job.

His sojourn in Berlin in 1807 and the first half of 1808 was the most trying period in his life; he was often close to starvation. A successful test composition, as a prerequisite for a musical post in Bamberg, led to an extended stay (1808–1813) in that southern city in the Upper Franconia region of Bavaria, where there are still various mementos of Hoffmann's sojourn, including a charming house-museum. There he composed, conducted, sang tenor, and painted stage sets, but was plagued by cabals and often endured privations (from 1809 to 1812 he unsuccessfully tried to supplement his income as a dealer of music published by Breitkopf & Härtel in Leipzig). His Leipzig connections made possible his debut as a music critic, and, also in 1809, he wrote his first important story (on a musical subject), "Ritter Gluck" (Chevalier Gluck—the famous composer).

Still in Bamberg, Hoffmann became enamored (for life) with his teenaged singing pupil Julie Marc (1796–1865); her engagement in 1812 to an unpromising boor was a devastating blow to him. Also by 1812, Hoffmann was reading heavily in the best early-Romantic German authors, especially Novalis (Friedrich von Hardenberg, 1772–1801) and Ludwig Tieck (1773–1853), and had made arrangements whereby Friedrich de la Motte Fouqué (1777–1843) would personally adapt his own masterpiece, the 1811 story, "Undine," as a libretto for a Hoffmann opera (which Hoffmann worked on for the next couple of years).

In 1813 and 1814 Hoffmann shuttled between Leipzig and Dresden,

---

3. Sometimes spelled Plozk in German. In Polish: Płock, pronounced approximately "pwutsk."

conducting operas and viewing at close range the street fighting that marked the end of Napoleon's stranglehold over Germany (Hoffmann was even wounded by a ricocheting bullet). In those two years he also wrote the story that some consider his best, "Der goldene Topf" (The Golden Pot; published in 1814 as Volume 3 of the *Fantasiestücke*). In 1814, Hoffmann was fired for insubordination, and moved back to Berlin permanently. There, his seniority having accrued even during the Napoleonic interregnum, he was attached to the supreme court. The same year was his big literary breakthrough, when the first three volumes of his *Fantasiestücke in Callots Manier* (Imaginative Pieces in the Manner of Callot) were published. That year he also began writing his long novel *Die Elixiere des Teufels* (The Devil's Elixirs; published in 1815 and 1816 as Volume 4 of the *Fantasiestücke*).

The success of the *Fantasiestücke* elicited numerous requests for story contributions to annual literary almanacs between 1815 and 1819. Many of his best tales were originally published in that fashion, being assembled into collected volumes later. In 1816, when Hoffmann enjoyed his greatest musical triumph, the Berlin world premiere of *Undine*, he also received an official position as a criminal jurist. In 1817 his story collection *Nachtstücke* (Night Pieces) was published; the first story in the first part was the brilliant "Der Sandmann" (The Sandman).[4]

Between 1819 and 1821 the *Serapionsbrüder* volumes were published (see the beginning of the next section of this Introduction, "The Individual Stories," and the subsections on the first three stories). Beginning in 1819, Hoffmann suffered increasingly from a variety of ailments, including stomach trouble, gout, and extreme nervousness. Yet his legal work never suffered (he was specifically commended for not allowing his extracurricular authorship to interfere with scrupulous and intelligent attention to his job),[5] and he turned out a vast amount of fiction, not hastily, but with much research and rewriting. Though Hoffmann was a winebibber, and was perpetually in financial straits, the old myth of his drunken bohemian existence is untenable. The major works of his last years were *Lebensansichten des Katers*

---

4. This story appears in German and English in Dover's dual-language volume *Five Great German Short Stories,* Appelbaum, ed., 1993 (0-486-27619-8).   5. He was impartial and even liberal as a judge and jurist. For instance, though he disagreed with many of the actions and aims of Friedrich Ludwig Jahn (1778–1852), the founder of gymnastic groups and a political agitator (Hoffmann was probably thinking of Jahn when he mentioned rabid "superpatriotic ascetics" near the end of the story "My Cousin's Corner Window"), he tried his best to end, or at least ameliorate, Jahn's imprisonment, which began in 1819.

Murr (The Tomcat Murr's Views on Life; 1820), *Prinzessin Brambilla*
(1821), and *Meister Floh* (Master Flea; 1822).

In 1821 Hoffmann was transferred to an appeals section of his court,
where his only duties were writing reports. Late that year, his terminal
illness, most likely locomotor ataxia, set in; by 1822 his creeping paral-
ysis made it necessary for him to dictate his stories, and prevented him
from showing up to answer malfeasance charges stemming from a
satirical passage in *Meister Floh.* After many agonies, hinted at in his
last great story, "My Cousin's Corner Window," he died on June 25.

Hoffmann is considered to be a representative of the late-Romantic
period in German literature, and even of the incipient Biedermeier.
His writings display typically Romantic ardor and sentimentality,
though his style can be somewhat old-fashioned, crotchety, and en-
dearingly pedantic, featuring long, involved sentences.[6] He is both a
realistic observer of life and an eccentric (and a connoisseur of ec-
centricity); he is a psychologist with a special interest in the insane,
and a philosopher preaching harmony with Nature; a liberal in politics
and social life, with a dislike of philistinism; a humorist and a master
of irony; and, above all, a visionary yearning for a fairyland that can reveal its existence amid the most ordinary everyday scenes, lending
temporary life even to inanimate objects.

Charming as the music is in works like Delibes's *Coppélia* (1870),
Offenbach's *Les contes d'Hoffmann* (1881), and Tchaikovsky's
Nutcracker (1892), they offer only a highly diluted notion of
Hoffmann's art. His truest disciples and emulators are literary men: in
America, Irving, Hawthorne (especially in "Rappacini's Daughter"),
and Poe; in Russia, Dostoyevsky (he was also greatly admired by
Pushkin, Gogol, and Turgenev); in France, where there was a verita-
ble Hoffmann craze, by Nodier, Balzac, Gautier, and many others.

The Individual Stories

Since the first three stories in this Dover volume appear in the collection *Die Serapionsbrüder,* and are given here in the wording, and
in the sequence, that they have in that collection, a short notice of it
seems advisable.

In 1818 the distinguished Berlin publisher Georg Reimer re-

---

6. Technical features include a liking for asyndeton (use of a comma instead of
"and") and the habit of omitting the auxiliary component of compound verbs.

quested Hoffmann to assemble into volumes for him the stories that had been appearing scattered in almanacs for a few years. The final collection, with material written between 1813 and 1821, including some new stories, appeared in four volumes (1819, 1819, 1820, and 1821) under the title (original spelling here only:) *Die Serapions-Brüder. Gesammelte Erzählungen und Mährchen* (The Serapion Brethren. Collected Stories and Tales).

With a few writer friends, Hoffmann had founded a *Seraphinen-Orden* (Order of Seraphim; also the name of a Swedish order of knighthood) in 1814, shortly after his definitive move to Berlin. In the frame story to his collection—inspired by Boccaccio's *Decameron* (ca. 1350), Marguerite d'Angoulême's *Heptameron* (1559), and, most recently, Tieck's *Phantasus* (1812–1816)—he converted this name to an order of Serapion, consisting of six members (one of them, Theodor, modeled on himself, and at least three of the others on personal writer friends) who tell and read one another stories, and frequently discuss the stories before and/or after they are told.

The first reunion of these friends, after many years apart, takes place on November 14 (1818), the day of the Saint Serapion who was martyred under the Roman emperor Decius (reigned 249–251). Before the stories collected from almanacs begin, one of the friends narrates his encounter with a mad ex-diplomat, living in the woods near Bamberg, who has assumed the identity of that saint; he is now perfectly adjusted to his environment, and "curing" him would be an undesirable interference. (Hoffmann had made a special study of mental patients while at Bamberg.) The members of the tiny society later enunciate the "Serapiontic principle": that a true poet must *really see* the life around him.

"Councilor Krespel." This very popular Hoffmann story is the basis of Act Three of Offenbach's opera. The term *Rat* (older spelling, *Rath*), rendered "councilor" here, refers to civil servants or courtiers of varying ranks; sometimes it is merely a courtesy title. The story, written in 1816, bears no title either in the *Serapionsbrüder* or in the almanac where it first appeared: *Das Frauentaschenbuch für das Jahr 1818* (Ladies' Almanac for 1818; published autumn 1817), edited by the above-mentioned Fouqué and published in Nuremberg by Johann Leonhard Schrag (1783–1858). In the almanac it was framed by a letter to Fouqué, dated September 22, 1816, in which Hoffmann expresses his regret at being too busy to supply a story for the almanac dated 1817, but adds in a postscript that he has had a vision of the eccentric

Krespel, and goes on to tell the story, beginning: "Dieser Rat Krespel war nämlich einer der . . ." (the beginning of the Dover text, which dispenses, however, with "Dieser" [This] and "nämlich" [you see,]).

In the *Serapionsbrüder*, the tale is the first regular story inserted into Section 1 of Volume I (1819). Hoffmann adapted the almanac version by omitting all the direct addresses to Fouqué and making a number of small changes. He leads into the story by a discussion of folly and madness following the pseudo-Serapion anecdote. The Theodor character then says: "I'm thinking just now about a man whose madcap humor actually caused half the town where he lived to denounce him as insane, despite the fact that no one could be as little prone to true, decided madness as that very man. The way I met him is just as oddly comical as the situation I found him in later, touching and affecting the depths of the soul. I'd like to tell you about it, in order to bring about a gentle transition from madness, through melancholy, to completely healthy reason. I merely fear, especially since music must play a big part in it, that you will . . . reproach me . . . for adding fantastic trimmings to my subject and inserting a great deal of my own invention, which won't be the case at all. . . . The man I wish to talk about is none other than Councilor Krespel in H—." Then the story begins exactly as in the almanac version, including the "Dieser" and the "nämlich." The Dover version of the opening sentence (like the addition of the title) is a standard feature of anthologized publications out of the context of the *Serapionsbrüder.* (It is after this story that the above-mentioned "Serapiontic principle" is enunciated in the course of the brethren's discussion.)

All three of the inserted stories in Section 1, Volume I, of the collection concern music; in a way, they represent the closing of Hoffmann's first period as a writer of fiction, in which musical subjects predominate (he had moved into fiction when he became a music critic). The title character of "Councilor Krespel" was inspired by Johann Bernhard Crespel (1747–1815), an eccentric friend of the Goethe family who designed his own house. But the protagonist is chiefly based on Hoffmann himself; highly autobiographical (and clearly reflecting the author's hopeless love for Julie Marc), the story has been considered typical of his early, "confessional" works, like many of those in the *Fantasiestücke.*

"The Mines at Falun." Written in December 1818[7] and very early

---

7. In a letter of December 15, 1818, Hoffmann requests reference books on Sweden.

1819, this story did not appear in any almanac, but was first published in the *Serapionsbrüder*, Vol. I (1819), Section 2, where it precedes Hoffmann's most celebrated story, "Nußknacker und Mausekönig" (Nutcracker and Mouse King). "The Mines of Falun" is presented as a story that the Serapion brother Theodor (Hoffmann himself) has just completed, and which he reads aloud to his friends. The discussion after the story is lively and includes amusing self-criticism: one friend asserts that, for all its imaginative trimmings, the story isn't as good as the simple report of the discovery of a well-preserved corpse at Falun, as told in Hoffmann's source (see next paragraph); another friend complains about all the specialized mining terms, which only experts will understand, and about the many Swedish words, which can be confusing.[8] But the friends concede that Theodor has written a good description of a split personality.

The source report, about a young man's body recognized by his former fiancée fifty years after his death, came from a book very dear to Hoffmann, *Ansichten von der Nachtseite der Naturwissenschaft* (Views of the Dark Side of the Natural Sciences; 1808), by Gotthilf Heinrich von Schubert (1780–1860). In addition, the above-mentioned Novalis had written a dithyramb to the fascination of mining in his uncompleted novel *Heinrich von Ofterdingen* (1800; published 1802 with additions by the above-mentioned Tieck).

In this Dover translation, very possibly for the first time in English, virtually every Swedish name and word has been either verified or changed to its correct modern form,[9] except for the names of the characters ("Pehrson," really a surname and not a given name, would most likely be Persson today, unless traditional spellings are retained in one's family; and "Eric Olawsen" is more likely to be Erik Olafsson). Some geographical data may be helpful:

Göteborg (often called Gothenburg in English), on the west coast of Sweden, is the nation's chief port and second largest city (after Stockholm); it is situated at the mouth of the Götaälv (Göta river). The Klippan area, now in the southwestern part of the city, formerly

---

8. Especially *öl* (beer; cognate with English "ale"), which means "oil" in German.
9. The only geographical name that eluded research is "Guffrisberg." "Bergfrälse" wasn't found in any dictionary, but it is clearly a *frälse* associated with mining; *frälse*, roughly defined in the text itself (and generally rendered as "franchise" in the translation), is connected with the word for "free," and originally meant a property free of taxes: the holder performed services for the crown, instead. "The word *masmästare* (which appears in Hoffmann's text as the Swedish-German hybrid "Masmeister") apparently means "foundry owner," but it's doubtful whether Hoffmann understood it that way, and the translation uses the more neutral "mine owner."

contained the East India docks, which were especially active in the 18th century. Masthuggstorget means literally "mast-cutting [market] square." The Haga area, due south of the fortified town, was Göteborg's first working-class suburb.

Falun (in pronunciation, the stress is on the first syllable) is the administrative center of Kopparberg (Copper Mine) county, which is more or less equivalent to the former province Dalarna (often called Dalecarlia in English), a hotbed of traditional Swedish folklore and folk arts. Copper was being extracted at Falun by the 11th century, and its mining company was the earliest Swedish industrial company with shareholders; the mines were worked until 1992. In the 17th century Falun was the second largest town in Sweden, and the world's foremost copper producer. The famous cave-in occurred on June 24, 1687 (the St. John's Day of the story); the resulting Great Pit is still a tourist attraction. The acid in the water at the bottom of the mines preserves organic matter, and Schubert's report was based on historical fact (though the man in question had been buried only 42 years). The church (mentioned in the story) was built in the 14th century and altered up to the 18th, and is the oldest building in town. The main square of Falun is now Stora Torget (Big Market).

Närke is a district in central Sweden, now a part of Örebro county. Gävle (old spelling, Gefle) is a town on the east coast, to the east of Falun. Ornäs is a town near Falun.

Mining mythology has been recorded from all over central and eastern Europe; in Hoffmann's day it appeared prominently in the folksong collection *Des Knaben Wunderhorn* (The Boy's Magic Horn; 1806–1808) and in the Grimm Brothers' *Deutsche Sagen* (German Legends; 1816–1818). In German lands, supernatural miners are frequently dwarfs, like those in "Snow White" and Wagner's *Rheingold*. A mine spirit in the form of a beautiful woman also occurs in the legends from the Urals on which Prokofiev based his ballet *The Stone Flower.*

Hoffmann's story features the close interpenetration of real and fantasy worlds. As in "The Sandman," the reader is intentionally left uncertain as to whether the hero is actually undergoing his weird experiences or just imagining them. The series of visions in the story not only indicates the hero's more than ambiguous attitude toward the women in his life; it also establishes brilliantly the correspondences between the two poles of his existence, the sea and the mine.

In 1842, Richard Wagner considered basing an opera on this story, but didn't proceed. He did, however, make use of plot elements from other Hoffmann stories in both *Tannhäuser* and *Die Meistersinger.*

"Mademoiselle de Scudéry." Written from March[10] to June of 1818, this story was first published in September 1819 in *Das Taschenbuch der Liebe und Freundschaft gewidmet für das Jahr 1820* (The Almanac Dedicated to Love and Friendship; 1820 Edition). This almanac was edited by Stephan Schütze (1771–1839) and published by Friedrich Wilmans (1764–1830) and his brother Heinrich in Frankfurt am Main. The public, fond of crime and horror stories at the time, made this edition of the brothers' annual spectacularly profitable, and in 1820 the brothers sent Hoffmann a bonus of fifty bottles of vintage Rüdesheimer wine.

The story was inserted, with no appreciable alterations, into Volume III, Section 6 (1820), of *Die Serapionsbrüder.* The situation there is as follows: one "brother" has just had a play produced, and an anecdote about Voltaire awaiting opening-night notices leads to a mention of his historical work *Le siècle de Louis XIV* (The Era of Louis XIV; first published, in Berlin [!], in 1751).

Oddly enough (and this is touched on briefly in the discussion after the story in *Die Serapionsbrüder*),[11] the direct inspiration for the story came from a treatise on the German mastersingers which Johann Christoph Wagenseil (1663–1708) appended to his 1697 chronicle of Nuremberg titled *De sacri Romani imperii libera civitate Noribergensi commentatio* (Commentary on the Free City Nuremberg of the Holy Roman Empire).[12] Wagenseil had visited Mlle de Scudéry in Paris, and she had told him about her verses (quoted in the story), which seemed to favor the robbers who were preying on courtiers; as a joke, a noblewoman had sent her a gift that purportedly came from the grateful robbers.

Hoffmann derived his information on *l'affaire des poisons* and on many historical characters (and even the surnames of the purely fictional characters) from Voltaire's book, but he used various other reference works as well. The *affaire des poisons,* actually a series of *affaires,* went on for years: the Marquise de Brinvilliers began her murders in 1666; the *chambre ardente* was instituted in 1679; "la Voisin" was executed in 1680. It is said that the king broke off the investigation after Mme de Montespan became implicated.[13]

10. In a letter of March 28, 1818, Hoffmann requests reference books.   11. That discussion also refers to a Venetian shoemaker who robbed and killed to gain money that he donated to St. Roch.   12. Hoffmann had read Wagenseil's treatise while preparing his slightly earlier story "Meister Martin der Küfner und seine Gesellen" (Master Martin the Cooper and His Journeymen).   13. Hoffmann's account of the terror in Paris, with people afraid to open a package for fear of inhaling poison, had its counterpart in the American anthrax scare in the fall of 2001.

A few words about the Parisian geography in the story: The palace where the heroine visits the king and Mme de Maintenon is the Louvre; the transfer of the court to Versailles began in 1678, and was far from complete in 1680, when the story takes place. The rue St-Honoré, where Mlle de Scudéry lives, runs north of the Louvre and the Tuileries Gardens. There is no rue Nicaise in Paris, at least at the present day; the one in the story is clearly within easy walking distance of the rue St-Honoré, and most of the other places mentioned aren't far away, either. The Place de Grève has been called the Place de l'Hôtel-de-Ville since 1806; on the right bank of the Seine, just opposite Notre-Dame, it was the scene of executions from 1310 to 1830. The hospital called the Hôtel-Dieu was the first (12th century) of the three by that name that have been built near Notre-Dame; the first one occupied both banks near the cathedral. The Pont Neuf cuts across the western tip of the Ile de la Cité, on which the cathedral and the Conciergerie prison are located. The other prison mentioned, the Bastille, is somewhat to the east of this area. St-Eustache is near the eastern end of the rue St-Honoré (in the former Les Halles area). The only areas in the story that are somewhat more remote are the fashionable Faubourg St-Germain (left bank, opposite the Tuileries; more or less the 6th arrondissement) and the folksy Faubourg St-Martin (northeastern Paris; site of the Gare du Nord, Gare de l'Est, and Canal St-Martin; more or less the 10th arrondissement).

The names of historical characters, extensively mangled in the German text, are spelled correctly in this edition, very possibly for the first time in an English translation. The principal real people (or real families), in proper alphabetical order, are:

Arnauld d'Andilly: a prominent 17th-century family connected with Jansenism at Port-Royal; no trace of a Pierre.

Argenson, Marc-René de Voyer, comte et marquis d' (1652–1721): in actuality he *replaced* La Reynie as chief of police and served in that capacity from 1697 to 1718.

Boileau-Despréaux, Nicolas (1636–1711): satirical poet, champion of the Greco-Roman authors in the famous "dispute between ancients and moderns."

Bouillon, Marie-Anne Mancini, duchesse de (1646–1714): a patroness of La Fontaine; involved in the Voisin poison scandal.

Brinvilliers, Marie-Madeleine d'Aubray, marquise de (1630–1676): poisoner; she did not manage to kill her sister; her capture at Liège is a true story, including the participation of a Desgrais, an officer in the Parisian mounted constabulary.

Desgrais: see preceding entry.

Dreux d'Aubray (first name unavailable; died 1666): father of Mme de Brinvilliers, murdered by her; chief magistrate in civil cases.

Fontanges, Marie-Angélique de Scoraille de Roussille, duchesse de (1661–1681): a rival of Mme de Montespan for the favor of the king.

Glaser, Christoph (died 1678): Swiss chemist involved with Mme de Brinvilliers and held under detention for a long time.

Godin de Sainte-Croix (first name unavailable; died 1672): poisoner.

Harlay de Champvallon, François de (1625–1695): archbishop of Paris from 1671.

Henrietta Anne (1644–1670): daughter of Charles I of England, sister-in-law of Louis XIV; it was rumored that she died of poison.

La Chapelle, Jean de (1655–1723): author; his first plays date from 1680 (see the story).

La Fare, de: there was a marquis and poet by that name (given names: Charles-Auguste; 1644–1712) who may be the man intended by Hoffmann.

La Reynie, Gabriel-Nicolas de (1625–1709): the first chief of Parisian police in the reign of Louis XIV (appointed 1667).

La Vallière, Louise de La Baume Le Blanc, duchesse de (1644–1710): became mistress of the king in 1661, retaining his favor even after the beginning of his liaison with Mme de Montespan; entered a convent in 1671, was recalled; permanently a nun from 1674.

Lesage: a poisoner.

Louis XIV (1638–1715): king of France.

Louvois, François-Michel Le Tellier, marquis de (1639–1691): minister of war; his ambition led him to encroach on many other departments of the government.

Luxembourg, François-Henri de Montmorency-Bouteville, duc de (1628–1695): a marshal of the realm from 1675; spent 14 months in the Bastille, 1679–1680, as an alleged client of poisoners, but his military career continued strong afterwards.

Maintenon, Françoise d'Aubigné, marquise de (1635–1719): an austerely pious companion of Louis XIV, who married her morganatically in 1684; most of her influence postdates the events in the story.

Montansier: possibly an error for Montausier, Julie d'Angennes, duchesse de (1607–1671), a leading literary patroness; or else, since she died too early for the story, the next duchesse de Montausier.

Montespan, Françoise-Athénaïs de Rochechouart de Mortemart, marquise de (1640–1707): became the king's favorite in 1667.

Perrault, Claude (1613–1688): physician and architect; see also footnote 5 in the text of this story.

Racine, Jean (1639–1699): foremost French playwright of his generation.

Scudéry, Madeleine de (1607–1701): author of long, sentimental novels (*Clélie* was written between 1654 and 1660, and not at the time of the story, though Hoffmann does give her her correct age), a spokeswoman for the *précieuse* movement in mid-century literature (ridiculed by Molière); after 1670 her writings became moralistic.

Soissons: an old family in which the title of count was hereditary; one comtesse de Soissons was really implicated in the *affaire des poisons.*

Vigoureux: a female accomplice of "la Voisin."

"Voisin, la" (Catherine Deshayes; ca. 1640–1680): midwife, fortune-teller, sorceress, poisoner.

The story is an excellent example of Hoffmann's frequently used technique of beginning *in medias res* and later revealing earlier events in flashbacks. It has been called a detective story, but the mystery is only one element and is cleared up long before the end, and even then not by ratiocination but by an eyewitness report. It is through her faith in human goodness that Mlle de Scudéry succeeds in bringing the truth to light, and not through any skills as a Miss Marple. Hoffmann does frequently generate a lot of suspense, however. The story is helped along by his training as an investigator of criminal cases, and by his interest in mental pathology, which is very well described ("the —— made me do it"). The king figures as a *deus ex machina,* as kings do in such 17th-century French plays as Corneille's *Le Cid* and Molière's *Tartuffe* (these French authors were strongly influenced by the Golden Age Spanish plays that Hoffmann himself admired so much).

The most important musical work based on this story is the opera *Cardillac* (1926; revised 1952) by Paul Hindemith (1895–1963).

"My Cousin's Corner Window." Written by Hoffmann on his deathbed, in the first half of April 1822, this story was first published in the Berlin periodical *Der Zuschauer* (The Spectator) in the issues of April 23, 25, 27, and 30, and May 2 and 4 (Nos. 49–54). The editor of the journal was Johann Daniel Symanski (1789–1857); the publisher, T. Trautwein. In 1823, Hoffmann's friend Julius Eduard Hitzig (1780–1849; one of the real-life Serapion Brethren) included the story in his book *Aus Hoffmanns Leben und Nachlaß* (From Hoffmann's Life and Literary Remains; Berlin, Ferdinand Dümmler). In 1825,

Hitzig included it in *Die letzten Erzählungen von E. T. A. Hoffmann* (The Last Stories of E. T. A. H.; same city and publisher as the 1823 volume).

The form of the story was suggested to Hoffmann by the 1798–99 monologues "Scarron am Fenster" (Scarron[14] at the Window), by Karl Friedrich Kretschmann (1738–1809). The locale reflects the apartment that Hoffmann himself occupied in Berlin from 1815 till his death. The address was Taubenstrasse 31, at the corner of Charlottenstrasse, a very central location. Taubenstrasse is some four blocks south of Unter den Linden; Charlottenstrasse is one block east of Friedrichstrasse. The house was a little southeast of the Brandenburg Gate and a little southwest of the Museum Island. It faced the Schauspielhaus (Theater) am Gendarmenmarkt (the market square of the story; the present-day Konzerthaus Berlin now stands where, or near where, that theater stood). Other Berlin localities are mentioned only fleetingly in the story, and are identified in footnotes.

This story has been neglected by English translators, but German critics consider it a pinnacle of Hoffmann's achievement, his best late short work, and a lasting monument of German literature. It vividly restates the Serapiontic Principle of accurate (and creative) seeing. Always referred to in German as an *Erzählung,* and grouped with more fictional narratives, "My Cousin's Corner Window" is not strictly a "story," being devoid of a plot (except for the ups and downs of the cousin's attitude toward life). Though much of it is in the form of dialogue,[15] it might be classified as an essay with a highly individual form.

The work is intensely autobiographical, not only reflecting the author's actual home, illness, and character (and, perhaps, some of his real acquaintances), but also (and this is among its chief merits) allowing us a glimpse into his method of creating fanciful constructs out of minutely observed reality. The market—for the shut-in, and for the Serapion brother—is the world, and the world is a stage (symbolized by the omnipresent theater building). The story asks us to meditate on the conflict between reality and appearance, the relativity of truth, the role of the mind in creating one's personal universe, and the role of our senses in cognition. Hoffmann's alert craving for social justice is constantly brought into play.

His artist's eye is also much in evidence, as he lovingly details arti-

14. On Scarron, see footnote 1 in the text of this story, page 221.   15. In the dialogue passages, quotation marks are intentionally absent from the main speeches, as if in a play script.

cles of dress and appreciates the picturesqueness of the market with its shifting variety of views and groupings. At one moment, he even appears to be describing a pointillist painting! This story must surely have been an inspiration for such later visual depicters of the colorful Berlin populace as Theodor Hosemann (1807–1875), who drew illustrations for Hoffmann works, and Heinrich Zille (1858–1929).

The Nature of This Edition

The German texts are complete and reliable; as stated above, the first three stories are reprinted in their *Serapionsbrüder* form. Following standard practice, the spelling and punctuation have been regularized and changed to follow 20th-century usage. (We have not, however, adopted the spelling reforms that were instituted in Germany in 1996, and still use the "ß" instead of "ss" following short vowels.) In addition, much new paragraphing has been introduced; Hoffmann's original paragraphs are often very long, sometimes running for several pages.[16]

The new English translation is absolutely complete, without the smaller or larger abridgments, condensations, or omissions of sentences (or even longer passages) occasionally introduced into some earlier translations. The rendering is as accurate as possible, but appropriate English equivalents replace untranslatable German idioms, and certain tics of Hoffmann's (such as asyndeton) are not slavishly imitated. As mentioned earlier, Swedish and French names and terms have been corrected in the English (only).

---

16. In general, individual speeches in direct address haven't been broken into more paragraphs, even if somewhat lengthy. An exception has been made, however, for Olivier's gigantic expository speeches in "Mademoiselle de Scudéry," and, even there, directly reported speeches within his narrative are kept in one paragraph, no matter how long. Following clear precedents, the German text does not use quotation marks at the beginning of paragraphs within Olivier's speeches.

Contents

Rat Krespel

Rat Krespel war einer der allerwunderlichsten Menschen, die mir jemals im Leben vorgekommen. Als ich nach H. zog, um mich einige Zeit dort aufzuhalten, sprach die ganze Stadt von ihm, weil soeben einer seiner allernärrischsten Streiche in voller Blüte stand. Krespel war berühmt als gelehrter, gewandter Jurist und als tüchtiger Diplomatiker. Ein nicht eben bedeutender, regierender Fürst in Deutschland hatte sich an ihn gewandt, um ein Memorial auszuarbeiten, das die Ausführung seiner rechtsbegründeten Ansprüche auf ein gewisses Territorium zum Gegenstand hatte, und das er dem Kaiserhofe einzureichen gedachte.

Das geschah mit dem glücklichsten Erfolg, und da Krespel einmal geklagt hatte, daß er nie eine Wohnung seiner Bequemlichkeit gemäß finden könne, übernahm der Fürst, um ihn für jenes Memorial zu lohnen, die Kosten eines Hauses, das Krespel ganz nach seinem Gefallen aufbauen lassen sollte. Auch den Platz dazu wollte der Fürst nach Krespels Wahl ankaufen lassen; das nahm Krespel indessen nicht an, vielmehr blieb er dabei, daß das Haus in seinem vor dem Tor in der schönsten Gegend belegenen Garten erbaut werden solle. Nun kaufte er alle nur möglichen Materialien zusammen und ließ sie herausfahren; dann sah man ihn, wie er tagelang in seinem sonderbaren Kleide (das er übrigens selbst angefertigt nach bestimmten eigenen Prinzipien) den Kalk löschte, den Sand siebte, die Mauersteine in regelmäßige Haufen aufsetzte und so weiter. Mit irgendeinem Baumeister hatte er nicht gesprochen, an irgendeinen Riß nicht gedacht.

An einem guten Tage ging er indessen zu einem tüchtigen Maurermeister in H. und bat ihm, sich morgen bei Anbruch des Tages mit sämtlichen Gesellen und Burschen, vielen Handlangern und so weiter in dem Garten einzufinden und sein Haus zu bauen.

Councilor Krespel

Councilor Krespel was one of the most eccentric people I've ever met in my life. When I moved to H—— in order to spend some time there, the whole town was talking about him because one of his most ridiculous larks was in full swing just then. Krespel was renowned as a learned, skillful jurist and an excellent diplomat. One of the ruling princes in Germany, not a particularly important one, had called on him to draft a petition that would help him make good his legally grounded claims on a certain territory, a petition he would present to the imperial court.

This had the most happy success, and since Krespel had once complained that he could never find a home comfortable enough for him, the prince, as a reward for that petition, assumed the costs of a house which Krespel might order constructed exactly to his tastes. The prince was also willing to purchase the site for it wherever Krespel chose, but Krespel didn't accept that offer; instead, he insisted on building the house on his garden plot, situated outside of town in the loveliest neighborhood. Now he bought and assembled all possible materials and had them delivered to the site; then he could be seen day in and day out in his peculiar clothing (which he, incidentally, had tailored himself following his own firm principles) slaking lime, sifting sand, stacking the building stones in regular piles, and so on. He hadn't conferred with any architect or thought of any blueprints.

Instead of that, one fine day he visited a capable master mason in H—— and asked him to show up in his garden the next morning at dawn with all his journeymen and apprentices, a lot of hod carriers, and so forth, and begin building his house.

Der Baumeister fragte natürlicherweise nach dem Bauriß und erstaunte nicht wenig, als Krespel erwiderte, es bedürfe dessen gar nicht, und es werde sich schon alles, wie es sein solle, fügen. Als der Meister anderen Morgens mit seinen Leuten an Ort und Stelle kam, fand er einen im regelmäßigen Viereck gezogenen Graben, und Krespel sprach: «Hier soll das Fundament meines Hauses gelegt werden, und dann bitte ich die vier Mauern so lange heraufzuführen, bis ich sage, nun ist's hoch genug.»

«Ohne Fenster und Türen, ohne Quermauern?» fiel der Meister, wie über Krespels Wahnsinn erschrocken, ein.

«So wie ich Ihnen es sage, bester Mann», erwiderte Krespel sehr ruhig, «das übrige wird sich alles finden.» Nur das Versprechen reicher Belohnung konnte den Meister bewegen, den unsinnigen Bau zu unternehmen; aber nie ist einer lustiger geführt worden, denn unter beständigem Lachen der Arbeiter, die die Arbeitsstätte nie verließen, da es Speis und Trank vollauf gab, stiegen die vier Mauern unglaublich schnell in die Höhe, bis eines Tages Krespel rief: «Halt!»

Da schwieg Kell und Hammer, die Arbeiter stiegen von den Gerüsten herab, und indem sie den Krespel im Kreise umgaben, sprach es aus jedem lachenden Gesicht: «Aber wie nun weiter?»

«Platz!» rief Krespel, lief nach einem Ende des Gartens und schritt dann langsam auf sein Viereck los, dicht an der Mauer schüttelte er unwillig den Kopf, lief nach dem andern Ende des Gartens, schritt wieder auf das Viereck los und machte es wie zuvor. Noch einige Male wiederholte er das Spiel, bis er endlich, mit der spitzen Nase hart an die Mauer anlaufend, laut schrie: «Heran, heran, ihr Leute, schlagt mir die Tür ein, hier schlagt mir eine Tür ein!»

Er gab Länge und Breite genau nach Fuß und Zoll an, und es geschah, wie er geboten. Nun schritt er hinein in das Haus und lächelte wohlgefällig, als der Meister bemerkte, die Mauern hätten gerade die Höhe eines tüchtigen zweistöckigen Hauses. Krespel ging in dem innern Raum bedächtig auf und ab, hinter ihm her die Maurer mit Hammer und Hacke, und sowie er rief: «Hier ein Fenster, sechs Fuß hoch, vier Fuß breit! – dort ein Fensterchen, drei Fuß hoch, zwei Fuß breit!» so wurde es flugs eingeschlagen.

Gerade während dieser Operation kam ich nach H., und es war höchst ergötzlich anzusehen, wie hunderte von Menschen um den Garten herumstanden und allemal laut aufjubelten, wenn die Steine

Naturally this contractor asked for the plans and was not a little surprised when Krespel answered that there was no need for any and that everything would turn out the right way. When the master arrived at the site with his staff the next morning, he found that a ditch had been dug in the form of a perfect square, and Krespel said: "Here's where the foundations of my house are to be laid, and then I request you to keep building up the four walls until I say they're high enough."

"Without windows and doors? Without cross walls?" the master interjected, as if alarmed at Krespel's madness.

"Just as I tell you, my good man," Krespel replied with perfect calm, "all the rest will come out all right." It was only the promise of a substantial payment that was able to persuade the master to undertake that senseless construction; but no job was ever executed so merrily, because, accompanied by the incessant laughter of the workmen, who never left the construction site since there was plenty to eat and drink, the four walls rose with incredible speed, until one day Krespel shouted "Stop!"

Then the trowels and hammers fell silent, the workmen descended from the scaffolding, and while they formed a circle around Krespel, every laughing face seemed to ask: "Well, what's coming now?"

"Give me room!" Krespel shouted; he ran to one end of the garden and then paced slowly toward his square; right in front of the wall, he shook his head in displeasure, then he ran to the other end of the garden, again walked up to the square, and shook his head again. He repeated these actions a few more times until finally, running so close to the wall that he nearly touched it with his pointy nose, he yelled loudly: "This way, this way, people! Pierce the doorway for me, pierce a door for me here!"

He gave exact measurements in feet and inches for its height and width, and his orders were carried out. Now he stepped inside the house and smiled graciously when the contractor remarked that the walls were exactly as high as a good two-story house. Krespel walked to and fro thoughtfully in the interior space, the masons following him with hammers and picks, and whenever he shouted: "Here a window, six feet high, four feet wide! There a small window, three feet high, two feet wide!" they were broken through immediately.

It was precisely at this stage of the proceedings that I arrived in H——, and it was very entertaining to watch the hundreds of onlookers standing around the garden and raising loud hurrahs

herausflogen und wieder ein neues Fenster entstand, da, wo man es
gar nicht vermutet hatte. Mit dem übrigen Ausbau des Hauses und
mit allen Arbeiten, die dazu nötig waren, machte es Krespel auf
ebendieselbe Weise, indem sie alles an Ort und Stelle nach seiner au-
genblicklichen Angabe verfertigen mußten. Die Possierlichkeit des
ganzen Unternehmens, die gewonnene Überzeugung, daß alles am
Ende sich besser zusammengeschickt als zu erwarten stand, vorzüglich aber Krespels Freigebigkeit, die ihm freilich nichts kostete, erhielt aber alle bei guter Laune.

So wurden die Schwierigkeiten, die die abenteuerliche Art zu
bauen herbeiführen mußte, überwunden, und in kurzer Zeit stand ein
völlig eingerichtetes Haus da, welches von der Außenseite den tollsten Anblick gewährte, da kein Fenster dem andern gleich war und so
weiter, dessen innere Einrichtung aber eine ganz eigene Wohlbehaglichkeit erregte. Alle, die hineinkamen, versicherten dies, und ich
selbst fühlte es, als Krespel nach näherer Bekanntschaft mich hinein-
führte.

Bis jetzt hatte ich nämlich mit dem seltsamen Manne noch nicht
gesprochen, der Bau beschäftigte ihn so sehr, daß er nicht einmal sich
bei dem Professor M . . . Dienstags, wie er sonst pflegte, zum
Mittagessen einfand und ihm, als er ihn besonders eingeladen, sagen
ließ, vor dem Einweihungsfeste seines Hauses käm er mit keinem
Tritt aus der Tür. Alle Freunde und Bekannten verspitzten sich auf
ein großes Mahl, Krespel hatte aber niemanden gebeten als sämtliche
Meister, Gesellen, Bursche und Handlanger, die sein Haus erbaut. Er
bewirtete sie mit den feinsten Speisen; Maurerburschen fraßen rücksichtslos Rebhuhnpasteten, Tischlerjungen hobelten mit Glück an ge-
bratenen Fasanen, und hungrige Handlanger langten diesmal sich
selbst die vortrefflichsten Stücke aus dem Trüffelfrikassee zu.

Des Abends kamen die Frauen und Töchter, und es begann ein
großer Ball. Krespel walzte etwas weniges mit den Meisterfrauen,
setzte sich dann aber zu den Stadtmusikanten, nahm eine Geige und
dirigierte die Tanzmusik bis zum hellen Morgen.

Den Dienstag nach diesem Feste, welches den Rat Krespel als
Volksfreund darstellte, fand ich ihn endlich zu meiner nicht geringen
Freude bei dem Professor M. . . . Verwunderlicheres als Krespels
Betragen kann man nicht erfinden. Steif und ungelenk in der
Bewegung, glaubte man jeden Augenblick, er würde irgendwo
anstoßen, irgendeinen Schaden anrichten, das geschah aber nicht,
und man wußte es schon, denn die Hausfrau erblaßte nicht im min-
desten, als er mit gewaltigem Schritt um den mit den schönsten

every time the stones flew out and a new window was created in a place that no one had suspected. Krespel handled the rest of the construction, and all the work it entailed, in the same way; the men had to accomplish everything on the spot following the instructions he gave at that moment. But the amusing nature of the entire enterprise, the growing realization that, after all, everything was working out better than could be expected, and especially Krespel's generosity, which of course cost him nothing, kept everyone in good spirits.

And so the difficulties that such a reckless mode of building necessarily caused were overcome, and before long a fully equipped house stood on the site; from outside, it looked decidedly peculiar, because no two windows were the same, and so forth, but the interior arrangement inspired a unique feeling of comfort. Everyone who went in testified to that, and I myself felt it when Krespel and I became better acquainted and he invited me in.

You see, until then I had not yet conversed with that strange man, who had been so occupied with the construction that he didn't even show up for lunch at Professor M——'s house on Tuesdays, as he normally did; when he was given a special invitation to do so, he sent word to the professor that he wouldn't set a foot out of his door before his housewarming. All of his friends and acquaintances were looking forward eagerly to a great banquet, but Krespel had invited no one except all the master masons, journeymen, apprentices, and hod carriers who had built his house. He treated them to the finest food; apprentice masons unfeelingly devoured partridge pies, apprentice carpenters successfully planed away at roast pheasants, and hungry hod carriers now carried the choicest bits of the truffle fricassee to their mouths.

In the evening their wives and daughters arrived, and a big dance began. Krespel waltzed a little with the masters' wives, but then he sat in with the town musicians, picked up a fiddle, and led the dance music till the break of day.

On the Tuesday after that party, which had portrayed Councilor Krespel as a friend of the people, I finally had the great pleasure of finding him at Professor M——'s. No one can invent more eccentric behavior than Krespel's. Stiff and awkward in his movements, he made you think that at any moment he would bump into something and cause some damage, but that never happened, and you realized it wouldn't because the professor's wife didn't turn at all pale when he swerved with

Tassen besetzten Tisch sich herumschwang, als er gegen den bis zum
Boden reichenden Spiegel manövrierte, als er selbst einen Blumen-
topf von herrlich gemaltem Porzellan ergriff und in der Luft herum-
schwenkte, als ob er die Farben spielen lassen wolle.

Überhaupt besah Krespel vor Tische alles in des Professors Zimmer
auf das genaueste, er langte sich auch wohl, auf den gepolsterten
Stuhl steigend, ein Bild von der Wand herab und hing es wieder auf.
Dabei sprach er viel und heftig; bald (bei Tische wurde es auffallend)
sprang er schnell von einer Sache auf die andere, bald konnte er von
einer Idee gar nicht loskommen; immer sie wieder ergreifend, geriet
er in allerlei wunderliche Irrgänge und konnte sich nicht
wiederfinden, bis ihn etwas anderes erfaßte. Sein Ton war bald rauh
und heftig schreiend, bald leise gedehnt, singend, aber immer paßte
er nicht zu dem, was Krespel sprach.

Es war von Musik die Rede, man rühmte einen neuen Komponisten, da lächelte Krespel und sprach mit seiner leisen, singenden
Stimme: «Wollt ich doch, daß der schwarzgefiederte Satan den verruchten Tonverdreher zehntausend Millionen Klafter tief in den
Abgrund der Hölle schlüge!» – Dann fuhr er heftig und wild heraus:
«Sie ist ein Engel des Himmels, nichts als reiner, Gott geweihter
Klang und Ton! – Licht und Sternbild alles Gesanges!» – Und dabei
standen ihm Tränen in den Augen. Man mußte sich erinnern, daß vor
einer Stunde von einer berühmten Sängerin gesprochen worden.

Es wurde ein Hasenbraten verzehrt, ich bemerkte, daß Krespel die
Knochen auf seinem Teller vom Fleische sorglich säuberte und
genaue Nachfrage nach den Hasenpfoten hielt, die ihm des
Professors fünfjähriges Mädchen mit sehr freundlichem Lächeln
brachte. Die Kinder hatten überhaupt den Rat schon während des
Essens sehr freundlich angeblickt, jetzt standen sie auf und nahten
sich ihm, jedoch in scheuer Ehrfurcht und nur auf drei Schritte. «Was
soll denn das werden», dachte ich im Innern.

Das Dessert wurde aufgetragen; da zog der Rat ein Kistchen aus
der Tasche, in dem eine kleine stählerne Drehbank lag, die schrob er
sofort an den Tisch fest, und nun drechselte er mit unglaublicher
Geschicklichkeit und Schnelligkeit aus den Hasenknochen allerlei
winzig kleine Döschen und Büchschen und Kügelchen, die die
Kinder jubelnd empfingen. Im Moment des Aufstehens von der Tafel
fragte des Professors Nichte: «Was macht denn unsere Antonie, lieber
Rat?»

Krespel schnitt ein Gesicht, als wenn jemand in eine bittere
Pomeranze beißt und dabei aussehen will, als wenn er Süßes

mighty stride around the table set with the most beautiful cups, when he maneuvered toward the full-length mirror, or when he even seized a flowerpot of splendidly painted porcelain and shook it around in the air as if he wanted to let the colors play.

In general, before lunch Krespel inspected everything in the professor's room most minutely, even climbing onto the uphol- stered armchair, detaching a picture from the wall, and hanging it back up. All the while, he spoke a lot, and emphatically; at times (this became conspicuous during the meal) he would jump quickly from one topic to another, at other times he was unable to let go of one and the same notion; returning to it time and again, he would go off onto all sorts of odd tangents and couldn't find the thread of his thoughts again until a different one took hold of him. His tone was now rough, a violent shout, now a quiet singsong drawl, but it never suited his subject matter.

The conversation turned to music and a new composer was praised; then Krespel smiled and said in his quiet, singsong voice: "How I wish that black-feathered Satan would drive that atrocious note-twister ten billion fathoms deep into the abyss of hell!" Then he exclaimed violently and wildly: "She's an angel from heaven, nothing but pure sound and tone consecrated to God! The light and constellation of all singing!" And there were tears in his eyes as he said it. We had to think back and recall that, an hour earlier, we had been discussing a famous soprano.

We were eating roast hare, and I noticed that Krespel care- fully removed all the meat from the bones in his serving and made a special inquiry after the hare's paws, which the profes- sor's five-year-old girl brought him with a very friendly smile. In general, the children had bestowed very friendly glances on the councilor even during the meal; now they got up and ap- proached him, but with shy respect, keeping three paces away. "What will come of this?" I asked myself.

Dessert was served; then the councilor drew from his pocket a little case, which contained a small steel lathe; he immediately screwed it to the table, and then with incredible skill and speed he shaped the hare bones into all sorts of tiny little containers, boxes, and spheres, which the children received joyfully. Just as we arose from the table, the professor's niece asked: "How is our Antonie doing, dear councilor?"

Krespel grimaced like a man who had bitten into a sour or- ange and wants to look as if he's enjoying its sweetness; but that

genossen; aber bald verzog sich dies Gesicht zur graulichen Maske, aus der recht bitterer, grimmiger, ja, wie es mir schien, recht teuflischer Hohn herauslachte. «Unsere? Unsere liebe Antonie?» frug er mit gedehntem, unangenehm singenden Tone.

Der Professor kam schnell heran; in dem strafenden Blick, den er der Nichte zuwarf, las ich, daß sie eine Saite berührt hatte, die in Krespels Innerm widrig dissonieren mußte. «Wie steht es mit den Violinen?» frug der Professor recht lustig, indem er den Rat bei beiden Händen erfaßte. Da heiterte sich Krespels Gesicht auf, und er erwiderte mit seiner starken Stimme: «Vortrefflich, Professor, erst heute hab ich die treffliche Geige von Amati, von der ich neulich erzählte, welch ein Glücksfall sie mir in die Hände gespielt, erst heute habe ich sie aufgeschnitten. Ich hoffe, Antonie wird das übrige sorgfältig zerlegt haben.»

«Antonie ist ein gutes Kind», sprach der Professor.

«Ja wahrhaftig, das ist sie!» schrie der Rat, indem er sich schnell umwandte und, mit einem Griff Hut und Stock erfassend, schnell zur Türe hinaussprang. Im Spiegel erblickte ich, daß ihm helle Tränen in den Augen standen.

Sobald der Rat fort war, drang ich in den Professor, mir doch nur gleich zu sagen, was es mit den Violinen und vorzüglich mit Antonien für eine Bewandtnis habe. «Ach», sprach der Professor, «wie denn der Rat überhaupt ein ganz wunderlicher Mensch ist, so treibt er auch das Violinbauen auf ganz eigne tolle Weise.»

«Violinbauen?» fragte ich ganz erstaunt.

«Ja», fuhr der Professor fort, «Krespel verfertigt nach dem Urteil der Kenner die herrlichsten Violinen, die man in neuerer Zeit nur finden kann; sonst ließ er manchmal, war ihm eine besonders gelungen, andere darauf spielen, das ist aber seit einiger Zeit ganz vorbei. Hat Krespel eine Violine gemacht, so spielt er selbst eine oder zwei Stunden darauf, und zwar mit höchster Kraft, mit hinreißendem Ausdruck, dann hängst er sie aber zu den übrigen, ohne sie jemals wieder zu berühren oder von andern berühren zu lassen. Ist nur irgendeine Violine von einem alten vorzüglichen Meister aufzutreiben, so kauft sie der Rat um jeden Preis, den man ihm stellt. Ebenso wie seine Geigen, spielt er sie aber nur ein einziges Mal, dann nimmt er sie auseinander, um ihre innere Struktur genau zu untersuchen, und wirft, findet er nach seiner Einbildung nicht das, was er gerade suchte, die Stücke unmutig in einen großen Kasten, der schon voll Trümmer zerlegter Violinen ist.»

«Wie ist es aber mit Antonien?» frug ich schnell und heftig.

«Das ist nun», fuhr der Professor fort, «das ist nun eine Sache, die

grimace was soon distorted into a horrible expression that bespoke bitter, furious, and (it seemed to me) downright diabolical scorn. "Our? Our dear Antonie?" he asked in a drawling, unpleasantly singsong tone.

The professor was on the spot at once; from the reproachful glance he cast at his niece I could tell that she had touched a chord that must necessarily create an unpleasant dissonance in Krespel's mind. "How are things with your violins?" the professor asked very cheerfully, taking hold of the councilor's two hands. Then Krespel's face became serene, and he replied in his louder tone: "Excellent, professor. That wonderful Amati violin, which, as I told you, recently came into my hands by a great stroke of luck—just today I cut it open. I hope that Antonie has carefully disassembled the rest of it."

"Antonie is a good girl," said the professor.

"She is indeed!" the councilor cried, turning around swiftly, seizing his hat and stick, and quickly leaping out the door. In the mirror I caught sight of bright tears in his eyes.

As soon as the councilor left, I urged the professor to tell me at once the story of the violins, and especially all about Antonie. "Ah," said the professor, "just as the councilor is a most eccentric person in general, so he conducts his violin making in an odd way that's all his own."

"Violin making?" I asked in great amazement.

"Yes," the professor continued, "in the judgment of connoisseurs Krespel makes the most splendid violins that are to be found nowadays; in the past, when one turned out especially well, he'd sometimes let other people play it, but that hasn't been the case for quite a while now. After Krespel completes a violin, he himself plays it for an hour or two—and as passionately as he can, with captivating expressiveness—then he hangs it up with the rest, never touching it again or allowing anyone else to touch it. If some violin by some outstanding old master comes on the market, the councilor buys it at any price that's asked. Just as with his own violins, however, he plays it only once, then he takes it apart to examine its inner structure thoroughly; if he doesn't find what his imagination led him to look for, he angrily tosses the pieces into a big chest that's already filled with the wreckage of dissected violins."

"But what about Antonie?" I asked quickly and impetuously.

"Well, that," the professor continued, "that is a matter that

den Rat mich könnte in höchstem Grade verabscheuen lassen, wenn
ich nicht überzeugt wäre, daß bei dem im tiefsten Grunde bis zur
Weichlichkeit gutmütigen Charakter des Rates es damit eine besondere geheime Bewandtnis haben müsse. Als vor mehreren Jahren
der Rat hierher nach H. kam, lebte er anachoretisch mit einer alten
Haushälterin in einem finstern Hause auf der —straße. Bald erregte
er durch seine Sonderbarkeiten die Neugierde der Nachbarn, und
sogleich, als er dies merkte, suchte und fand er Bekanntschaften.
Eben wie in meinem Hause gewöhnte man sich überall so an ihn,
daß er unentbehrlich wurde. Seines rauhen Äußeren unerachtet,
liebten ihn sogar die Kinder, ohne ihn zu belästigen, denn trotz aller
Freundlichkeit behielten sie eine gewisse scheue Ehrfurcht, die ihn
vor allem Zudringlichen schützte. Wie er die Kinder durch allerlei
Künste zu gewinnen weiß, haben Sie heute gesehen. Wir hielten ihn
alle für einen Hagestolz, und er widersprach dem nicht. Nachdem
er sich einige Zeit hier aufgehalten, reiste er ab, niemand wußte
wohin, und kam nach einigen Monaten wieder. Den andern Abend
nach seiner Rückkehr waren Krespels Fenster ungewöhnlich er-
leuchtet, schon dies machte die Nachbarn aufmerksam, bald vernahm man aber die ganz wunderherrliche Stimme eines
Frauenzimmers, von einem Pianoforte begleitet. Dann wachten die
Töne einer Violine auf und stritten in regem, feurigen Kampfe mit
der Stimme. Man hörte gleich, daß es der Rat war, der spielte. – Ich
selbst mischte mich unter die zahlreiche Menge, die das wundervolle Konzert vor dem Hause des Rates versammelt hatte, und ich
muß Ihnen gestehen, daß gegen die Stimme, gegen den ganz eigenen, tief in das Innerste dringenden Vortrag der Unbekannten mir
der Gesang der berühmtesten Sängerinnen, die ich gehört, matt
und ausdruckslos schien. Nie hatte ich eine Ahnung von diesen lang
ausgehaltenen Tönen, von diesen Nachtigallwirbeln, von diesem
Auf- und Abwogen, von diesem Steigen bis zur Stärke des
Orgellautes, von diesem Sinken bis zum leisesten Hauch. Nicht
einer war, den der süßeste Zauber nicht umfing, und nur leise
Seufzer gingen in der tiefen Stille auf, wenn die Sängerin schwieg.
Es mochte schon Mitternacht sein, als man den Rat sehr heftig
reden hörte, eine andere männliche Stimme schien, nach dem Tone
zu urteilen, ihm Vorwürfe zu machen, dazwischen klagte ein
Mädchen in abgebrochenen Reden. Heftiger und heftiger schrie
der Rat, bis er endlich in jenen gedehnten, singenden Ton fiel, den
Sie kennen. Ein lauter Schrei des Mädchens unterbrach ihn, dann
wurde es totenstille, bis plötzlich es die Treppe herabpolterte, und

could make me abhor the councilor utterly, if I weren't convinced
that, given the councilor's character, which is fundamentally good-
natured to the point of softness, there must be a special secret involved. When the councilor came here to H—— several years ago,
he lived like a hermit with an elderly housekeeper in a dark house
on ——strasse. Soon his peculiarities aroused the curiosity of his
neighbors, and as soon as he became aware of that, he sought and
found acquaintances. Just as in my house, people everywhere got
so used to him that he became indispensable. Disregarding his
rough exterior, even the children loved him, though they didn't
pester him because, despite all his friendliness, they somehow remained shyly respectful in their dealings with him, and this protected him from any impertinence. You've seen today how he's
able to win over the children by all sorts of tricks. We all thought
he was a confirmed bachelor, and he didn't contradict that view.
After living here for some time, he went on a trip, no one knew
where, and returned a few months later. On the second evening
after his return, Krespel's windows were lighted up, contrary to
his custom, and that alone made his neighbors take notice; but
soon they could hear the truly marvelous voice of a woman, accompanied by a piano. Then the tones of a violin were awakened
and fought a lively, fiery battle with the voice. You could tell at
once it was the councilor playing.—I myself mingled with the numerous crowd that the wonderful concert had drawn together
outside the councilor's house, and I must confess to you that,
compared with that voice, compared with the unknown woman's
unique execution, which penetrated to one's very soul, the singing
of the most famous sopranos I ever heard seemed dull and ex-
pressionless. Never had I had any previous notion of those long-
held notes, those nightingale trills, that rising and descending
surge, that crescendo reaching the strength of an organ's tone,
that diminuendo dwindling to the softest whisper. No one among
us was unaffected by that sweet sorcery, and nothing but quiet
sighs arose from the deep silence after the singer had ceased. It
was probably already midnight when we heard the councilor
speaking violently; another man's voice seemed, to judge from its
tone, to be reproaching him, while a girl was lamenting intermit-
tently. The councilor was shouting more and more violently until
he finally subsided into that drawling, singsong tone you're familiar with. He was interrupted by a loud cry from the girl, then it became deathly still until there was a sudden clattering down the

ein junger Mensch schluchzend herausstürzte, der sich in eine nahe
stehende Postchaise warf und rasch davonfuhr. Tags darauf erschien
der Rat sehr heiter, und niemand hatte den Mut, ihn nach der
Begebenheit der vorigen Nacht zu fragen. Die Haushälterin sagte
aber auf Befragen, daß der Rat ein bildhübsches, blutjunges
Mädchen mitgebracht, die er Antonie nenne, und die eben so schön
gesungen. Auch sei ein junger Mann mitgekommen, der sehr
zärtlich mit Antonien getan und wohl ihr Bräutigam sein müsse. Der
habe aber, weil es der Rat durchaus gewollt, schnell abreisen
müssen. – In welchem Verhältnis Antonie mit dem Rat steht, ist bis
jetzt ein Geheimnis, aber so viel ist gewiß, daß er das arme Mädchen
auf die gehässigste Weise tyrannisiert. Er bewacht sie wie der
Doktor Bartolo im «Barbier von Sevillien» seine Mündel; kaum darf
sie sich am Fenster blicken lassen. Führt er sie auf inständiges
Bitten einmal in Gesellschaft, so verfolgt er sie mit Argusblicken
und leidet durchaus nicht, daß sich irgendein musikalischer Ton
hören lasse, viel weniger daß Antonie singe, die übrigens auch in
seinem Hause nicht mehr singen darf. Antoniens Gesang in jener
Nacht ist daher unter dem Publikum der Stadt zu einer Phantasie
und Gemüt aufregenden Sage von einem herrlichen Wunder geworden, und selbst die, welche sie gar nicht hörten, sprechen oft, versucht sich eine Sängerin hier am Orte: «Was ist denn das für ein
gemeines Quinkelieren? – Nur Antonie vermag zu singen.» –
    Ihr wißt, daß ich auf solche phantastische Dinge ganz versessen bin,
und könnt wohl denken, wie notwendig ich es fand, Antoniens
Bekanntschaft zu machen. Jene Äußerungen des Publikums über
Antoniens Gesang hatte ich selbst schon öfters vernommen, aber ich
ahnte nicht, daß die Herrliche am Orte sei und in den Banden des
wahnsinnigen Krespels wie eines tyrannischen Zauberers liege.
Natürlicherweise hörte ich auch sogleich in der folgenden Nacht
Antoniens wunderbaren Gesang, und da sie mich in einem herrlichen
Adagio (lächerlicherweise kam es mir vor, als hätte ich es selbst kom-
poniert) auf das rührendste beschwor, sie zu retten, so war ich bald
entschlossen, ein zweiter Astolfo, in Krespels Haus wie in Alzinens
Zauberburg einzudringen und die Königin des Gesanges aus
schmachvollen Banden zu befreien.

stairs and a young man dashed out, sobbing, leaped into a post chaise that was waiting nearby, and drove off rapidly. The next day, the councilor looked quite serene, and no one was bold enough to ask him about the events of the preceding night. But when his housekeeper was questioned, she said that the councilor had brought home a beautiful, very young lady whom he called Antonie, and it was she who had sung so well. A young man had also come along, who had acted very affectionately with Antonie, and must be her fiancé. But, at the councilor's firm insistence, he had had to depart quickly.—Antonie's relationship to the councilor is still a mystery, but this much is certain: he tyrannizes over the poor girl in the most hateful way. He guards her just as Doctor Bartolo guards his ward in *The Barber of Seville;*[1] she's scarcely allowed to show herself at the window. If he ever brings her along on a visit, after incessant pleading, he follows her around with Argus eyes, and absolutely refuses to have any music played, let alone to have Antonie sing; what's more, even at home she isn't allowed to sing anymore. Antonie's singing that night has therefore become for the town public a fantasy and a soul-stirring legend about a splendid miracle; even people who didn't hear her often say, when some soprano tries her luck in this tone: 'What sort of commonplace twittering is this? Only Antonie knows how to sing.'"

You know that I'm totally obsessed with matters like this, which intrigue the imagination, and you can easily conceive how essential I considered it to make Antonie's acquaintance. I myself had already often heard those declarations of the public concerning Antonie's singing, but I had had no notion that the splendid creature was in town, held captive by the lunatic Krespel as if by some tyrannical sorcerer. Naturally, that very night I heard Antonie's marvelous singing in my dreams, and when she most feelingly besought me in a splendid adagio (which, comically, seemed to me like a composition of my own) to rescue her, I was soon determined to break into Krespel's house, like a new Astolfo entering Alcina's enchanted castle,[2] and to liberate the queen of song from her shameful chains.

1. Probably a reference to Paisiello's opera of 1782, still very popular at the time (if not to Beaumarchais's original play of 1775). Rossini's opera, first performed in 1816, the year in which this story was written, was not yet the internationally famous success it later became.   2. Astolfo and Alcina are characters in Ariosto's *Orlando furioso* (1532).

Es kam alles anders, wie ich es mir gedacht hatte; denn kaum hatte ich den Rat zwei- bis dreimal gesehen und mit ihm eifrig über die beste Struktur der Geigen gesprochen, als er mich selbst einlud, ihn in seinem Hause zu besuchen. Ich tat es, und er zeigte mir den Reichtum seiner Violinen. Es hingen deren wohl dreißig in einem Kabinett, unter ihnen zeichnete sich eine durch alle Spuren der hohen Altertümlichkeit (geschnitzten Löwenkopf und so weiter) aus, und sie schien, höher gehängt und mit einer darüber angebrachten Blumenkrone, als Königin den andern zu gebieten.

«Diese Violine», sprach Krespel, nachdem ich ihn darum befragt, «diese Violine ist ein sehr merkwürdiges, wunderbares Stück eines unbekannten Meisters, wahrscheinlich aus Tartinis Zeiten. Ganz überzeugt bin ich, daß in der innern Struktur etwas Besonderes liegt, und daß, wenn ich sie zerlegte, sich mir ein Geheimnis erschließen würde, dem ich längst nachspürte, aber – lachen Sie mich nur aus, wenn Sie wollen – dies tote Ding, dem ich selbst doch nur erst Leben und Laut gebe, spricht oft aus sich selbst zu mir auf wunderliche Weise, und es war mir, da ich zum ersten Male darauf spielte, als wär ich nur der Magnetiseur, der die Somnambule zu erregen vermag, daß sie selbsttätig ihre innere Anschauung in Worten verkündet. – Glauben Sie ja nicht, daß ich geckhaft genug bin, von solchen Phantastereien auch nur das mindeste zu halten, aber eigen ist es doch, daß ich es nie über mich erhielt, jenes dumme, tote Ding dort aufzuschneiden. Lieb ist es mir jetzt, daß ich es nicht getan, denn seitdem Antonie hier ist, spiele ich ihr zuweilen etwas auf dieser Geige vor. – Antonie hört es gern – gar gern.»

Die Worte sprach der Rat mit sichtlicher Rührung, das ermutigte mich zu den Worten: «O mein bester Herr Rat, wollten Sie das nicht in meiner Gegenwart tun?»

Krespel schnitt aber sein süßsaures Gesicht und sprach mit gedehntem, singendem Ton: «Nein, mein bester Herr Studiosus!» Damit war die Sache abgetan. Nun mußte ich noch mit ihm allerlei, zum Teil kindische Raritäten besehen; endlich griff er in ein Kistchen und holte ein zusammengelegtes Papier heraus, das er mir in die Hand drückte, sehr feierlich sprechend: «Sie sind ein Freund der Kunst, nehmen Sie dies Geschenk als ein teures Andenken, das Ihnen ewig über alles wert bleiben muß.» Dabei schob er mich bei beiden Schultern sehr sanft nach der Tür zu und umarmte mich an der

But everything happened differently from my expectations; for, hardly had I met the councilor two or three times and spoken to him enthusiastically about the best way to make violins, when he himself invited me to visit him at home. I did so, and he showed me his great collection of violins. About thirty of them were hanging in a small room, among which one was distinguished by every sign of great antiquity (carved lion's head and so on); hung higher than the rest, and with a crown of flowers placed above it, it seemed like a queen lording it over all the others.

"This violin," Krespel said after I asked him about it, "this violin is a very remarkable, marvelous instrument made by an unknown master, probably in Tartini's[3] day. I'm completely convinced that there's something special about its inner structure, and that, if I took it apart, a secret would be revealed to me that I have long sought to discover, but—laugh at me if you like—this inanimate object, which, after all, only derives its life and sound from me, often spontaneously speaks to me in a strange way, and, when I first played it, I felt as if I were merely the hypnotist capable of inspiring his sleeping subject to put her inward feelings into words, of her own accord. Don't think I'm silly enough to believe in such fantasies at all, but it is the strange fact that I have never been able to bring myself to cut open that stupid, dead thing there. Now I'm glad I never did, because ever since Antonie has been here, I sometimes play her something on this violin. Antonie likes to hear it, she likes it very much."

The councilor uttered those words with visible emotion, which encouraged me to say: "My dear councilor, won't you play something on it while I'm here?"

But Krespel displayed his sweet-and-sour grimace and said in a drawling, singsong tone: "No, my student friend!" And that was the end of the matter. Now he compelled me to join him in inspecting all sorts of curios, some of them childish; finally he reached into a small case and pulled out a folded piece of paper, which he thrust into my hand, saying most solemnly: "You are a friend of art; take this present as a precious souvenir, which you will surely value above all else forever." Saying that, he took me by both shoulders and shoved me very gently toward the door,

---

3. Giuseppe Tartini, violinist and composer, 1692–1770.

Schwelle. Eigentlich wurde ich doch von ihm auf symbolische Weise zur Tür hinausgeworfen.

Als ich das Papierchen aufmachte, fand ich ein ungefähr ein Achtelzoll langes Stückchen einer Quinte und dabei geschrieben: «Von der Quinte, womit der selige Stamitz seine Geige bezogen hatte, als er sein letztes Konzert spielte.»

Die schnöde Abfertigung, als ich Antoniens erwähnte, schien mir zu beweisen, daß ich sie wohl nie zu sehen bekommen würde; dem war aber nicht so, denn als ich den Rat zum zweiten Male besuchte, fand ich Antonien in seinem Zimmer, ihm helfend bei dem Zusammensetzen einer Geige. Antoniens Äußeres machte auf den ersten Anblick keinen starken Eindruck, aber bald konnte man nicht loskommen von dem blauen Auge und den holden Rosenlippen der ungemein zarten, lieblichen Gestalt. Sie war sehr blaß, aber wurde etwas Geistreiches und Heiteres gesagt, so flog in süßem Lächeln ein feuriges Inkarnat über die Wangen hin, das jedoch bald im rötlichen Schimmer erblaßte. Ganz unbefangen sprach ich mit Antonien und bemerkte durchaus nichts von den Argusblicken Krespels, wie sie der Professor ihm angedichtet hatte, vielmehr blieb er ganz in gewöhnlichem Geleise, ja, er schien sogar meiner Unterhaltung mit Antonien Beifall zu geben.

So geschah es, daß ich öfter den Rat besuchte, und wechselseitiges Aneinandergewöhnen dem kleinen Kreise von uns dreien eine wunderbare Wohlbehaglichkeit gab, die uns bis ins Innerste hinein erfreute. Der Rat blieb mit seinen höchst seltsamen Skurrilitäten mir höchst ergötzlich; aber doch war es wohl nur Antonie, die mit unwiderstehlichem Zauber mich hinzog und mich manches ertragen ließ, dem ich sonst, ungeduldig wie ich damals war, entronnen. In das Eigentümliche, Seltsame des Rates mischte sich nämlich gar zu oft Abgeschmacktes und Langweiliges, vorzüglich zuwider war es mir aber, daß er, sobald ich das Gespräch auf Musik, insbesondere auf Gesang lenkte, mit seinem diabolisch lächelnden Gesicht und seinem widrig singenden Tone einfiel, etwas Heterogenes, mehrenteils Gemeines, auf die Bahn bringend.

An der tiefen Betrübnis, die dann aus Antoniens Blicken sprach, merkte ich wohl, daß es nur geschah, um irgendeine Aufforderung zum Gesange mir abzuschneiden. Ich ließ nicht nach. Mit den Hindernissen, die mir der Rat entgegenstellte, wuchs mein Mut, sie

embracing me on the threshold. Actually he was symbolically throwing me out.

When I unfolded the scrap of paper, I found a little piece of an E-string about an eighth of an inch long, with the words: "From the E-string with which the late Stamitz[4] fitted his violin when he played his last concert."

My scornful dismissal when I mentioned Antonie was like a proof to me that I'd probably never get to meet her; but that wasn't the case, for, on my second visit to the councilor, I found Antonie in his room, helping him to assemble a violin. At first glance Antonie's looks didn't make a strong impression, but before long it was impossible to look away from the blue eyes and sweet rosy lips of that unusually gentle and lovely girl. She was very pale, but at any witty or merry remark, her sweet smile was accompanied by a bright flush on her cheeks, which soon subsided into a pinkish glow. I spoke to Antonie without embarrassment, and failed to detect even one of those Argus-like stares from Krespel which the professor had ascribed to him; rather, he behaved in his customary way and even seemed to approve of my conversation with Antonie.

And so it came about that I visited the councilor frequently, and that our getting accustomed to one another lent a wonderful sense of coziness to our little circle of three, giving us all profound pleasure. With his very peculiar and bizarre notions, the councilor continued to be most entertaining to me; but, most likely, it was Antonie alone who attracted me with an irresistible magic and allowed me to endure many things that I would otherwise have fled from, impatient as I was in those days. You see, the councilor's individual and peculiar behavior was all too often tinged with tastelessness and tiresomeness; I was especially put off—whenever I brought music, particularly singing, into the conversation—by his diabolically smiling face and his repellently singsong tone, as he interrupted me, introducing some totally different, usually commonplace, subject.

From the deep sorrow in Antonie's facial expression at such times I realized perfectly that he was doing so only to prevent me from asking her to sing. I persisted. As the councilor placed more and more obstacles in my way, my boldness in surmount-

---

4. Karl Stamitz, violinist and composer, 1746–1801.

zu übersteigen, ich mußte Antoniens Gesang hören, um nicht in
Träumen und Ahnungen dieses Gesanges zu verschwimmen.

Eines Abends war Krespel bei besonders guter Laune; er hatte eine
alte Cremoneser Geige zerlegt und gefunden, daß der Stimmstock
um eine halbe Linie schräger als sonst gestellt war. Wichtige, die
Praxis bereichernde Erfahrung! – Es gelang mir, ihn über die wahre
Art des Violinenspielens in Feuer zu setzen. Der großen, wahrhafti-
gen Sängern abgehorchte Vortrag der alten Meister, von dem Krespel
sprach, führte von selbst die Bemerkung herbei, daß jetzt gerade
umgekehrt der Gesang sich nach den erkünstelten Sprüngen und
Läufen der Instrumentalisten verbilde.

«Was ist unsinniger», rief ich, vom Stuhle aufspringend, hin zum
Pianoforte laufend und es schnell öffnend, «was ist unsinniger als
solche vertrackte Manieren, welche, statt Musik zu sein, dem Tone
über den Boden hingeschütteter Erbsen gleichen.» Ich sang manche
der modernen Fermaten, die hin und herlaufen und schnurren wie
ein tüchtig losgeschnürter Kreisel, einzelne schlechte Akkorde dazu
anschlagend.

Übermäßig lachte Krespel und schrie: «Haha! mich dünkt, ich höre
unsere deutschen Italiener oder unsere italienischen Deutschen, wie
sie sich in einer Arie von Pucitta oder Portogallo oder sonst einem
Maestro di Capella oder vielmehr Schiavo d'un primo uomo
übernehmen.»

«Nun», dachte ich, «ist der Zeitpunkt da.» «Nicht wahr», wandte
ich mich zu Antonien, «nicht wahr, von dieser Singerei weiß
Antonie nichts?» und zugleich intonierte ich ein herrliches, seelen-
volles Lied vom alten Leonardo Leo. Da glühten Antoniens
Wangen, Himmelsglanz blitzte aus den neubeseelten Augen, sie
sprang an das Pianoforte – sie öffnete die Lippen – aber in demselben Augenblick drängte sie Krespel fort, ergriff mich bei den
Schultern und schrie im kreischenden Tenor – «Söhnchen –
Söhnchen – Söhnchen».

Und gleich fuhr er fort, sehr leise singend und in höflich gebeugter
Stellung meine Hand ergreifend: «In der Tat, mein höchst
verehrungswürdiger Herr Studiosus, in der Tat, gegen alle Lebensart,
gegen alle guten Sitten würde es anstoßen, wenn ich laut und lebhaft
den Wunsch äußerte, daß Ihnen hier auf der Stelle gleich der höllische Satan mit glühenden Krallenfäusten sanft das Genick abstieße

ing them grew; I just had to hear Antonie sing if I wanted to avoid losing myself in dreams and premonitions of her singing.

One evening, Krespel was in a particularly good mood; he had taken apart an old violin from Cremona and had discovered that its sound post was inclined a twenty-fourth of an inch more than usual. An important find, one that enriched his practical knowledge! I succeeded in arousing his enthusiasm over the true method of playing the violin. Krespel's remarks on the performance of the old masters, which had been modeled on that of great, natural singers, led naturally to my observation that nowadays it was just the opposite, and singing was being disfigured by imitating the artificial leaps and runs of instrumental music.

"What is more senseless," I cried, jumping out of my chair, running over to the piano, and rapidly opening it, "what is more senseless than such complicated mannerisms, which, instead of being music, sound like peas being spilled out on the floor?" I sang several of our modern cadenzas, which run to and fro, humming like a violently released top, and I struck a few bad chords to go with my singing.

Krespel laughed immoderately and shouted: "Ha, ha! I seem to hear our German Italians or our Italian Germans, biting off more than they can chew in an aria by Pucitta[5] or Portogallo[6] or some other *maestro di cappella*,[7] or rather *schiavo d'un primo uomo*."[8]

"Now," I thought, "the time has come." "Isn't it so," I said, turning to Antonie, "isn't it so that Antonie knows nothing of that sort of yowling?" And at the same time I started to play a splendid, soulful song by the old master Leonardo Leo.[9] Antonie's cheeks blazed, a heavenly radiance flashed from her freshly animated eyes, she dashed over to the piano—she opened her lips—but at that very moment Krespel forced her away, seized me by the shoulders, and yelled in a shrill tenor: "Young man! Young man! Young man!"

And he continued at once, in a very quiet singsong, while he bowed courteously and took my hand: "Indeed, my most honored student friend, indeed it would run counter to all gentlemanly conduct and good manners if I were to utter loud and strong the wish that Satan from hell would immediately, right here, gently break your neck with his flaming clawed fists, in that

5. Vincenzo Pucitta, 1778–1861. 6. Marco Antonio Portogallo, 1762–1830.
7. Conductor (often also composer). 8. Slave of a principal (male) singer.
9. 1694–1746.

und Sie auf die Weise gewissermaßen kurz expedierte; aber davon
abgesehen, müssen Sie eingestehen, Liebwertester, daß es bedeutend
dunkelt, und da heute keine Laterne brennt, könnten Sie, würfe ich
Sie auch gerade nicht die Treppe herab, doch Schaden leiden an
Ihren lieben Gebeinen. Gehen Sie fein zu Hause und erinnern Sie
sich freundschaftlichst Ihres wahren Freundes, wenn Sie ihn etwa nie
mehr – verstehen Sie wohl? – nie mehr zu Hause antreffen sollten!»
– Damit umarmte er mich und drehte sich, mich festhaltend, langsam
mit mir zur Türe heraus, so daß ich Antonien mit keinem Blick mehr
anschauen konnte.

Ihr gesteht, daß es in meiner Lage nicht möglich war, den Rat zu
prügeln, welches doch eigentlich hätte geschehen müssen. Der
Professor lachte mich sehr aus und versicherte, daß ich es nun mit
dem Rat auf immer verdorben hätte. Den schmachtenden, ans
Fenster heraufblickenden Amoroso, den verliebten Abenteurer zu
machen, dazu war Antonie mir zu wert, ich möchte sagen, zu heilig.
Im Innersten zerrissen, verließ ich H., aber wie es zu gehen pflegt, die
grellen Farben des Phantasiegebildes verblaßten, und Antonie – ja
selbst Antoniens Gesang, den ich nie gehört, leuchtete oft in mein
tiefstes Gemüt hinein, wie ein sanfter tröstender Rosenschimmer.

Nach zwei Jahren war ich schon in B. angestellt, als ich eine Reise
nach dem südlichen Deutschland unternahm. Im duftigen Abendrot
erhoben sich die Türme von H.; sowie ich näher und näher kam, ergriff mich ein unbeschreibliches Gefühl der peinlichsten Angst; wie
eine schwere Last hatte es sich über meine Brust gelegt, ich konnte
nicht atmen; ich mußte heraus aus dem Wagen ins Freie. Aber bis
zum physischen Schmerz steigerte sich meine Beklemmung. Mir war
es bald, als hörte ich die Akkorde eines feierlichen Chorals durch die
Lüfte schweben – die Töne wurden deutlicher, ich unterschied
Männerstimmen, die einen geistlichen Choral absangen. – «Was ist
das? – was ist das?» rief ich, indem es wie ein glühender Dolch durch
meine Brust fuhr!

«Sehen Sie denn nicht», erwiderte der neben mir fahrende
Postillon, «sehen Sie es denn nicht? da drüben auf dem Kirchhof begraben sie einen!» In der Tat befanden wir uns in der Nähe des Kirch-
hofes, und ich sah einen Kreis schwarzgekleideter Menschen um ein
Grab stehen, das man zuzuschütten im Begriff stand. Die Tränen
stürzten mir aus den Augen, es war, als begrübe man dort alle Lust,
alle Freude des Lebens. Rasch vorwärts von dem Hügel her-

manner getting rid of you quickly, so to speak; but, aside from that, my dearest fellow, you must admit that it's really dark out and, since there's no streetlamp on tonight, even if I don't actually throw you down the stairs, you might still suffer an injury to your dear bones. Go home like a nice boy and remember your true friend most kindly, in case you should never again—understand?—never again find him at home!" Therewith he embraced me and, holding onto me tight, slowly turned around and around until we were both out the door, so that I couldn't catch another sight of Antonie.

You'll admit that, in my situation, it wasn't possible to beat up the councilor, though that's what really should have been done. The professor had a good laugh at my expense and assured me that I had now ruined my relationship with the councilor forever. Antonie meant too much to me, I'd even say she was too sacred to me, for me to play the languishing *amoroso*[10] gazing up at her window, or the love-smitten adventurer. In mental disarray I left H——, but, as things usually turn out, the vivid colors of my imaginings faded, and Antonie—yes, even Antonie's singing, which I never heard—often radiated deep into my spirit like a gentle, consoling pinkish glow.

Two years later, I already had a position in B—— when I went on a trip to the south of Germany. The towers of H—— loomed in the fragrant sunset; as I got nearer and nearer, I was seized by an indescribable feeling of the most painful anguish; a heavy load seemed to have settled on my chest, and I couldn't breathe; I had to get out of the coach into the fresh air. But my oppression increased to the point of physical pain. Soon I thought I heard the chords of a solemn chorale drifting through the air—the sounds became clearer, I could distinguish men's voices singing a sacred chorale. "What's going on? What's going on?" I cried, while a red-hot dagger seemed to be piercing my bosom!

"Don't you see?" replied the stagecoach driver, who was driving alongside me. "Don't you see? Over there in the churchyard someone's being buried!" And in fact we were now close to the churchyard, and I saw a group of people dressed in black standing around a grave that was just being filled in with earth. Tears burst from my eyes; it was as if all of life's pleasure and joy were being buried there. After walking ahead rapidly down the hill, I

---

10. Lover.

abgeschritten, konnte ich nicht mehr in den Kirchhof hineinsehen, der Choral schwieg, und ich bemerkte unfern des Tores schwarzgekleidete Menschen, die von dem Begräbnis zurückkamen. Der Professor mit seiner Nichte am Arm, beide in tiefer Trauer, schritten dicht bei mir vorüber, ohne mich zu bemerken. Die Nichte hatte das Tuch vor die Augen gedrückt und schluchzte heftig.

Es war mir unmöglich, in die Stadt hineinzugehen; ich schickte meinen Bedienten mit dem Wagen nach dem gewohnten Gasthofe und lief in die mir wohlbekannte Gegend heraus, um so eine Stimmung loszuwerden, die vielleicht nur physische Ursachen, Erhitzung auf der Reise und so weiter haben konnte. Als ich in die Allee kam, welche nach einem Lustorte führt, ging vor mir das sonderbarste Schauspiel auf.

Rat Krespel wurde von zwei Trauermännern geführt, denen er durch allerlei seltsame Sprünge entrinnen zu wollen schien. Er war, wie gewöhnlich, in seinen wunderlichen, grauen, selbst zugeschnittenen Rock gekleidet, nur hing von dem kleinen, dreieckigen Hütchen, das er martialisch auf ein Ohr gedrückt, ein sehr langer, schmaler Trauerflor herab, der in der Luft hin- und herflatterte. Um den Leib hatte er ein schwarzes Degengehenk geschnallt, doch statt des Degens einen langen Violinbogen hineingesteckt. Eiskalt fuhr es mir durch die Glieder; «der ist wahnsinnig», dacht ich, indem ich langsam folgte.

Die Männer führten den Rat bis an sein Haus, da umarmte er sie mit lautem Lachen. Sie verließen ihn, und nun fiel sein Blick auf mich, der dicht neben ihm stand. Er sah mich lange starr an, dann rief er dumpf: «Willkommen, Herr Studiosus! – Sie verstehen es ja auch» – damit packte er mich beim Arm und riß mich fort in das Haus – die Treppe herauf in das Zimmer hinein, wo die Violinen hingen. Alle waren mit schwarzem Flor umhüllt; die Violine des alten Meisters fehlte, an ihrem Platze hing ein Zypressenkranz. – Ich wußte was geschehen – «Antonie! ach Antonie!» schrie ich auf in trostlosem Jammer.

Der Rat stand wie erstarrt mit übereinandergeschlagenen Armen neben mir. Ich zeigte nach dem Zypressenkranz. «Als sie starb», sprach der Rat sehr dumpf und feierlich, «als sie starb, zerbrach mit dröhnendem Krachen der Stimmstock in jener Geige, und der Resonanzboden riß sich auseinander. Die Getreue konnte nur mit ihr, in ihr leben; sie liegt bei ihr im Sarge, sie ist mit ihr begraben worden.»

Tief erschüttert sank ich in einen Stuhl, aber der Rat fing an, mit rauhem Ton ein lustig Lied zu singen, und es war recht graulich

no longer had a view of the churchyard; the chorale ceased, and not far from the town gate I noticed people dressed in black who were returning from the burial. The professor and his niece, who was holding his arm, walked right past me without noticing me. His niece had her handkerchief pressed to her eyes, and was sobbing violently.

It was impossible for me to enter town; I sent my valet with the coach to my usual inn, while I ran out to the neighborhood I knew so well, in order to free myself in that way of a mood which was possibly due merely to physical causes, such as over-heating on the journey. When I arrived at the avenue that leads to a pleasure resort, the oddest scene was displayed to me.

Councilor Krespel was being led by two male mourners, from whom he seemed to be trying to escape by making all sorts of strange jumps. As usual, he was dressed in his eccentric gray coat, which he himself had tailored; but now his small three-cornered hat, which he had pulled down over one ear in martial fashion, had attached to it a very long, narrow crape band that was fluttering to and fro in the breeze. Around his waist he had buckled a black sword belt, but instead of the sword he had thrust a long violin bow into it. I felt an icy chill all over my body; "He's gone mad," I said to myself, as I followed them slowly.

The men led the councilor up to his house, whereupon he embraced them with a loud laugh. They left him there, and now his glance fell on me; I was standing right beside him. He stared at me rigidly for a long while, then called in a muffled tone: "Welcome, student! Of course, you understand!" With those words he grabbed my arm and dragged me into the house—up the stairs and into the room where the violins hung. They were all draped in black mourning; the old master violin was missing, a cypress wreath hanging in its place. I knew what had happened: "Antonie! oh, Antonie!" I cried in inconsolable grief.

The councilor stood there beside me with crossed arms as if numb. I pointed to the cypress wreath. "When she died," the councilor said very tonelessly and solemnly, "when she died, the sound post of that violin broke with a rumbling noise, and its belly broke apart. The faithful thing could only live with her, through her; it's now lying in the coffin with her, it's been buried with her."

In my deep emotion I sank into a chair, but the councilor began singing a jolly song in a rough voice, and it was truly

anzusehen, wie er auf einem Fuße dazu herumsprang, und der Flor
(er hatte den Hut auf dem Kopfe) im Zimmer und an den aufge-
hängten Violinen herumstrich; ja, ich konnte mich eines überlauten
Schreies nicht erwehren, als der Flor bei einer raschen Wendung des
Rates über mich herfuhr; es war mir, als wollte er mich verhüllt her-
abziehen in den schwarzen, entsetzlichen Abgrund des Wahnsinns.

Da stand der Rat plötzlich stille und sprach in seinem singenden
Ton: «Söhnchen? – Söhnchen? – warum schreist du so? hast du den
Totenengel geschaut? – das geht allemal der Zeremonie vorher!» –
Nun trat er in die Mitte des Zimmers, riß den Violinbogen aus dem
Gehenke, hielt ihn mit beiden Händen über den Kopf und zerbrach
ihn, daß er in viele Stücke zersplitterte.

Laut lachend rief Krespel: «Nun ist der Stab über mich gebrochen,
meinst du, Söhnchen? nicht wahr? Mitnichten, mitnichten, nun bin
ich frei – frei – frei – Heisa frei! – Nun bau ich keine Geigen mehr –
keine Geigen mehr – heisa keine Geigen mehr.» – Das sang der Rat
nach einer schauerlich lustigen Melodie, indem er wieder auf einem
Fuße herumsprang.

Voll Grauen wollte ich schnell zur Türe heraus, aber der Rat hielt
mich fest, indem er sehr gelassen sprach: «Bleiben Sie, Herr
Studiosus, halten Sie diese Ausbrüche des Schmerzes, der mich mit
Todesmartern zerreißt, nicht für Wahnsinn, aber es geschieht nur
alles deshalb, weil ich mir vor einiger Zeit einen Schlafrock anfertigte,
in dem ich aussehen wollte wie das Schicksal oder wie Gott!»

Der Rat schwatzte tolles, grauliches Zeug durcheinander, bis er ganz
erschöpft zusammensank; auf mein Rufen kam die alte Haushälterin
herbei, und ich war froh, als ich mich nur wieder im Freien befand. –
Nicht einen Augenblick zweifelte ich daran, daß Krespel wahnsinnig
geworden, der Professor behauptete jedoch das Gegenteil.

«Es gibt Menschen», sprach er, «denen die Natur oder ein besonderes Verhängnis die Decke wegzog, unter der wir andern unser
tolles Wesen unbemerkter treiben. Sie gleichen dünngehäuteten
Insekten, die im regen, sichtbaren Muskelspiel mißgestaltet erscheinen, ungeachtet sich alles bald wieder in die gehörige Form
fügt. Was bei uns Gedanke bleibt, wird dem Krespel alles zur Tat. –
Den bittern Hohn, wie der in das irdische Tun und Treiben
eingeschachtete Geist ihn wohl oft bei der Hand hat, führt Krespel
aus in tollen Gebärden und geschickten Hasensprüngen. Das ist aber
sein Blitzableiter. Was aus der Erde steigt, gibt er wieder der Erde,

horrible to see him hopping around on one foot while he sang; he had kept his hat on, and the crape band swished around in the room, grazing the hanging violins; yes, I couldn't help uttering an extremely loud cry when the councilor made a sudden turn and the band stroked me; I felt as if it were trying to cover me and drag me down into the frightful black abyss of madness.

Then the councilor suddenly came to a halt and said in his singsong tone: "Young man? Young man? Why are you yelling like that? Did you see the angel of death? That always precedes the ceremony!" Then he stepped into the middle of the room, yanked the violin bow out of his belt, held it over his head with both hands, and broke it into bits.

With a loud laugh Krespel shouted: "Now the staff has been broken over me,[11] right, young man? True? Not at all, not at all, now I'm free, free, free! Free, hurrah! Now I won't make any more violins, any more violins, any more violins, hurrah!" The councilor sang those words to a gruesomely jolly tune while hopping around on one foot again.

Horror-stricken, I wanted to dash out, but the councilor held onto me, as he said very calmly: "Stay here, student, don't take these outbursts of a sorrow that rends me apart with the tortures of death as a sign of madness; all this is merely happening because some time ago I made myself a dressing gown in which I wanted to look like fate or like God!"

The councilor babbled all sorts of crazy, horrible nonsense until he collapsed from sheer exhaustion; at my call his old housekeeper appeared, and I was glad to find myself outdoors once more. I didn't doubt for a moment that Krespel had gone mad, but the professor asserted just the opposite.

"There are people," he said, "from whom Nature, or some particular destiny, has removed the covering beneath which the rest of us perform our crazy actions more unobservedly. They resemble those thin-skinned insects which appear misshapen because we can see the lively play of their muscles, even though everything soon resumes its proper form. What for us remains a secret thought, becomes an outward action in Krespel's case. That bitter scorn which our spirit, encased in the world's hubbub, surely often finds ready to hand—Krespel acts it out with crazy gestures and nimble, harelike leaps. But that is his lightning rod. That

---

11. In earlier times, a staff was symbolically broken over the head of a criminal condemned to death before he was executed.

aber das Göttliche weiß er zu bewahren; und so steht es mit seinem
innern Bewußtsein recht gut, glaub ich, unerachtet der scheinbaren,
nach außen herausspringenden Tollheit. Antoniens plötzlicher Tod
mag freilich schwer auf ihm lasten, aber ich wette, daß der Rat schon
morgenden Tages seinen Eselsritt im gewöhnlichen Geleise weiter
forttrabt.»

Beinahe geschah es so, wie der Professor es vorausgesagt. Der Rat
schien andern Tages ganz der vorige, nur erklärte er, daß er niemals
mehr Violinen bauen und auch auf keiner jemals mehr spielen wolle.
Das hat er, wie ich später erfuhr, gehalten.

Des Professors Andeutungen bestärkten meine innere Überzeugung, daß das nähere, so sorgfältig verschwiegene Verhältnis
Antoniens zum Rat, ja daß selbst ihr Tod eine schwer auf ihm la-
stende, nicht abzubüßende Schuld sein könne. Nicht wollte ich H.
verlassen, ohne ihm das Verbrechen, welches ich ahnete, vorzuhal-
ten; ich wollte ihn bis ins Innerste hinein erschüttern und so das of-
fene Geständnis der gräßlichen Tat erzwingen. Je mehr ich der Sache
nachdachte, desto klarer wurde es mir, daß Krespel ein Bösewicht
sein müsse, und desto feuriger, eindringlicher wurde die Rede, die
sich wie von selbst zu einem wahren, rhetorischen Meisterstück
formte.

So gerüstet und ganz erhitzt, lief ich zu dem Rat. Ich fand ihn, wie
er mit sehr ruhiger, lächelnder Miene Spielsachen drechselte. «Wie
kann nur», fuhr ich auf ihn los, «wie kann nur auf einen Augenblick
Frieden in Ihre Seele kommen, da der Gedanke an die gräßliche Tat
Sie mit Schlangenbissen peinigen muß?»

Der Rat sah mich verwundert an, den Meißel beiseite legend.
«Wieso, mein Bester?» fragte er; – «setzen Sie sich doch gefälligst auf
jenen Stuhl!»

Aber eifrig fuhr ich fort, indem ich, mich selbst immer mehr er-
hitzend, ihn geradezu anklagte, Antonien ermordet zu haben, und
ihm mit der Rache der ewigen Macht drohte. Ja, als nicht längst
eingeweihte Justizperson, erfüllt von meinem Beruf, ging ich so weit,
ihn zu versichern, daß ich alles anwenden würde, der Sache auf die
Spur zu kommen und so ihn dem weltlichen Richter schon hienieden
in die Hände zu liefern. – Ich wurde in der Tat etwas verlegen, da
nach dem Schlusse meiner gewaltigen, pomphaften Rede der Rat,
ohne ein Wort zu erwidern, mich sehr ruhig anblickte, als erwarte er,
ich müsse noch weiter fortfahren. Das versuchte ich auch in der Tat,
aber es kam nun alles so schief, ja, so albern heraus, daß ich gleich
wieder schwieg.

which arises from the earth he returns to the earth, but he knows how to preserve the divine; and so his inner consciousness is in fine shape, I think, in spite of his apparent lunacy, so conspicuous outwardly. Of course, Antonie's sudden death may be weighing him down heavily, but I'll wager that, as early as tomorrow, the councilor will continue to trot along in his customary routine."

It turned out almost exactly as the professor had foretold. The next day, the councilor appeared to be completely his old self; only, he declared that he would never again make violins or even play one. As I later learned, he kept that word.

The professor's suggestions strengthened my inner conviction that Antonie's relationship to the councilor, which was intimate and kept so carefully under wraps, and, in fact, even her death, might constitute a guilt weighing on him heavily and impossible to atone. I didn't want to leave H—— before confronting him with the crime I suspected him of. I wanted to shake him to his very depths and thus wring from him an open confession of his grisly deed. The more I thought over the case, the surer I felt that Krespel must be a criminal, and the more impassioned and forcible became the speech I was preparing in my mind, which, as if spontaneously, was shaping itself into a true masterpiece of rhetoric.

Thus armed, and in great excitement, I ran to the councilor's house. I found him carving toys, his expression calm and smiling. "How can it be?" I blurted out. "How can peace enter your soul for even a moment while the thought of your grisly deed must be torturing you with a serpent's sting?"

The councilor looked at me in amazement, laying aside his chisel. "What do you mean, my friend?" he asked. "Please do sit down on that chair!"

But in my zeal I continued; as I got more and more excited, I accused him directly of having murdered Antonie, and I threatened him with the vengeance of the eternal Power. Yes, as a newly fledged man of law, my head full of my profession, I went so far as to assure him that I would take every measure to track down his crime and thus hand him over to an earthly judge while he was still among the living. In fact, I got somewhat embarrassed when, at the end of my tremendous and pompous speech, the councilor said not a word in reply, but merely looked at me very calmly as if expecting me to continue. Indeed, I attempted to, but it all came out wrong and I sounded so foolish that I immediately shut up again.

Krespel weidete sich an meiner Verlegenheit, ein boshaftes, ironisches Lächeln flog über sein Gesicht. Dann wurde er aber sehr ernst, und sprach mit feierlichem Tone: «Junger Mensch! du magst mich für närrisch, für wahnsinnig halten, das verzeihe ich dir, da wir beide in demselben Irrenhause eingesperrt sind, und du mich darüber, daß ich Gott der Vater zu sein wähne, nur deshalb schiltst, weil du dich für Gott den Sohn hältst; wie magst du dich aber unterfangen, in ein Leben eindringen zu wollen, seine geheimsten Fäden erfassend, das dir fremd blieb und bleiben mußte? – Sie ist dahin und das Geheimnis gelöst!»

Krespel hielt inne, stand auf und schritt die Stube einige Male auf und ab. Ich wagte die Bitte um Aufklärung; er sah mich starr an, faßte mich bei der Hand und führte mich an das Fenster, beide Flügel öffnend. Mit aufgestützten Armen legte er sich hinaus, und so in den Garten herabblickend, erzählte er mir die Geschichte seines Lebens. – Als er geendet, verließ ich ihn gerührt und beschämt.

Mit Antonien verhielt es sich kürzlich in folgender Art. – Vor zwanzig Jahren trieb die bis zur Leidenschaft gesteigerte Liebhaberei, die besten Geigen alter Meister aufzusuchen und zu kaufen, den Rat nach Italien. Selbst baute er damals noch keine und unterließ daher auch das Zerlegen jener alten Geigen. In Venedig hörte er die berühmte Sängerin Angela —i, welche damals auf dem Teatro di S. Benedetto in den ersten Rollen glänzte. Sein Enthusiasmus galt nicht der Kunst allein, die Signora Angela freilich auf die herrlichste Weise übte, sondern auch wohl ihrer Engelsschönheit. Der Rat suchte Angelas Bekanntschaft, und trotz aller seiner Schroffheit gelang es ihm, vorzüglich durch sein keckes und dabei höchst ausdrucksvolles Violinspiel sie ganz für sich zu gewinnen.

Das engste Verhältnis führte in wenigen Wochen zur Heirat, die deshalb verborgen blieb, weil Angela sich weder vom Theater, noch von dem Namen, der die berühmte Sängerin bezeichnete, trennen oder ihm auch nur das übeltönende «Krespel» hinzufügen wollte. – Mit der tollsten Ironie beschrieb Krespel die ganz eigene Art, wie Signora Angela, sobald sie seine Frau geworden, ihn marterte und quälte. Aller Eigensinn, alles launische Wesen sämtlicher erster Sängerinnen sei, wie Krespel meinte, in Angelas kleine Figur hineingebannt worden. Wollte er sich einmal in Positur setzen, so schickte ihm Angela ein genzes Heer von Abbates, Maestro, Akademikos über den Hals, die, unbekannt mit seinem eigentlichen Verhältnis, ihn als den unerträglichsten, unhöflichsten Liebhaber,

Krespel was enjoying my embarrassment immensely; a malicious, ironical smile spread over his face. But then he became quite serious, and he said in solemn tones: "My boy, you may consider me a fool or a madman, for which I forgive you, because we're both locked up in the same madhouse, and you are reproaching me for imagining I'm God the Father merely because you imagine that you're God the Son; but how dare you presume to force your way into a person's life, and seize its most secret threads, when it has remained closed to you, and had to remain so? She is dead, and the mystery is solved!"

Krespel stopped, stood up, and paced up and down the room a few times. I ventured on a request for an explanation; he stared at me, took my hand, and led me to the window, opening both casements. Resting his arms on the sill, he leaned far out and, gazing down at the garden in that manner, he told me the story of his life. When he was done, I left his house, feeling both moved and ashamed.

In brief, his relationship to Antonie was as follows. Twenty years earlier, the councilor's hobby (which had escalated into a passion) for seeking out and purchasing the best violins of the old masters compelled him to visit Italy. At the time he was not yet making any himself, and so he didn't dissect those old violins, either. In Venice he heard the famous soprano Angela —i, who was then brilliantly performing the main roles at the Teatro San Benedetto. His enthusiasm was not for her art alone, though Signora Angela was a magnificent singer, but also surely for her angelic beauty. The councilor sought Angela's acquaintance, and despite all his rough edges he succeeded, primarily by means of his bold and yet extremely expressive violin playing, in winning her over completely.

In a few weeks, their intimate relationship led to marriage, which was kept secret because Angela didn't want to give up either the theater or the name she had made famous, refusing even to tack onto it the ugly-sounding "Krespel." With the most madcap irony Krespel described the unique fashion in which Signora Angela tortured and tormented him as soon as she became his wife. In Krespel's opinion, all the egotism and all the capriciousness of the whole race of leading ladies had been locked up in Angela's diminutive body by enchantment. Whenever he tried to defend himself, Angela called down upon him a whole army of abbés, maestros, and academicians who, unacquainted with his true relationship to her, berated him as a

der sich in die liebenswürdige Laune der Signora nicht zu schicken
wisse, ausfilzten.

Gerade nach einem solchen stürmischen Auftritt war Krespel auf
Angelas Landhaus geflohen und vergaß, auf seiner Cremoneser Geige
phantasierend, die Leiden des Tages. Doch nicht lange dauerte es, als
Signora, die dem Rat schnell nachgefahren, in den Saal trat. Sie war
gerade in der Laune, die Zärtliche zu spielen, sie umarmte den Rat
mit süßen, schmachtenden Blicken, sie legte das Köpfchen auf seine
Schulter. Aber der Rat, in die Welt seiner Akkorde verstiegen, geigte
fort, daß die Wände widerhallten, und es begab sich, daß er mit Arm
und Bogen die Signora etwas unsanft berührte.

Die sprang aber voller Furie zurück; «bestia tedesca» schrie sie auf,
riß dem Rat die Geige aus der Hand und zerschlug sie an dem
Marmortisch in tausend Stücke. Der Rat blieb, erstarrt zur Bildsäule,
vor ihr stehen, dann aber, wie aus dem Traume erwacht, faßte er
Signora mit Riesenstärke, warf sie durch das Fenster ihres eigenen
Lusthauses und floh, ohne sich weiter um etwas zu bekümmern, nach
Venedig – nach Deutschland zurück.

Erst nach einiger Zeit wurde es ihm recht deutlich, was er getan;
obschon er wußte, daß die Höhe des Fensters vom Boden kaum
fünf Fuß betrug, und ihm die Notwendigkeit, Signora bei obbe-
wandten Umständen durchs Fenster zu werfen, ganz einleuchtete,
so fühlte er sich doch von peinlicher Unruhe gequält, um so mehr,
da Signora ihm nicht undeutlich zu verstehen gegeben, daß sie
guter Hoffnung sei. Er wagte kaum Erkundigungen einzuziehen,
und nicht wenig überraschte es ihn, als er nach ungefähr acht
Monaten einen gar zärtlichen Brief von der geliebten Gattin erhielt, worin sie jenes Vorganges im Landhause mit keiner Silbe erwähnte, und der Nachricht, daß sie von einem herzallerliebsten
Töchterchen entbunden, die herzlichste Bitte hinzufügte, daß der
Marito amato e padre felicissimo doch nur gleich nach Venedig
kommen möge.

Das tat Krespel nicht, erkundigte sich vielmehr bei einem ver-
trauten Freunde nach den näheren Umständen und erfuhr, daß
Signora damals, leicht wie ein Vogel, in das weiche Gras herabge-
sunken sei, und der Fall oder Sturz durchaus keine andere als psy-
chische Folgen gehabt habe. Signora sei nämlich nach Krespels
heroischer Tat wie umgewandelt; von Launen, närrischen
Einfällen, von irgendeiner Quälerei ließe sie durchaus nichts mehr

most unbearable and discourteous lover unable to indulge the Signora in her charming caprices.

Right after one such stormy scene, Krespel had taken refuge in Angela's country villa; improvising on his Cremona violin, he forgot the sorrows of the day. But before very long, the Signora, who had quickly driven in pursuit of the councilor, walked into the room. Her whim of the moment was to play the affectionate wife; she embraced the councilor with sweet, languishing glances, she rested her little head on his shoulder. But the councilor, lost in the world of his chords, kept on playing, making the walls echo, and he happened to touch the Signora rather ungently with his arm and the bow.

She leapt back in a rage; *"Bestia tedesca!"*[12] she screamed, as she tore the violin out of the councilor's hand and smashed it to smithereens against the marble table. The councilor just stood there in front of her, as motionless as a statue, but then, as if awakened from a dream, he seized the Signora with the strength of a giant, threw her out the window of her own villa, and, with no concern for anything else, fled to Venice, and from there back to Germany.

It took some time before the nature of his action became really clear to him; even though he knew that the window was scarcely five feet from the ground, and he was fully convinced that it had been perfectly necessary to throw the Signora out the window, given the circumstances, nevertheless he felt tormented by a painful unease, all the more so because the Signora had given him to understand in unequivocal terms that she was pregnant. He hardly dared to make inquiries about her, and he was not a little surprised when, about eight months later, he received a quite affectionate letter from his beloved spouse, in which she made not the slightest mention of that event in the villa, but accompanied the news that she had given birth to a lovely little girl with a very cordial invitation to the *marito amato e padre felicissimo*[13] to come to Venice at once.

Krespel didn't comply; instead, he asked a close friend of his to look into the details of the situation, and he learned that, on that occasion, the Signora, who was as light as a bird, had landed on soft grass, and her fall or plunge had had only psychological consequences. To wit: after Krespel's heroic exploit the Signora was like a changed woman; she showed absolutely no further signs of whims, foolish caprices, or any tendency to torture people, and

---

12. "German animal!"   13. "Beloved husband and most happy father."

verspüren, und der Maestro, der für das nächste Karneval komponiert, sei der glücklichste Mensch unter der Sonne, weil Signora
seine Arien ohne hunderttausend Abänderungen, die er sich sonst
gefallen lassen mußte, singen wolle. Übrigens habe man alle
Ursache, meinte der Freund, es sorgfältig zu verschweigen, wie
Angela kuriert wurde, da sonst jedes Tages Sängerinnen durch die
Fenster fliegen würden.

Der Rat geriet nicht in geringe Bewegung, er bestellte Pferde, er
setzte sich in den Wagen. «Halt!» rief er plötzlich. – «Wie»,
murmelte er dann in sich hinein, «ist's denn nicht ausgemacht, daß,
sobald ich mich blicken lasse, der böse Geist wieder Kraft und
Macht erhält über Angela? – Da ich sie schon zum Fenster heraus-
geworfen, was soll ich nun in gleichem Falle tun? was ist mir noch
übrig?»

Er stieg wieder aus dem Wagen, schrieb einen zärtlichen Brief
an seine genesene Frau, worin er höflich berührte, wie zart es von
ihr sei, ausdrücklich es zu rühmen, daß das Töchterchen gleich
ihm ein kleines Mal hinter dem Ohre trage, und – blieb in
Deutschland.

Der Briefwechsel dauerte sehr lebhaft fort. – Versicherungen der
Liebe – Einladungen – Klagen über die Abwesenheit der Geliebten –
verfehlte Wünsche – Hoffnungen und so weiter flogen hin und her
von Venedig nach H., von H. nach Venedig.

Angela kam endlich nach Deutschland und glänzte, wie bekannt,
als Primadonna auf dem großen Theater in F. Ungeachtet sie gar nicht
mehr jung war, riß sie doch alles hin mit dem unwiderstehlichen
Zauber ihres wunderbar herrlichen Gesanges. Ihre Stimme hatte
damals nicht im mindesten verloren. Antonie war indessen
herangewachsen, und die Mutter konnte nicht genug dem Vater
schreiben, wie in Antonien eine Sängerin vom ersten Range aufblühe.
In der Tat bestätigten dies die Freunde Krespels in F., die ihm zuset-
zten, doch nur einmal nach F. zu kommen, um die seltne Erscheinung
zwei ganz sublimer Sängerinnen zu bewundern. Sie ahneten nicht, in
welchem nahen Verhältnis der Rat mit diesem Paare stand. Krespel
hätte gar zu gern die Tochter, die recht in seinem Innersten lebte, und
die ihm öfters als Traumbild erschien, mit leiblichen Augen gesehen,
aber sowie er an seine Frau dachte, wurde es ihm ganz unheimlich zumute, und er blieb zu Hause unter seinen zerschnittenen Geigen
sitzen.

Ihr werdet von dem hoffnungsvollen jungen Komponisten B . . . in
F. gehört haben, der plötzlich verscholl, man wußte nicht wie; (oder

the *maestro* who had composed an opera for the coming Carnival season was the luckiest man under the sun because the Signora was willing to sing his arias without making the hundred thousand alterations he had formerly had to put up with. Moreover, the councilor's friend thought, there was every reason to conceal carefully the manner in which Angela was cured, or else no day would go by without some soprano sailing through a window.

The councilman was stirred to considerable activity; he ordered horses and took a seat in the coach. "Stop!" he suddenly shouted. Then he muttered to himself: "What! Isn't it a sure thing that, the minute I show myself, the evil spirit will once again regain power over Angela? Since I've already thrown her out the window, what am I to do if the same case should arise? What is there left for me?"

He got out of the coach again; he wrote an affectionate letter to his wife, now a mother, in which he politely acknowledged how nice it had been of her to report with pride that the baby girl had the same small mole behind her ear that he had; and— he stayed in Germany.

The correspondence continued in lively fashion. Assurances of love, invitations, laments over the absence of the loved one, unfulfilled wishes, hopes, and so on and so forth, sped back and forth from Venice to H—— and from H—— to Venice.

Finally Angela came to Germany, and, as is well known, achieved a great success as a prima donna at the principal theater in F——. Even though she was no longer young, she captivated everyone with the irresistible magic of her miraculously fine singing. Her voice hadn't suffered at all from her misadventure. Meanwhile Antonie had grown up, and her mother couldn't say enough to her father, in letters, about Antonie's promising future as a soprano of the first rank. Indeed, this judgment was confirmed by Krespel's friends in F——, who badgered him with requests to come to F—— to marvel at the unusual phenomenon of two quite sublime sopranos in the same place. They had no idea how closely related the councilor was to those two women. Krespel would really have liked to see with his own eyes that daughter who occupied his thoughts and often appeared in his dreams, but the moment he thought about his wife, he got quite alarmed, and he stayed home with his dissected violins.

You must have heard about B——, the promising young composer in F——, who suddenly dropped out of sight, without any-

kanntet ihr ihn vielleicht selbst?) Dieser verliebte sich in Antonien so
sehr, daß er, da Antonie seine Liebe recht herzlich erwiderte, der
Mutter anlag, doch nur gleich in eine Verbindung zu willigen, die die
Kunst heilige. Angela hatte nichts dagegen, und der Rat stimmte um
so lieber bei, als des jungen Meisters Kompositionen Gnade gefunden
vor seinem strengen Richterstuhl. Krespel glaubte Nachricht von der
vollzogenen Heirat zu erhalten, statt derselben kam ein schwarz
gesiegelter Brief, von fremder Hand überschrieben.

Der Doktor R . . . meldete dem Rat, daß Angela an den Folgen
einer Erkältung im Theater heftig erkrankt und gerade in der
Nacht, als am andern Tage Antonie getraut werden sollte, gestorben
sei. Ihm, dem Doktor, habe Angela entdeckt, daß sie Krespels Frau
und Antonie seine Tochter sei; er möge daher eilen, sich der
Verlassenen anzunehmen. So sehr auch der Rat von Angelas
Hinscheiden erschüttert wurde, war es ihm doch bald, als sei ein
störendes, unheimliches Prinzip aus seinem Leben gewichen, und
er könne nun erst recht frei atmen. Noch denselben Tag reiste er ab
nach F.

Ihr könnt nicht glauben, wie herzzerreißend mir der Rat den
Moment schilderte, als er Antonien sah. Selbst in der Bizarrerie
seines Ausdrucks lag eine wunderbare Macht der Darstellung, die
auch nur anzudeuten ich gar nicht imstande bin. – Alle Liebenswürdigkeit, alle Anmut Angelas wurde Antonien zuteil, der aber die
häßliche Kehrseite ganz fehlte. Es gab kein zweideutig Pferdefüß-
chen, das hin und wieder hervorgucken konnte.

Der junge Bräutigam fand sich ein, Antonie, mit zartem Sinn den
wunderlichen Vater im tiefsten Innern richtig auffassend, sang eine
jener Motetten des alten Padre Martini, von denen sie wußte, daß
Angela sie dem Rat in der höchsten Blüte ihrer Liebeszeit unaufhörlich vorsingen mußte. Der Rat vergoß Ströme von Tränen, nie hatte
er selbst Angela so singen gehört. Der Klang von Antoniens Stimme
war ganz eigentümlich und seltsam, oft dem Hauch der Äolsharfe, oft
dem Schmettern der Nachtigall gleichend. Die Töne schienen nicht
Raum haben zu können in der menschlichen Brust.

Antonie, vor Freude und Liebe glühend, sang und sang alle ihre
schönsten Lieder, und B . . . spielte dazwischen, wie es nur die won-
netrunkene Begeisterung vermag. Krespel schwamm erst in
Entzücken, dann wurde er nachdenklich – still – in sich gekehrt.
Endlich sprang er auf, drückte Antonien an seine Brust und bat sehr

one knowing how; maybe you even knew him personally. He fell so deeply in love with Antonie that, when Antonie warmly reciprocated his love, he entreated her mother to consent at once to a union that was hallowed by art. Angela had no objections, and the councilor was all the more agreeable because the young master's compositions had found favor in his severe judgment. Krespel was expecting news that the wedding had taken place; instead of that, a black-sealed letter arrived, addressed in an unfamiliar hand.

Doctor R—— reported to the councilor that Angela had fallen seriously ill after catching cold in the theater, and had died on the very night before Antonie was to be married. Angela had revealed to him, the doctor, that she was Krespel's wife and Antonie was his daughter; he therefore urged him to make haste and take charge of the unprotected girl. Though the councilor was greatly moved by Angela's passing, he soon felt as if a disruptive, uncanny force had vanished from his life, and that he could now breathe freely for the first time. That very day he set out for F——.

You won't believe how heartrendingly the councilor depicted to me the moment when he first saw Antonie. Despite the oddity of the words he used, he displayed a marvelous narrative power, which I'm quite incapable of even hinting at. All of Angela's charm and grace had been passed on to Antonie, but entirely without the ugly side of her mother's nature. There was no ambiguous "fly in the ointment" that might make its presence known at odd times.

Her young fiancé arrived. Antonie's loving spirit gave her a clear insight into the real nature of her eccentric father; she sang one of those motets by old Padre Martini[14] which she knew the councilor had made Angela sing for him incessantly when their love affair was at its height. The councilor shed streams of tears; he had never heard Angela sing that well. The sound of Antonie's voice was altogether unique and unusual, often resembling the whisper of an Aeolian harp, often the full-throated singing of a nightingale. It seemed as if such tones couldn't be contained in a human breast.

Antonie, aglow with joy and love, went on singing all her most beautiful songs, and B—— played in between, as only a man in rapturous enthusiasm can. At first Krespel was filled with delight, then he became pensive, quiet, shut up in himself. Finally he leaped up, pressed Antonie to his bosom, and said in a low,

14. Giambattista Martini, 1706–1784.

leise und dumpf: «Nicht mehr singen, wenn du mich liebst – es drückt
mir das Herz ab – die Angst – die Angst – Nicht mehr singen.» –

«Nein», sprach der Rat andern Tages zum Doktor R . . . , «als
während des Gesanges ihre Röte sich zusammenzog in zwei dunkel-
rote Flecke auf den blassen Wangen, da war es nicht mehr dumme
Familienähnlichkeit, da war es das, was ich gefürchtet.»

Der Doktor, dessen Miene vom Anfang des Gesprächs von tiefer
Bekümmernis zeugte, erwiderte: «Mag es sein, daß es von zu früher
Anstrengung im Singen herrührt, oder hat die Natur es verschuldet,
genug, Antonie leidet an einem organischen Fehler in der Brust, der
eben ihrer Stimme die wundervolle Kraft und den seltsamen, ich
möchte sagen, über die Sphäre des menschlichen Gesangen hin-
austönenden Klang gibt. Aber auch ihr früher Tod ist die Folge
davon, denn singt sie fort, so gebe ich ihr noch höchstens sechs
Monate Zeit.»

Den Rat zerschnitt es im Innern wie mit hundert Schwertern.
Es war ihm, als hinge zum ersten Male ein schöner Baum die
wunderherrlichen Blüten in sein Leben hinein, und der solle
recht an der Wurzel zersägt werden, damit er nie mehr zu grünen
und zu blühen vermöge. Sein Entschluß war gefaßt. Er sagte
Antonien alles, er stellte ihr die Wahl, ob sie dem Bräutigam folgen und seiner und der Welt Verlockung nachgeben, so aber früh
untergehen, oder ob sie dem Vater noch in seinen alten Tagen nie
gefühlte Ruhe und Freude bereiten, so aber noch jahrelang leben
wolle.

Antonie fiel dem Vater schluchzend in die Arme, er wollte, das
Zerreißende der kommenden Momente wohl fühlend, nichts
Deutlicheres vernehmen. Er sprach mit dem Bräutigam, aber
unerachtet dieser versicherte, daß nie ein Ton über Antoniens
Lippen gehen solle, so wußte der Rat doch wohl, daß selbst B . . .
nicht der Versuchung würde widerstehen können, Antonien singen zu hören, wenigstens von ihm selbst komponierte Arien. Auch
die Welt, das musikalische Publikum, mocht es auch unterrichtet
sein von Antoniens Leiden, gab gewiß die Ansprüche nicht auf,
denn dies Volk ist ja, kommt es auf Genuß an, egoistisch und
grausam.

Der Rat verschwand mit Antonien aus F. und kam nach H.
Verzweiflungsvoll vernahm B . . . die Abreise. Er vorfolgte die Spur,
holte den Rat ein und kam zugleich mit ihm nach H. – «Nur einmal
ihn sehen und dann sterben», flehte Antonie.

«Sterben? – sterben?» rief der Rat in wildem Zorn, eiskalter

muffled voice: "Don't sing anymore, if you love me; it oppresses my heart—fear—fear—don't sing anymore."

"No," the councilor said to Doctor R—— the next day, "when, in the course of her singing, her blush became concentrated into two dark-red spots on her pale cheeks, it was no longer some silly family resemblance; it was what I had feared."

The doctor, whose expression at the beginning of the conversation had bespoken deep concern, replied: "Whether it's the result of premature overexertion in singing, or whether Nature is to blame, suffice it to say that Antonie is suffering from a defect in her chest organs, the very defect which gives her voice its marvelous power and its strange timbre, which I might say goes beyond the sphere of human vocalism. But an early death will be another consequence of it, because if she continues to sing, I give her not more than six months."

The councilor felt as if a hundred swords were cutting up his insides. It seemed to him as if for the first time in his life a beautiful tree was putting forth marvelous blossoms for him, and that very tree was to be sawn off at its roots so it could never again grow green and bloom. His decision was made. He told Antonie everything and gave her the choice of following her fiancé and yielding to his and the world's temptations, in which case she would die young, or else of offering her father in his declining days the repose and joy he had never yet known, in which case, however, she could live for many years more.

Antonie fell into her father's arms, sobbing; no doubt foreseeing how painful the coming period would be, he wouldn't let her make any clearer statement. He spoke to her fiancé, but, even though the young man assured him that no note would ever pass Antonie's lips, the councilor knew very well that even B—— wouldn't be able to resist the temptation to hear Antonie sing, at least arias that he himself composed. Even the world at large, the musical public, even if informed of Antonie's illness, certainly wouldn't give up its claims on her, because, where their pleasure is concerned, that crowd is selfish and cruel.

The councilor disappeared from F—— along with Antonie, and set out for H——. B—— was in despair on hearing of their departure. He followed their tracks, caught up with the councilor, and arrived in H—— at the same time that he did. "Let me see him just once and then die," Antonie pleaded.

"Die? Die?" shouted the councilor in wild anger, as an icy

Schauer durchbebte sein Inneres. – Die Tochter, das einzige
Wesen auf der weiten Welt, das nie gekannte Lust in ihm entzündet, das allein ihn mit dem Leben versöhnte, riß sich gewaltsam los
von seinem Herzen, und er wollte, daß das Entsetzliche geschehe.
– B . . . mußte an den Flügel, Antonie sang, Krespel spielte lustig
die Geige, bis sich jene roten Flecken auf Antoniens Wangen
zeigten. Da befahl er einzuhalten; als nun aber B . . . Abschied
nahm von Antonien, sank sie plötzlich mit einem lauten Schrei
zusammen.

«Ich glaubte» (so erzählte mir Krespel), «ich glaubte, sie wäre, wie
ich es vorausgesehen, nun wirklich tot und blieb, da ich einmal mich
selbst auf die höchste Spitze gestellt hatte, sehr gelassen und mit mir
einig. Ich faßte den B . . . , der in seiner Erstarrung schafsmäßig und
albern anzusehen war, bei den Schultern und sprach: (der Rat fiel in
seinen singenden Ton) «Da Sie, verehrungswürdigster Klaviermeister,
wie Sie gewollt und gewünscht, Ihre liebe Braut wirklich ermordet
haben, so können Sie nun ruhig abgehen, es wäre denn, Sie wollten
so lange gütigst verziehen, bis ich Ihnen den blanken Hirschfänger
durch das Herz renne, damit so meine Tochter, die, wie Sie sehen,
ziemlich verblaßt, einige Couleur bekomme durch Ihr sehr wertes
Blut. – Rennen Sie nur geschwind, aber ich könnte Ihnen auch ein
flinkes Messerchen nachwerfen!» – Ich muß wohl bei diesen Worten
etwas graulich ausgesehen haben; denn mit einem Schrei des tiefsten
Entsetzens sprang er, sich von mir losreißend, fort durch die Türe, die
Treppe herab.»

Wie der Rat nun, nachdem B . . . fortgerannt war, Antonien, die
bewußtlos auf der Erde lag, aufrichten wollte, öffnete sie tief-
seufzend die Augen, die sich aber bald wieder zum Tode zu schließen
schienen. Da brach Krespel aus in lautes, trostloses Jammern. Der
von der Haushälterin herbeigerufene Arzt erklärte Antoniens
Zustand für einen heftigen, aber nicht im mindesten gefährlichen
Zufall, und in der Tat erholte sich diese auch schneller, als der Rat es
nur zu hoffen gewagt hatte. Sie schmiegte sich nun mit der innigsten,
kindlichsten Liebe an Krespel; sie ging ein in seine Lieb-
lingsneigungen – in seine tollen Launen und Einfälle. Sie half ihm
alte Geigen auseinanderlegen und neue zusammenleimen. «Ich will
nicht mehr singen, aber für dich leben», sprach sie oft sanft lächelnd
zum Vater, wenn jemand sie zum Gesange aufgefordert und sie es
abgeschlagen hatte.

Solche Momente suchte der Rat indessen ihr soviel möglich zu er-
sparen, und daher kam es, daß er ungern mit ihr in Gesellschaft ging

chill ran through him.—His daughter, the only being in the whole world that had kindled never-before-known pleasure in him, who alone reconciled him to life, tore herself away forcefully from his heart, and he allowed the horror to occur. B—— had to go to the piano, Antonie sang, Krespel played the violin merrily, until those red spots appeared on Antonie's cheeks. Then he gave orders to cease; but when B—— was taking leave of Antonie, she suddenly collapsed with a loud cry.

"I thought," said Krespel in his narrative, "I thought she was now really dead, as I had foreseen; since I had already raised myself to the highest pitch, I remained very calm and at one with myself. I seized B——, who looked sheepish and stupid as he stood by rigidly; taking him by the shoulders, I said [here the councilor lapsed into his singsong tone]: 'Most honorable piano virtuoso, since you have accomplished what you intended and desired, and have actually murdered your dear fiancée, you can now leave in peace, unless you're kind enough to tarry until I pierce your heart with my drawn dagger, so that my daughter, who is rather pale, as you see, can gain a little color from your most respectable blood. Run away quickly, though I might still fling a swift stiletto at you!' When I uttered those words, I must have looked somewhat fearsome, because with a cry of deepest horror he tore himself away from me, and leapt out the door and down the stairs."

After B—— had run away, when the councilor tried to raise up Antonie, who was lying unconscious on the floor, with a deep sigh she opened her eyes, which soon, however, seemed to close again in death. Then Krespel burst into a loud, inconsolable lament. The doctor, who had been summoned by the house-keeper, pronounced Antonie's condition to be a serious, but in no way life-threatening attack, and indeed she recovered more quickly than the councilor had dared hope. From then on, she clung to Krespel with the most heartfelt, childlike love; she hu-mored his favorite propensities, his daft whims and notions. She helped him take apart old violins and glue together new ones. "I shall not sing again, but only live for you," she often told her fa-ther with a gentle smile, whenever someone had asked her to sing and she had refused.

Meanwhile, the councilor tried to save her from similar occa-sions as much as possible, and that's why he didn't like to take her along on visits, and why he carefully avoided all music. He

und alle Musik sorgfältig vermied. Er wußte es ja wohl, wie schmerz-
lich es Antonien sein mußte, der Kunst, die sie in solch hoher
Vollkommenheit geübt, ganz zu entsagen.

Als der Rat jene wunderbare Geige, die er mit Antonien begrub,
gekauft hatte und zerlegen wollte, blickte ihn Antonie sehr wehmütig
an und sprach leise bittend: «Auch diese?» – Der Rat wußte selbst
nicht, welche unbekannte Macht ihn nötigte, die Geige unzerschnit-
ten zu lassen und darauf zu spielen. Kaum hatte er die ersten Töne
angestrichen, als Antonie laut und freudig rief: «Ach, das bin ich ja –
ich singe ja wieder.»

Wirklich hatten die silberhellen Glockentöne des Instruments
etwas ganz eigenes Wundervolles, sie schienen in der menschlichen Brust erzeugt. Krespel wurde bis in das Innerste gerührt,
er spielte wohl herrlicher als jemals, und wenn er in kühnen
Gängen mit voller Kraft, mit tiefem Ausdruck auf- und nieder-
stieg, dann schlug Antonie die Hände zusammen und rief
entzückt: «Ach, das habe ich gut gemacht! das habe ich gut
gemacht!»

Seit dieser Zeit kam eine große Ruhe und Heiterkeit in ihr Leben.
Oft sprach sie zum Rat: «Ich möchte wohl etwas singen, Vater!» Dann
nahm Krespel die Geige von der Wand und spielte Antoniens schönste Lieder, sie war recht aus dem Herzen froh.

Kurz vor meiner Ankunft war es in einer Nacht dem Rat so, als
höre er im Nebenzimmer auf seinem Pianoforte spielen, und bald
unterschied er deutlich, daß B . . . nach gewöhnlicher Art
präludierte. Er wollte aufstehen, aber wie eine schwere Last lag es
auf ihm, wie mit eisernen Banden gefesselt, vermochte er sich nicht
zu regen und zu rühren. Nun fiel Antonie ein in leisen, hinge-
hauchten Tönen, die immer steigend und steigend zum
schmetternden Fortissimo wurden, dann gestalteten sich die wunderbaren Laute zu dem tief ergreifenden Liede, welches B . . . einst
ganz im frommen Stil der alten Meister für Antonie komponiert
hatte.

Krespel sagte, unbegreiflich sei der Zustand gewesen, in dem er
sich befunden, denn eine entsetzliche Angst habe sich gepaart mit
nie gefühlter Wonne. Plötzlich umgab ihn eine blendende Klarheit,
und in derselben erblickte er B . . . und Antonien, die sich umschlungen hielten und sich voll seligem Entzücken anschauten. Die
Töne des Liedes und des begleitenden Pianofortes dauerten fort,
ohne daß Antonie sichtbar sang oder B . . . das Fortepiano
berührte.

was quite aware how painful it must be to Antonie to renounce entirely the art which she had practiced with such supreme perfection.

When the councilor bought that marvelous violin which he buried with Antonie, and he wanted to take it apart, Antonie looked at him with great melancholy and said softly and beseechingly: "This one, too?" The councilor himself didn't know what unknown force prevailed on him to leave the violin undissected and to play it. Scarcely had he bowed the first few notes when Antonie cried out loud in joy: "Oh, it's me—I'm singing again!"

In truth, the bright, silvery, bell-like tones of the instrument had something uniquely marvelous in them, they seemed to have been generated in a human breast. Krespel was stirred to his very depths; he played more magnificently than ever, and whenever he executed bold passagework with full strength, ascending and descending the scales with great expressivity, Antonie would clap her hands and call in rapture: "Oh, I did that well! I did that well!"

From that time on, a great repose and serenity entered her life. She often said to the councilor: "I'd like to sing something, father!" Then Krespel would take the violin down from the wall and he'd play Antonie's most beautiful songs, and she was thoroughly happy.

One night, shortly before my arrival, the councilor thought he heard his piano being played in the next room, and he could soon tell distinctly that B—— was beginning a piece in his usual style. He wanted to get up, but a heavy load seemed to weigh him down; as if fettered with bands of iron, he was unable to move or stir. Now Antonie joined in, in soft, whispered tones, which continued to grow stronger until they reached a resounding fortissimo; then those wonderful sounds formed themselves into that deeply affecting song which B—— had once composed for Antonie, exactly in the pious style of the old masters.

Krespel said that he couldn't comprehend the state he was in at that moment, for a horrible anguish was combined with a rapture he had never felt before. Suddenly things became dazzlingly clear to him, and in that clarity he caught sight of B—— and Antonie, who were embracing each other and gazing at each other in blissful delight. The notes of the song and of its piano accompaniment continued to sound, though Antonie wasn't visibly singing and B—— wasn't touching the piano.

Der Rat fiel nun in eine Art dumpfer Ohnmacht, in der das Bild mit den Tönen versank. Als er erwachte, war ihm noch jene fürchterliche Angst aus dem Traume geblieben. Er sprang in Antoniens Zimmer. Sie lag mit geschlossenen Augen, mit holdselig lächelndem Blick, die Hände fromm gefaltet, auf dem Sofa, als schliefe sie und träume von Himmelswonne und Freudigkeit. Sie war aber tot.

Then the councilor fell into a sort of numb faint, in which that image subsided along with the sounds. When he awoke, he still felt that terrible anguish from his dream. He dashed into Antonie's room. She was lying on the sofa with her eyes shut, her face smiling sweetly, her hands piously clasped, as if she were asleep and dreaming of heavenly rapture and joyousness. But she was dead.

Die Bergwerke zu Falun

An einem heitern sonnenhellen Juliustage hatte sich alles Volk zu
Götaborg auf der Reede versammelt. Ein reicher Ostindienfahrer,
glücklich heimgekehrt aus dem fernen Lande, lag im Klippa-Hafen
vor Anker und ließ die langen Wimpel, die schwedischen Flaggen,
lustig hinauswehen in die azurblaue Luft, während Hunderte von
Fahrzeugen, Böten, Kähnen, vollgepfropft mit jubelnden Seeleuten
auf den spiegelblanken Wellen der Götaelf hin und her
schwammen und die Kanonen von Masthuggetorg ihre weithallen-
den Grüße hinüberdonnerten in das weite Meer. Die Herren von der
ostindischen Kompagnie wandelten am Hafen auf und ab, und
berechneten mit lächelnden Gesichtern den reichen Gewinn, der
ihnen geworden, und hatten ihre Herzensfreude daran, wie ihr
gewagtes Unternehmen nun mit jedem Jahr mehr und mehr gedeihe
und das gute Götaborg im schönsten Handelsflor immer frischer und
herrlicher emporblühe. Jeder sah auch deshalb die wackern Herrn
mit Lust und Vergnügen an und freute sich mit ihnen, denn mit
ihrem Gewinn kam ja Saft und Kraft in das rege Leben der ganzen
Stadt.

Die Besatzung des Ostindienfahrers, wohl an die hundertundfunf-
zig Mann stark, landete in vielen Böten die dazu ausgerüstet, und
schickte sich an ihren Hönsning zu halten. So ist nämlich das Fest
geheißen, das bei derlei Gelegenheit von der Schiffsmannschaft
gefeiert wird, und das oft mehrere Tage dauert. Spielleute in wunderlicher bunter Tracht zogen vorauf mit Geigen, Pfeifen, Oboen
und Trommeln, die sie wacker rührten, während andere allerlei
lustige Lieder dazu absangen. Ihnen folgten die Matrosen zu Paar
und Paar. Einige mit bunt bebänderten Jacken und Hüten schwan-
gen flatternde Wimpel, andere tanzten und sprangen, und alle
jauchzten und jubelten, daß das helle Getöse weit in den Lüften er-
hallte.

So ging der fröhliche Zug fort über die Werfte – durch die

The Mines at Falun

On a clear, sunny July day everyone in Göteborg had assembled at the roadstead. A richly laden East Indiaman, which had returned from that distant region after a successful voyage, lay at anchor in the Klippan harbor, and let its long pennons and Swedish banners wave merrily against the azure sky, while hundreds of craft, launches, and lighters, crammed with jubilant sailors, moved to and fro on the mirror-bright billows of the Göta river, and the cannons in the Masthuggstorget rumbled their echoing salutes over the broad sea. The gentlemen of the East India Company were walking back and forth on the docks, smiling as they calculated the substantial profit they had gained, and were glad at heart that their risky enterprise was now thriving more and more each year, and their beloved Göteborg was continuing to blossom ever more vigorously and splendidly in the most excellent commercial prosperity. On that account, everyone felt pleasure and contentment at the sight of those honest gentlemen and shared their joy, because their profit brought energy and strength into the busy life of the entire city.

The crew of the East Indiaman, some hundred and fifty men strong, landed in numerous specially equipped launches, and hastened to participate in their *hönsning*. That is the name of the celebration held by the crew on such occasions, one that often lasts several days. Musicians in odd, colorful costumes led the way with fiddles, fifes, oboes, and snare drums which they beat lustily, while others sang all sorts of jolly songs to the music. They were followed by the seamen in pairs. Some of them, with colorful ribbons on their jackets and hats, were waving fluttering pennons, others were dancing and leaping, and all of them were whooping and hurrahing, so that their noisy racket echoed far and wide through the air.

The cheerful procession continued across the docks in that manner, through the suburbs, until the men reached the suburb

Vorstädte bis nach der Haga-Vorstadt, wo in einem Gästgifvaregard
tapfer geschmaust und gezecht werden sollte.

Da floß nun das schönste Öl in Strömen und Bumper auf Bumper
wurde geleert. Wie es denn nun bei Seeleuten, die heimkehren von
weiter Reise, nicht anders der Fall ist, allerlei schmucke Dirnen
gesellten sich alsbald zu ihnen, der Tanz begann, und wilder und
wilder wurde die Lust und lauter und toller der Jubel.

Nur ein einziger Seemann, ein schlanker hübscher Mensch, kaum
mocht er zwanzig Jahr alt sein, hatte sich fortgeschlichen aus dem
Getümmel, und draußen einsam hingesetzt auf die Bank, die neben
der Tür des Schenkhauses stand.

Ein paar Matrosen traten zu ihm, und einer von ihnen rief laut auflachend: «Elis Fröbom! – Elis Fröbom! – Bist du mal wieder ein
recht trauriger Narr worden, und verträdelst die schöne Zeit mit
dummen Gedanken? – Hör, Elis, wenn du von unserm Hönsning
wegbleibst, so bleib lieber auch ganz weg vom Schiff! – Ein or-
dentlicher tüchtiger Seemann wird doch so aus dir niemals werden.
Mut hast du zwar genug, und tapfer bist du auch in der Gefahr, aber
saufen kannst du gar nicht, und behältst lieber die Dukaten in der
Tasche, als sie hier gastlich den Landratzen zuzuwerfen. – Trink,
Bursche! oder der Seeteufel Näcken – der ganze Troll soll dir über
den Hals kommen!»

Elis Fröbom sprang hastig von der Bank auf, schaute den
Matrosen an mit glühendem Blick, nahm den mit Branntwein bis an
den Rand gefüllten Becher und leerte ihn mit einem Zuge. Dann
sprach er: «Du siehst, Joens, daß ich saufen kann wie einer von euch,
und ob ich ein tüchtiger Seemann bin, mag der Kapitän entscheiden.
Aber nun halt dein Lästermaul, und schier dich fort! – Mir ist eure
wilde Tollheit zuwider. – Was ich hier draußen treibe, geht dich
nichts an!»

«Nun, nun», erwiderte Joens, «ich weiß es ja, du bist ein
Neriker von Geburt, und die sind alle trübe und traurig, und
haben keine rechte Lust am wackern Seemannsleben! – Wart nur,
Elis, ich werde dir jemand herausschicken, du sollst bald wegge-
bracht werden von der verhexten Bank, an die dich der Näcken
genagelt hat.»

Nicht lange dauerte es, so trat ein gar feines schmuckes Mädchen
aus der Tür des Gästgifvaregard und setzte sich hin neben dem trüb-
sinnigen Elis, der sich wieder verstummt und in sich gekehrt auf die

of Haga, where they intended to have a hearty eating and drinking bout in a *gästgivargård*.[1]

Then the finest *öl*[2] flowed in rivers, and one bumper after another was drained. Next, as is regularly the case when sailors return to home port after a long voyage, all sorts of pretty chippies soon came to keep them company; a dance struck up, and their revelry became increasingly wilder, and their shouting louder and madder.

Only one solitary seaman, a good-looking, slender fellow, who was scarcely twenty years old, had slipped away from the merriment and had sat down alone outside on the bench next to the inn door.

A couple of sailors came up to him, one of whom called with a loud burst of laughter: "Elis Fröbom! Elis Fröbom! Have you turned into a really sad fool once again, wasting this wonderful occasion in stupid thoughts? Listen, Elis, if you stay away from our *hönsning*, you may just as well stay away from the ship altogether! If you act this way, you'll never become a proper, able sailor. I know you have plenty of courage, and you're brave, too, when there's any danger, but you don't know how to drink, and you'd rather keep your ducats in your pocket than toss them to the landlubbers here for entertainment. Drink, lad! Or else the sea devil, the *näcken,* and his whole gang of trolls will drop in on you!"

Elis Fröbom leaped up from the bench hastily, glared at the sailor with burning eyes, took the goblet, which was filled to the brim with brandy, and emptied it in one draft. Then he said: "You see, Jöns, that I can drink as well as any of you, and whether or not I'm an able sailor—that's for the captain to decide. But for now, shut your blaspheming mouth and beat it! I can't stand the wild, crazy ways of you and yours. What I'm doing out here is none of your business!"

"Now, now," Jöns replied, "I know very well that you were born in Närke, and that all the people there are gloomy and sad, and can't properly enjoy an honest sailor's life! Just you wait, Elis, I'm going to send someone out to you who'll soon draw you away from that enchanted bench to which the *näcken* has fastened you!"

Before very long, a really delicate, pretty girl stepped out of the door of the *gästgivargård* and sat down next to the melancholy Elis, who had fallen silent again and had sat back down on

1. Inn (Swedish word).   2. Beer (Swedish word; later in the story the form *aehl* is used).

Bank niedergelassen hatte. Man sah es dem Putz, dem ganzen Wesen
der Dirne wohl an, daß sie sich leider böser Lust geopfert, aber noch
hatte das wilde Leben nicht seine zerstörende Macht geübt an den
wunderlieblichen sanften Zügen ihres holden Antlitzes. Keine Spur
von zurückstoßender Frechheit, nein, eine stille sehnsüchtige Trauer
lag in dem Blick der dunkeln Augen.

«Elis! – wollt Ihr denn gar keinen Teil nehmen an der Freude Eurer
Kameraden? – Regt sich denn gar keine Lust in Euch, da Ihr wieder
heimgekommen und, der bedrohlichen Gefahr der trügerischen
Meereswellen entronnen, nun wieder auf vaterländischem Boden steht?»

So sprach die Dirne mit leiser, sanfter Stimme, indem sie den Arm
um den Jüngling schlang. Elis Fröbom, wie aus tiefem Traum
erwachend, schaute dem Mädchen ins Auge, er faßte ihre Hand, er
drückte sie an seine Brust, man merkte wohl, daß der Dirne süß
Gelispel recht in sein Inneres hineingeklungen.

«Ach», begann er endlich, wie sich besinnend, «ach, mit meiner
Freude, mit meiner Lust ist es nun einmal gar nichts. Wenigstens
kann ich durchaus nicht einstimmen in die Toberei meiner
Kameraden. Geh nur hinein, mein gutes Kind, juble und jauchze mit
den andern, wenn du es vermagst, aber laß den trüben, traurigen Elis
hier draußen allein; er würde dir nur alle Lust verderben. – Doch
wart! – Du gefällst mir gar wohl, und sollst an mich fein denken, wenn
ich wieder auf dem Meere bin.»

Damit nahm er zwei blanke Dukaten aus der Tasche, zog ein schönes
ostindisches Tuch aus dem Busen, und gab beides der Dirne. *Der* traten
aber die hellen Tränen in die Augen, sie stand auf, sie legte die Dukaten
auf die Bank, sie sprach: «Ach, behaltet doch nur Eure Dukaten, die
machen mich nur traurig, aber das schöne Tuch, das will ich tragen Euch
zum teuern Andenken, und Ihr werdet mich wohl übers Jahr nicht mehr
finden wenn Ihr Hönsning haltet hier in der Haga.»

Damit schlich die Dirne, nicht mehr zurückkehrend in das Schenk-
haus, beide Hände vors Gesicht gedrückt, fort über die Straße.

Aufs neue versank Elis Fröbom in seine düstre Träumerei, und rief
endlich, als der Jubel in der Schenke recht laut und toll wurde: «Ach
läg ich doch nur begraben in dem tiefsten Meeresgrunde! – denn im
Leben gibt's keinen Menschen mehr, mit dem ich mich freuen sollte!»

Da sprach eine tiefe rauhe Stimme dicht hinter ihm: «Ihr müßt gar
großes Unglück erfahren haben, junger Mensch, daß Ihr Euch schon
jetzt, da das Leben Euch erst recht aufgehen sollte, den Tod wünschet.»

Elis schaute sich um, und gewahrte einen alten Bergmann, der mit
übereinandergeschlagenen Armen an die Plankenwand des Schenk-

the bench, lost in thought. The tart's finery and overall appearance showed that she had unfortunately sacrificed herself to men's lust, but her reckless way of life had not yet had a destructive effect on the extremely charming and gentle features of her lovely face. There was no trace of repellent insolence—no, there was a quiet, yearning sadness in the gaze of her dark eyes.

"Elis! Don't you want to join in your shipmates' joy? Have you no feeling of pleasure at having come home again and at standing on your native soil again, after escaping the menacing peril of the treacherous sea waves?"

Thus spoke the harlot, in a quiet, gentle tone, as she put her arm around the young man. Elis Fröbom, as if awakening from a deep dream, looked the girl in the eye, seized her hand, and pressed her to his heart; it was plain to see that the harlot's soft sweet words had struck a real chord in his soul.

"Ah," he finally began, as if reflecting, "ah, my joy and pleasure are now things of the past. At least, I absolutely can't take part in my shipmates' carousing. Please go in, my sweet girl, whoop and hurrah with the others, if you can, but leave gloomy, sad Elis out here alone; he'd only spoil all your fun. But wait! I like you very much, and I want you to remember me when I'm at sea again."

Saying that, he took two bright ducats from his pocket, drew a beautiful East Indian shawl from inside his shirt, and gave it all to the harlot. Her eyes were filled with bright tears; she stood up, placed the ducats on the bench, and said: "Oh, please keep your ducats—they just make me sad—but I'll wear this beautiful shawl as a dear memento of you, and a year from now you probably won't find me again when you celebrate your *hönsning* here in Haga."

With those words the harlot, deciding not to return to the inn, covered her face with both hands and departed down the street.

Once again Elis Fröbom lapsed into his dreary reverie, finally exclaiming, when the racket in the inn became truly wild and madcap: "Oh, if I were only buried in the deepest part of the sea! For there's no one left in my life with whom I can rejoice!"

Then a deep, rough voice right behind him said: "You must have undergone a great misfortune, young man, to be wishing to die so early, when life should be just starting out for you."

Elis looked behind him and espied an old miner, who stood leaning against the frame wall of the inn, his arms crossed;

hauses angelehnt stand, und mit ernstem durchdringenden Blick auf ihn herabschaute.

Sowie Elis den Alten länger ansah, wurde es ihm, als trete in tiefer wilder Einsamkeit, in die er sich verloren geglaubt, eine bekannte Gestalt ihm freundlich tröstend entgegen. Er sammelte sich, und erzählte, wie sein Vater ein tüchtiger Steuermann gewesen, aber in demselben Sturme umgekommen, aus dem er gerettet worden auf wunderbare Weise. Seine beiden Brüder wären als Soldaten geblieben in der Schlacht, und er allein habe seine arme verlassene Mutter erhalten mit dem reichen Solde, den er nach jeder Ostindienfahrt empfangen. Denn Seemann habe er doch nun einmal, von Kindesbeinen an dazu bestimmt, bleiben müssen, und da habe es ihm ein großes Glück gedünkt, in den Dienst der ostindischen Kompagnie treten zu können. Reicher als jemals sei diesmal der Gewinn ausgefallen, und jeder Matrose habe noch außer dem Sold ein gut Stück Geld erhalten, so daß er, die Tasche voll Dukaten, in heller Freude hingelaufen sei nach dem kleinen Häuschen, wo seine Mutter gewohnt. Aber fremde Gesichter hätten ihn aus dem Fenster angeguckt, und eine junge Frau, die ihm endlich die Tür geöffnet, und der er sich zu erkennen gegeben, habe ihm mit kaltem rauhem Ton berichtet, daß seine Mutter schon vor drei Monaten gestorben, und daß er die paar Lumpen, die, nachdem die Begräbniskosten berichtigt, noch übriggeblieben, auf dem Rathause in Empfang nehmen könne.

Der Tod seiner Mutter zerreiße ihm das Herz, er fühle sich von aller Welt verlassen, einsam wie auf ein ödes Riff verschlagen, hülflos, elend. Sein ganzes Leben auf der See erscheine ihm wie ein irres zweckloses Treiben, ja, wenn er daran denke, daß seine Mutter, vielleicht schlecht gepflegt von fremden Leuten, so ohne Trost sterben müssen, komme es ihm ruchlos und abscheulich vor, daß er überhaupt zur See gegangen, und nicht lieber daheim geblieben, seine arme Mutter nährend und pflegend. Die Kameraden hätten ihn mit Gewalt fortgerissen zum Hönsning, und er selbst habe geglaubt, daß der Jubel um ihn her, ja auch wohl das starke Getränk, seinen Schmerz betäuben werde, aber statt dessen sei es ihm bald geworden, als sprängen alle Adern in seiner Brust, und er müsse sich verbluten.

«Ei», sprach der alte Bergmann, «ei, du wirst bald wieder in See stechen, Elis, und dann wird dein Schmerz vorüber sein in weniger Zeit. Alte Leute sterben, das ist nun einmal nicht anders, und deine Mutter hat ja, wie du selbst gestehst, nur ein armes mühseliges Leben verlassen.»

the man was looking down at him with a grave, penetrating gaze.

When Elis took a longer look at the old man, he felt as if, amid the great, painful loneliness in which he believed himself lost, a familiar figure were coming to greet him with friendly consolation. He pulled himself together, and told his story: His father had been an excellent helmsman, but had perished in the very storm from which he had been miraculously saved. His two brothers, soldiers, had fallen in battle, and he alone had supported his poor, forsaken mother out of the rich pay he had received after each voyage to the East Indies. For, destined from childhood to be a sailor, he had had to remain in that calling, and so he had thought himself very fortunate to be able to enter the service of the East India Company. This time the profits were greater than ever before, and on top of the regular pay, each sailor had been given a substantial bonus, so that, his pocket full of ducats, he had dashed in great joy to the little cottage in which his mother had lived. But strange faces had looked at him through the window, and a young woman, who had finally opened the door and to whom he had made his identity known, had informed him in a cold, coarse manner that his mother had died three months earlier, and that the few rags that had remained after the funeral expenses were paid could be collected at the city hall.

His mother's death (he continued) had broken his heart, and he felt deserted by the whole world, as solitary as if shipwrecked on a barren reef, helpless, miserable. His entire life at sea now appeared to be a pointless, directionless activity; yes, when he thought of how his mother, perhaps inadequately cared for by strangers, had had to die that way without consolation, it seemed to have been criminal and loathsome of him to have ever gone to sea at all, instead of staying home to support and tend to his poor mother. His shipmates had dragged him off to the *hönsning* unwillingly, and he himself had thought that the hubbub around him, as well as the alcohol, might deaden his pain, but instead he had soon felt as if all the veins in his chest were bursting and he'd bleed to death.

"Well," the old miner said, "well, you'll soon put out to sea again, Elis, and then your sorrow will be over pretty soon. Old people die, that's the way it goes, and, as you yourself admit, the life your mother left behind was a poor and troubled one."

«Ach», erwiderte Elis, «ach, daß niemand an meinen Schmerz glaubt, ja daß man mich wohl albern und töricht schilt, das ist es ja eben, was mich hinausstößt aus der Welt. – Auf die See mag ich nicht mehr, das Leben ekelt mich an. Sonst ging mir wohl das Herz auf, wenn das Schiff, die Segel wie stattliche Schwingen ausbreitend, über das Meer dahinfuhr, und die Wellen in gar lustiger Musik plätscherten und sausten, und der Wind dazwischen pfiff durch das knätternde Tauwerk. Da jauchzte ich fröhlich mit den Kameraden auf dem Verdeck, und dann – hatte ich in stiller dunkler Nacht die Wache, da gedachte ich der Heimkehr und meiner guten alten Mutter, wie die sich nun wieder freuen würde, wenn Elis zurückgekommen! – Hei! da konnt ich wohl jubeln auf dem Hönsning, wenn ich dem Mütterchen die Dukaten in den Schoß geschüttet, wenn ich ihr die schönen Tücher und wohl noch manch anderes Stück seltner Ware aus dem fernen Lande hingereicht. Wenn ihr dann vor Freude die Augen hell aufleuchteten, wenn sie die Hände einmal über das andere zusammenschlug, ganz erfüllt von Vergnügen und Lust, wenn sie geschäftig hin und her trippelte, und das schönste Aehl herbeiholte, das sie für Elis aufbewahrt. Und saß ich denn nun abends bei der Alten, dann erzählte ich ihr von den seltsamen Leuten, mit denen ich verkehrt, von ihren Sitten und Gebräuchen, von allem Wunderbaren, was mir begegnet auf der langen Reise. Sie hatte ihre große Lust daran, und redete wieder zu mir von den wunderbaren Fahrten meines Vaters im höchsten Norden, und tischte mir dagegen manches schauerliche Seemannsmärlein auf, das ich schon hundertmal gehört, und an dem ich mich doch gar nicht satt hören konnte! – Ach! wer bringt mir diese Freude wieder! – Nein, niemals mehr auf die See. – Was sollt ich unter den Kameraden, die mich nur aushöhnen würden, und wo sollt ich Lust hernehmen zur Arbeit, die mir nur ein mühseliges Treiben um nichts dünken würde!»

«Ich höre Euch», sprach der Alte, al Elis schwieg, «ich höre Euch mit Vergnügen reden, junger Mensch, so wie ich schon seit ein paar Stunden, ohne daß Ihr mich gewahrtet, Euer ganzes Betragen beobachtete, und meine Freude daran hatte. Alles, was Ihr tatet, was Ihr spracht, beweist, daß Ihr ein tiefes, in sich selbst gekehrtes, frommes, kindliches Gemüt habt, und eine schönere Gabe konnte Euch der hohe Himmel gar nicht verleihen. Aber zum Seemann habt Ihr Eure Lebetage gar nicht im mindesten getaugt. Wie sollte Euch stillem, wohl gar zum Trübsinn geneigten Neriker (daß Ihr das seid, seh ich an den Zügen Eures Gesichts, an Eurer ganzen Haltung), wie sollte Euch das wilde unstete Leben auf der See zusagen. Ihr tut wohl

"Ah," Elis replied, "the very thing that makes me withdraw from society is that nobody believes in my sorrow, and that people must find me stupid and foolish. I don't want to return to sea; that life disgusts me. In the past, my heart used to leap up when the ship skimmed over the ocean, spreading its sails like mighty wings, and the waves made merry music as they slapped and crashed, the breeze all the while whistling through the rattling lines. At such times, I'd whoop happily with my shipmates on deck, and then, if I was on watch on a quiet, dark night, I'd think about homecoming and how glad my kind old mother would be when her Elis was back again! Yes, in those days I was able to kick up a row at the *hönsning*, after pouring my ducats into my mother's lap, after making her a present of beautiful shawls and many another piece of rare merchandise from that faraway land; when her eyes flashed brightly with joy, when she clapped her hands time and again, filled with contentment and pleasure, when she bustled to and fro and brought out the finest beer, which she had been saving for her Elis! Then I'd sit with the old woman in the evening, telling her about the unusual people I had rubbed elbows with, about their manners and customs, about all the remarkable things that had happened to me during the long voyage. She took a great pleasure in it, and she'd tell me again about my father's wonderful voyages to the far north, treating me to many a frightening sailor's yarn that I'd already heard a hundred times, but which I nevertheless could never hear often enough! Ah, who can restore that joy to me? No, never again to sea! What would I do among my shipmates, who'd only laugh at me, and how would I find joy in my work, which would only seem like a lot of labor for nothing?"

"I hear you," said the old man when Elis finished, "I hear you speak with great pleasure, young man, just as I've taken great joy in observing all of your conduct, without your noticing me, for a couple of hours now. Everything you've done and said proves that you have a deep, reflective, pious, and childlike nature, and a finer gift heaven above couldn't have lent you. But, all your life, you've been not in the least good as a sailor. How could the wild, unsettled life at sea suit you, a quiet man from Närke, who's probably inclined to be melancholy? (I can see you're from there by your features and all your body language.) You're probably doing the right thing by giving up that life for

daran, daß Ihr dies Leben aufgebt für immer. Aber die Hände werdet Ihr doch nicht in den Schoß legen? – Folgt meinem Rat, Elis Fröbom! geht nach Falun, werdet ein Bergmann. Ihr seid jung, rüstig, gewiß bald ein tüchtiger Knappe, dann Hauer, Steiger und immer höher herauf. Ihr habt tüchtige Dukaten in der Tasche, die legt Ihr an, verdient dazu, kommt wohl gar zum Besitz eines Bergmannshemmans, habt Eure eigne Kuxe in der Grube. Folgt meinem Rat, Elis Fröbom, werdet ein Bergmann!»

Elis Fröbom erschrak beinahe über die Worte des Alten. «Wie», rief er, «was ratet Ihr mir? Von der schönen freien Erde, aus dem heitern sonnenhellen Himmel, der mich umgibt, labend, erquickend, soll ich hinaus – hinab in die schauerliche Höllentiefe und dem Maulwurf gleich wühlen und wühlen nach den Erzen und Metallen, schnöden Gewinns halber?»

«So ist», rief der Alte erzürnt, «so ist nun das Volk, es verachtet das, was es nicht zu erkennen vermag. Schnöder Gewinn! Als ob alle grausame Quälerei auf der Oberfläche der Erde, wie sie der Handel herbeiführt, sich edler gestalte als die Arbeit des Bergmanns, dessen Wissenschaft, dessen unverdrossenem Fleiß die Natur ihre geheimsten Schatzkammern erschließt. Du sprichst von schnödem Gewinn, Elis Fröbom! – ei, es möchte hier wohl noch Höheres gelten. Wenn der blinde Maulwurf in blindem Instinkt die Erde durchwühlt, so möcht es wohl sein, daß in der tiefsten Teufe bei dem schwachen Schimmer des Grubenlichts des Menschen Auge hellsehender wird, ja daß es endlich, sich mehr und mehr erkräftigend, in dem wunderbaren Gestein die Abspieglung dessen zu erkennen vermag, was oben über den Wolken verborgen. Du weißt nichts von dem Bergbau, Elis Fröbom, laß dir davon erzählen.»

Mit diesen Worten setzte sich der Alte hin auf die Bank neben Elis, und begann sehr ausführlich zu beschreiben, wie es bei dem Bergbau hergehe, und mühte sich, mit den lebendigsten Farben dem Unwissenden alles recht deutlich vor Augen zu bringen. Er kam auf die Bergwerke von Falun, in denen er, wie er sagte, seit seiner frühen Jugend gearbeitet, er beschrieb die große Tagesöffnung mit den schwarzbraunen Wänden, die dort anzutreffen, er sprach von dem

good. But you surely won't sit around idle? Take my advice, Elis Fröbom! Go to Falun and become a miner. You're young and spry, and I'm sure you'll soon become a capable pitman, then a hewer, a supervisor,[3] and so on up the ranks. You've got plenty of ducats in your pocket; when you invest them, and earn more, you'll get to own a miner's homestead and have your own mine[4] in the complex. Take my advice, Elis Fröbom, become a miner!"

Elis Fröbom was almost alarmed at the old man's words. "What!" he shouted; "what advice are you giving me? You want me to abandon the beautiful, free earth, the clear, sunny sky that surrounds me, refreshing and restoring me, and to descend into the frightful depths of hell and, like a mole, to burrow and burrow in search of ore and metal, for the sake of vile gain?"

"That's how they are," shouted the old man angrily, "that's how people are, showing contempt for things they can't understand! Vile gain! As if all the cruel torments on the earth's surface, which are the consequence of commerce, are somehow nobler than the labor of the miner, to whose knowledge and tireless industry Nature reveals her most secret treasure chambers! You speak of vile gain, Elis Fröbom! Ah, loftier things may prevail here. Even if the blind mole burrows in the earth out of blind instinct, it may very well be that, at the very bottom of the mine, in the feeble light of the miner's lamp, a man's eyes see more clearly and finally, his sight growing ever stronger, are able to discern in the marvelous configuration of stone the reflection of that which lies concealed up above the clouds. You know nothing about mining, Elis Fröbom; let me tell you about it."

With those words the old man sat down on the bench beside Elis, and began to describe mining activities in great detail, striving to depict everything to the ignorant man's eyes distinctly and in the liveliest colors. He then spoke of the Falun mines, in which, as he said, he had worked since his early youth; he described the huge pit entrance that was to be found there, with its dark-brown sides; he spoke of the mine's immeasurable

3. A *Knappe* is the lowest rank of qualified miner, doing miscellaneous tasks; a *Hauer* does the actual excavation at the working face; a *Steiger* is a below-ground foreman, supervisor, or "deputy." 4. *Hemman* is a Swedish word. *Kuxe* are literally shares (stock certificates) in a mine, but the term is used in this story to mean a single mine, individually owned and run, within an entire mining region or complex.

unermeßlichen Reichtum der Erzgrube an dem schönsten Gestein.
Immer lebendiger und lebendiger wurde seine Rede, immer glühender sein Blick. Er durchwanderte die Schachten wie die Gänge eines
Zaubergartens. Das Gestein lebte auf, die Fossile regten sich, der
wunderbare Pyrosmalith, der Almandin blitzten im Schein der
Grubenlichter – die Bergkristalle leuchteten und flimmerten
durcheinander.

Elis horchte hoch auf; des Alten seltsame Weise, von den unterirdischen Wundern zu reden, als stehe er gerade in ihrer Mitte, erfaßte sein ganzes Ich. Er fühlte seine Brust beklemmt, es war ihm, als
sei er schon hinabgefahren mit dem Alten in die Tiefe, und ein
mächtiger Zauber halte ihn unten fest, so daß er nie mehr das
freundliche Licht des Tages schauen werde. Und doch war es ihm
wieder, als habe ihm der Alte eine neue unbekannte Welt erschlossen,
in die er hineingehöre, und aller Zauber dieser Welt sei ihm schon
zur frühsten Knabenzeit in seltsamen geheimnisvollen Ahnungen
aufgegangen.

«Ich habe», sprach endlich der Alte, «ich habe Euch, Elis Fröbom,
alle Herrlichkeit eines Standes dargetan, zu dem Euch die Natur
recht eigentlich bestimmte. Geht nur mit Euch selbst zu Rate, und tut
dann, wie Euer Sinn es Euch eingibt!»

Damit sprang der Alte hastig auf von der Bank, und schritt von dannen, ohne Elis weiter zu grüßen oder sich nach ihm umzuschauen.
Bald war er seinem Blick entschwunden.

In dem Schenkhause war es indessen still geworden. Die Macht des
starken Aehls (Biers), des Branntweins hatte gesiegt. Manche vom
Schiffsvolk waren fortgeschlichen mit ihren Dirnen, andere lagen in
den Winkeln und schnarchten. Elis, der nicht mehr einkehren konnte
in das gewohnte Obdach, erhielt auf sein Bitten ein kleines Kämmer-
lein zur Schlafstelle.

Kaum hatte er sich, müde und matt, wie er war, hingestreckt auf
sein Lager, als der Traum über ihm seine Fittiche rührte. Es war ihm,
als schwämme er in einem schönen Schiff mit vollen Segeln auf dem
spiegelblanken Meer, und über ihm wölbe sich ein dunkler Wolkenhimmel. Doch wie er nun in die Wellen hinabschaute, erkannte er
bald, daß das, was er für das Meer gehalten, eine feste durchsichtige
funkelnde Masse war, in deren Schimmer das ganze Schiff auf wunderbare Weise zerfloß, so daß er auf dem Kristallboden stand, und
über sich ein Gewölbe von schwarz flimmerndem Gestein erblickte.
Gestein war das nämlich, was er erst für den Wolkenhimmel gehalten.
Von unbekannter Macht fortgetrieben, schritt er vorwärts, aber in

wealth of the finest minerals. His talk became more vivid all the time, his eyes shone ever more brightly. He traveled through the shafts as through the walks of an enchanted garden. The minerals took on life, the fossils began to move, the remarkable pyrosmalite and the almandine glittered in the light of the miners' lamps; the rock crystals flared and emitted crisscrossing rays.

Elis was extremely attentive; the old man's peculiar way of depicting the subterranean marvels, as if he were right in the midst of them, captivated his entire being. He felt a pressure on his chest; it seemed as if he had already journeyed down into the depths with the old man and as if he were being held prisoner there by some powerful spell, so that he would never again behold the friendly light of day. And yet, he also felt as if the old man had disclosed a new, unfamiliar world to him, one in which he belonged; and that all the magic of that world had already appeared to him in his earliest boyhood as strange and mysterious premonitions.

"Now," the old man finally said, "now, Elis Fröbom, I have introduced to you all the magnificence of a vocation for which Nature has distinctly destined you. Think it over carefully, and then do what your own mind tells you to!"

Saying that, the old man jumped up from the bench hastily and strode away, without uttering a word of farewell to Elis or looking back at him. Soon he was gone from Elis's sight.

Meanwhile it had become quiet in the inn. The power of the strong beer and the brandy had conquered. Many of the seamen had slipped away with their tarts, others were lying in the corners, snoring. Elis, who could no longer return to his accustomed residence, asked for and obtained a small room to sleep in.

Weary and exhausted as he was, scarcely had he stretched out on his bed when a dream beat its wings over him. He thought he was sailing on a fine ship, all canvas spread, over the mirror-bright sea, with a dark, cloudy sky arching over him. But, looking down at the waves, he soon realized that what he had taken to be the sea was a solid mass, transparent and sparkling, in the glow of which the entire ship miraculously dissolved, leaving him standing on the crystalline floor, as he caught sight of a vault of blackly glimmering stone overhead. You see, what he had first taken to be the cloudy sky was stone. Impelled by an unfamiliar force, he walked forward, but at that moment everything around

dem Augenblick regte sich alles um ihn her, und wie kräuselnde
Wogen erhoben sich aus dem Boden wunderbare Blumen und
Pflanzen von blinkendem Metall, die ihre Blüten und Blätter aus der
tiefsten Tiefe emporrankten, und auf anmutige Weise ineinander ver-
schlangen.

Der Boden war so klar, daß Elis die Wurzeln der Pflanzen deutlich
erkennen konnte, aber bald immer tiefer mit dem Blick eindringend,
erblickte er ganz unten – unzählige holde jungfräuliche Gestalten,
die sich mit weißen glänzenden Armen umschlungen hielten, und aus
ihren Herzen sproßten jene Wurzeln, jene Blumen und Pflanzen
empor, und wenn die Jungfrauen lächelten, ging ein süßer Wohllaut
durch das weite Gewölbe, und höher und freudiger schossen die wunderbaren Metallblüten empor. Ein unbeschreibliches Gefühl von
Schmerz und Wollust ergriff den Jüngling, eine Welt von Liebe,
Sehnsucht, brünstigem Verlangen ging auf in seinem Innern. «Hinab
– hinab zu euch», rief er, und warf sich mit ausgebreiteten Armen auf
den kristallenen Boden nieder. Aber *der* wich unter ihm, und er
schwebte wie in schimmerndem Äther.

«Nun, Elis Fröbom, wie gefällt es dir in dieser Herrlichkeit?» – So
rief eine starke Stimme. Elis gewahrte neben sich den alten
Bergmann, aber so wie er ihn mehr und mehr anschaute, wurde er
zur Riesengestalt aus glühendem Erz gegossen. Elis wollte sich
entsetzen, aber in dem Augenblick leuchtete es auf aus der Tiefe wie
ein jäher Blitz und das ernste Antlitz einer mächtigen Frau wurde
sichtbar. Elis fühlte, wie das Entzücken in seiner Brust immer
steigend und steigend zur zermalmenden Angst wurde. Der Alte
hatte ihn umfaßt und rief: «Nimm dich in acht, Elis Fröbom, das ist
die Königin, noch magst du heraufschauen.»

Unwillkürlich drehte er das Haupt, und wurde gewahr wie die
Sterne des nächtlichen Himmels durch eine Spalte des Gewölbes
leuchteten. Eine sanfte Stimme rief wie in trostlosem Weh seinen
Namen. Es war die Stimme seiner Mutter. Er glaubte ihre Gestalt zu
schauen oben an der Spalte. Aber es war ein holdes junges Weib, die
ihre Hand tief hinabstreckte in das Gewölbe und seinen Namen rief.
«Trage mich empor», rief er dem Alten zu, «ich gehöre doch der
Oberwelt an und ihrem freundlichen Himmel.»

«Nimm dich in acht», sprach der Alte dumpf, «nimm dich in acht,
Fröbom! – sei treu der Königin, der du dich ergeben.» Sowie nun
aber der Jüngling wieder hinabschaute in das starre Antlitz der
mächtigen Frau, fühlte er, daß sein Ich zerfloß in dem glänzenden
Gestein. Er kreischte auf in namenloser Angst und erwachte aus dem

him moved, and like curling waves there arose from the ground marvelous flowers and plants of shining metal; their blossoms and leaves wound like vines out of the very depths, intertwining attractively.

The ground was so clear that Elis could distinctly make out the roots of the plants, but soon, as his sight penetrated more and more deeply, he espied at the very bottom—innumerable figures of lovely maidens, embracing one another with their gleaming white arms; and it was from their hearts that those roots, flowers, and plants were sprouting upward; and when the maidens smiled, a sweet, euphonious sound rang through the extensive vault, and the metallic flowers shot upward, taller and more joyous. An indescribable feeling of pain and pleasure seized upon the young man, a world of love, longing, and ardent desire awoke within him. "Down, down to where you are!" he called, and, with arms outspread, he threw himself onto the crystalline ground. But it vanished below him, and he was floating as if in the glimmering sky.

"Now, Elis Fröbom, how do you like this splendor?" A powerful voice had uttered those words. Elis became aware of the old miner standing beside him, but as he continued to look at him, he grew to the size of a giant made of red-hot cast metal. Elis was on the point of feeling terror, but at that moment there was a flash from the depths like a sudden stroke of lightning, and the grave countenance of a regal woman became visible. Elis felt the rapture in his bosom steadily heightening into a crushing anxiety. The old man had embraced him and was shouting: "Watch out, Elis Fröbom, it's the queen; you may still look upward."

He turned his head involuntarily and saw the stars of the night sky twinkling through a rift in the vault. A gentle voice called his name, as if in inconsolable distress. It was his mother's voice. He thought he could discern her figure up above at the rift. But it was a pretty young woman, who was extending her hand far into the vault and calling his name. "Carry me up!" he shouted to the old man. "I belong to the upper world, after all, and to its friendly sky."

"Watch out," said the old man in muffled tones, "watch out, Fröbom! Be faithful to the queen, to whom you have devoted yourself!" But when the young man now looked down again into the rigid face of the regal woman, he felt his self dissolving in the shining stone. He shrieked in nameless dread and awoke from

wunderbaren Traum, dessen Wonne und Entsetzen tief in seinem Innern widerklang.

«Es konnte», sprach Elis, als er sich mit Mühe gesammelt, zu sich selbst, «es konnte wohl nicht anders sein, es mußte mir solch wunderliches Zeug träumen. Hat mir doch der alte Bergmann so viel erzählt von der Herrlichkeit der unterirdischen Welt, daß mein ganzer Kopf davon erfüllt ist, noch in meinem ganzen Leben war mir nicht so zumute als eben jetzt. – Vielleicht träume ich noch fort – Nein nein – ich bin wohl nur krank, hinaus ins Freie, der frische Hauch der Seeluft wird mich heilen!»

Er raffte sich auf und rannte nach dem Klippa-Hafen, wo der Jubel des Hönsnings aufs neue sich erhob. Aber bald gewahrte er, wie alle Lust an ihm vorüberging, wie er keinen Gedanken in der Seele festhalten konnte, wie Ahnungen, Wünsche, die er nicht zu nennen vermochte, sein Inneres durchkreuzten. – Er dachte mit tiefer Wehmut an seine verstorbene Mutter, dann war es ihm aber wieder, als sehne er sich nur noch einmal jener Dirne zu begegnen, die ihn gestern so freundlich angesprochen. Und dann fürchtete er wieder, träte auch die Dirne aus dieser oder jener Gasse ihm entgegen, so würd es am Ende der alte Bergmann sein, vor dem er sich, selbst konnte er nicht sagen warum, entsetzen müsse. Und doch hätte er wieder auch von dem Alten sich gern mehr erzählen lassen von den Wundern des Bergbaues.

Von all diesen treibenden Gedanken hin und her geworfen, schaute er hinein in das Wasser. Da wollt es ihm bedünken, als wenn die silbernen Wellen erstarrten zum funkelnden Glimmer, in dem nun die schönen großen Schiffe zerfließen, als wenn die dunklen Wolken, die eben heraufzogen an dem heitern Himmel, sich hinabsenken würden und verdichten zum steinernen Gewölbe. – Er stand wieder in seinem Traum, er schaute wieder das ernste Antlitz der mächtigen Frau, und die verstörende Angst des sehnsüchtigsten Verlangens erfaßte ihn aufs neue. –

Die Kameraden rüttelten ihn auf aus der Träumerei, er mußte ihrem Zuge folgen. Aber nun war es, als flüstre eine unbekannte Stimme ihm unaufhörlich ins Ohr: «Was willst du noch hier? – fort! – fort – in den Bergwerken zu Falun ist deine Heimat. – Da geht alle Herrlichkeit dir auf, von der du geträumt – fort, fort nach Falun!»

Drei Tage trieb sich Elis Fröbom in den Straßen von Götaborg umher, unaufhörlich verfolgt von den wunderlichen Gebilden seines Traums, unaufhörlich gemahnt von der unbekannten Stimme.

Am vierten Tage stand Elis an dem Tore, durch welches der Weg

that peculiar dream, the rapture and terror of which reechoed deep down within him.

"No," said Elis to himself, after laboriously collecting his thoughts, "it couldn't be any other way: I had to dream such crazy stuff. After all, the old miner told me so much about the splendor of the world below ground that my head is chock full of it; never in my whole life have I felt the way I do right now. Maybe I'm still dreaming. No, no, I'm probably just ill. Out into the open air! The fresh breeze from the sea will cure me!"

He pulled himself up and ran to the Klippan harbor, where the *hönsning* hubbub was starting all over again. But he soon noticed that all the fun meant nothing to him, that he was unable to keep one thought steady in his mind, that premonitions and wishes which he couldn't define were crisscrossing in his head. In deep sadness he thought of his deceased mother, but at the next moment he felt as if he were yearning to meet just once more that harlot who had spoken to him in such a friendly way the day before. Next, he was afraid that even if the girl were to walk toward him out of one narrow lane or another, it would turn out to be the old miner, in whose presence he'd necessarily feel terror, though he couldn't say why. And yet, even from the old man, he would have liked to hear more about the wonders of mining.

Buffeted to and fro by all these contradictory thoughts, he looked into the water. And then it seemed to him as if the silvery waves were becoming rigid in a sparkling glow, in which the beautiful big ships were now dissolving, and as if the dark clouds that had just gathered in the clear sky would descend and solidify into a stone vault. He was back in his dream; again he beheld the grave countenance of the regal woman, and the searing anxiety of the most yearning desire gripped him once more.

His shipmates shook him out of his reverie and made him join their procession. But now an unfamiliar voice seemed to be whispering ceaselessly in his ear: "What business do you still have here? Away! Away! Your home is in the mines at Falun. That is where all the splendor you've dreamed of will be revealed to you. Away, away to Falun!"

For three days Elis Fröbom roamed through the streets of Göteborg, incessantly pursued by the strange figures of his dream, incessantly admonished by the unfamiliar voice.

On the fourth day, Elis stood at the city gate through which

nach Gefle führt. Da schritt eben ein großer Mann vor ihm hindurch.
Elis glaubte den alten Bergmann erkannt zu haben und eilte un-
widerstehlich fortgetrieben ihm nach, ohne ihn zu erreichen.
Rastlos ging es nun fort und weiter fort.

Elis wußte deutlich, daß er sich auf dem Wege nach Falun befinde,
und eben dies beruhigte ihn auf besondere Weise, denn gewiß war es
ihm, daß die Stimme des Verhängnisses durch den alten Bergmann zu
ihm gesprochen, der ihn nun auch seiner Bestimmung entgegen-
führe.

In der Tat sah er auch manchmal, vorzüglich wenn der Weg ihm
ungewiß werden wollte, den Alten, wie er aus einer Schlucht, aus
dickem Gestrüpp, aus dunklem Gestein plötzlich hervortrat, und vor
ihm, ohne sich umzuschauen, daherschritt, dann aber schnell wieder
verschwand.

Endlich nach manchem mühselig durchwanderten Tage erblickte
Elis in der Ferne zwei große Seen, zwischen denen ein dicker Dampf
aufstieg. So wie er mehr und mehr die Anhöhe westlich erklimmte,
unterschied er in dem Rauch ein paar Türme und schwarze Dächer.
Der Alte stand vor ihm riesengroß, zeigte mit ausgestrecktem Arm
hin nach dem Dampf und verschwand wieder im Gestein.

«Das ist Falun!» rief Elis, «das ist Falun, das Ziel meiner Reise!» –
Er hatte recht, denn Leute, die ihm hinterher wanderten, bestätigten
es, daß dort zwischen den Seen Runn und Warpann die Stadt Falun
liege, und daß er soeben den Guffrisberg hinansteige, wo die große
Pinge oder Tagesöffnung der Erzgrube befindlich.

Elis Fröbom schritt guten Mutes vorwärts, als er aber vor dem
ungeheuern Höllenschlunde stand, da gefror ihm das Blut in den
Adern und er erstarrte bei dem Anblick der fürchterlichen Zerstörung.

Bekanntlich ist die große Tagesöffnung der Erzgrube zu Falun an
zwölfhundert Fuß lang, sechshundert Fuß breit und einhundertund-
achtzig Fuß tief. Die schwarzbraunen Seitenwände gehen anfangs
größtenteils senkrecht nieder; dann verflächen sie sich aber gegen die
mittlere Tiefe durch ungeheuern Schutt und Trümmerhalden. In
diesen und an den Seitenwänden blickt hin und wieder die Zimme-
rung alter Schächte hervor, die aus starken, dicht aufeinandergelegten
und an den Enden ineinandergefugten Stämmen nach Art des
gewöhnlichen Blockhäuserbaues aufgeführt sind. Kein Baum, kein
Grashalm sproßt in dem kahlen zerbröckelten Steingeklüft, und in
wunderlichen Gebilden, manchmal riesenhaften versteinerten
Tieren, manchmal menschlichen Kolossen ähnlich, ragen die zacki-

the road to Gävle leads. A tall man was just walking through it ahead of him. Elis thought he had recognized the old miner, and he hastened after him, under an irresistible compulsion, but failed to overtake him.

Now his journey went on and on without repose.

Elis knew distinctly that he was on the way to Falun, and it was precisely that knowledge which made him strangely calm, for he was sure that the voice of destiny had spoken to him through the old miner, who was now also guiding him toward his true calling.

In fact, there were times, especially if he started to be unsure of the right path, when he even saw the old man suddenly emerge from a ravine, dense underbrush, or dark rocks, and walk ahead of him, without looking back; but then he would quickly vanish again.

Finally, after many a day of tedious walking, Elis espied in the distance two large lakes, between which a dense vapor ascended. As he climbed the slope higher and higher to the west, he could make out in the smoke a couple of towers and black roofs. The old man stood before him as tall as a giant, pointing toward the vapor with his extended arm, and once again disappeared among the rocks.

"That's Falun!" Elis exclaimed. "That's Falun, my journey's end!" He was right, for people walking behind him confirmed the fact that the town of Falun lay there between lakes Runn and Varpan, and that he was just then ascending mount Guffris, where the great funnel-shaped opening of the mining pit was located.

Elis Fröbom strode forward cheerfully, but when he stopped in front of that vast hellish maw, the blood froze in his veins and he stiffened at the sight of that fearful ruin.

As is well known, the great opening of the mining pit at Falun is about twelve hundred feet long, six hundred feet wide, and one hundred eighty feet deep. The dark-brown sides are generally vertical at the outset, but then, around the middle of the descent, the vast dumps of rubble and debris make them more level. In these dumps and on the sides one can see here and there the timberwork of old shafts, constructed of powerful logs piled closely on top of one another, and mortised at the ends, in typical log-cabin fashion. No tree, not even a blade of grass, grows in that bare, scree-covered crevasse, and jagged masses of rock that loom up all around it form strange figures, in some places like gigantic petrified animals, in others like human

gen Felsenmassen ringsumher empor. Im Abgrunde liegen in wilder Zerstörung durcheinander Steine, Schlacken – ausgebranntes Erz, und ein ewiger betäubender Schwefeldunst steigt aus der Tiefe, als würde unten der Höllensud gekocht, dessen Dämpfe alle grüne Lust der Natur vergiften. Man sollte glauben, hier sei Dante herabgestiegen und habe den Inferno geschaut mit all seiner trostlosen Qual, mit all seinem Entzetzen.°

Als nun Elis Fröbom hinabschaute in den ungeheueren Schlund, kam ihm in den Sinn was ihm vor langer Zeit der alte Steuermann seines Schiffs erzählt. Dem war es, als er einmal im Fieber gelegen, plötzlich gewesen, als seien die Wellen des Meeres verströmt, und unter ihm habe sich der unermeßliche Abgrund geöffnet, so daß er die scheußlichen Untiere der Tiefe erblicke, die sich zwischen Tausenden von seltsamen Muscheln, Korallenstauden, zwischen wunderlichem Gestein in häßlichen Verschlingungen hin und her wälzten bis sie mit aufgesperrtem Rachen zum Tode erstarrt liegen geblieben. Ein solches Gesicht, meinte der alte Seemann, bedeute den baldigen Tod in den Wellen, und wirklich stürzte er auch bald darauf unversehens von dem Verdeck in das Meer und war rettungslos verschwunden. Daran dachte Elis, denn wohl bedünkte ihm der Abgrund wie der Boden der von den Wellen verlassenen See, und das schwarze Gestein, die blaulichen, roten Schlacken des Erzes schienen ihm abscheuliche Untiere, die ihre häßlichen Polypenarme nach ihm ausstreckten. – Es geschah, daß eben einige Bergleute aus der Teufe emporstiegen, die in ihrer dunklen Grubentracht, mit ihren schwarz verbrannten Gesichtern, wohl anzusehen waren wie häßliche Unholde, die, aus der Erde mühsam hervorgekrochen, sich den Weg bahnen wollten bis auf die Oberfläche.

Elis fühlte sich von tiefen Schauern durchbebt und, was dem Seemann noch niemals geschehen, ihn ergriff der Schwindel; es war ihm, als zögen unsichtbare Hände ihn hinab in den Schlund.

Mit geschlossenen Augen rannte er einige Schritte fort, und erst als er weit von der Pinge den Guffrisberg wieder hinabstieg und er hinaufblickte zum heitern sonnenhellen Himmel, war ihm alle Angst jenes schauerlichen Anblicks entnommen. Er atmete wieder frei und rief recht aus tiefer Seele: «O Herr meines Lebens, was sind alle Schauer des Meeres gegen das Entsetzen, was dort in dem öden

---

°S. die Beschreibung der großen Pinge zu Falun in Hausmanns Reise durch Skandinavien. V. Teil. Seite 96 ff.

colossi. In the abyss there lies a wildly confused havoc of stones and slag (burnt-out ore), and a perpetually anesthetizing sulfuric vapor arises from the deep, as if someone down there were cooking that hellish broth the vapors of which poison all of Nature's green joy. One would think it was here that Dante descended and beheld the Inferno with all its inconsolable tortures and all its horror.°

As Elis Fröbom now gazed down into that vast maw, he recalled a story that the old helmsman on his ship had told him long before. When that man was lying ill with fever, it suddenly seemed to him that the waves of the sea had flowed away, and that the measureless abyss had opened beneath him, so that he could see the horrible monsters of the deep, wallowing to and fro in ugly intertwinings, amid thousands of unusual shellfish, coral bushes, and peculiar minerals, until they stiffened to death and just lay there with wide-open jaws. A vision like that, the old seaman had said, foretells a forthcoming death in the ocean, and, in fact, shortly thereafter he unexpectedly fell off the deck into the sea and disappeared beyond any possibility of rescue. Elis now recalled this, because the abyss before him was like the bottom of the sea abandoned by its waters, and the black stones and the bluish and red slag seemed to him like repellent monsters extending their ugly, octopus-like arms in his direction. At that very moment, a few miners ascended from the bottom, and with their dark uniforms and their soot-blackened faces, they might very well resemble ugly evil creatures that had laboriously crawled out of the earth and were trying to find their way to the surface.

Elis felt himself thoroughly shaken by a strong shudder, and—something that had never before happened to the sailor— he became dizzy; he felt as if invisible hands were pulling him down into the maw.

With eyes closed he ran a few paces away, and only when he was far from the opening, descending mount Guffris, and he looked up at the clear, sunny sky, was he relieved of all the anxiety caused by that frightful view. He breathed freely once more and exclaimed from the very depths of his soul: "O Lord of my life, what are all the terrors of the sea compared with the horror

---

° [Footnote in original text:] "See the description of the great mine opening at Falun in Hausmann's Journey Through Scandinavia, Part V, pp. 96 ff." [Johann Friedrich Ludwig Hausmann (1782–1859), *Reise durch Skandinavien in den Jahren 1806–1807.*]

Steingeklüft wohnt! – Mag der Sturm toben, mögen die schwarzen
Wolken hinabtauchen in die brausenden Wellen, bald siegt doch
wieder die schöne herrliche Sonne und vor ihrem freundlichen
Antlitz verstummt das wilde Getöse, aber nie dringt ihr Blick in jene
schwarze Höhlen, und kein frischer Frühlingshauch erquickt dort
unten jemals die Brust. – Nein, zu euch mag ich mich nicht gesellen,
ihr schwarzen Erdwürmer, niemals würd ich mich eingewöhnen können in euer trübes Leben!»

Elis gedachte in Falun zu übernachten und dann mit dem frühesten Morgen seinen Rückweg anzutreten nach Götaborg.

Als er auf den Marktplatz, der Helsingtorget geheißen, kam, fand
er eine Menge Volks versammelt.

Ein langer Zug von Bergleuten in vollem Staat mit
Grubenlichtern in den Händen, Spielleute voraus, hielt eben vor
einem stattlichen Hause. Ein großer schlanker Mann von mit-
tleren Jahren trat heraus, und schaute mit mildem Lächeln
umher. An dem freien Anstande, an der offnen Stirn, an den
dunkelblau leuchtenden Augen mußte man den echten Dalkarl
erkennen. Die Bergleute schlossen einen Kreis um ihn, jedem
schüttelte er treuherzig die Hand, mit jedem sprach er freundliche Worte.

Elis Fröbom erfuhr auf Befragen, daß der Mann Pehrson Dahlsjö
sei, Masmeister Altermann und Besitzer einer schönen Bergsfrälse
bei Stora-Kopparberg. Bergsfrälse sind in Schweden Ländereien
geheißen, die für die Kupfer- und Silberbergwerke verliehen wurden.
Die Besitzer solcher Frälsen haben Kuxe in den Gruben, für deren
Betrieb sie zu sorgen gehalten sind.

Man erzählte dem Elis weiter, daß eben heute der Bergsthing
(Gerichtstag) geendigt, und daß dann die Bergleute herumzögen bei
dem Bergmeister, dem Hüttenmeister und den Altermännern, überall aber gastlich bewirtet würden.

Betrachtete Elis die schönen stattlichen Leute mit den freien
freundlichen Gesichtern, so konnte er nicht mehr an jene Erdwürmer
in der großen Pinge denken. Die helle Fröhlichkeit, die, als Pehrson
Dahlsjö hinaustrat, wie aufs neue angefacht durch den ganzen Kreis
aufloderte, war wohl ganz anderer Art als der wilde tobende Jubel der
Seeleute beim Hönsning.

Dem stillen ernsten Elis ging die Art, wie sich diese Bergmänner
freuten, recht tief ins Herz. Es wurde ihm unbeschreiblich wohl zumute, aber der Tränen konnt er sich vor Rührung kaum enthalten, als
einige der jüngeren Knappen ein altes Lied anstimmten, das in gar

that dwells in that barren crevasse there! Let the storm rage, let the black clouds dip down into the roaring waves—soon the beautiful, splendid sun will conquer again, and the wild tumult will fall silent before its friendly countenance, but its gaze never penetrates those black caverns, and no fresh spring breeze ever refreshes one's breast down there. No, I don't want to join you, you black earthworms; I'd never be able to get used to your dismal existence!"

Elis intended to spend the night in Falun and then start back for Göteborg at the earliest light.

When he arrived at the market square, called Hälsingtorget, he found a great number of people assembled there.

A long procession of miners, in their best finery, carrying their work lamps and preceded by musicians, was just coming to a halt in front of an imposing house. A tall, slender middle-aged man stepped out of the house and looked all around with a kindly smile. From his frank behavior, from his open brow, from his gleaming dark-blue eyes, it was impossible not to recognize a true Dalecarlian. The miners formed a circle around him; he shook everyone's hand warmly and spoke friendly words to each and all.

Asking who this man was, Elis Fröbom learned that he was Pehrson Dahlsjö, mine manager, guildsman, and owner of a fine *bergsfrälse* near Stora-Kopparberg. *Bergsfrälse* is the Swedish term for a piece of land rented out for mining copper and silver. The owners of such franchises have their own individual mines within the pit complex, which they are expected to manage themselves.

Elis was told further that the *bergsting* (miners' legal sessions) had just been concluded, and that on such occasions the miners visited the homes of the mine owner, the foundry owner, and the guild officials, and were entertained as guests everywhere.

When Elis observed those good-looking, dignified people, with their frank, friendly faces, he could no longer think of those earthworms in the big pit opening. The bright cheerfulness, which seemed to be newly kindled by Pehrson Dahlsjö's appearance, and now flared up throughout the throng, was surely different in nature from the wild, tumultuous merrymaking of the sailors at their *hönsning*.

The way in which these miners celebrated was quite after the heart of quiet, serious Elis. He became indescribably happy, but he could scarcely refrain from tears of emotion when a few of the younger pitmen struck up an old song—the very simple tune

einfacher in Seele und Gemüt dringender Melodie den Segen des
Bergbaues pries.

Als das Lied geendet, öffnete Pehrson Dahlsjö die Türe seines
Hauses und alle Bergleute traten nacheinander hinein. Elis folgte unwillkürlich und blieb an der Schwelle stehen, so daß er den ganzen
geräumigen Flur übersehen konnte, in dem die Bergleute auf Bänken
Platz nahmen. Ein tüchtiges Mahl stand auf einem Tisch bereitet.

Nun ging die hintere Türe dem Elis gegenüber auf, und eine holde,
festlich geschmückte Jungfrau trat hinein. Hoch und schlank gewach-
sen, die dunklen Haare in vielen Zöpfen über der Scheitel aufge-
flochten, das nette schmucke Mieder mit reichen Spangen zusam-
mengenestelt, ging sie daher in der höchsten Anmut der blühendsten
Jugend. Alle Bergleute standen auf und ein leises freudiges
Gemurmel lief durch die Reihen: «Ulla Dahlsjö – Ulla Dahlsjö! – Wie
hat Gott gesegnet unsern wackern Altermann mit dem schönen frommen Himmelskinde!» – Selbst den ältesten Bergleuten funkelten die
Augen, als Ulla ihnen so wie allen übrigen die Hand bot zum
freundlichen Gruß. Dann brachte sie schöne silberne Krüge,
schenkte treffliches Aehl, wie es denn nun in Falun bereitet wird, ein,
und reichte es dar den frohen Gästen, indem aller Himmelsglanz der
unschuldvollsten Unbefangenheit ihr holdes Antlitz überstrahlte.

Sowie Elis Fröbom die Jungfrau erblickte, war es ihm, als schlüge
ein Blitz durch sein Innres und entflamme alle Himmelslust, allen
Liebesschmerz – alle Inbrunst, die in ihm verschlossen. – Ulla
Dahlsjö war es, die ihm in dem verhängnisvollen Traum die rettende
Hand geboten; er glaubte nun die tiefe Deutung jenes Traums zu er-
raten, und pries, des alten Bergmanns vergessend, das Schicksal, dem
er nach Falun gefolgt. –

Aber dann fühlte er sich, auf der Türschwelle stehend, ein un-
beachteter Fremdling, elend, trostlos, verlassen und wünschte, er sei
gestorben, ehe er Ulla Dahlsjö geschaut, da er doch nun vergehen
müsse in Liebe und Sehnsucht. Nicht das Auge abzuwenden vermochte er von der holden Jungfrau, und als sie nun bei ihm ganz nahe
vorüberstreifte, rief er mit leiser bebender Stimme ihren Namen.
Ulla schaute sich um und erblickte den armen Elis, der, glühende
Röte im ganzen Gesicht, mit niedergesenktem Blick dastand – erstarrt – keines Wortes mächtig.

Ulla trat auf ihn zu und sprach mit süßem Lächeln: «Ei Ihr seid ja
wohl ein Fremdling, lieber Freund! das gewahre ich an Eurer
seemännischen Tracht! – Nun! – warum steht Ihr denn so auf der
Schwelle? – Kommt doch nur hinein und freut Euch mit uns!» –

of which went right to one's heart and soul—in praise of the
blessings of a miner's life.

When the song was over, Pehrson Dahlsjö opened the door of
his house, and all the miners entered one after the other. Elis
followed them involuntarily, coming to a halt on the threshold,
so that he had a full view of the spacious hall, in which the miners sat down on benches. A copious meal was ready on a table.

Now the back door opposite Elis opened, and a lovely, fes-
tively adorned maiden walked in. With her tall, slim figure, her
dark hair piled on top of her head in numerous braids, and her
dainty, pretty bodice fastened with costly brooches, she exuded
the extreme charm of blossoming youth. All the miners stood
up, and a quiet, joyful murmur spread through their ranks: "Ulla
Dahlsjö! Ulla Dahlsjö! How God has blessed our honest guild
official with that beautiful, pious child from heaven!" The eyes
of even the oldest miners were sparkling when Ulla offered
them her hand (as she did to all the rest) in friendly greeting.
Then she fetched beautiful silver jugs, poured that excellent
beer which is brewed in Falun, and handed it to the happy
guests, while all the heavenly glow of the most innocent candor
shone on her lovely face.

As soon as Elis Fröbom caught sight of the maiden, he felt as
if a lightning bolt were ripping through him and igniting all the
heavenly pleasure, all the love-pain, all the passion that slum-
bered within him. It was Ulla Dahlsjö who had extended her res-
cuing hand to him in that fateful dream; he now thought he could
guess the hidden meaning of that dream, and, forgetting the old
miner, he blessed the destiny that had brought him to Falun.

But then, standing on the threshold, he felt that he was a
stranger there, unregarded, wretched, comfortless, forsaken;
and he wished he had died before seeing Ulla Dahlsjö, since
now he would have to perish of love and longing. He was unable
to look away from the lovely maiden, and when she now passed
by him very closely, he spoke her name in a quiet, trembling
voice. Ulla looked around and caught sight of poor Elis; his
whole face was a flaming red as he stood there with eyes cast
down, rigid, incapable of speech.

Ulla walked up to him and said with a sweet smile: "Oh, you
must be a stranger, my dear friend! I can tell that from your
sailor's clothes! Well, why are you standing on the threshold like
that? Do come in and enjoy yourself with us!" Thereupon she

Damit nahm sie ihn bei der Hand, zog ihn in den Flur und reichte ihm einen vollen Krug Aehl! «Trinkt», sprach sie, «trinkt, mein lieber Freund, auf guten gastlichen Willkommen!»

Dem Elis war es, als läge er in dem wonnigen Paradiese eines herrlichen Traums, aus dem er gleich erwachen und sich unbeschreiblich elend fühlen werde. Mechanisch leerte er den Krug. In dem Augenblick trat Pehrson Dahlsjö an ihn heran und fragte, nachdem er ihm die Hand geschüttelt zum freundlichen Gruß, von wannen er käme und was ihn hingebracht nach Falun.

Elis fühlte die wärmende Kraft des edlen Getränks in allen Adern. Dem wackern Pehrson ins Auge blickend, wurde ihm heiter und mutig zu Sinn. Er erzählte, wie er, Sohn eines Seemanns, von Kindesbeinen an auf der See gewesen, wie er eben von Ostindien zurückgekehrt, seine Mutter, die er mit seinem Solde gehegt und gepflegt, nicht mehr am Leben gefunden, wie er sich nun ganz verlassen auf der Welt fühle, wie ihm nun das wilde Leben auf der See ganz und gar zuwider geworden, wie seine innerste Neigung ihn zum Bergbau treibe, und wie er hier in Falun sich mühen werde, als Knappe unterzukommen. Das letzte, so sehr allem entgegen, was er vor wenigen Augenblicken beschlossen, fuhr ihm ganz unwillkürlich heraus, es war ihm, als hätte er dem Altermann gar nichts anders eröffnen können, ja als wenn er eben seinen innersten Wunsch ausgesprochen, an den er bisher selbst nur nicht geglaubt.

Pehrson Dahlsjö sah den Jüngling mit sehr ernstem Blick an, als wollte er sein Innerstes durchschauen, dann sprach er: «Ich mag nicht vermuten, Elis Fröbom, daß bloßer Leichtsinn Euch von Euerem bisherigen Beruf forttreibt, und daß Ihr nicht alle Mühseligkeit, alle Beschwerde des Bergbaues vorher reiflich erwägt habt, ehe Ihr den Entschluß gefaßt, sich ihm zu ergeben. Es ist ein alter Glaube bei uns, daß die mächtigen Elemente, in denen der Bergmann kühn waltet, ihn vernichten, strengt er nicht sein ganzes Wesen an, die Herrschaft über sie zu behaupten, gibt er noch andern Gedanken Raum, die die Kraft schwächen, welche er ungeteilt der Arbeit in Erd und Feuer zuwenden soll. Habt Ihr aber Euern innern Beruf genugsam geprüft und ihn bewährt gefunden, so seid Ihr zur guten Stunde gekommen. In meiner Kuxe fehlt es an Arbeitern. Ihr könnt, wenn Ihr wollt, nun gleich bei mir bleiben und morgenden Tages mit dem Steiger anfahren, der Euch die Arbeit schon anweisen wird.»

Das Herz ging dem Elis auf bei Pehrson Dahlsjös Rede. Er dachte nicht mehr an die Schrecken des entsetzlichen Höllenschlundes, in

took his hand, drew him into the hall, and handed him a full jug
of beer. "Drink," she said, "drink, my dear friend, to a cheerful
welcome as a guest!"

Elis felt as if he were in the blissful paradise of a wonderful
dream, from which he'd immediately awaken to find himself indescribably miserable. He drained the jug mechanically. At that
moment Pehrson Dahlsjö stepped up to him and, after shaking
his hand in friendly greeting, asked him where he was from and
what had brought him to Falun.

Elis could sense the warming strength of that noble brew in
every vein. Looking honest Pehrson in the eye, he became
serene and courageous in his mind. He told him that, the son of
a sailor, he had been going to sea since childhood; that he had
just returned from the East Indies to find that his mother, whom
he had sheltered and supported on his pay, was no longer living;
that he now felt all alone in the world; that the reckless life of a
sailor had grown altogether repellent to him; that his natural in-
clination was urging him to become a miner; and that here in
Falun he would strive to find work as a pitman. The last remark,
so clearly contrary to all of his decisions of a few moments previously, was blurted out quite involuntarily; he felt as if he could
make no other declaration to the guild official, as if, in fact, he
had just made public his most deeply cherished desire, one in
which he himself had simply not believed up till then.

Pehrson Dahlsjö gazed at the young man very gravely, as if trying to read his true intentions; then he said: "Elis Fröbom, I
wouldn't wish to presume that it is mere frivolity that is driving
you away from your previous calling; and that you haven't already
carefully considered all the labors and difficulties of mining before making the decision to devote yourself to it. We have an old
belief that the mighty elements amid which the miner boldly
holds sway will destroy him if he doesn't exert his entire being to
maintain his dominion over them, and if he allows himself other
thoughts, which weaken the strength he must apply undividedly
to his work in earth and fire. But if you have sufficiently tested
your inner vocation and have found it firm, then you have arrived
at an opportune moment. Workers are needed in my mine. If you
wish, you can now stay at my house and go down tomorrow with
the supervisor, who will show you what to do."

Elis's heart leapt up at Pehrson Dahlsjö's words. He no longer
thought about the terrors of that horrible maw of hell into which

den er geschaut. Daß er nun die holde Ulla täglich sehen, daß er mit ihr unter einem Dache wohnen werde, das erfüllte ihn mit Wonne und Entzücken; er gab den süßesten Hoffnungen Raum.

Pehrson Dahlsjö tat den Bergleuten kund, wie sich eben ein junger Knappe zum Bergdienst bei ihm gemeldet, und stellte ihnen den Elis Fröbom vor.

Alle schauten wohlgefällig auf den rüstigen Jüngling und meinten, mit seinem schlanken kräftigen Gliederbau sei er ganz zum Bergmann geboren, und an Fleiß und Frömmigkeit werd es ihm gewiß auch nicht fehlen.

Einer von den Bergleuten, schon hoch in Jahren, näherte sich und schüttelte ihm treuherzig die Hand, indem er sagte, daß er der Obersteiger in der Kuxe Pehrson Dahlsjös sei, und daß er sich's recht angelegen sein lassen werde, ihn sorglich in allem zu unterrichten, was ihm zu wissen nötig. Elis mußte sich zu ihm setzen, und sogleich begann der Alte beim Kruge Aehl weitläuftig über die erste Arbeit der Knappen zu sprechen.

Dem Elis kam wieder der alte Bergmann aus Götaborg in den Sinn und auf besondere Weise wußte er beinahe alles, was der ihm gesagt, zu wiederholen. «Ei», rief der Obersteiger voll Erstaunen, «Elis Fröbom, wo habt Ihr denn die schönen Kenntnisse her? – Nun da kann es Euch ja gar nicht fehlen, Ihr müßt in kurzer Zeit der tüchtigste Knappe in der Zeche sein!»

Die schöne Ulla, unter den Gästen auf und ab wandelnd und sie bewirtend, nickte oft freundlich dem Elis zu und munterte ihn auf recht froh zu sein. Nun sei er, sprach sie, ja nicht mehr fremd, sondern gehöre ins Haus und nicht mehr das trügerische Meer, nein! – Falun mit seinen reichen Bergen sei seine Heimat! – Ein ganzer Himmel voll Wonne und Seligkeit tat sich dem Jüngling auf bei Ullas Worten. Man merkte es wohl, daß Ulla gern bei ihm weilte, und auch Pehrson Dahlsjö betrachtete ihn in seinem stillen ernsten Wesen mit sichtlichem Wohlgefallen.

Das Herz wollte dem Elis doch mächtig schlagen, als er wieder bei dem rauchenden Höllenschlunde stand und, eingehüllt in die Bergmannstracht, die schweren mit Eisen beschlagenen Dalkarlschuhe an den Füßen, mit dem Steiger hinabfuhr in den tiefen Schacht. Bald wollten heiße Dämpfe, die sich auf seine Brust legten, ihn ersticken, bald flackerten die Grubenlichter von dem schneidend kalten Luftzuge, der die Abgründe durchströmte. Immer tiefer und tiefer ging es hinab, zuletzt auf kaum ein Fuß breiten eisernen Leitern, und

he had gazed. The idea of seeing lovely Ulla daily and living under one roof with her filled him with rapture and delight; he permitted himself the sweetest hopes.

Pehrson Dahlsjö informed the miners that a young pitman had just applied to him for a job, and he introduced Elis Fröbom to them.

Everyone looked contentedly at the sturdy young man and felt that, with his slim, strong build, he was born to be a miner; he surely wouldn't fall short in diligence and godliness, either.

One of the miners, a man advanced in years, approached and shook his hand warmly, saying that he was chief below-ground supervisor in Pehrson Dahlsjö's individual mine, and that he would take it upon himself conscientiously to instruct him carefully in all he needed to know. Elis was made to sit down next to him, and the old man, over his jug of beer, immediately began to speak at length about the first duties of pitmen.

Elis once again recalled the old miner in Göteborg, and in a strange way he was able to repeat almost everything that he had told him. "My!" exclaimed the chief supervisor, filled with amazement. "Elis Fröbom, where did you acquire all that wonderful knowledge? Now it just can't fail, and before very long you'll surely be the most competent pitman in the mine!"

Beautiful Ulla, walking to and fro among the guests and waiting on them, often gave Elis a friendly nod and encouraged him to enjoy himself. Now, she said, he was no longer a stranger but a member of the household; no longer the treacherous sea, no, Falun with its rich mountains was now his home! A heaven full of rapture and bliss disclosed itself to the young man at Ulla's words. It was clear to see that Ulla enjoyed his company, and Pehrson Dahlsjö, too, observed his quiet, earnest nature with visible satisfaction.

All the same, Elis's heart was on the point of pounding mightily when he once again stood near the smoking hellish maw and, clad in miner's uniform, his heavy iron-studded Dalecarlian shoes on his feet, descended with the supervisor into the deep shaft. At times hot vapors, gathering on his chest, almost stifled him; at other times the miners' lamps flickered in the bitingly cold air current that blew through the depths. They continued farther and farther downward, until they finally descended iron ladders barely a foot wide, and Elis Fröbom saw clearly that all

Elis Fröbom merkte wohl, daß alle Geschicklichkeit, die er sich als
Seemann im Klettern erworben, ihm hier nichts helfen könne.

Endlich standen sie in der tiefsten Teufe und der Steiger gab dem
Elis die Arbeit an, die er hier verrichten sollte.

Elis gedachte der holden Ulla, wie ein leuchtender Engel sah er
ihre Gestalt über sich schweben und vergaß alle Schrecken des
Abgrundes, alle Beschwerden der mühseligen Arbeit. Es stand nun
einmal fest in seiner Seele, daß nur dann, wenn er sich bei Pehrson
Dahlsjö mit aller Macht des Gemüts, mit aller Anstrengung, die nur
der Körper dulden wolle, dem Bergbau ergebe, vielleicht dereinst die
süßesten Hoffnungen erfüllt werden könnten, und so geschah es, daß
er in unglaublich kurzer Zeit es dem geübtesten Bergmann in der
Arbeit gleichtat.

Mit jedem Tage gewann der wackre Pehrson Dahlsjö den fleißigen
frommen Jüngling mehr lieb und sagte es ihm öfters unverhohlen,
daß er in ihm nicht sowohl einen tüchtigen Knappen, als einen
geliebten Sohn gewonnen. Auch Ullas innige Zuneigung tat sich
immer mehr und mehr kund. Oft, wenn Elis zur Arbeit ging und irgend Gefährliches im Werke war, bat, beschwor sie ihn, die hellen
Tränen in den Augen, doch nur ja sich vor jedem Unglück zu hüten.
Und wenn er dann zurückkam, sprang sie ihm freudig entgegen, und
hatte immer das beste Aehl zur Hand oder sonst ein gut Gericht bereitet, ihn zu erquicken.

Das Herz bebte dem Elis vor Freude, als Pehrson Dahlsjö einmal
zu ihm sprach, daß, da er ohnedies ein gut Stück Geld mitgebracht, es
bei seinem Fleiß, bei seiner Sparsamkeit ihm gar nicht fehlen könne,
künftig zum Besitztum eines Berghemmans oder wohl gar einer
Bergfrälse zu gelangen, und daß dann wohl kein Bergbesitzer zu
Falun ihn abweisen werde, wenn er um die Hand der Tochter werbe.
Er hätte nun gleich sagen mögen, wie unaussprechlich er Ulla liebe,
und wie er alle Hoffnung des Lebens auf ihren Besitz gestellt. Doch
unüberwindliche Scheu, mehr aber wohl noch der bange Zweifel, ob
Ulla, wie er manchmal ahne, ihn auch wirklich liebe, verschlossen ihm
den Mund.

Es begab sich, daß Elis Fröbom einmal in der tiefsten Teufe arbeitete in dicken Schwefeldampf gehüllt, so daß sein Grubenlicht
nur schwach durchdämmerte und er die Gänge des Gesteins kaum
zu unterscheiden vermochte. Da hörte er, wie aus noch tieferm
Schacht ein Klopfen heraustönte, als werde mit dem Puchhammer
gearbeitet. Da dergleichen Arbeit nun nicht wohl in der Teufe
möglich, und Elis wohl wußte, daß außer ihm heute niemand her-

the nimbleness in climbing he had attained as a sailor was of no use to him here.

At last they were standing on the very bottom, and the supervisor told Elis what sort of work he was to do there.

Elis thought about lovely Ulla; he saw her image hovering over him like a gleaming angel, and he forgot all the terrors of the abyss, all the difficulties of the tedious work. He was now certain in his mind that, only if he dedicated himself to mining in Pehrson Dahlsjö's employ with the full force of his spirit, with every exertion his body could stand, might his sweetest hopes perhaps be fulfilled one day; and thus it came about that, in an unbelievably short while, his work was equal to that of the most experienced miner.

Every day, honest Pehrson Dahlsjö grew fonder of the diligent, pious young man, and often told him right out that in him he had gained not so much a competent pitman as a beloved son. Ulla's secret liking for him became more and more evident, as well. Often, when Elis went to work and some dangerous procedure was being carried out, she would beg and implore him, with bright tears in her eyes, to guard himself well against any accident. Then, when he came back, she'd run happily to meet him, and always had the best beer ready, or had prepared some tasty dish, to refresh him.

Elis's heart jumped with joy when Pehrson Dahlsjö once told him that, since he had already brought along a substantial amount of money, with his industriousness and thriftiness he couldn't fail to acquire a miner's homestead or even a mining franchise one day, and that then probably no mine owner in Falun would refuse him if he sought his daughter's hand. Elis would have liked to state at once how absolutely in love with Ulla he was, and how he had pinned every hope of his life on possessing her. But his insurmountable shyness, and even more, perhaps, the fearful doubt whether Ulla really loved him, too, as much as he sometimes suspected, sealed his lips.

It came about that, one day, Elis Fröbom was working at the deepest level, enveloped in dense sulfur fumes, so that his lamp cut through the gloom only feebly and he was scarcely able to distinguish the lodes in the rockface. Then he heard the rumble of hammering from a yet deeper shaft, as if someone were working with a rock-crushing mallet. Since work of that sort wasn't possible at the very bottom, and Elis knew that no one beside himself

abgefahren, da der Steiger eben die Leute im Förderschacht anstellte, so wollte ihm das Pochen und Hämmern ganz unheimlich bedünken. Er ließ Handfäustel und Eisen ruhen und horchte zu den hohl anschlagenden Tönen, die immer näher und näher zu kommen schienen. Mit eins gewahrte er dicht neben sich einen schwarzen Schatten und erkannte, da eben ein schneidender Luftstrom den Schwefeldampf verblies, den alten Bergmann von Götaborg, der ihm zur Seite stand.

«Glück auf!» rief der Alte, «Glück auf, Elis Fröbom, hier unten im Gestein! – Nun wie gefällt dir das Leben, Kamerad?» – Elis wollte fragen, auf welche wunderbare Art der Alte in den Schacht gekommen; *der* schlug aber mit seinem Hammer an das Gestein mit solcher Kraft, daß Feuerfunken umherstoben und es wie ferner Donner im Schacht widerhallte, und rief dann mit entsetzlicher Stimme: «Das ist hier ein herrlicher Trappgang, aber du schnöder schuftiger Geselle schauest nichts als einen Trum, der kaum eines Strohhalms mächtig. – Hier unten bist du ein blinder Maulwurf, dem der Metallfürst ewig abhold bleiben wird, und oben vermagst du auch nichts zu unternehmen, und stellst vergebens dem Garkönig nach. – Hei! des Pehrson Dahlsjö Tochter Ulla willst du zum Weibe gewinnen, deshalb arbeitest du hier ohne Lieb und Gedanken. – Nimm dich in acht, du falscher Gesell, daß der Metallfürst, den du verhöhnst, dich nicht faßt und hinabschleudert, daß deine Glieder zerbröckeln am scharfen Gestein. – Und nimmer wird Ulla dein Weib, das sag ich dir!»

Dem Elis wallte der Zorn auf vor den schnöden Worten des Alten. «Was tust du», rief er, «was tust du hier in dem Schacht meines Herrn Pehrson Dahlsjö, in dem ich arbeite mit aller Kraft und wie es meines Berufs ist? Hebe dich hinweg, wie du gekommen, oder wir wollen sehen, wer hier unten einer dem andern zuerst das Gehirn einschlägt.» – Damit stellte sich Elis Fröbom trotzig vor den Alten hin und schwang sein eisernes Handfäustel, mit dem er gearbeitet, hoch empor. Der Alte lachte höhnisch auf, und Elis sah mit Entsetzen, wie er behende gleich einer Eichkatz' die schmalen Sprossen der Leiter heraufhüpfte und in dem schwarzen Geklüft verschwand.

Elis fühlte sich wie gelähmt an allen Gliedern, die Arbeit wollte nicht mehr vonstatten gehen, er stieg herauf. Als der alte Obersteiger,

had come down that day, because the supervisor had just summoned everyone to work in the hoisting shaft, the pounding and
hammering seemed quite uncanny to him. He let his hand hammer and his iron spike rest, and listened to the hollow sounds that
seemed to be coming closer and closer. All at once he became
aware of a black shadow right next to him and, as a biting air current blew away the sulfur fumes for a moment, he recognized the
old miner from Göteborg, who was standing beside him.

"Good luck!"[5] the old man exclaimed. "Good luck, Elis Fröbom,
down here amid the rocks! Now how do you like the life, com-
rade?" Elis wanted to ask in what miraculous way the old man had
arrived in the shaft, but his visitor swung his hammer against the
rock with such force that sparks flew all around and there was an
echo in the shaft that sounded like distant thunder; then the man
cried in a terrifying voice: "What we have here is a splendid
Trappgang,[6] but you, you base, shabby fellow, see nothing there
but a *Trum*[6] that could scarcely support a straw. Down here you're
a blind mole, who will always be disliked by the Prince of Metals,
and up there you're equally incapable of any enterprise, and you're
pursuing the 'refined ore' in vain. Ha! You want to win Pehrson
Dahlsjö's daughter Ulla for your wife, and that's why you're working here lovelessly and mindlessly. Watch out, you faithless man, or
the Prince of Metals, whom you hold in contempt, will seize you
and hurl you down where your limbs will shatter against the sharp
rocks! And Ulla will never be your wife, that I can tell you!"

Elis was filled with anger at the old man's base speech. "What
are you doing here?" he shouted. "What are you doing here in
my master Pehrson Dahlsjö's shaft, where I work with all my
strength, in accordance with my profession? Get out of here the
way you came, or we'll see which one of us down here is the first
to beat out the other's brains!" Saying that, Elis stepped in front
of the old man defiantly, swinging high in the air the small iron
hammer with which he had been working. The old man burst
into a scornful laugh, and Elis saw to his horror how he hopped
up the narrow rungs of the ladder as nimbly as a squirrel and disappeared in the black crevasse.

Elis felt paralyzed all over; he was unable to continue his
work, and he ascended. When the elderly chief supervisor, who

---

5. *Glück auf!* is a traditional miner's greeting.   6. These words have been intentionally left in German in this passage because Elis (and presumably the
reader) is not supposed to understand them until they're explained.

der eben aus dem Förderschacht gestiegen, ihn gewahrte, rief er: «Um Christus willen, was ist dir widerfahren, Elis, du siehst blaß und verstört aus wie der Tod! – Gelt! – der Schwefeldampf, den du noch nicht gewohnt, hat es dir angetan? – Nun – trink, guter Junge, das wird dir wohltun.» – Elis nahm einen tüchtigen Schluck Branntwein aus der Flasche, die ihm der Obersteiger darbot, und erzählte dann erkräftigt alles, was sich unten im Schacht begeben, sowie auf welche Weise er die Bekanntschaft des alten unheimlichen Bergmanns in Götaborg gemacht.

Der Obersteiger hörte alles ruhig an, dann schüttelte er aber bedenklich den Kopf und sprach: «Elis Fröbom, das ist der alte Torbern gewesen, dem du begegnet, und ich merke nun wohl, daß das mehr als ein Märlein ist, was wir uns hier von ihm erzählen. Vor mehr als hundert Jahren gab es hier in Falun einen Bergmann, namens Torbern. Er soll einer der ersten gewesen sein, der den Bergbau zu Falun recht in Flor gebracht hat, und zu seiner Zeit war die Ausbeute bei weitem reicher als jetzt. Niemand verstand sich damals auf den Bergbau so als Torbern, der in tiefer Wissenschaft erfahren, dem ganzen Bergwesen in Falun vorstand. Als sei er mit besonderer höherer Kraft ausgerüstet, erschlossen sich ihm die reichsten Gänge und kam noch hinzu, daß er ein finstrer tiefsinniger Mann war, der ohne Weib und Kind, ja ohne eigentliches Obdach in Falun zu haben, beinahe niemals ans Tageslicht kam, sondern unaufhörlich in den Teufen wühlte, so konnte es nicht fehlen, daß bald von ihm die Sage ging, er stehe mit der geheimen Macht, die im Schoß der Erde waltet und die Metalle kocht, im Bunde. Auf Torberns strenge Ermahnungen nicht achtend, der unaufhörlich Unglück prophezeite, sobald nicht wahre Liebe zum wunderbaren Gestein und Metall den Bergmann zur Arbeit antreibe, weitete man in gewinnsüchtiger Gier die Gruben immer mehr und mehr aus, bis endlich am Johannistage des Jahres eintausendsechshundertundsiebenundachtzig sich der fürchterliche Bergsturz ereignete, der unsere ungeheure Pinge schuf, und dabei den ganzen Bau dergestalt verwüstete, daß erst nach vielem Mühen und mit vieler Kunst mancher Schacht wieder hergestellt werden konnte. Von Torbern war nichts mehr zu hören und zu sehn, und gewiß schien es, daß er in der Teufe arbeitend durch den Einsturz verschüttet. – Bald darauf, und zwar, als die Arbeit immer besser und besser vonstatten ging, behaupteten die Hauer, sie hätten im Schacht den alten Torbern gesehen, der ihnen allerlei guten

had just climbed out of the hoisting shaft, noticed him, he called: "For Christ's sake, what has happened to you, Elis? You look as pale and haggard as death! I imagine that the sulfur fumes, which you aren't used to, have affected you. Now, have a drink, my dear boy, it'll do you good." Elis took a hefty gulp of brandy from the bottle that the chief supervisor offered him, and then, feeling stronger, he told him everything that had occurred down in the shaft, and also how he had made the acquaintance of the uncanny old miner in Göteborg.

The chief supervisor listened to it all calmly, but then he shook his head dubiously and said: "Elis Fröbom, the man you met is old Torbern, and I now realize that what we tell each other about him here is no mere yarn. Over a hundred years ago here in Falun there was a miner named Torbern. He's said to have been one of the first men to make mining in Falun really prosperous, and in his day the yield was much greater than it is now. At that time nobody understood mining as well as Torbern did; having accumulated vast knowledge, he was in charge of all mining operations in Falun. As if he were endowed with some special higher power, the richest lodes revealed themselves to him; in addition, he was a gloomy, pensive man, with no wife or child, or even any real domicile in Falun, so that he almost never came to the surface, but incessantly burrowed in the deepest galleries; therefore, pretty soon, it was inevitable for a legend to be attached to him to the effect that he was in league with the secret force that holds sway at the earth's core and 'cooks' the metals. Paying no heed to Torbern's severe warnings—he was constantly prophesying disaster unless a true love for marvelous minerals and metals inspired the miners' labor—the pits were increasingly expanded in a sick greed for profit, until finally, on St. John's Day[7] of the year sixteen hundred and eighty-seven, the terrible cave-in occurred that created our immense pit opening and, at the same time, destroyed the whole complex so thoroughly that only after great efforts and with great skill was it possible to restore many shafts to operation. No more was to be heard or seen of Torbern, and it appeared certain that he had been working at the bottom and was buried by the cave-in. Shortly afterward, and, in fact, when work was continuing to pick up again, the hewers claimed to have seen old Torbern in the shaft; he had given them

7. June 24.

Rat erteilt und die schönsten Gänge gezeigt. Andere hatten den Alten oben an der Pinge umherstreichend erblickt, bald wehmütig klagend, bald zornig tobend. Andere Jünglinge kamen so wie du hieher und behaupteten, ein alter Bergmann habe sie ermahnt zum Bergbau und hieher gewiesen. Das geschah allemal, wenn es an Arbeitern mangeln wollte, und wohl mochte der alte Torbern auch auf diese Weise für den Bergbau sorgen. – Ist es nun wirklich der alte Torbern gewesen, mit dem du Streit gehabt im Schacht, und hat er von einem herrlichen Trappgange gesprochen, so ist es gewiß, daß dort eine reiche Eisenader befindlich, der wir morgen nachspüren wollen. – Du hast nämlich nicht vergessen, daß wir hier die eisengehaltige Ader im Gestein, Trappgang nennen, und daß Trum eine Ader von dem Gange ist, die sich in verschiedene Teile zerschlägt und wohl gänzlich auseinandergeht.»

Als Elis Fröbom, von mancherlei Gedanken hin und her geworfen, eintrat in Pehrson Dahlsjös Haus, kam ihm nicht wie sonst Ulla freundlich entgegen. Mit niedergeschlagenem Blick, und, wie Elis zu bemerken glaubte, mit verweinten Augen saß Ulla da und neben ihr ein stattlicher junger Mann, der ihre Hand festhielt in der seinigen und sich mühte allerlei Freundliches, Scherzhaftes vorzubringen, worauf Ulla aber nicht sonderlich achtete. – Pehrson Dahlsjö zog den Elis, der, von trüber Ahnung ergriffen, den starren Blick auf das Paar heftete, fort ins andere Gemach und begann: «Nun Elis Fröbom, wirst du bald deine Liebe zu mir, deine Treue beweisen können, denn, habe ich dich schon immer wie meinen Sohn gehalten, so wirst du es nun wirklich werden ganz und gar. Der Mann, den du bei mir siehst, ist der reiche Handelsherr, Eric Olawsen geheißen, aus Götaborg. Ich geb ihm auf sein Werben meine Tochter zum Weibe; er zieht mit ihr nach Götaborg und du bleibst dann allein bei mir, Elis, meine einzige Stütze im Alter. – Nun, Elis, du bleibst stumm? – du erbleichst, ich hoffe nicht, daß dir mein Entschluß mißfällt, daß du jetzt, da meine Tochter mich verlassen muß, auch von mir willst! – doch ich höre Herrn Olawsen meinen Namen nennen – ich muß hinein!»

Damit ging Pehrson wieder in das Gemach zurück.

Elis fühlte sein Inneres von tausend glühenden Messern zerfleischt – Er hatte keine Worte, keine Tränen. – In wilder Verzweiflung rannte er aus dem Hause fort – fort – bis zur großen Pinge. Bot das unge-

all sorts of good advice and had showed them the finest lodes. Others had caught sight of the old man roaming about up at the opening; at times he was lamenting sorrowfully, at times raging in anger. Other young men arrived here the way you did, claiming that an old miner had encouraged them to become miners themselves and had directed them here. That happened every time there was a shortage of workmen, and old Torbern was probably looking out for our mining operations that way, too. Now, if it was really old Torbern that you quarreled with in the shaft, and if he spoke about a splendid *Trappgang*, there's no doubt that a rich vein of iron is located there, which we'll look into tomorrow. I'm sure you haven't forgotten that we here call an iron-bearing vein in the rock a *Trappgang*,[8] or that a *Trum*[9] is a vein from the lode that divides into various parts and then runs out altogether."

When Elis Fröbom, buffeted to and fro by a multitude of thoughts, entered Pehrson Dahlsjö's house, Ulla didn't come to give him a friendly greeting as usual. Her eyes cast down and, as Elis thought he observed, with eyes red from weeping, Ulla sat there; beside her was an imposing young man who held her hand tightly in his own and strove to come up with all sorts of friendly or humorous remarks, to which Ulla, however, was paying no special attention. Pehrson Dahlsjö drew Elis away into another room when he found him staring at the couple, prey to a dismal foreboding. He began: "Now, Elis Fröbom, you'll soon be able to prove your love for me and your fidelity, because, if I've always considered you as my son before this, you'll now become one for real. The man you see in my house is a wealthy merchant, named Eric Olawsen, from Göteborg. He has asked for my daughter's hand, and I've consented; he'll take her to Göteborg and then you'll be the only one with me, Elis, the sole prop of my old age. Well, Elis, you have nothing to say? You're turning pale! I hope you don't dislike my decision, so that, now, when my daughter has to leave me, you'll want to desert me, as well! But I hear Mr. Olawsen calling my name; I must go in there!"

With those words, Pehrson returned to that room.

Elis felt as if his insides were being slashed to shreds by a thousand red-hot knives. He couldn't speak, couldn't weep. In wild despair he ran out of the house and away, away, until he

---

8. The word literally means a lode of trap(rock).   9. An apophysis, or small, trivial branching vein of ore.

heuere Geklüft schon im Tageslicht einen entsetzlichen Anblick dar, so war vollends jetzt, da die Nacht eingebrochen und die Mondesscheibe erst aufdämmerte, das wüste Gestein anzusehen, als wühle und wälze unten eine zahllose Schar gräßlicher Untiere, die scheußliche Ausgeburt der Hölle, sich durcheinander am rauchenden Boden und blitze herauf mit Flammenaugen und strecke die riesigen Krallen aus nach dem armen Menschenvolk. –

«Torbern – Torbern!» schrie Elis mit furchtbarer Stimme, daß die öden Schlüfte widerhallten – «Torbern, hier bin ich! – Du hattest recht, ich war ein schuftiger Gesell, daß ich alberner Lebenshoffnung auf der Oberfläche der Erde mich hingab! – Unten liegt mein Schatz, mein Leben, mein alles! – Torbern! – steig herab mit mir, zeig mir die reichsten Trappgänge, da will ich wühlen und bohren und arbeiten und das Licht des Tages fürder nicht mehr schauen! – Torbern! – Torbern – steig herab mit mir!»

Elis nahm Stahl und Stein aus der Tasche, zündete sein Grubenlicht an und stieg hinab in den Schacht, den er gestern befahren, ohne daß sich der Alte sehen ließ. Wie ward ihm, als er in der tiefsten Teufe deutlich und klar den Trappgang erblickte, so daß er seiner Salbänder Streichen und Fallen zu erkennen vermochte.

Doch als er fester und fester den Blick auf die wunderbare Ader im Gestein richtete, war es, als ginge ein blendendes Licht durch den ganzen Schacht, und seine Wände wurden durchsichtig wie der reinste Kristall. Jener verhängnisvolle Traum, den er in Götaborg geträumt, kam zurück. Er blickte in die paradiesischen Gefilde der herrlichsten Metallbäume und Pflanzen, an denen wie Früchte, Blüten und Blumen feuerstrahlende Steine hingen. Er sah die Jungfrauen, er schaute das hohe Antlitz der mächtigen Königin. Sie erfaßte ihn, zog ihn hinab, drückte ihn an ihre Brust, da durchzuckte ein glühender Strahl sein Inneres und sein Bewußtsein war nur das Gefühl, als schwämme er in den Wogen eines blauen durchsichtig funkelnden Nebels. –

«Elis Fröbom, Elis Fröbom!» – rief eine starke Stimme von oben herab und der Widerschein von Fackeln fiel in den Schacht. Pehrson Dahlsjö selbst war es, der mit dem Steiger hinabkam, um den Jüngling, den sie wie im hellen Wahnsinn nach der Pinge rennen gesehen, zu suchen.

Sie fanden ihn wie erstarrt stehend, das Gesicht gedrückt in das kalte Gestein.

«Was», rief Pehrson ihn an, «was machst du hier unten zur Nachtzeit, unbesonnener junger Mensch! – Nimm deine Kraft

reached the big pit opening. If the immense crevasse was horrible to look at even in daylight, now, after nightfall, with the moon's disk just beginning to appear, the rocky desert looked entirely as if, down below, a numberless troop of hideous monsters, the disgusting spawn of hell, were burrowing and wallowing in a tangle on the steaming bottom, sending flashes upward from their eyes of flame and stretching out their gigantic talons at poor mankind.

"Torbern! Torbern!" Elis cried in a frightful voice that made the barren gullies echo. "Torbern, here I am! You were right, I was a shabby fellow, devoting myself to foolish hopes on the surface of the earth! It is down below that my treasure lies, my life, my all! Torbern, come down with me and show me the richest iron lodes; there I'll burrow and bore and work and never again behold the light of day! Torbern, Torbern, come down with me!"

Elis took his steel and flint from his pocket, lit his work lamp, and descended into the shaft that he had worked the day before, without the old man showing himself. How he felt when, at the very bottom, he saw the iron lode so distinctly and clearly that he could distinguish its horizontal and vertical boundaries!

But, as he directed his gaze at the marvelous vein in the rock more and more steadily, a dazzling light seemed to traverse the entire shaft, and its walls became as transparent as the purest crystal. The fateful dream he had dreamt in Göteborg recurred. He was gazing into the Eden-like regions of the most splendid metallic trees and plants, on which hung fruit, blossoms, and flowers that were flamingly radiant gems. He saw the maidens, he saw the noble countenance of the regal queen. She seized him, drew him down, and pressed him to her bosom; then a burning ray quivered through him, and he had no consciousness beyond the feeling that he was floating in the billows of a blue mist that sparkled in its transparency.

"Elis Fröbom! Elis Fröbom!" a strong voice called down from above, and the reflected glow of torches fell into the shaft. It was Pehrson Dahlsjö himself coming down with the supervisor to look for the young man, whom they had seen running toward the pit opening, as if in sheer madness.

They found him standing as if paralyzed, his face pressed against the cold rock.

"What," Pehrson called to him, "what are you doing down here at night, you careless young person? Gather your strength

zusammen und steige mit uns herauf, wer weiß was du oben Gutes erfahren wirst!»

In tiefem Schweigen stieg Elis herauf, in tiefem Schweigen folgte
er dem Pehrson Dahlsjö, der nicht aufhörte, ihn tapfer auszuschelten,
daß er sich in solche Gefahr begeben.

Der Morgen war hell aufgegangen, als sie ins Haus traten. Ulla
stürzte mit einem lauten Schrei dem Elis an die Brust, und nannte ihn
mit den süßesten Namen. Aber Pehrson Dahlsjö sprach zu Elis: «Du
Tor! mußte ich es denn nicht längst wissen, daß du Ulla liebtest, und
wohl nur ihretwegen mit so vielem Fleiß und Eifer in der Grube arbeitetest? Mußte ich nicht längst gewahren, daß auch Ulla dich liebte
recht aus dem tiefsten Herzensgrunde? Konnte ich mir einen bessern
Eidam wünschen, als einen tüchtigen fleißigen frommen Bergmann,
als eben dich, mein braver Elis? – Aber daß ihr schwiegt, das ärgerte,
das kränkte mich.»

«Haben wir», unterbrach Ulla den Vater, «haben wir denn selbst
gewußt, daß wir uns so unaussprechlich liebten?»

«Mag», fuhr Pehrson Dahlsjö fort, «mag dem sein, wie ihm wolle,
genug, ich ärgerte mich, daß Elis nicht offen und ehrlich von seiner
Liebe zu mir sprach und deshalb, und weil ich dein Herz auch prüfen
wollte, förderte ich gestern das Märchen mit Herrn Eric Olawsen zu-
tage, worüber du bald zugrunde gegangen wärst. Du toller Mensch! –
Herr Eric Olawsen ist ja längst verheiratet und dir, braver Elis
Fröbom, gebe ich meine Tochter zum Weibe, denn ich wiederhole es,
keinen bessern Schwiegersohn konnt ich mir wünschen.»

Dem Elis rannten die Tränen herab vor lauter Wonne und
Freude. Alles Lebensglück war so unerwartet auf ihn herabgekom-
men und es mußte ihn beinahe bedünken, er stehe abermals im
süßen Traum! –

Auf Pehrson Dahlsjös Gebot sammelten sich die Bergleute mittags
zum frohen Mahl.

Ulla hatte sich in ihren schönsten Schmuck gekleidet und sah anmutiger aus als jemals, so daß alle einmal über das andere riefen: «Ei,
welche hochherrliche Braut hat unser wackrer Elis Fröbom erworben! – Nun! – der Himmel segne beide in ihrer Frömmigkeit und
Tugend!»

Auf Elis Fröboms bleichem Gesicht lag noch das Entsetzen der
Nacht und oft starrte er vor sich hin wie entrückt allem was ihn
umgab.

«Was ist dir, mein Elis?» fragte Ulla. Elis drückte sie an seine Brust
und sprach: «Ja ja! – Du bist wirklich mein und nun ist ja alles gut!»

and climb up with us. Who knows what sort of good news you'll
hear up above!"

In deep silence Elis climbed up, in deep silence he followed
Pehrson Dahlsjö, who didn't cease giving him a good scolding
for having exposed himself to such great danger.

It was already bright morning when they entered the house.
With a loud cry Ulla threw herself on Elis's breast, calling him
the most endearing names. But Pehrson Dahlsjö said to Elis:
"You fool! Wouldn't I have known for some time that you loved
Ulla, and were probably working so diligently and eagerly in the
mine solely for her sake? Wouldn't I have noticed long since that
Ulla loved you, too, from the very bottom of her heart? Could I
wish for a better son-in-law than a competent, industrious, God-
fearing miner—than you yourself, my good Elis? But the silence
of the two of you—that vexed me, that hurt me."

"Did we," Ulla interrupted her father, "did we ourselves know
that we loved each other so inexpressibly?"

"However," continued Pehrson Dahlsjö, "however that may
be, suffice it to say that I was vexed because Elis didn't speak to
me about his love openly and honestly; for that reason, and because I wanted to test his inclinations, yesterday I concocted
that story about Mr. Eric Olawsen, which almost led to your
death. You lunatic! Mr. Eric Olawsen was married long ago, and
it's to you, my good Elis Fröbom, that I give my daughter's hand,
because I repeat: I couldn't wish for a better son-in-law."

Tears streamed down Elis's face out of sheer bliss and joy. All
of life's happiness had been bestowed on him so unexpectedly,
and he surely almost thought he was once again having a sweet
dream!

At Pehrson Dahlsjö's invitation the miners assembled at noon
for a joyful meal.

Ulla was dressed in her best finery and looked more charming
than ever, so that everyone exclaimed repeatedly: "My, what a
magnificent bride our honest Elis Fröbom has won! Now, may
heaven bless both of those pious and virtuous people!"

Elis Fröbom's pale face still showed signs of his nocturnal terror, and he often stared blankly as if detached from everything
around him.

"What's wrong, my Elis?" Ulla asked. Elis pressed her to his
heart and said: "Yes, yes! You're really mine, and now everything
is all right!"

Mitten in aller Wonne war es dem Elis manchmal, als griffe auf einmal eine eiskalte Hand in sein Inneres hinein und eine dunkle
Stimme spräche: «Ist es denn nun noch dein Höchstes, daß du Ulla
erworben? Du armer Tor! – Hast du nicht das Antlitz der Königin
geschaut?»

Er fühlte sich beinahe übermannt von einer unbeschreiblichen
Angst, der Gedanke peinigte ihn, es werde nun plötzlich einer von
den Bergleuten riesengroß sich vor ihm erheben, und er werde zu
seinem Entsetzen den Torbern erkennen, der gekommen, ihn
fürchterlich zu mahnen an das unterirdische Reich der Steine und
Metalle, dem er sich ergeben!

Und doch wußte er wieder gar nicht, warum ihm der gespenstische
Alte feindlich sein, was überhaupt sein Bergmannshantieren mit
seiner Liebe zu schaffen haben solle.

Pehrson merkte wohl Elis Fröboms verstörtes Wesen und schrieb
es dem überstandenen Weh, der nächtlichen Fahrt in den Schacht zu.
Nicht so Ulla, die, von geheimer Ahnung ergriffen, in den Geliebten
drang, ihr doch nur zu sagen, was ihm denn Entsetzliches begegnet,
das ihn ganz von ihr hinwegreiße. Dem Elis wollte die Brust zer-
springen. – Vergebens rang er darnach, der Geliebten von dem wunderbaren Gesicht, das sich ihm in der Teufe aufgetan, zu erzählen. Es
war, als verschlösse ihm eine unbekannte Macht mit Gewalt den
Mund, als schaue aus seinem Innern heraus das furchtbare Antlitz der
Königin, und nenne er ihren Namen, so würde, wie bei dem Anblick
des entsetzlichen Medusenhaupts, sich alles um ihn her versteinen
zum düstern schwarzen Geklüft! – Alle Herrlichkeit, die ihn unten in
der Teufe mit der höchsten Wonne erfüllt, erschien ihm jetzt wie eine
Hölle voll trostloser Qual, trügerisch ausgeschmückt zur verderblichsten Verlockung!

Pehrson Dahlsjö gebot, daß Elis Fröbom einige Tage hindurch daheim bleiben solle, um sich ganz von der Krankheit zu erholen, in die
er gefallen schien. In dieser Zeit verscheuchte Ullas Liebe, die nun
hell und klar aus ihrem kindlichen frommen Herzen ausströmte, das
Andenken an die verhängnisvollen Abenteuer im Schacht. Elis lebte
ganz auf in Wonne und Freude und glaubte an sein Glück, das wohl
keine böse Macht mehr verstören könne.

Als er wieder hinabfuhr in den Schacht, kam ihm in der Teufe
alles ganz anders vor wie sonst. Die herrlichsten Gänge lagen offen
ihm vor Augen, er arbeitete mit verdoppeltem Eifer, er vergaß
alles, er mußte sich, auf die Oberfläche hinaufgestiegen, auf
Pehrson Dahlsjö, ja auf seine Ulla besinnen, er fühlte sich wie in

In the midst of all his rapture Elis sometimes felt as if an ice-cold hand were suddenly seizing him inwardly and a dark voice were saying: "Is having won Ulla the greatest achievement you can imagine? You poor fool! Haven't you beheld the counte-nance of the queen?"

He felt nearly overcome by an unspeakable anxiety, and he was plagued by the thought that one of the miners would sud-denly grow to a gigantic height before his eyes, and that, to his horror, he would recognize Torbern, who had come to give him a frightening reminder of the subterranean realm of stone and metal to which he had dedicated himself!

And yet, on reflection, he knew no reason why the spectral old man should be hostile to him, or what his mining activities had to do with his love at all.

Pehrson clearly observed Elis Fröbom's distraught condition, and attributed it to the sorrow he had undergone and his noctur-nal descent into the shaft. Not so Ulla, who, in the grip of a secret foreboding, urged her sweetheart to tell her what sort of horror he had confronted, a horror that was tearing him away from her so completely. Elis's heart nearly broke. He struggled in vain to tell his darling about the miraculous vision that had been disclosed to him at the bottom of the shaft. It was as if some unknown force were violently closing his lips, as if the fearsome countenance of the queen were gazing out from within him, and, were he to speak her name, everything around him—as at the sight of the terrible head of Medusa—would become petrified into a dismal black crevasse! All the splendor that had filled him with the highest rap-ture down at the bottom now appeared to him like a hell full of in-consolable torments, deceptively adorned to lure him to his doom!

Pehrson Dahlsjö ordered Elis Fröbom to stay home for a few days to make a full recovery from the illness he seemed to have contracted. During that time, Ulla's love, which now flowed in a bright, clear stream from her childlike, pious heart, dispelled his recollections of those fateful adventures in the shaft. Elis re-vived completely in bliss and joy, and believed in his good for-tune, which no evil power could disturb any longer.

When he descended into the shaft again, everything at the bot-tom looked different to him than ever before. The finest lodes of ore were clearly visible to him, he worked with redoubled enthu-siasm, he forgot everything else; after ascending to the surface, he had to make an effort to recall Pehrson Dahlsjö, and even his Ulla;

zwei Hälften geteilt, es war ihm, als stiege sein besseres, sein
eigentliches Ich hinab in den Mittelpunkt der Erdkugel und ruhe
aus in den Armen der Königin, während er in Falun sein düsteres
Lager suche. Sprach Ulla mit ihm von ihrer Liebe und wie sie so
glücklich miteinander leben würden, so begann er von der Pracht
der Teufen zu reden, von den unermeßlich reichen Schätzen, die
dort verborgen lägen, und verwirrte sich dabei in solch wunderliche
unverständliche Reden, daß Angst und Beklommenheit das arme
Kind ergriff und sie gar nicht wußte, wie Elis sich auf einmal so in
seinem ganzen Wesen geändert. – Dem Steiger, Pehrson Dahlsjön
selbst verkündete Elis unaufhörlich in voller Lust, wie er die reich-
haltigsten Adern, die herrlichsten Trappgänge entdeckt, und wenn
sie dann nichts fanden als taubes Gestein, so lachte er höhnisch und
meinte, freilich verstehe er nur allein die geheimen Zeichen, die
bedeutungsvolle Schrift, die die Hand der Königin selbst hinein-
grabe in das Steingeklüft, und genug sei es auch eigentlich, diese
Zeichen zu verstehen, ohne das, was sie verkündeten, zu Tage zu
fördern.

Wehmütig blickte der alte Steiger den Jüngling an, der mit wild
funkelndem Blick von dem glanzvollen Paradiese sprach, das im
tiefen Schoß der Erde aufleuchte.

«Ach, Herr», lispelte der Alte Pehrson Dahlsjön leise ins Ohr, «ach,
Herr! dem armen Jungen hat's der böse Torbern angetan!»

«Glaubt», erwiderte Pehrson Dahlsjö, «glaubt nicht an solche
Bergmannsmärlein, Alter! – Dem tiefsinnigen Neriker hat die Liebe
den Kopf verrückt, das ist alles. Laßt nur erst die Hochzeit vorüber
sein, dann wird's sich schon geben mit den Trappgängen und
Schätzen und dem ganzen unterirdischen Paradiese!»

Der von Pehrson Dahlsjö bestimmte Hochzeittag kam endlich
heran. Schon einige Tage vorher war Elis Fröbom stiller, ernster, in
sich gekehrter gewesen als jemals, aber auch nie hatte er sich so
ganz in Liebe der holden Ulla hingegeben als in dieser Zeit. Er
mochte sich keinen Augenblick von ihr trennen, deshalb ging er
nicht zur Grube; er schien an sein unruhiges Bergmannstreiben gar
nicht zu denken, denn kein Wort von dem unterirdischen Reich
kam über seine Lippen. Ulla war ganz voll Wonne; alle Angst, wie
vielleicht die bedrohlichen Mächte des unterirdischen Geklüfts,
von denen sie oft alte Bergleute reden gehört, ihren Elis ins
Verderben locken würden, war verschwunden. Auch Pehrson
Dahlsjö sprach lächelnd zum alten Steiger: «Seht Ihr wohl, daß Elis
Fröbom nur schwindlicht geworden im Kopfe vor Liebe zu meiner
Ulla!»

he felt split in two; it seemed to him that his better, true self was descending into the center of the globe and reposing in the arms of the queen while he was seeking out his dreary bed in Falun. If Ulla spoke to him about their love, and how happy their life together was going to be, he started to talk about the glory of the pit bottom and the measurelessly rich treasures that were hidden there; and, as he spoke, he entangled himself in such oddly incomprehensible expressions that fear and anguish overcame the poor girl, and she had no idea how Elis's nature could have changed so completely all at once. To the supervisor, to Pehrson Dahlsjö himself, Elis constantly reported with the greatest pleasure how he had discovered the most abundant veins of ore, the most splendid iron deposits, and when they subsequently found nothing but ordinary rock, he'd laugh scornfully, saying that, naturally, he alone understood the secret signs, the meaningful ciphers that the hand of the queen herself engraved in the rockface, and that actually, moreover, it was enough to understand those signs without needing to excavate the riches they indicated.

The elderly supervisor would turn a melancholy gaze at the young man, who, his eyes sparkling wildly, spoke of the radiant paradise shining in the deep womb of the earth.

"Oh, master," the old man softly whispered in Pehrson Dahlsjö's ear, "oh, master, the poor boy has been spellbound by that evil Torbern!"

"Don't," Pehrson Dahlsjö replied, "don't believe in such miners' yarns, old man! The pensive lad from Närke has had his head turned by love, that's all. Just let the wedding be over, then we'll hear the last of those iron deposits and treasures and that entire paradise below ground!"

The day that Pehrson Dahlsjö had set for the wedding finally arrived. A few days before, Elis Fröbom was already more quiet, grave, and introspective than ever, but, in addition, he had never surrendered himself so completely to his love for beautiful Ulla than during those days. He didn't want to leave her for even a moment, so he didn't go to the pit; apparently he gave no thought to his restless mining activity, because not a word about the subterranean realm passed his lips. Ulla was completely filled with rapture; all her fears that the menacing forces of the subterranean crevasse, of which she had often heard old miners speak, might perhaps lure Elis to his undoing, had vanished. Even Pehrson Dahlsjö said with a smile to the old supervisor: "Now you must see that Elis Fröbom only got dizzy in the head out of love for my Ulla!"

Am frühen Morgen des Hochzeitstages – es war der Johannistag – klopfte Elis an die Kammer seiner Braut. Sie öffnete und fuhr erschrocken zurück, als sie den Elis erblickte schon in den Hochzeitskleidern, todbleich, dunkel sprühendes Feuer in den Augen. «Ich will», sprach er mit leiser schwankender Stimme, «ich will dir nur sagen, meine herzgeliebte Ulla, daß wir dicht an der Spitze des höchsten Glücks stehen, wie es nur dem Menschen hier auf Erden beschieden. Mir ist in dieser Nacht alles entdeckt worden. Unten in der Teufe liegt in Chlorit und Glimmer eingeschlossen der kirschrot funkelnde Almandin, auf den unsere Lebenstafel eingegraben, den mußt du von mir empfangen als Hochzeitsgabe. Er ist schöner als der herrlichste blutrote Karfunkel, und wenn wir, in treuer Liebe verbunden, hineinblicken in sein strahlendes Licht, können wir es deutlich erschauen, wie unser Inneres verwachsen ist mit dem wunderbaren Gezweige, das aus dem Herzen der Königin im Mittelpunkt der Erde emporkeimt. Es ist nur nötig, daß ich diesen Stein hinauffördere zu Tage, und das will ich nunmehro tun. Gehab dich so lange wohl, meine herzgeliebte Ulla! – bald bin ich wieder hier.»

Ulla beschwor den Geliebten mit heißen Tränen doch abzustehen von diesem träumerischen Unternehmen, da ihr großes Unglück ahne; doch Elis Fröbom versicherte, daß er ohne jenes Gestein niemals eine ruhige Stunde haben würde, und daß an irgendeine bedrohliche Gefahr gar nicht zu denken sei. Er drückte die Braut innig an seine Brust und schied von dannen.

Schon waren die Gäste versammelt, um das Brautpaar nach der Kopparbergs-Kirche, wo nach gehaltenem Gottesdienst die Trauung vor sich gehen sollte, zu geleiten. Eine ganze Schar zierlich geschmückter Jungfrauen, die, nach der Sitte des Landes, als Brautmädchen der Braut voranziehen sollten, lachten und scherzten um Ulla her. Die Musikanten stimmten ihre Instrumente und versuchten einen fröhlichen Hochzeitsmarsch. – Schon war es beinahe Mittag, noch immer ließ sich Elis Fröbom nicht sehen. Da stürzten plötzlich Bergleute herbei, Angst und Entsetzen in den bleichen Gesichtern, und meldeten, wie eben ein fürchterlicher Bergfall die ganze Grube, in der Dahlsjös Kuxe befindlich, verschüttet.

«Elis – mein Elis, du bist hin – hin!» – So schrie Ulla laut auf und fiel wie tot nieder. – Nun erfuhr erst Pehrson Dahlsjö von dem Steiger, daß Elis am frühen Morgen nach der großen Pinge gegangen und hinabgefahren, sonst hatte, da Knappen und Steiger zur Hochzeit geladen, niemand in dem Schacht gearbeitet. Pehrson Dahlsjö, alle Bergleute eilten hinaus, aber alle Nachforschungen, so wie sie nur

Early in the morning of the wedding day—it was St. John's Day—Elis knocked at his bride's bedroom door. She opened it and recoiled in fright when she saw Elis already in his wedding clothes, deathly pale, with a flame in his eyes that flashed darkly. "I only want," he said in a quiet, wavering voice, "I only want to tell you, my dearly beloved Ulla, that we are close to the pinnacle of the greatest good fortune that can fall to the lot of people here on earth. Everything was revealed to me last night. Down there at the bottom of the shaft, enclosed in chlorite and mica, is the almandine that sparkles cherry-red, and on it our life chart is engraved; you must receive it from me as a wedding present. It's more beautiful than the most splendid blood-red garnet, and when we, joined in true love, gaze into its radiant light, we'll be able to see distinctly that our inner being is intimately connected with the marvelous branching plant that springs from the heart of the queen at the earth's center. All that's necessary is for me to bring that stone to light, and that's what I intend to do right now. Till then, good-bye, my dearly beloved Ulla! I'll be back soon."

With scalding tears Ulla implored her sweetheart to desist from that fantastic enterprise, because she foresaw a great misfortune; but Elis Fröbom assured her that, without that stone, he would never know a moment of repose, and there was no reason to fear any lurking danger. He pressed his bride warmly to his heart, and left.

The guests were already assembled to escort the bride and groom to the Kopparberg church, where they were to be married after the regular service. A whole troop of prettily adorned young women, who, in accordance with local custom, were to walk ahead of the bride as bridesmaids, were laughing and joking around Ulla. The musicians were tuning their instruments and trying out a cheerful wedding march. It was already nearly noon, but Elis Fröbom was still nowhere in sight. Then some miners suddenly rushed onto the scene, fear and horror on their pale faces, and reported that a tremendous landslide had just buried the entire pit in which Dahlsjö's mine was located.

"Elis, my Elis, you're lost, lost!" Ulla shouted this loudly and then fainted as if dead. Now for the first time Pehrson Dahlsjö heard from the supervisor that, early in the morning, Elis had gone to the big opening and had descended; no one else had been working in the shaft because both pitmen and supervisors had been invited to the wedding. Pehrson Dahlsjö and all the

selbst mit der höchsten Gefahr des Lebens möglich, blieben
vergebens. Elis Fröbom wurde nicht gefunden. Gewiß war es, daß der
Erdsturz den Unglücklichen im Gestein begraben; und so kam Elend
und Jammer über das Haus des wackern Pehrson Dahlsjö, in dem
Augenblick, als er Ruhe und Frieden für seine alten Tage sich zu
bereiten gedacht.

Längst war der wackre Masmeister Altermann Pehrson Dahlsjö
gestorben, längst seine Tochter Ulla verschwunden, niemand in Falun
wußte von beiden mehr etwas, da seit Fröboms unglückseligem
Hochzeitstage wohl an die funfzig Jahre verflossen. Da geschah es,
daß die Bergleute, als sie zwischen zwei Schachten einen Durchschlag
versuchten, in einer Teufe von dreihundert Ellen im Vitriolwasser den
Leichnam eines jungen Bergmanns fanden, der versteinert schien, als
sie ihn zu Tage förderten.

Es war anzusehen, als läge der Jüngling in tiefem Schlaf, so
frisch, so wohlerhalten waren die Züge seines Antlitzes, so ohne alle
Spur der Verwesung seine zierliche Bergmannskleider, ja selbst die
Blumen an der Brust. Alles Volk aus der Nähe sammelte sich um
den Jüngling, den man heraufgetragen aus der Pinge, aber niemand
kannte die Gesichtszüge des Leichnams, und keiner der Bergleute
vermochte sich auch zu entsinnen, daß irgendeiner der Kameraden
verschüttet. Man stand im Begriff, den Leichnam weiter
fortzubringen nach Falun, als aus der Ferne ein steinaltes eisgraues
Mütterchen auf Krücken hinankeuchte. «Dort kommt das
Johannismütterchen!» riefen einige von den Bergleuten. Diesen
Namen hatten sie der Alten gegeben, die sie schon seit vielen
Jahren bemerkt, wie sie jedesmal am Johannistage erschien, in die
Tiefe schauend, die Hände ringend, in den wehmütigsten Tönen
ächzend und klagend an der Pinge umherschlich und dann wieder
verschwand.

Kaum hatte die Alte den erstarrten Jüngling erblickt, als sie beide
Krücken fallen ließ, die Arme hoch emporstreckte zum Himmel und
mit dem herzzerschneidendsten Ton der tiefsten Klage rief: «O Elis
Fröbom – o mein Elis – mein süßer Bräutigam!» Und damit kauerte
sie neben dem Leichnam nieder und faßte die erstarrte Hände und
drückte sie an ihre im Alter erkaltete Brust, in der noch, wie heiliges
Naphthafeuer unter der Eisdecke, ein Herz voll heißer Liebe schlug.
«Ach», sprach sie dann, sich im Kreise umschauend, «ach niemand,
niemand von euch kennt mehr die arme Ulla Dahlsjö, dieses
Jünglings glückliche Braut vor funfzig Jahren! – Als ich mit Gram und

miners rushed out, but all their searches, which could only be undertaken at the risk of their lives, remained fruitless. Elis Fröbom wasn't found. There was no doubt that the landslide had buried the unfortunate man among the rocks. And so misery and grief came over the house of honest Pehrson Dahlsjö at the very moment when he thought he had secured peace and repose for his declining years.

The honest mine manager and guildsman Pehrson Dahlsjö was long dead, and his daughter Ulla was long gone from view; no one in Falun knew anything about either of them anymore, because some fifty years had elapsed since Fröbom's unfortunate wedding day. But then it came about that some miners who were working on a crosscut between two shafts found the corpse of a young miner in a pool of acidic water at a depth of three hundred ells; it seemed to be petrified when they brought it up to the surface.

The young man looked as if he were merely fast asleep, so fresh and well-preserved were his facial features, so free from any sign of rotting were his handsome miner's clothes, and even the flowers on his bosom. Everyone in the vicinity gathered around the young man, who had been carried out of the pit opening, but nobody recognized the features of the corpse; nor could any of the miners recall that any of their fellow workers had been buried in that manner. They were about to pick up the body and take it to Falun, when in the distance an ancient, gray-haired old woman came panting up on crutches. "Here comes St. John's lady!" a few of the miners called. They had given the old woman that nickname because for many years they had seen her appear every St. John's Day; she'd gaze into the depths, wring her hands, walk around the opening, moaning and lamenting in the most melancholy tones, and then depart again.

Scarcely had the old woman caught sight of the rigid youth when she dropped both crutches, raised her arms high into the sky, and called in the most heartrending accents of deepest grief: "O Elis Fröbom, O my Elis, my sweet bridegroom!" Saying that, she squatted down beside the corpse, seized its stiff hands, and pressed them to her breast, which had grown cold with age but in which a heart filled with ardent love still beat, like a sacred naphtha flame beneath the ice cover. "Ah," she then said, looking around the bystanders, "ah, none, none of you knows poor Ulla Dahlsjö anymore, this young man's happy bride fifty years

Jammer fortzog nach Ornäs, da tröstete mich der alte Torbern und sprach, ich würde meinen Elis, den das Gestein begrub am Hochzeitstage, noch wiedersehen hier auf Erden, und da bin ich jahraus jahrein hergekommen und habe, ganz Sehnsucht und treue Liebe, hinabgeschaut in die Tiefe. – Und heute ist mir ja wirklich solch seliges Wiedersehen vergönnt! – O mein Elis – mein geliebter Bräutigam!»

Aufs neue schlug sie die dürren Arme um den Jüngling, als wolle sie ihn nimmer lassen, und alle standen tief bewegt ringsumher.

Leiser und leiser wurden die Seufzer, wurde das Schluchzen der Alten, bis es dumpf vertönte.

Die Bergleute traten hinan, sie wollten die arme Ulla aufrichten, abe sie hatte ihr Leben ausgehaucht auf dem Leichnam des erstarrten Bräutigams. Man bemerkte, daß der Körper des Unglücklichen, der fälschlicherweise für versteinert gehalten, in Staub zu zerfallen begann.

In der Kopparbergs-Kirche, dort wo vor funfzig Jahren das Paar getraut werden sollte, wurde die Asche des Jünglings beigesetzt und mit ihr die Leiche der bis in den bittern Tod getreuen Braut.

ago! When I moved away to Ornäs in my grief and sorrow, old Torbern comforted me, saying that I'd still see my Elis, who was buried by rocks on our wedding day, here on earth once more; and so I've come here every year and, my heart full of yearning and true love, I've gazed down into the depths. And today that blessed reunion has really been vouchsafed to me! O my Elis, my beloved bridegroom!"

Once again she threw her withered arms around the young man, as if she would never leave him again, and all the onlookers stood around them, deeply touched.

The old woman's sighs became softer and softer, as did her sobs, until they came to a muffled end.

The miners walked over to poor Ulla, intending to help her up, but she had breathed her last over the corpse of her stiff bridegroom. They noticed that the body of the unfortunate man, which they had mistakenly thought was petrified, was beginning to crumble into dust.

In the Kopparberg church, where the couple were to have been wed fifty years earlier, the young man's ashes were laid to rest, and with them the body of the bride who had remained faithful to him to the bitter end.

Das Fräulein von Scuderi

Erzählung aus dem Zeitalter Ludwig des Vierzehnten

In der Straße St. Honoré war das kleine Haus gelegen, welches
Magdaleine von Scuderi, bekannt durch ihre anmutigen Verse, durch
die Gunst Ludwig XIV. und der Maintenon, bewohnte.

Spät um Mitternacht – es mochte im Herbste des Jahres 1680 sein
– wurde an dieses Haus hart und heftig angeschlagen, daß es im
ganzen Flur laut widerhallte. – Baptiste, der in des Fräuleins kleinem
Haushalt Koch, Bedienten und Türsteher zugleich vorstellte, war mit
Erlaubnis seiner Herrschaft über Land gegangen zur Hochzeit seiner
Schwester, und so kam es, daß die Martiniere, des Fräuleins Kammerfrau, allein im Hause noch wachte.

Sie hörte die wiederholten Schläge, es fiel ihr ein, daß Baptiste
fortgegangen, und sie mit dem Fräulein ohne weitern Schutz im
Hause geblieben sei; aller Frevel von Einbruch, Diebstahl und Mord,
wie er jemals in Paris verübt worden, kam ihr in den Sinn, es wurde
ihr gewiß, daß irgendein Haufen Meuter, von der Einsamkeit des
Hauses unterrichtet, da draußen tobe und, eingelassen, ein böses
Vorhaben gegen die Herrschaft ausführen wolle, und so blieb sie in
ihrem Zimmer, zitternd und zagend und den Baptiste verwünschend
samt seiner Schwester Hochzeit.

Unterdessen donnerten die Schläge immer fort, und es war ihr,
als rufe eine Stimme dazwischen: «So macht doch nur auf um
Christus willen, so macht doch nur auf!» Endlich in steigender
Angst ergriff die Martiniere schnell den Leuchter mit der brennen-
den Kerze und rannte hinaus auf den Flur; da venahm sie ganz deutlich die Stimme des Anpochenden: «Um Christus willen, so macht
doch nur auf!»

«In der Tat», dachte die Martiniere, «so spricht doch wohl kein
Räuber; wer weiß, ob nicht gar ein Verfolgter Zuflucht sucht bei
meiner Herrschaft, die ja geneigt ist zu jeder Wohltat. Aber laßt uns
vorsichtig sein!» – Sie öffnete ein Fenster und rief hinab, wer denn da

Mademoiselle de Scudéry

Story from the Era of Louis XIV

The little house which Madeleine de Scudéry—known for her charming verses—occupied, thanks to the favor of Louis XIV and Mme de Maintenon, was situated in the rue St-Honoré.

Late at night, around midnight—it may have been in the fall of the year 1680—there was such hard and violent knocking at the door of that house that the entire entrance hall loudly re-echoed with it. Baptiste, who represented cook, butler, and porter in the lady's small household, had gone out of town, with the permission of his mistress, to attend his sister's wedding, and so Mme Martinière, the lady's chambermaid, was the only one in the house still up and about.

Hearing the repeated knocks, she recalled that Baptiste was away, and that she was left in the house with the lady but with no further protection; recollecting all the crimes of burglary, theft, and murder that were prevalent in Paris at the time, she was now sure that some gang of malefactors, informed that they were alone in the house, was raging outside and, if admitted, would carry out some evil design against her mistress; therefore she remained in her room, trembling and hesitant, and cursing Baptiste and his sister's wedding.

Meanwhile the blows continued to thunder on the door, and it seemed to her that a voice was also shouting: "Please open up, in the name of Christ, please open up!" Finally, her fear mounting, Martinière quickly seized the candlestick with the burning taper and ran out to the vestibule; there she heard quite distinctly the voice of the man who was knocking: "In the name of Christ, please open up!"

"Actually," Martinière thought, "no robber would speak that way; who knows—maybe some persecuted man is seeking refuge with my mistress, who's a benefactress by nature, after all. But let's be cautious!" She opened a window and called

99

unten in später Nacht so an der Haustür tobe und alles aus dem
Schlafe wecke, indem sie ihrer tiefen Stimme so viel Männliches zu
geben sich bemühte, als nur möglich.

In dem Schimmer der Mondesstrahlen, die eben durch die finstern
Wolken brachen, gewahrte sie eine lange, in einen hellgrauen Mantel
gewickelte Gestalt, die den breiten Hut tief in die Augen gedrückt
hatte. Sie rief nun mit lauter Stimme, so, daß es der unten vernehmen
konnte: «Baptiste, Claude, Pierre, steht auf und seht einmal zu,
welcher Taugenichts uns das Haus einschlagen will!»

Da sprach es aber mit sanfter, beinahe klagender Stimme von
unten herauf: «Ach! la Martiniere, ich weiß ja, daß Ihr es seid, liebe
Frau, so sehr Ihr Eure Stimme zu verstellen trachtet, ich weiß ja, daß
Baptiste über Land gegangen ist und Ihr mit Eurer Herrschaft allein
im Hause seid. Macht mir nur getrost auf, befürchtet nichts. Ich muß
durchaus mit Eurem Fräulein sprechen, noch in dieser Minute.»

«Wo denkt Ihr hin», erwiderte die Martiniere, «mein Fräulein wollt
Ihr sprechen mitten in der Nacht? Wißt Ihr denn nicht, daß sie längst
schläft, und daß ich sie um keinen Preis wecken werde aus dem ersten süßesten Schlummer, dessen sie in ihren Jahren wohl bedarf.»

«Ich weiß», sprach der Untenstehende, «ich weiß, daß Euer
Fräulein soeben das Manuskript ihres Romans, ‹Clelia› geheißen, an
dem sie rastlos arbeitet, beiseite gelegt hat und jetzt noch einige Verse
aufschreibt, die sie morgen bei der Marquise de Maintenon vorzule-
sen gedenkt. Ich beschwöre Euch, Frau Martiniere, habt die
Barmherzigkeit und öffnet mir die Türe. Wißt, daß es darauf
ankommt, einen Unglücklichen vom Verderben zu retten, wißt, daß
Ehre, Freiheit, ja das Leben eines Menschen abhängt von diesem
Augenblick, in dem ich Euer Fräulein sprechen muß. Bedenkt, daß
Eurer Gebieterin Zorn ewig auf Euch lasten würde, wenn sie erführe,
daß Ihr es waret, die den Unglücklichen, welcher kam, ihre Hilfe zu
erflehen, hartherzig von der Türe wieset.»

«Aber warum sprecht Ihr denn meines Fräuleins Mitleid an in
dieser ungewöhnlichen Stunde, kommt morgen zu guter Zeit
wieder», so sprach die Martiniere herab; da erwiderte der unten:
«Kehrt sich denn das Schicksal, wenn es verderbend wie der tötende
Blitz einschlägt, an Zeit und Stunde? Darf, wenn nur ein Augenblick
Rettung noch möglich ist, die Hilfe aufgeschoben werden? Öffnet mir
die Türe, fürchtet doch nur nichts von einem Elenden, der schutzlos,
verlassen von aller Welt, verfolgt, bedrängt von einem ungeheuern
Geschick, Euer Fräulein um Rettung anflehen will aus drohender
Gefahr!»

down, asking who was making such a racket at the door down there so late at night, waking everyone up; she strove to speak in a deep voice and sound as much as possible like a man.

In the glimmer of the moonbeams, which were just breaking through the dark clouds, she espied a tall figure enveloped in a light-gray cloak, his broad-brimmed hat pulled far down over his face. Now she called loudly, so the man below could hear her: "Baptiste, Claude, Pierre, get up and go see what sort of a good-for-nothing is trying to break our house down!"

But then, in a gentle, almost sorrowful tone, the words came from below: "Oh, Martinière, I know it's you, dear lady, however much you try to disguise your voice; I know that Baptiste is out of town and you're alone in the house with your mistress. Set your mind at ease and open the door; have no fear. I must absolutely talk with your lady, and this very minute!"

"What are you thinking of?" Martinière replied. "You want to speak with my lady in the middle of the night? Don't you know she went to bed some time ago, and that for nothing in the world would I awaken her from her first sleep, the sweetest of all, which she surely needs at her age?"

"I know," said the man below, "I know that your lady has just put aside the manuscript of her novel *Clélie,* which she's working on tirelessly, and is now still writing down some verses which she intends to read to the Marquise de Maintenon tomorrow. I implore you, Mme Martinière, be merciful and open the door! I'll have you know that it's a matter of saving an unfortunate man from ruin; that a human being's honor, freedom, and even life, are dependent on this moment, in which I must speak with your lady. Reflect that your mistress's anger would pursue you eternally, should she learn that it was you who hardheartedly turned away the unfortunate man who came to beseech her aid."

"But why are you soliciting my lady's sympathy at this unusual hour? Come back tomorrow at a decent time," Martinière called down; and the man below answered: "When fate strikes as ruinously as a fatal lightning flash, does it care about time and hours? When rescue is possible only at the very moment, may aid be postponed? Let me in, and please fear nothing from a miserable man, defenseless, abandoned by the world, persecuted, oppressed by a monstrous fate, who wants to implore your lady to save him from the danger that threatens him!"

Die Martiniere vernahm, wie der Untenstehende bei diesen
Worten vor tiefem Schmerz stöhnte und schluchzte; dabei war der
Ton von seiner Stimme der eines Jünglings, sanft und eindringend tief
in die Brust. Sie fühlte sich im Innersten bewegt, ohne sich weiter
lange zu besinnen, holte sie die Schlüssel herbei.

Sowie sie die Türe kaum geöffnet, drängte sich ungestüm die im
Mantel gehüllte Gestalt hinein und rief, der Martiniere vorbeischrei-
tend in den Flur, mit wilder Stimme: «Führt mich zu Euerm
Fräulein!» Erschrocken hob die Martiniere den Leuchter in die Höhe,
und der Kerzenschimmer fiel in ein todbleiches, furchtbar entstelltes
Jünglingsantlitz. Vor Schrecken hätte die Martiniere zu Boden sinken
mögen, als nun der Mensch den Mantel auseinanderschlug und der
blanke Griff eines Stiletts aus dem Brustlatz hervorragte. Es blitzte der
Mensch sie an mit funkelnden Augen und rief noch wilder als zuvor:
«Führt mich zu Euerm Fräulein, sage ich Euch!»

Nun sah die Martiniere ihr Fräulein in der dringendsten Gefahr,
alle Liebe zu der teuren Herrschaft, in der sie zugleich die fromme,
treue Mutter ehrte, flammte stärker auf im Innern und erzeugte
einen Mut, dessen sie wohl selbst sich nicht fähig geglaubt hätte. Sie
warf die Türe ihres Gemachs, die sie offen gelassen, schnell zu, trat
vor dieselbe und sprach stark und fest: «In der Tat, Euer tolles
Betragen hier im Hause paßt schlecht zu Euern kläglichen Worten da
draußen, die, wie ich nun wohl merke, mein Mitleiden sehr zu un-
rechter Zeit erweckt haben. Mein Fräulein sollt und werdet Ihr jetzt
nicht sprechen. Habt Ihr nichts Böses im Sinn, dürft Ihr den Tag
nicht scheuen, so kommt morgen wieder und bringt Eure Sache an! –
jetzt schert Euch aus dem Hause!»

Der Mensch stieß einen dumpfen Seufzer aus, blickte die
Martiniere starr an mit entzetzlichem Blick und griff nach dem Stilett.
Die Martiniere befahl im stillen ihre Seele dem Herrn, doch blieb sie
standhaft und sah dem Menschen keck ins Auge, indem sie sich fester
an die Türe des Gemachs drückte, durch welches der Mensch gehen
mußte, um zu dem Fräulein zu gelangen. «Laßt mich zu Eurem
Fräulein, sage ich Euch», rief der Mensch nochmals.

«Tut, was Ihr wollt», erwiderte die Martiniere, «ich weiche nicht
von diesem Platz, vollendet nur die böse Tat, die Ihr begonnen, auch
Ihr werdet den schmachvollen Tod finden auf dem Greveplatz, wie
Eure verruchten Spießgesellen.»

«Ha», schrie der Mensch auf, «Ihr habt recht, la Martiniere! ich
sehe aus, ich bin bewaffnet wie ein verruchter Räuber und Mörder,
aber meine Spießgesellen sind nicht gerichtet, sind nicht gerich-

Martinière could hear the man below moaning and sobbing in profound sorrow as he spoke those words; at the same time, the tone of his voice was that of a young man, soft and heart-piercing. She felt agitated in her mind; without stopping to think any longer, she fetched the keys.

Scarcely had she opened the door when the figure wrapped in the cloak forced its way in impetuously and, striding past Martinière in the vestibule, shouted wildly: "Take me to your lady!" In her fright Martinière raised the candlestick, and the light of the taper fell upon the deathly pale, horribly distorted face of a young man. Martinière could almost have collapsed with fear when the fellow now spread out his cloak, and the bright handle of a stiletto protruded from his doublet. The fellow glared at her with flashing eyes and shouted even more wildly than before: "Take me to your lady, I tell you!"

Now Martinière pictured her lady as being in the most urgent peril; all her love for her dear mistress, in whom she also revered a pious, faithful mother, flared up more brightly within her, generating courage that she surely hadn't thought herself capable of. She quickly slammed the door to her room, which she had left open, took a stand in front of it, and said loudly and firmly: "To tell the truth, your wild behavior here in the house doesn't live up to your sorrowful words outside, which, as I now see, aroused my sympathy very inopportunely. You may and shall not speak with my lady at this time. If you have no evil in mind, you don't need to shun daylight; so come back tomorrow to state your case! For now, get out of the house!"

The fellow uttered a muffled sigh, stared at Martinière with a frightening gaze, and reached for his stiletto. Martinière silently commended her soul to the Lord, but she remained steadfast, boldly looking the fellow in the eye, while pressing more firmly against the door to her room, which the fellow would have to cross in order to reach her lady. "Admit me to your lady, I tell you," the fellow shouted again.

"Do with me as you like," Martinière replied, "I'm not stepping away from this spot. Carry out the evil deed you've begun, and you too will die a shameful death on the Place de Grève, like your wicked accomplices."

"Ha!" the fellow shouted. "You're right, Martinière! I look like, and I'm armed like, a wicked robber and murderer, but my accomplices haven't been condemned, they haven't been

tet!» – Und damit zog er, giftige Blicke schießend auf die zum Tode geängstete Frau, das Stilett heraus.

«Jesus!» rief sie, den Todesstoß erwartend, aber in dem Augenblick ließ sich auf der Straße das Geklirr von Waffen, der Huftritt von Pferden hören. «Die Marechaussee – die Marechaussee. Hilfe, Hilfe!» schrie die Martiniere.

«Entsetzliches Weib, du willst mein Verderben – nun ist alles aus, alles aus! – nimm! – nimm; gib das dem Fräulein heute noch – morgen, wenn du willst» – dies leise murmelnd, hatte der Mensch der Martiniere den Leuchter weggerissen, die Kerzen verlöscht und ihr ein Kästchen in die Hände gedrückt. «Um deiner Seligkeit willen, gib das Kästchen dem Fräulein», rief der Mensch und sprang zum Hause hinaus.

Die Martiniere war zu Boden gesunken, mit Mühe stand sie auf und tappte sich in der Finsternis zurück in ihr Gemach, wo sie ganz erschöpft, keines Lautes mächtig, in den Lehnstuhl sank. Nun hörte sie die Schlüssel klirren, die sie im Schloß der Haustüre hatte stecken lassen. Das Haus wurde zugeschlossen, und leise unsichere Tritte nahten sich dem Gemach. Festgebannt, ohne Kraft sich zu regen, erwartete sie das Gräßliche; doch wie geschah ihr, als die Türe aufging und sie bei dem Scheine der Nachtlampe auf den ersten Blick den ehrlichen Baptiste erkannte; der sah leichenblaß aus und ganz verstört.

«Um aller Heiligen willen», fing er an, «um aller Heiligen willen, sagt mir, Frau Martiniere, was ist geschehen? Ach die Angst! die Angst! – Ich weiß nicht, was es war, aber fortgetrieben hat es mich von der Hochzeit gestern abend mit Gewalt! – Und nun komme ich in die Straße. Frau Martiniere, denk ich, hat einen leisen Schlaf, die wird's wohl hören, wenn ich leise und säuberlich anpoche an die Haustüre und mich hereinlassen. Da kommt mir eine starke Patrouille entgegen, Reuter, Fußvolk, bis an die Zähne bewaffnet, und hält mich an und will mich nicht fortlassen. Aber zum Glück ist Desgrais dabei, der Marechaussee-Lieutenant, der mich recht gut kennt; der spricht, als sie mir die Laterne unter die Nase halten: ‹Ei, Baptiste, wo kommst du her des Wegs in der Nacht? Du mußt fein im Hause bleiben und es hüten. Hier ist es nicht geheuer, wir denken noch in dieser Nacht einen guten Fang zu machen.› Ihr glaubt gar nicht, Frau Martiniere, wie mir diese Worte aufs Herz fielen. Und nun trete ich auf die Schwelle, und da stürzt ein verhüllter Mensch aus dem Hause, das

condemned!" And with those words, darting poisonous glances at the woman, who was scared to death, he drew his stiletto.

"Jesus!" she cried, expecting a fatal blow, but at that moment the clanking of swords and the hoofbeats of horses could be heard in the street. "The *maréchaussée*, the *maréchaussée!*[1] Help! Help!" Martinière cried.

"Terrible woman, you want me to be destroyed! Now it's all over, all over! Here! Here! Give this to your lady today—tomorrow, if you like!" Quietly muttering those words, the fellow had torn the candlestick from Martinière's grasp, doused the taper, and thrust a small box into her hands. "As you desire your salvation, give your lady this box!" the fellow shouted, and dashed out of the house.

Martinière had fallen to the floor; she stood up with difficulty and groped her way back to her room in the dark; there she collapsed onto her armchair, totally exhausted and unable to make a sound. Now she heard the clinking of the keys she had left in the lock of the front door. Someone locked the door, and quiet, uncertain steps approached her room. Pinned to the spot, without the strength to move, she awaited the coming horror; but what was her surprise when her door opened and by the glow of the night light she immediately recognized honest Baptiste! He looked as pale as a corpse and completely distraught.

"In the name of all the saints," he began, "by all the saints, tell me, Mme Martinière, what has happened? Oh, my fear! My fear! I don't know how it was, but I felt driven away from the wedding last night by force! And now I arrive at our street. Mme Martinière, think I to myself, is a light sleeper, she'll surely hear me if I tap lightly and decently at the front door, and she'll let me in. Then a numerous patrol rides up, horsemen, men on foot, all armed to the teeth; they stop me and won't let me pass. But fortunately Desgrais is among them, the *maréchaussée* lieutenant, who knows me well; when they held their lantern under my nose, he said: 'Well, Baptiste, where are you coming from at night? You ought to stay put in your house and guard it. It isn't safe here, and this very night we hope to make a good catch.' Mme Martinière, you wouldn't believe how strongly those words affected me! And now I walk up to our threshold, and a cloaked man bursts out of the house, a drawn stiletto in his fist, and

---

1. Mounted constabulary.

blanke Stilett in der Faust, und rennt mich um und um – das Haus ist offen, die Schlüssel stecken im Schlosse – sagt, was hat das alles zu bedeuten?»

Die Martiniere, von ihrer Todesangst befreit, erzählte, wie sich alles begeben. Beide, sie und Baptiste, gingen in den Hausflur, sie fanden den Leuchter auf dem Boden, wo der fremde Mensch ihn im Entfliehen hingeworfen. «Es ist nur zu gewiß», sprach Baptiste, «daß unser Fräulein beraubt und wohl gar ermordet werden sollte. Der Mensch wußte, wie Ihr erzählt, daß Ihr allein wart mit dem Fräulein, ja sogar, daß sie noch wachte bei ihren Schriften; gewiß war es einer von den verfluchten Gaunern und Spitzbuben, die bis ins Innere der Häuser dringen, alles listig auskundschaftend, was ihnen zur Ausführung ihrer teuflischen Anschläge dienlich. Und das kleine Kästchen, Frau Martiniere, das, denk ich, werfen wir in die Seine, wo sie am tiefsten ist. Wer steht uns dafür, daß nicht irgendein verruchter Unhold unserm guten Fräulein nach dem Leben trachtet, daß sie, das Kästchen öffnend, nicht tot niedersinkt wie der alte Marquis von Tournay, als er den Brief aufmachte, den er von unbekannter Hand erhalten! –»

Lange ratschlagend, beschlossen die Getreuen endlich, dem Fräulein am andern Morgen alles zu erzählen und ihr auch das geheimnisvolle Kästchen einzuhändigen, das ja mit gehöriger Vorsicht geöffnet werden könne. Beide, erwägten sie genau jeden Umstand der Erscheinung des verdächtigen Fremden, meinten, daß wohl ein besonderes Geheimnis im Spiele sein könne, über das sie eigenmächtig nicht schalten dürften, sondern die Enthüllung ihrer Herrschaft überlassen müßten. –

Baptistes Besorgnisse hatten ihren guten Grund. Gerade zu der Zeit war Paris der Schauplatz der verruchtesten Greueltaten, gerade zu der Zeit bot die teuflischste Erfindung der Hölle die leichtesten Mittel dazu dar.

Glaser, ein deutscher Apotheker, der beste Chemiker seiner Zeit, beschäftigte sich, wie es bei Leuten von seiner Wissenschaft wohl zu geschehen pflegt, mit alchimistischen Versuchen. Er hatte es darauf abgesehen, den Stein der Weisen zu finden. Ihm gesellte sich ein Italiener zu, namens *Exili.* Diesem diente aber die Goldmacherkunst nur zum Vorwande. Nur das Mischen, Kochen, Sublimieren der Giftstoffe, in denen Glaser sein Heil zu finden hoffte, wollte er erlernen, und es gelang ihm endlich, jenes feine Gift zu bereiten, das ohne Geruch, ohne Geschmack, entweder auf der Stelle oder langsam tötend, durchaus keine Spur im menschlichen Körper zurückläßt und

knocks me over—the house door is open, the keys are in the lock—tell me, what does it all mean?"

Martinière, freed from her fear of death, told him everything that had occurred. The two of them, she and Baptiste, returned to the vestibule and found the candlestick on the floor, where the stranger had thrown it while escaping. "It's all too certain," Baptiste said, "that our lady was to have been robbed and even killed. As you tell me, the fellow knew you were alone with our lady, and even that she was still awake writing; he was surely one of those damned rogues and thieves who manage to get inside houses and craftily spy out everything useful to them for carrying out their devilish plans. As for that little box, Mme Martinière, I think we should throw it into the deepest part of the Seine. Who can guarantee that some wicked monster doesn't have a design on our good lady's life, that when she opens the box she won't fall dead like the old Marquis de Tournay when he opened the letter he had received from a person unknown?"

After lengthy deliberations the loyal servants finally decided to tell their lady everything the next morning, and also to hand over the mysterious box to her, so it could be opened with appropriate caution. When they weighed closely every circumstance of the appearance of the suspicious stranger, both were of the opinion that a particular secret might be involved, one whose discovery they shouldn't undertake on their own, but ought to leave to their mistress.

Baptiste's worries were well founded. Precisely at that time Paris was the scene of the most wicked crimes; precisely at that time the most diabolical invention from hell offered the easiest means to commit them.

Glaser, a German pharmacist and the best chemist of his era, was occupied with experiments in alchemy, a regular practice with followers of his science. He had made up his mind to find the philosopher's stone. His collaborator was an Italian named Exili. But the latter used the art of gold-making merely as a pretext. All he wanted to learn was how to mix, brew, and sublimate the toxic substances by means of which Glaser hoped to make his fortune; and he finally succeeded in preparing that subtle poison which, odorless and flavorless, killing either at once or slowly, leaves no trace in the human body and eludes all the skill

alle Kunst, alle Wissenschaft der Ärzte täuscht, die, den Giftmord nicht ahnend, den Tod einer natürlichen Ursache zuschreiben müssen. So vorsichtig Exili auch zu Werke ging, so kam er doch in den Verdacht des Giftverkaufs und wurde nach der Bastille gebracht.

In dasselbe Zimmer sperrte man bald darauf den Hauptmann Godin de Sainte Croix ein. Dieser hatte mit der Marquise de Brinvillier lange Zeit in einem Verhältnisse gelebt, welches Schande über die ganze Familie brachte, und endlich, da der Marquis unempfindlich blieb für die Verbrechen seiner Gemahlin, ihren Vater, Dreux d'Aubray, Zivil-Lieutenant zu Paris, nötigte, das verbrecherische Paar durch einen Verhaftsbefehl zu trennen, den er wider den Hauptmann auswirkte. Leidenschaftlich, ohne Charakter, Frömmigkeit heuchelnd und zu Lastern aller Art geneigt von Jugend auf, eifersüchtig, rachsüchtig bis zur Wut, konnte dem Hauptmann nichts willkommner sein als Exilis teuflisches Geheimnis, das ihm die Macht gab, alle seine Feinde zu vernichten. Er wurde Exilis eifriger Schüler und tat es bald seinem Meister gleich, so daß er, aus der Bastille entlassen, allein fortzuarbeiten imstande war.

Die Brinvillier war ein entartetes Weib, durch Sainte Croix wurde sie zum Ungeheuer. Er vermochte sie nach und nach, erst ihren eignen Vater, bei dem sie sich befand, ihn mit verruchter Heuchelei im Alter pflegend, dann ihre beiden Brüder und endlich ihre Schwester zu vergiften; den Vater aus Rache, die andern der reichen Erbschaft wegen. Die Geschichte mehrerer Giftmörder gibt das entsetzliche Beispiel, daß Verbrechen der Art zur unwiderstehlichen Leidenschaft werden. Ohne weitern Zweck, aus reiner Lust daran, wie der Chemiker Experimente macht zu seinem Vergnügen, haben oft Giftmörder Personen gemordet, deren Leben oder Tod ihnen völlig gleich sein konnte.

Das plötzliche Hinsterben mehrerer Armen im Hotel Dieu erregte später den Verdacht, daß die Brote, welche die Brinvillier dort wöchentlich auszuteilen pflegte, um als Muster der Frömmigkeit und des Wohltuns zu gelten, vergiftet waren. Gewiß ist es aber, daß sie Taubenpasteten vergiftete und sie den Gästen, die sie geladen, vorsetzte. Der Chevalier du Guet und mehrere andere Personen fielen als Opfer dieser höllischen Mahlzeiten. Sainte Croix, sein Gehilfe la Chaussee, die Brinvillier wußten lange Zeit hindurch ihre gräßlichen Untaten in undurchdringliche Schleier zu hüllen; doch welche verruchte List verworfener Menschen vermag zu bestehen, hat die ewige Macht des Himmels beschlossen, schon hier auf Erden die Frevler zu richten!

and science of doctors, who fail to suspect poisoning and are compelled to attribute the death to natural causes. But, as cautiously as Exili proceeded, he nevertheless fell under suspicion of selling poison and was taken to the Bastille.

Soon after, Captain Godin de Sainte-Croix was locked up in the same cell. For a long time this man had had an affair with the Marquise de Brinvilliers which had brought shame on her entire family; finally, when the marquis showed no reaction to his wife's crime, the situation compelled her father, Dreux d'Aubray, head of the civil court in Paris, to separate the criminal pair by obtaining an order to arrest the captain. Passionate, of weak character, a religious hypocrite, inclined to every kind of vice since his youth, jealous, and vengeful to the point of frenzy, the captain could find nothing more welcome than Exili's diabolical secret, which gave him the power to exterminate all his enemies. He became Exili's devoted pupil and was soon as proficient as his teacher, so that, when released from the Bastille, he was able to continue on his own.

Mme de Brinvilliers was a degenerate woman; Sainte-Croix turned her into a monster. He gradually induced her to poison first her own father, with whom she was living, tending to him with wicked hypocrisy in his old age, then her two brothers, and finally her sister: her father in revenge, the others because of the sizeable inheritance. The history of several poisoners reveals the horrible fact that crimes of that type become an irresistible compulsion with them. With no ulterior motive, just for the sheer pleasure of it, the way a chemist performs experiments for his own satisfaction, poisoners have often murdered people whose life or death could have meant nothing at all to them.

The sudden death of several paupers in the Hôtel-Dieu later aroused the suspicion that the loaves which Mme de Brinvilliers was accustomed to distribute there every week, in order to appear as a model of piety and charity, were poisoned. But it is beyond doubt that she poisoned pigeon pies and served them to her invited guests. The Chevalier du Guet and several other persons fell victim to those diabolical dinners. Sainte-Croix, his assistant La Chaussée, and Mme de Brinvilliers were long able to hide their awful misdeeds beneath impenetrable veils, but what evil cunning of depraved people can prevail when the eternal power of heaven has once determined to judge the criminals while still here on earth?

Die Gifte, welche Sainte Croix bereitete, waren so fein, daß, lag das Pulver (poudre de succession nannten es die Pariser) bei der Bereitung offen, ein einziger Atemzug hinreichte, sich augenblicklich den Tod zu geben. Sainte Croix trug deshalb bei seinen Operationen eine Maske von feinem Glase. Diese fiel eines Tags, als er eben ein fertiges Giftpulver in eine Phiole schütten wollte, herab, und er sank, den feinen Staub des Giftes einatmend, augenblicklich tot nieder.

Da er ohne Erben verstorben, eilten die Gerichte herbei, um den Nachlaß unter Siegel zu nehmen. Da fand sich in einer Kiste verschlossen das ganze höllische Arsenal des Giftmords, das dem verruchten Sainte Croix zu Gebote gestanden, aber auch die Briefe der Brinvillier wurden aufgefunden, die über ihre Untaten keinen Zweifel ließen. Sie floh nach Lüttich in ein Kloster. Desgrais, ein Beamter der Marechaussee, wurde ihr nachgesendet. Als Geistlicher verkleidet, erschien er in dem Kloster, wo sie sich verborgen. Es gelang ihm, mit dem entsetzlichen Weibe einen Liebeshandel anzuknüpfen und sie zu einer heimlichen Zusammenkunft in einem einsamen Garten vor der Stadt zu verlocken. Kaum dort angekommen, wurde sie aber von Desgrais' Häschern umringt, der geistliche Liebhaber verwandelte sich plötzlich in den Beamten der Marechaussee und nötigte sie in den Wagen zu steigen, der vor dem Garten bereit stand und, von den Häschern umringt, geradeswegs nach Paris abfuhr. La Chaussee war schon früher enthauptet worden, die Brinvillier litt denselben Tod, ihr Körper wurde nach der Hinrichtung verbrannt und die Asche in die Lüfte zerstreut.

Die Pariser atmeten auf, als das Ungeheuer von der Welt war, das die heimliche mörderische Waffe ungestraft richten konnte gegen Feind und Freund. Doch bald tat es sich kund, daß des verruchten La Croix' entsetzliche Kunst sich fortvererbt hatte. Wie ein unsichtbares tückisches Gespenst schlich der Mord sich ein in die engsten Kreise, wie sie Verwandtschaft – Liebe – Freundschaft nur bilden können, und erfaßte sicher und schnell die unglücklichen Opfer. Der, den man heute in blühender Gesundheit gesehen, wankte morgen krank und siech umher, und keine Kunst der Ärzte konnte ihn vor dem Tode retten. Reichtum – ein einträgliches Amt – ein schönes, vielleicht zu jugendliches Weib – das genügte zur Verfolgung auf den Tod.

Das grausamste Mißtrauen trennte die heiligsten Bande. Der Gatte zitterte vor der Gattin – der Vater vor dem Sohn – die Schwester vor

The poisons that Sainte-Croix prepared were so subtle that, if the powder (which the Parisians dubbed *poudre de succession*)[2] lay about loose during the preparation, a single inhalation of it was enough to cause death at once. Therefore Sainte-Croix wore a mask of thin glass while he worked. One day, when he was just about to pour a completed poisonous powder into a vial, his mask fell off and, breathing in the fine powder of the poison, he fell dead on the spot.

Since he had died without heirs, court officers rushed over to put his belongings under a seal. Locked away in a chest they found the entire hellish arsenal of poisoning that had been at the disposal of the wicked Sainte-Croix; but they also found letters from Mme de Brinvilliers, which left no doubt as to her misdeeds. She escaped to a convent in Liège. Desgrais, an officer of the *maréchaussée,* was sent after her. Disguised as a priest, he came to the convent where she was hiding. He succeeded in entering into a liaison with the horrible woman, luring her to a secret tryst in a solitary garden outside of town. Scarcely had she arrived there, however, when she was surrounded by Desgrais's bailiffs; her ecclesiastical lover was suddenly transformed into the *maréchaussée* officer, and forced her to enter the coach that was waiting in front of the garden and immediately departed for Paris, bailiffs all around it. La Chaussée had already been beheaded; Mme de Brinvilliers suffered the same death; after her execution her body was burned and the ashes scattered in the wind.

The people of Paris were relieved when the world was rid of the monster that had been able to wield its secret murderous weapon against friend and foe with impunity. But it soon became known that the horrible art of the wicked Sainte-Croix had been inherited. Like an invisible, crafty ghost, murder insinuated itself into the closest groups that consanguinity, love, or friendship can form, and seized swiftly and surely on its unfortunate victims. A man obviously in perfect health one day, staggered about sick and suffering on the next, and no medical skill could save him from death. Wealth, a lucrative position, a wife who was beautiful and perhaps too young—any of that sufficed for hounding him to death.

The most cruel distrust tore apart the most sacred bonds. Husband was afraid of wife, father of son, sister of brother. Food

---

2. "Inheritance powder."

dem Bruder. – Unberührt blieben die Speisen, blieb der Wein bei dem Mahl, das der Freund den Freunden gab, und wo sonst Lust und Scherz gewaltet, spähten verwilderte Blicke nach dem verkappten Mörder. Man sah Familienväter ängstlich in entfernten Gegenden Lebensmittel einkaufen und in dieser, jener schmutzigen Garküche selbst bereiten, in ihrem eigenen Hause teuflischen Verrat fürchtend. Und doch war manchmal die größte, bedachteste Vorsicht vergebens.

Der König, dem Unwesen, das immer mehr überhandnahm, zu steuern, ernannte einen eigenen Gerichtshof, dem er ausschließlich die Untersuchung und Bestrafung dieser heimlichen Verbrechen übertrug. Das war die sogenannte Chambre ardente, die ihre Sitzungen unfern der Bastille hielt, und welcher la Regnie als Präsident vorstand. Mehrere Zeit hindurch blieben Regnies Bemühungen, so eifrig sie auch sein mochten, fruchtlos; dem verschlagenen Desgrais war es vorbehalten, den geheimsten Schlupfwinkel des Verbrechens zu entdecken.

In der Vorstadt Saint Germain wohnte ein altes Weib, la Voisin geheißen, die sich mit Wahrsagen und Geisterbeschwören abgab, und mit Hilfe ihrer Spießgesellen, le Sage und le Vigoureux, auch selbst Personen, die eben nicht schwach und leichtgläubig zu nennen, in Furcht und Erstaunen zu setzen wußte. Aber sie tat mehr als dieses. Exilis Schülerin wie la Croix, bereitete sie wie dieser das feine, spurlose Gift und half auf diese Weise ruchlosen Söhnen zur frühen Erbschaft, entarteten Weibern zum andern, jüngern Gemahl. Desgrais drang in ihr Geheimnis ein, sie gestand alles, die Chambre ardente verurteilte sie zum Feuertode, den sie auf dem Greveplatze erlitt.

Man fand bei ihr eine Liste aller Personen, die sich ihrer Hilfe bedient hatten; und so kam es, daß nicht allein Hinrichtung auf Hinrichtung folgte, sondern auch schwerer Verdacht selbst auf Personen von hohem Ansehen lastete. So glaubte man, daß der Kardinal Bonzy bei der la Voisin das Mittel gefunden, alle Personen, denen er als Erzbischof von Narbonne Pensionen bezahlen mußte, in kurzer Zeit hinsterben zu lassen. So wurden die Herzogin von Bouillon, die Gräfin von Soissons, deren Namen man auf der Liste gefunden, der Verbindung mit dem teuflischen Weibe angeklagt, und selbst François Henri de Montmorenci, Boudebelle, Herzog von Luxemburg, Pair und Marschall des Reichs, blieb nicht verschont. Auch ihn verfolgte die furchtbare Chambre ardente. Er stellte sich

and wine were left untouched at dinners that friend offered friend; where pleasure and jollity had once reigned, haggard glances watched out for a disguised murderer. Heads of families were to be seen anxiously buying foodstuffs in remote neighborhoods and preparing them themselves in this or that filthy cookshop, since they feared diabolical treachery in their own homes. But, despite all that, at times the greatest, most circumspect caution was in vain.

The king, in order to counteract this bad situation, which was increasingly widespread, appointed a special court, to which he gave the exclusive task of investigating and punishing these secret crimes. It was the so-called *chambre ardente*,[3] which held its sessions not far form the Bastille, with La Reynie as chief judge. For some time La Reynie's efforts, zealous as they were, remained fruitless; it was reserved for the cunning Desgrais to discover the most secret hiding place of crime.

In the faubourg Saint-Germain lived an old woman named Voisin, who practiced fortune-telling and spirit-conjuring and, with the aid of her accomplices Lesage and the woman Vigoureux, was able to instill fear and amazement even in people who couldn't exactly be called weak and credulous. But she did more than that. A pupil of Exili like Sainte-Croix, like him, too, she prepared that subtle, odorless poison, thus helping nefarious sons gain an early inheritance, and degenerate women gain a new, younger husband. Desgrais uncovered her secret, she made a full confession, and the *chambre ardente* condemned her to death by burning, which she underwent on the Place de Grève.

Among her belongings was found a list of all the persons who had made use of her services; and thus it came about that, not only did one execution follow another, but, in addition, strong suspicion fell even on persons of high rank. It was thought, for instance, that Cardinal Bonzy had acquired from the Voisin woman the means of quickly killing everyone to whom he was bound to pay pensions as archbishop of Narbonne. Likewise the Duchesse de Bouillon and the Comtesse de Soissons, whose names were found on the list, were accused of being connected with that diabolical woman, and even François-Henri de Montmorency-Bouteville, Duc de Luxembourg, peer and marshal of the realm, wasn't spared. He, too, was pursued by the *chambre ardente*. He turned himself in to be a prisoner in the

---

3. "Burning room"; it was lit by torches.

selbst zum Gefängnis in der Bastille, wo ihn Louvois' und la Regnies Haß in ein sechs Fuß langes Loch einsperren ließ. Monate vergingen, ehe es sich vollkommen ausmittelte, daß des Herzogs Verbrechen keine Rüge verdienen konnte. Er hatte sich einmal von le Sage das Horoskop stellen lassen.

Gewiß ist es, daß blinder Eifer den Präsidenten la Regnie zu Gewaltstreichen und Grausamkeiten verleitete. Das Tribunal nahm ganz den Charakter der Inquisition an, der geringfügigste Verdacht reichte hin zu strengen Einkerkerung, und oft war es dem Zufall überlassen, die Unschuld des auf den Tod Angeklagten darzutun. Dabei war Regnie von garstigem Ansehen und heimtückischem Wesen, so daß er bald den Haß derer auf sich lud, deren Rächer oder Schützer zu sein er berufen wurde. Die Herzogin von Bouillon, von ihm im Verhöre gefragt, ob sie den Teufel gesehen, erwiderte: «Mich dünkt, ich sehe ihn in diesem Augenblick!»

Während nun auf dem Greveplatz das Blut Schuldiger und Verdächtiger in Strömen floß, und endlich der heimliche Giftmord seltner und seltner wurde, zeigte sich ein Unheil anderer Art, welches neue Bestürzung verbreitete. Eine Gaunerbande schien es darauf angelegt zu haben, alle Juwelen in ihren Besitz zu bringen. Der reiche Schmuck, kaum gekauft, verschwand auf unbegreifliche Weise, mochte er verwahrt sein, wie er wollte. Noch viel ärger war es aber, daß jeder, der es wagte, zur Abendzeit Juwelen bei sich zu tragen, auf offener Straße oder in finstern Gängen der Häuser beraubt, ja wohl gar ermordet wurde.

Die mit dem Leben davongekommen, sagten aus, ein Faustschlag auf den Kopf habe sie wie ein Wetterstrahl niedergestürzt, und aus der Betäubung erwacht, hätten sie sich beraubt und am ganz andern Orte als da, wo sie der Schlag getroffen, wiedergefunden. Die Ermordeten, wie sie beinahe jeden Morgen auf der Straße oder in den Häusern lagen, hatten alle dieselbe tödliche Wunde. Einen Dolchstich ins Herz, nach dem Urteil der Ärzte so schnell und sicher tötend, daß der Verwundete, keines Lautes mächtig, zu Boden sinken mußte. Wer war an dem üppigen Hofe Ludwig des XIV., der nicht in einen geheimen Liebeshandel verstrickt, spät zur Geliebten schlich und manchmal ein reiches Geschenk bei sich trug?

Als stünden die Gauner mit Geistern im Bunde, wußten sie genau, wenn sich so etwas zutragen sollte. Oft erreichte der Unglückliche nicht das Haus, wo er Liebesglück zu genießen dachte, oft fiel er auf der Schwelle, ja vor dem Zimmer der Geliebten, die mit Entsetzen den blutigen Leichnam fand.

Bastille, where the hatred of Louvois and La Reynie had him confined in a dungeon only six feet long. Months went by before it was fully ascertained that the duke's wrongdoing deserved no reprimand. He had merely had Lesage cast his horoscope once.

Without doubt, chief judge La Reynie's blind zeal led him to tyrannical acts and cruelties. The tribunal took on altogether the character of the Inquisition; the slightest suspicion was enough to have someone harshly imprisoned, and it was frequently left to chance to prove the innocence of a man accused of a capital crime. At the same time, La Reynie was nasty to look at and spiteful by nature, so that he soon won the hatred of those whose avenger or protector it was his calling to be. The Duchesse de Bouillon, whom he asked during an interrogation whether she had ever seen the Devil, replied: "I think I'm looking at him right now!"

Now, while the blood of the guilty and the suspected was flowing in rivers on the Place de Grève, and secret poisonings were finally becoming more and more infrequent, an evil of a different kind showed its face and spread new alarm. A gang of thieves seemed to have made it their goal to come into possession of all the jewelry around. As soon as a costly item was purchased, it disappeared in an incomprehensible way, no matter how securely protected. But what was much worse: everyone who dared to carry jewelry on his person in the evening was robbed, and even murdered, right out on the street or in dark corridors in houses.

Those who had escaped with their lives declared that they had been felled by a punch on the head like a thunderbolt; once regaining consciousness, they had found themselves robbed and lying far away from the place where they had been struck. Those who had been killed—and someone was found on the street or in a house nearly every morning—all bore the same fatal wound: a dagger blow to the heart, which, in the opinion of the doctors, killed so swiftly and surely that the wounded man, deprived of speech, could only collapse on the ground. Who was there at the sensual court of Louis XIV who wasn't involved in some secret love affair, and didn't surreptitiously visit his sweetheart late at night, sometimes carrying an expensive present?

As if the thieves were in league with spirits, they knew precisely when a visit of that sort was going to occur. Often the unfortunate man didn't reach the house in which he hoped to enjoy the blessings of love; often he died on his sweetheart's threshold, or even just outside her room, where she discovered the bleeding corpse to her horror.

Vergebens ließ Argenson, der Polizeiminister, alles aufgreifen in
Paris, was von dem Volk nur irgend verdächtig schien, vergebens
wütete la Regnie und suchte Geständnisse zu erpressen, vergebens
wurden Wachen, Patrouillen verstärkt, die Spur der Täter war nicht
zu finden. Nur die Vorsicht, sich bis an die Zähne zu bewaffnen und
sich eine Leuchte vortragen zu lassen, half einigermaßen, und doch
fanden sich Beispiele, daß der Diener mit Steinwürfen geängstet,
und der Herr in demselben Augenblick ermordet und beraubt
wurde.

Merkwürdig war es, daß aller Nachforschungen auf allen Plätzen,
wo Juwelenhandel nur möglich war, unerachtet, nicht das mindeste
von den geraubten Kleinodien zum Vorschein kam, und also auch hier
keine Spur sich zeigte, die hätte verfolgt werden können.

Desgrais schäumte vor Wut, daß selbst seiner List die Spitzbuben
zu entgehen wußten. Das Viertel der Stadt, in dem er sich gerade befand, blieb verschont, während in dem andern, wo keiner Böses
geahnt, der Raubmord seine reichen Opfer erspähte.

Desgrais besann sich auf das Kunststück, mehrere Desgrais zu
schaffen, sich untereinander so ähnlich an Gang, Stellung, Sprache,
Figur, Gesicht, daß selbst die Häscher nicht wußten, wo der rechte
Desgrais stecke. Unterdessen lauschte er, sein Leben wagend,
allein in den geheimsten Schlupfwinkeln und folgte von weitem
diesem oder jenem, der auf seinen Anlaß einen reichen Schmuck
bei sich trug. *Der* blieb unangefochten; also auch von *dieser*
Maßregel waren die Gauner unterrichtet. Desgrais geriet in
Verzweiflung.

Eines Morgens kommt Desgrais zu dem Präsidenten la Regnie,
blaß, entstellt, außer sich. – «Was habt Ihr, was für Nachrichten? –
Fandet Ihr die Spur?» ruft ihm der Präsident entgegen.

«Ha – gnädiger Herr», fängt Desgrais an, vor Wut stammelnd, «ha,
gnädiger Herr – gestern in der Nacht – unfern des Louvre ist der
Marquis de la Fare angefallen worden in meiner Gegenwart.»

«Himmel und Erde», jauchzt la Regnie auf vor Freude – «wir
haben sie!»

«O hört nur», fällt Desgrais mit bitterm Lächeln ein, «o hört nur
erst, wie sich alles begeben. – Am Louvre steh ich also und passe, die
ganze Hölle in der Brust, auf die Teufel, die meiner spotten. Da
kommt mit unsicherm Schritt, immer hinter sich schauend, eine
Gestalt dicht bei mir vorüber, ohne mich zu sehen. Im
Mondesschimmer erkenne ich den Marquis de la Fare. Ich konnt ihn

It was in vain that D'Argenson, the chief of police, had every commoner in Paris rounded up who seemed in the least suspicious; it was in vain that La Reynie raged and sought to wring out confessions; it was in vain that watches and patrols were reinforced—no trace of the perpetrators was to be found. Only the precaution of arming oneself to the teeth and being proceeded by a torchbearer helped to some degree, and yet there were cases where the servant was distracted by having stones thrown at him while at the same time his master was killed and robbed.

It was odd that, despite all searches in all venues where it was possible for jewelry to change hands, not one of the stolen pieces showed up, and that therefore here, too, there was no clue that could be followed up.

Desgrais foamed with rage because the thieves were able to elude even his wiles. The neighborhood of town where he happened to be located was spared, while in another, where no one had foreseen trouble, the robbers and killers lay in wait successfully for their wealthy victims.

Desgrais thought of the stratagem of hiring several doubles of himself, so similar to one another in gait, posture, speech, figure, and face that even his bailiffs didn't know where the real Desgrais was. Meanwhile, at the risk of his life, he'd be listening all alone in the most secret hiding places, and he'd follow at a distance someone or other who was carrying some costly jewelry at his instigation. Such people were never attacked, and so the thieves must have been informed of that measure, as well. Desgrais fell into despair.

One morning Desgrais came to chief judge La Reynie pale, haggard, beside himself. "What have you got, what sort of news? Have you found their track?" the judge called to him.

"Ah, Your Honor," Desgrais began, stammering in his rage, "ah, Your Honor—last night—not far from the Louvre, the Marquis de La Fare was assailed in my presence."

"Heaven and earth!" La Reynie exclaimed jubilantly. "We've got them!"

"Please hear me out," Desgrais interrupted with a bitter smile, "please listen first to all that happened. So, I was waiting by the Louvre, with all of hell boiling within me, on the lookout for those devils who are laughing at me. Then a figure passed right by me, walking unsteadily, constantly looking over his shoulder, and not noticing me. In the moonlight I recognized the Marquis de La

da erwarten, ich wußte, wo er hinschlich. Kaum ist er zehn – zwölf
Schritte bei mir vorüber, da springt wie aus der Erde herauf eine
Figur, schmettert ihn nieder und fällt über ihn her. Unbesonnen,
überrascht von dem Augenblick, der den Mörder in meine Hand
liefern konnte, schrie ich laut auf und will mit einem gewaltigen
Sprunge aus meinem Schlupfwinkel heraus auf ihn zusetzen; da ver-
wickle ich mich in den Mantel und falle hin. Ich sehe den Menschen
wie auf den Flügeln des Windes forteilen, ich rapple mich auf, ich
renne ihm nach – laufend stoße ich in mein Horn – aus der Ferne
antworten die Pfeifen der Häscher – es wird lebendig – Waffengeklirr,
Pferdegetrappel von allen Seiten. – ‹Hierher – hierher – Desgrais –
Desgrais!› schreie ich, daß es durch die Straßen hallt. – Immer sehe
ich den Menschen vor mir im hellen Mondschein, wie er, mich zu
täuschen, da – dort – einbiegt; wir kommen in die Straße Nicaise, da
scheinen seine Kräfte zu sinken, ich strenge die meinigen doppelt an
– noch fünfzehn Schritte höchstens hat er Vorsprung.»

«Ihr holt ihn ein – Ihr packt ihn, die Häscher kommen» ruft la
Regnie mit blitzenden Augen, indem er Desgrais beim Arm ergreift,
als sei *der* der fliehende Mörder selbst.

«Fünfzehn Schritte», fährt Desgrais mit dumpfer Stimme und
mühsam atmend fort, «fünfzehn Schritte vor mir springt der Mensch
auf die Seite in den Schatten und verschwindet durch die Mauer.»

«Verschwindet? – durch die Mauer! – Seid Ihr rasend?» ruft la
Regnie, indem er zwei Schritte zurücktritt und die Hände zusam-
menschlägt.

«Nennt mich», fährt Desgrais fort, sich die Stirne reibend wie einer,
den böse Gedanken plagen, «nennt mich, gnädiger Herr, immerhin
einen Rasenden, einen törichten Geisterseher, aber es ist nicht anders, als wie ich es Euch erzähle. Erstarrt stehe ich vor der Mauer, als
mehrere Häscher atemlos herbeikommen; mit ihnen der Marquis de
la Fare, der sich aufgerafft, den bloßen Degen in der Hand. Wir zün-
den die Fackeln an, wir tappen an der Mauer hin und her; keine Spur
einer Türe, eines Fensters, einer Öffnung. Es ist eine starke steinerne
Hofmauer, die sich an das Haus lehnt, in dem Leute wohnen, gegen
die auch nicht der leiseste Verdacht aufkommt. Noch heute habe ich
alles in genauen Augenschein genommen. – Der Teufel selbst ist es,
der uns foppt.»

Desgrais' Geschichte wurde in Paris bekannt. Die Köpfe waren erfüllt von den Zaubereien, Geisterbeschwörungen, Teufelsbündnissen
der Voisin, des Vigoureux, des berüchtigten Priesters le Sage; und wie
es denn nun in unserer ewigen Natur liegt, daß der Hang zum Über-

Fare. I could have expected him there; I knew where he was sneaking off to. Scarcely had he taken ten or twelve steps past me when another figure leaped up, as if out of the earth, knocked him down, and jumped on top of him. Thoughtlessly, in my surprise at the occasion that might deliver the murderer into my hands, I yelled out loud, intending to make a mighty leap out of my hiding place and attack him; but I got tangled up in my cloak and I fell down. I saw the fellow dash away as if on the wings of the wind; I picked myself up and ran after him—while running I blew my horn—from the distance my bailiffs' whistles replied—things were getting lively—clanking of swords, clipclop of horses on all sides. 'This way! This way! It's Desgrais! It's Desgrais!' I shouted, loud enough to make the streets ring. I can still see the fellow in front of me in the bright moonlight, doubling back and forth to give me the slip. We arrived at the rue Nicaise, where his strength seemed to give out; I redoubled my own efforts—now he was only fifteen paces ahead of me at the most."

"You caught up with him—you seized him, your bailiffs arrived," shouted La Reynie with flashing eyes, gripping Desgrais by the arm, as if he were the fleeing killer himself.

"Fifteen paces," Desgrais continued in a hollow voice, breathing heavily, "fifteen paces in front of me the fellow sprang to one side into the shadows and vanished through the wall."

"Vanished? Through the wall? Are you crazy?" yelled La Reynie, recoiling two paces and clapping his hands.

"Call me," Desgrais continued, rubbing his brow like a man troubled by bad thoughts, "call me a madman if you like, Your Honor, or a foolish visionary, but it happened exactly as I told you. I stood there rigidly in front of the wall as several bailiffs ran up to me out of breath; with them was the Marquis de La Fare, who had picked himself up and now held his drawn sword. We lit the torches, we groped back and forth along the wall: no trace of a door, window, or other opening. It's a solid stone enclosing wall that abuts the house, which is occupied by people who aren't in the least subject to suspicion. Today again I inspected everything scrupulously. It's the Devil himself who's making a fool of us."

Desgrais's story became known in Paris. People's heads were filled with the spells, conjurations, and hellish alliances of Voisin, Vigoureux, and the infamous priest Lesage; and since it's an ineradicable part of our nature that our leanings toward the

natürlichen, zum Wunderbaren alle Vernunft überbietet, so glaubte man bald nichts Geringeres, als daß, wie Desgrais nur im Unmut gesagt, wirklich der Teufel selbst die Verruchten schütze, die ihm ihre Seelen verkauft. Man kann es sich denken, daß Desgrais' Geschichte mancherlei tollen Schmuck erhielt. Die Erzählung davon mit einem Holzschnitt darüber, eine gräßliche Teufelsgestalt vorstellend, die vor dem erschrockenen Desgrais in die Erde versinkt, wurde gedruckt und an allen Ecken verkauft. Genug, das Volk einzuschüchtern und selbst den Häschern allen Mut zu nehmen, die nun zur Nachtzeit mit Zittern und Zagen die Straßen durchirrten, mit Amuletten behängt und eingeweicht in Weihwasser.

Argenson sah die Bemühungen der Chambre ardente scheitern und ging den König an, für das neue Verbrechen einen Gerichtshof zu ernennen, der mit noch ausgedehnterer Macht den Tätern nachspüre und sie strafe. Der König, überzeugt, schon der Chambre ardente zu viel Gewalt gegeben zu haben, erschüttert von dem Greuel unzähliger Hinrichtungen, die der blutgierige la Regnie veranlaßt, wies den Vorschlag gänzlich von der Hand.

Man wählte ein anderes Mittel, den König für die Sache zu beleben.

In den Zimmern der Maintenon, wo sich der König nachmittags aufzuhalten und wohl auch mit seinen Ministern bis in die späte Nacht hinein zu arbeiten pflegte, wurde ihm ein Gedicht überreicht im Namen der gefährdeten Liebhaber, welche klagten, daß, gebiete ihnen die Galanterie, der Geliebten ein reiches Geschenk zu bringen, sie allemal ihr Leben daransetzen müßten. Ehre und Lust sei es, im ritterlichen Kampf sein Blut für die Geliebte zu verspritzen; anders verhalte es sich aber mit dem heimtückischen Anfall des Mörders, wider den man sich nicht wappnen könne. Ludwig, der leuchtende Polarstern aller Liebe und Galanterie, der möge hellaufstrahlend die finstre Nacht zerstreuen und so das schwarze Geheimnis, das darin verborgen, enthüllen. Der göttliche Held, der seine Feinde niedergeschmettert, werde nun auch sein siegreich funkelndes Schwert zucken und, wie Herkules die lernäische Schlange, wie Theseus den Minotaur, das bedrohliche Ungeheuer bekämpfen, das alle Liebeslust wegzehre und alle Freude verdüstre in tiefes Leid, in trostlose Trauer.

So ernst die Sache auch war, so fehlte es diesem Gedicht doch nicht, vorzüglich in der Schilderung, wie die Liebhaber auf dem heimlichen Schleichwege zur Geliebten sich ängstigen müßten, wie die Angst schon alle Liebeslust, jedes schöne Abenteuer der Galanterie im Aufkeimen töte, an geistreich-witzigen Wendungen.

supernatural and miraculous outstrip all our reason, people soon believed no less than what Desgrais had said merely out of bad temper: that the Devil was really protecting those wicked criminals, who had sold their souls to him. It may easily be imagined that many irresponsible embroideries were added to Desgrais's story. A report of it, adorned by a woodcut depicting a horrible devil sinking into the earth before an astonished Desgrais, was printed and sold everywhere. This was enough to intimidate the populace and even steal their courage from the bailiffs, who now roamed through the streets at night trembling and hesitant, wearing amulets and sopping with holy water.

D'Argenson saw the efforts of the *chambre ardente* wrecked, and requested the king to appoint a court for the new series of crimes, a body that would track down and punish the perpetrators with even broader powers. The king, convinced that he had given even the *chambre ardente* too many powers, and shaken by the horror of the numberless executions occasioned by the bloodthirsty La Reynie, rejected the proposal out of hand.

Another means was chosen to win over the king to the cause.

In Mme de Maintenon's apartment, where the king usually spent the afternoon and sometimes also worked with his ministers till late at night, a poem was handed to him in the name of the endangered lovers, who lamented that, if gallantry demanded that they bring expensive presents to their sweethearts, they always had to risk their lives to do so. It was an honor and pleasure to shed their blood for their sweethearts in chivalrous battle, but it was a different story with the malicious attacks of the murderer, against which they couldn't arm themselves. Louis, the gleaming polestar of all love and gallantry, should beam brightly and dispel the darkness of night, thus revealing the black mystery that was hidden in it. The divine hero, who had crushed his enemies, would now also draw his victoriously flashing sword and, as Hercules fought the hydra of Lerna, and Theseus the Minotaur, he would fight the threatening monster that was eradicating all the pleasure of love and darkening all its joy, turning them into deep sorrow and comfortless mourning.

As serious as the matter actually was, this poem wasn't lacking in cleverly witty turns of phrase, especially in its description of how worried the lovers must be as they stole their way secretly to their sweethearts, and how their fear nipped in the bud all their pleasure in love and each beautiful adventure in gallantry.

Kam nun noch hinzu, daß beim Schluß alles in einen hochtrabenden Panegyrikus auf Ludwig den XIV. ausging, so konnte es nicht fehlen, daß der König das Gedicht mit sichtlichem Wohlgefallen durchlas. Damit zustande gekommen, drehte er sich, die Augen nicht weg-wendend von dem Papier, rasch um zur Maintenon, las das Gedicht noch einmal mit lauter Stimme ab und fragte dann, anmutig lächelnd, was sie von den Wünschen der gefährdeten Liebhaber halte. Die Maintenon, ihrem ernsten Sinne treu und immer in der Farbe einer gewissen Frömmigkeit, erwiderte, daß geheime verbotene Wege eben keines besondern Schutzes würdig, die entsetzlichen Verbrecher aber wohl besonderer Maßregeln zu ihrer Vertilgung wert wären.

Der König, mit dieser schwankenden Antwort unzufrieden, schlug das Papier zusammen und wollte zurück zu dem Staatssekretär, der in dem andern Zimmer arbeitete, als ihm bei einem Blick, den er seitwärts warf, die Scuderi ins Auge fiel, die zugegen war und eben unfern der Maintenon auf einem kleinen Lehnsessel Platz genommen hatte. Auf diese schritt er nun los; das anmutige Lächeln, das erst um Mund und Wangen spielte und das verschwunden, gewann wieder Oberhand, und dicht vor dem Fräulein stehend und das Gedicht wieder auseinanderfaltend, sprach er sanft:

«Die Marquise mag nun einmal von den Galanterien unserer ver-liebten Herren nichts wissen und weicht mir aus auf Wegen, die nichts weniger als verboten sind. Aber Ihr, mein Fräulein, was haltet Ihr von dieser dichterischen Supplik?»

Die Scuderi stand ehrerbietig auf von ihrem Lehnsessel, ein flüchtiges Rot überflog wie Abendpurpur die blassen Wangen der alten würdigen Dame, sie sprach, sich leise verneigend, mit nieder-geschlagenen Augen:

> Un amant, qui craint les voleurs,
> n'est point digne d'amour.

Der König, ganz erstaunt über den ritterlichen Geist dieser weni-gen Worte, die das ganze Gedicht mit seinen ellenlangen Tiraden zu Boden schlugen, rief mit blitzenden Augen: «Beim heiligen Dionys, Ihr habt recht, Fräulein! Keine blinde Maßregel, die den Unschul-digen trifft mit dem Schuldigen, soll die Feigheit schützen; mögen Argenson und la Regnie das Ihrige tun!» –

Alle die Greuel der Zeit schilderte nun die Martiniere mit den

Moreover, since the end of the poem turned into a bombastic panegyric to Louis XIV, the king couldn't fail to read it with visible satisfaction. After he finished it, he quickly turned toward Mme de Maintenon, still not taking his eyes off the paper, read the poem again (this time aloud), and then, with a charming smile, asked her what she thought about the wishes of the endangered lovers. Mme de Maintenon, in line with her earnest temperament, always tinged with a certain sanctimoniousness, replied that secret, forbidden ways didn't deserve any special protection, although the terrible criminals merited special measures for their extirpation.

The king, dissatisfied with that equivocal reply, folded the paper and was about to rejoin the secretary of state working in the next room, when a sidelong glance of his made him notice Mlle de Scudéry, who was in attendance and had just taken a seat in a small armchair not far from Mme de Maintenon. He now walked toward her; the charming smile that had played around his lips and cheeks earlier, but had disappeared, gained the upper hand again; coming to a halt right in front of the lady and unfolding the poem again, he said softly:

"The marquise apparently refuses to have anything to do with the gallantry of our enamored gentlemen, and she is evading me in 'ways' that are anything but 'forbidden.' But you, mademoiselle, what's your opinion of this poetic petition?"

Mlle de Scudéry stood up respectfully from her armchair; a fleeting blush spread over the worthy old lady's cheeks like the glow of sunset, and with a slight curtsey and downcast eyes, she said:

A lover who fears thieves
Is not at all worthy of love.[4]

The king, quite amazed at the chivalrous spirit of those few words, which outdid the whole poem with its long, tedious tirades, exclaimed with flashing eyes: "By Saint Denis, you're right, mademoiselle! No blind measure that affects the innocent along with the guilty shall protect the cowardly; let Argenson and La Reynie do what they can!"

Martinière now depicted all the horrors of the era in the

---

4. In French in Hoffmann's text, here and later.

lebhaftesten Farben, als sie am andern Morgen ihrem Fräulein
erzählte, was sich in voriger Nacht zugetragen, und übergab ihr zitternd und zagend das geheimnisvolle Kästchen. Sowohl sie als
Baptiste, der ganz verblaßt in der Ecke stand und, vor Angst und
Beklommenheit die Nachtmütze in den Händen knetend, kaum
sprechen konnte, baten das Fräulein auf das wehmütigste um aller
Heiligen willen, doch nur mit möglichster Behutsamkeit das Kästchen
zu öffnen. Die Scuderi, das verschlossene Geheimnis in der Hand
wiegend und prüfend, sprach lächelnd:
«Ihr seht beide Gespenster! – Daß ich nicht reich bin, daß bei mir
keine Schätze, eines Mordes wert, zu holen sind, das wissen die verruchten Meuchelmörder da draußen, die wie ihr selbst sagt, das
Innerste der Häuser erspähen, wohl ebensogut als ich und ihr. Auf
mein Leben soll es abgesehen sein? Wem kann was an dem Tode
liegen einer Person von dreiundsiebzig Jahren, die niemals andere
verfolgte als die Bösewichter und Friedenstörer in den Romanen, die
sie selbst schuf, die mittelmäßige Verse macht, welche niemandes
Neid erregen können, die nichts hinterlassen wird, als den Staat des
alten Fräuleins, das bisweilen an den Hof ging, und ein paar Dutzend
gut eingebundene Bücher mit vergoldetem Schnitt! Und du,
Martiniere, du magst nun die Erscheinung des fremden Menschen so
schreckhaft beschreiben, wie du willst, doch kann ich nicht glauben,
daß er Böses im Sinne getragen.»
«Also!» –
Die Martiniere prallte drei Schritte zurück, Baptiste sank mit
einem dumpfen Ach! halb in die Knie, als das Fräulein nun an einen
hervorragenden stählernen Knopf drückte, und der Deckel des
Kästchens mit Geräusch aufsprang.
Wie erstaunte das Fräulein, als ihr aus dem Kästchen ein Paar
goldne, reich mit Juwelen besetzte Armbänder und eben ein solcher
Halsschmuck entgegenfunkelten. Sie nahm das Geschmeide heraus,
und indem sie die wundervolle Arbeit des Halsschmucks lobte,
beäugelte die Martiniere die reichen Armbänder und rief ein Mal
über das andere, daß ja selbst die eitle Montespan nicht solchen
Schmuck besitze.
«Aber was soll das, was hat das zu bedeuten?» sprach die Scuderi.
In dem Augenblick gewahrte sie auf dem Boden des Kästchens einen
kleinen zusammengefalteten Zettel. Mit Recht hoffte sie den
Aufschluß des Geheimnisses darin zu finden. Der Zettel, kaum hatte
sie, was er enthielt, gelesen, entfiel ihren zitternden Händen. Sie warf
einen sprechenden Blick zum Himmel und sank dann, wie halb ohn-

liveliest colors when she told her lady next morning what had occurred the night before, handing her, with trembling and hesitation, the mysterious little box. She as well as Baptiste, who was
standing in the corner quite pale and, kneading his nightcap in
his hands in his fear and distress, could hardly speak, urged their
lady in the most mournful tone, and calling on all the saints, to
open the box only with the most extreme caution. Mlle de
Scudéry, weighing the concealed mystery in her hand and examining it, said with a smile:

"You're both seeing ghosts! That I'm not wealthy, that no treasures worth a murder are to be found in my house, the wicked
killers out there know just as well as you and I, since, as you say,
they spy out the interiors of houses. Do you think there's a design on my life? Who can be interested in the death of a person
who's seventy-three years old and has never persecuted anyone
except the criminals and disturbers of the peace in the novels
she herself wrote, a person who composes mediocre verses that
are incapable of arousing anyone's envy, and who has nothing to
bequeath but the finery of an old lady who occasionally attended
court and a couple of dozen well-bound books with gilded
edges? And you, Martinière, you can describe the appearance of
that stranger as scarily as you like, but I can't believe he had evil
intentions.

"Well, here goes!"

Martinière jumped three paces back, and Baptiste nearly fell
to his knees, uttering a feeble "Oh," when the lady now pressed
a protruding steel button and the cover of the box noisily flew
open.

What was the lady's surprise when a pair of golden bracelets,
richly studded with gems, and a necklace of the same description gleamed at her from the box! She took the jewelry out, and
while she was praising the marvelous workmanship on the necklace, Martinière ogled the costly bracelets, exclaiming time and
again that even the vain Mme de Montespan didn't own jewelry
like that.

"But why? What can this mean?" Mlle de Scudéry asked. At
that moment she noticed a small folded note at the bottom of
the box. She justifiably hoped to find the solution to the mystery
in it. Scarcely had she read the contents of the note when she let
it drop from her trembling hands. She cast a meaningful glance
at heaven and then collapsed into the armchair, as if partially in

mächtig, in den Lehnsessel zurück. Erschrocken sprang die
Martiniere, sprang Baptiste ihr bei. «O», rief sie nun mit von Tränen
halb erstickter Stimme, «o der Kränkung, o der tiefen Beschämung!
Muß mir das noch geschehen im hohen Alter! Hab ich denn im
törichten Leichtsinn gefrevelt, wie ein junges, unbesonnenes Ding? –
O Gott, sind Worte, halb im Scherz hingeworfen, solcher gräßlichen
Deutung fähig! – Darf dann mich, die ich, der Tugend getreu und der
Frömmigkeit, tadellos blieb von Kindheit an, darf dann mich das
Verbrechen des teuflischen Bündnisses zeihen?»

Das Fräulein hielt das Schnupftuch vor die Augen und weinte und
schluchzte heftig, so daß die Martiniere und Baptiste, ganz verwirrt
und beklommen, nicht wußten, wie ihrer guten Herrschaft beistehen
in ihrem großen Schmerz.

Die Martiniere hatte den verhängnisvollen Zettel von der Erde
aufgehoben. Auf demselben stand:

> Un amant, qui craint les voleurs,
> n'est point digne d'amour.

«Euer scharfsinniger Geist, hochverehrte Dame, hat uns, die
wir an der Schwäche und Feigheit das Recht des Stärkern üben
und uns Schätze zueignen, die auf unwürdige Weise vergeudet
werden sollten, von großer Verfolgung errettet. Als einen Beweis
unserer Dankbarkeit nehmet gütig diesen Schmuck an. Es ist das
Kostbarste, was wir seit langer Zeit haben auftreiben können,
wiewohl Euch, würdige Dame, viel schöneres Geschmeide
zieren sollte, als dieses nun eben ist. Wir bitten, daß Ihr uns Eure
Freundschaft und Euer huldvolles Andenken nicht entziehen
möget.

Die Unsichtbaren.»

«Ist es möglich», rief die Scuderi, als sie sich einigermaßen erholt
hatte, «ist es möglich, daß man die schamlose Frechheit, den verruchten Hohn so weit treiben kann?» – Die Sonne schien hell durch
die Fenstergardinen von hochroter Seide, und so kam es, daß die
Brillanten, welche auf dem Tische neben dem offenen Kästchen
lagen, in rötlichem Schimmer aufblitzten. Hinblickend, verhüllte die
Scuderi voll Entsetzen das Gesicht und befahl der Martiniere, das
fürchterliche Geschmeide, an dem das Blut der Ermordeten klebe,
augenblicklich fortzuschaffen. Die Martiniere, nachdem sie
Halsschmuck und Armbänder sogleich in das Kästchen verschlossen,
meinte, daß es wohl am geratensten sein würde, die Juwelen dem

a faint. In alarm Martinière and Baptiste hastened to her aid. "Oh," she now exclaimed in a voice half-stifled by tears, "oh, how mortifying, oh, the awful disgrace! Did I need this in my old age? Have I then transgressed out of foolish frivolity like a thoughtless young girl? Oh, God, are words quickly uttered half in jest subject to such a horrible interpretation? Am I, I who am faithful to virtue and piety, I who have remained blameless since I was a child, am I liable to be accused by criminals of being in league with the Devil?"

The lady held her handkerchief to her eyes and wept and sobbed violently, so that Martinière and Baptiste, altogether confused and distressed, didn't know how to assist their kind mistress in her great sorrow.

Martinière had picked up the fateful note from the floor. It read:

> "'A lover who fears thieves
> Is not at all worthy of love.'

"Deeply revered lady, your penetrating intelligence has saved us from severe persecution, while we maintain the right of the strong over the weak and cowardly, and appropriate to ourselves treasures that are to be squandered unworthily. As a token of our gratitude please accept this jewelry. It is the most costly that has fallen into our hands for some time, although, worthy lady, you should be adorned with much more beautiful jewels than these. We hope that you won't deprive us of your friendship and your gracious remembrance.

The Invisible Ones."

"Is it possible," Mlle de Scudéry exclaimed after recovering to some extent, "is it possible for shameless insolence and wicked mockery to go so far?" The sun was shining brightly through the window curtains of deep-red silk, so that the jewels lying on the table beside the open box flashed with a reddish glow. Looking at them, Mlle de Scudéry covered her face in fright and ordered Martinière to take away at once that frightful jewelry which was red with the blood of murdered men. After Martinière shut the necklace and bracelets away in the box immediately, she offered her opinion that it would probably be most advisable to hand the jewels over to the chief of police and to tell him the whole story

Polizeiminister zu übergeben und ihm zu vertrauen, wie sich alles mit der beängstigenden Erscheinung des jungen Menschen und der Einhändigung des Kästchens zugetragen.

Die Scuderi stand auf und schritt schweigend langsam im Zimmer auf und nieder, als sinne sie erst nach, was nun zu tun sei. Dann befahl sie dem Baptiste, einen Tragsessel zu holen, der Martiniere aber, sie anzukleiden, weil sie auf der Stelle hin wolle zur Marquise de Maintenon.

Sie ließ sich hintragen zur Marquise gerade zu der Stunde, wenn diese, wie die Scuderi wußte, sich allein in ihren Gemächern befand. Das Kästchen mit den Juwelen nahm sie mit sich.

Wohl mußte die Marquise sich hoch verwundern, als sie das Fräulein, sonst die Würde, ja trotz ihrer hohen Jahre die Liebenswürdigkeit, die Anmut selbst, eintreten sah, blaß, entstellt, mit wankenden Schritten. «Was um aller Heiligen willen ist Euch widerfahren?» rief sie der armen, beängsteten Dame entgegen, die, ganz außer sich selbst, kaum imstande, sich aufrecht zu erhalten, nur schnell den Lehnsessel zu erreichen suchte, den ihr die Marquise hinschob.

Endlich des Wortes wieder mächtig, erzählte das Fräulein, welche tiefe, nicht zu verschmerzende Kränkung ihr jener unbedachtsame Scherz, mit dem sie die Supplik der gefährdeten Liebhaber beantwortet, zugezogen habe. Die Marquise, nachdem sie alles von Moment zu Moment erfahren, urteilte, daß die Scuderi sich das sonderbare Ereignis viel zu sehr zu Herzen nehme, daß der Hohn verruchten Gesindels nie ein frommes, edles Gemüt treffen könne und verlangte zuletzt den Schmuck zu sehen.

Die Scuderi gab ihr das geöffnete Kästchen, und die Marquise konnte sich, als sie das köstliche Geschmeide erblickte, des lauten Ausrufs der Verwunderung nicht erwehren. Sie nahm den Halsschmuck, die Armbänder heraus und trat damit an das Fenster, wo sie bald die Juwelen an der Sonne spielen ließ, bald die zierliche Goldarbeit ganz nahe vor die Augen hielt, um nur recht zu erschauen, mit welcher wundervollen Kunst jedes kleine Häkchen der verschlungenen Ketten gearbeitet war.

Auf einmal wandte sich die Marquise rasch um nach dem Fräulein und rief: «Wißt Ihr wohl, Fräulein, daß diese Armbänder, diesen Halsschmuck niemand anders gearbeitet haben kann als René Cardillac?»

René Cardillac war damals der geschickteste Goldarbeiter in Paris, einer der kunstreichsten und zugleich sonderbarsten Menschen seiner Zeit. Eher klein als groß, aber breitschultrig und von starkem,

of the frightening visit of the young man who had consigned the box to them.

Mlle de Scudéry stood up and, in silence, slowly paced to and fro in the room, as if only now reflecting on what was to be done next. Then she ordered Baptiste to go out for a sedan chair, and Martinière to dress her, because she wanted to visit the Marquise de Maintenon at once.

She had herself carried to the marquise at the very hour when Mlle de Scudéry knew she would be alone in her apartment. She took along the box with the jewelry.

The marquise must have been greatly surprised to see the lady, who, despite her advanced age, was usually dignity, graciousness, and charm themselves, come in looking pale, her features distorted, her steps shaky. "By all the saints, what has happened to you?" she called to the poor distressed lady who, quite beside herself and hardly able to stand, was merely trying to reach quickly the armchair that the marquise was pushing toward her.

Finally able to speak again, the lady told what a deep, indelible mortification she had received as a result of that unconsidered jest of hers in reply to the petition of the endangered lovers. After the marquise heard it all in proper sequence, she declared that Mlle de Scudéry was taking the odd occurrence too much to heart, that the mockery of wicked rabble could never touch a pious, noble mind; finally she asked to see the jewelry.

Mlle de Scudéry opened the box and gave it to her; when the marquise caught sight of the costly jewelry, she couldn't help exclaiming loudly in amazement. She took out the necklace and the bracelets and walked to the window with them; there, she now let the sunlight play over the gems, now held the beautiful work of the goldsmith close to her eyes to get a good look at the marvelous skill with which each little hook of the braided chains was crafted.

All at once the marquise quickly turned around to face the lady and exclaimed: "Mademoiselle, are you aware that these bracelets and this necklace could have been made by no one except René Cardillac?"

At the time René Cardillac was the most skillful goldsmith in Paris, one of the most artistic and, at the same time, eccentric people of his day. Rather short than tall, but broad-shouldered

muskulösem Körperbau, hatte Cardillac, hoch in die Fünfzigerjahre vorgerückt, noch die Kraft, die Beweglichkeit des Jünglings. Von dieser Kraft, die ungewöhnlich zu nennen, zeugte auch das dicke, krause, rötliche Haupthaar und das gedrungene, gleißende Antlitz. Wäre Cardillac nicht in ganz Paris als der rechtlichste Ehrenmann, uneigennützig, offen, ohne Hinterhalt, stets zu helfen bereit, bekannt gewesen, sein ganz besonderer Blick aus kleinen, tiefliegenden, grün funkelnden Augen hätte ihn in den Verdacht heimlicher Tücke und Bosheit bringen können.

Wie gesagt, Cardillac war in seiner Kunst der Geschickteste nicht sowohl in Paris, als vielleicht überhaupt seiner Zeit. Innig vertraut mit der Natur der Edelsteine, wußte er sie auf eine Art zu behandeln und zu fassen, daß der Schmuck, der erst für unscheinbar gegolten, aus Cardillacs Werkstatt hervorging in glänzender Pracht. Jeden Auftrag übernahm er mit brennender Begierde und machte einen Preis, der, so geringe er war, mit der Arbeit in keinem Verhältnis zu stehen schien. Dann ließ ihm das Werk keine Ruhe, Tag und Nacht hörte man ihn in seiner Werkstatt hämmern und oft, war die Arbeit beinahe vollendet, mißfiel ihm plötzlich die Form, er zweifelte an der Zierlichkeit irgendeiner Fassung der Juwelen, irgendeines kleinen Häkchens – Anlaß genug, die ganze Arbeit wieder in den Schmelztiegel zu werfen und von neuem anzufangen. So wurde jede Arbeit ein reines, unübertreffliches Meisterwerk, das den Besteller in Erstaunen setzte.

Aber nun war es kaum möglich, die fertige Arbeit von ihm zu erhalten. Unter tausend Vorwänden hielt er den Besteller hin von Woche zu Woche, von Monat zu Monat. Vergebens bot man ihm das Doppelte für die Arbeit, nicht einen Louis mehr als den bedungenen Preis wollte er nehmen. Mußte er dann endlich dem Andringen des Bestellers weichen und den Schmuck herausgeben, so konnte er sich aller Zeichen des tiefsten Verdrusses, ja einer innern Wut, die in ihm kochte, nicht erwehren. Hatte er ein bedeutenderes, vorzüglich reiches Werk, vielleicht viele Tausende an Wert, bei der Kostbarkeit der Juwelen, bei der überzierlichen Goldarbeit, abliefern müssen, so war er imstande, wie unsinnig umherzulaufen, sich, seine Arbeit, alles um sich her verwünschend.

Aber sowie einer hinter ihm herrannte und laut schrie: «René Cardillac, möchtet Ihr nicht einen schönen Halsschmuck machen für meine Braut – Armbänder für mein Mädchen und so weiter», dann stand er plötzlich still, blitzte den an mit seinen kleinen Augen und fragte, die Hände reibend: «Was habt Ihr denn?»

and of a powerful, muscular build, Cardillac, though well into his fifties, still had a young man's strength and agility. This strength, which could be called unusual, was also testified to by his thick, curly, reddish hair and his shiny, square face. If Cardillac hadn't been well known all over Paris as the most upright man of honor, unselfish, frank, candid, and always ready to help others, his very special way of looking at you with his small, deepset, green-flashing eyes could have brought him under suspicion of being secretly sly and malicious.

As stated above, in his art Cardillac was the most skillful not merely in Paris but perhaps anywhere at that period. Thoroughly familiar with the nature of precious stones, he was able to handle them and set them in such a way that a jewel which had at first been considered plain and unpretentious left Cardillac's workshop in dazzling splendor. He accepted every commission with ardent zeal, setting a price that was so low, it seemed to be out of proportion to his labor. Then the task gave him no rest; day and night he could be heard hammering in his atelier, and often, when the job was nearly done, he took a sudden dislike to its shape, or had doubts about the attractiveness of some setting of the gems or of some small hook—sufficient reason to throw the whole thing back in the crucible and start all over again. And so every piece of work became an unsurpassable masterpiece, which astonished the purchaser.

But, at that point, it was barely possible to obtain the finished piece from him. With a thousand pretexts he put off the purchaser week after week, month after month. In vain they offered him twice what he had asked for the piece, he refused to take one *louis* more than the price agreed on. When he finally had to yield to the purchaser's pressure and deliver the jewelry, he couldn't help showing every sign of the greatest vexation—in fact, an inward rage boiling inside him. If he had had to hand over a particularly significant, especially costly item, worth thousands, perhaps, because the gems were so valuable and the goldsmith work was so intricate, he was capable of dashing about like a madman, cursing himself, his work, and everything around him.

But as soon as someone ran after him and shouted, "René Cardillac, won't you make a beautiful necklace for my fiancée?" or "bracelets for my girl," or the like, he would suddenly come to a halt, flash his little eyes at the man, and ask, while rubbing his hands: "Well, what have you got?"

Der zieht nun ein Schächtelchen hervor und spricht: «Hier sind
Juwelen, viel Sonderliches ist es nicht, gemeines Zeug, doch unter
Euern Händen» – Cardillac läßt ihn nicht ausreden, reißt ihm das
Schächtelchen aus den Händen, nimmt die Juwelen heraus, die wirk-
lich nicht viel wert sind, hält sie gegen das Licht und ruft voll
Entzücken:

«Ho ho – gemeines Zeug? – mitnichten! – hübsche Steine – herrliche Steine, laßt mich nur machen! – und wenn es Euch auf eine
Handvoll Louis nicht ankommt, so will ich noch ein paar Steinchen
hineinbringen, die Euch in die Augen funkeln sollen wie die liebe
Sonne selbst –»

Der spricht: «Ich überlasse Euch alles, Meister René, und zahle,
was Ihr wollt!» Ohne Unterschied, mag er nun ein reicher Bürgers-
mann oder ein vornehmer Herr vom Hofe sein, wirft sich Cardillac
ungestüm an seinen Hals und drückt und küßt ihn und spricht, nun
sei er wieder ganz glücklich, und in acht Tagen werde die Arbeit fertig sein. Er rennt über Hals und Kopf nach Hause, hinein in die
Werkstatt und hämmert darauf los, und in acht Tagen ist ein Meisterwerk zustande gebracht. Aber sowie der, der es bestellte, kommt, mit
Freuden die geforderte geringe Summe bezahlen und den fertigen
Schmuck mitnehmen will, wird Cardillac verdrießlich, grob, trotzig.

«Aber Meister Cardillac, bedenkt, morgen ist meine Hochzeit.»

«Was schert mich Eure Hochzeit, fragt in vierzehn Tagen wieder
nach.»

«Der Schmuck ist fertig, hier liegt das Geld, ich muß ihn haben.»

«Und ich sage Euch, daß ich noch manches an dem Schmuck ändern muß und ihn heute nicht herausgeben werde.»

«Und ich sage Euch, daß wenn Ihr mir den Schmuck, den ich Euch
allenfalls doppelt bezahlen will, nicht herausgebt im guten, Ihr mich
gleich mit Argensons dienstbaren Trabanten anrücken sehen sollt.»

«Nun so quäle Euch der Satan mit hundert glühenden Kneip-
zangen und hänge drei Zentner an den Halsschmuck, damit er Eure
Braut erdroßle!» – Und damit steckt Cardillac dem Bräutigam den
Schmuck in die Busentasche, ergreift ihn beim Arm, wirft ihn zur
Stubentür hinaus, daß er die ganze Treppe hinabpoltert, und lacht wie
der Teufel zum Fenster hinaus, wenn er sieht, wie der arme junge
Mensch, das Schnupftuch vor der blutigen Nase, aus dem Hause hin-
aushinkt.

Gar nicht zu erklären war es auch, daß Cardillac oft, wenn er mit
Enthusiasmus eine Arbeit übernahm, plötzlich den Besteller mit
allen Zeichen des im Innersten aufgeregten Gemüts, mit den er-

Then the man would take out a little case and say: "Here are some gems, nothing special, plain stuff, but in your hands—." Cardillac wouldn't let him finish; he'd tear the case out of his hands, take out the gems, which were truly not worth much, hold them to the light, and call in great delight:

"Ho, ho! Plain stuff? Not at all! Pretty stones! Splendid stones! Just leave it to me! And if you aren't worried about paying a few *louis* more, I'll even add a couple of small stones that will sparkle in your eyes like the dear sun itself."

The man would then say: "I leave it all to you, Master René, and I'll pay whatever you ask!" Making no distinction between a wealthy bourgeois and an aristocratic courtier, Cardillac would embrace him impetuously, squeeze him, kiss him, and say he was now completely happy again, and the job would be done in a week. He would dash home at breakneck speed, enter his workshop, and start hammering away, and in a week a masterpiece was produced. But as soon as the man who commissioned it came cheerfully to pay the low sum requested and take along the completed piece, Cardillac would become cross, rude, and defiant.

"But, Master Cardillac, stop and think, my wedding is tomorrow."

"What do I care about your wedding? Ask me for it again in two weeks."

"The jewelry is ready, here's the money, I've got to have it."

"And I tell you, I still have to make a lot of alterations to the piece, and I can't let it out of my hands today."

"And I tell you, if you don't willingly hand over the jewelry, for which I'll pay you double if it must be, you'll soon see me coming back with D'Argenson's trusty halberdiers."

"In that case, may Satan torment you with a hundred red-hot pincers and hang three hundredweights on the necklace, so it chokes your bride!" And with those words Cardillac would stick the jewelry into the bridegroom's breast pocket, grab him by the arm, and throw him out the parlor door, so that he clattered down the whole staircase; and he'd laugh out the window like a devil when he saw the poor young fellow limp out of the house, holding his handkerchief to his bloody nose.

Nor could anyone explain why frequently Cardillac, after accepting a commission with alacrity, would suddenly—showing every sign of a deeply agitated mind—beseech the purchaser

schütterndsten Beteuerungen, ja unter Schluchzen und Tränen bei
der Jungfrau und allen Heiligen beschwor, ihm das unternommene
Werk zu erlassen. Manche der von dem Könige, von dem Volke
hochgeachtetsten Personen hatten vergebens große Summen
geboten, um nur das kleinste Werk von Cardillac zu erhalten. Er
warf sich dem Könige zu Füßen und flehte um die Huld, nichts für
ihn arbeiten zu dürfen. Ebenso verweigerte er der Maintenon jede
Bestellung, ja, mit dem Ausdruck des Abscheues und Entsetzens
verwarf er den Antrag derselben, einen kleinen, mit den Emblemen
der Kunst verzierten Ring zu fertigen, den Racine von ihr erhalten
sollte.

«Ich wette», sprach daher die Maintenon, «ich wette, daß Cardillac,
schicke ich auch hin zu ihm, um wenigstens zu erfahren, für wen er
diesen Schmuck fertigte, sich weigert herzukommen, weil er vielleicht eine Bestellung fürchtet und doch durchaus nichts für mich
arbeiten will. Wiewohl er seit einiger Zeit abzulassen scheint von
seinem starren Eigensinn, denn wie ich höre, arbeitet er jetzt fleißiger
als je und liefert seine Arbeit ab auf der Stelle, jedoch noch immer mit
tiefem Verdruß und weggewandtem Gesicht.»

Die Scuderi, der auch viel daran gelegen, daß, sei es noch möglich,
der Schmuck bald in die Hände des rechtmäßigen Eigentümers
komme, meinte, daß man dem Meister Sonderling ja gleich sagen
lassen könne, wie man keine Arbeit, sondern nur sein Urteil über
Juwelen verlange. Das billigte die Marquise. Es wurde nach Cardillac
geschickt, und, als sei er schon auf dem Wege gewesen, trat er nach
Verlauf weniger Zeit in das Zimmer.

Er schien, als er die Scuderi erblickte, betreten und wie einer, der,
von dem Unerwarteten plötzlich getroffen, die Ansprüche des
Schicklichen, wie sie der Augenblick darbietet, vergißt, neigte er sich
zuerst tief und ehrfurchtsvoll vor dieser ehrwürdigen Dame und
wandte sich dann erst zur Marquise. *Die* frug ihn hastig, indem sie auf
das Geschmeide wies, das auf dem dunkelgrün behängten Tisch
funkelte, ob das seine Arbeit sei. Cardillac warf kaum einen Blick
darauf und packte, der Marquise ins Gesicht starrend, Armbänder
und Halsschmuck schnell ein in das Kästchen, das daneben stand und
das er mit Heftigkeit von sich wegschob.

Nun sprach er, indem ein häßliches Lächeln auf seinem roten
Antlitz gleißte: «In der Tat, Frau Marquise, man muß René Cardillacs
Arbeit schlecht kennen, um nur einen Augenblick zu glauben, daß irgendein anderer Goldschmied in der Welt solchen Schmuck fassen
könne. Freilich ist das meine Arbeit.»

with the most moving asseverations, even with sobs and tears, to release him from the commission in the name of the Holy Virgin and all the saints. Many a person among those most highly esteemed by the king and by the people had offered large sums in vain to obtain even the smallest item from Cardillac. He threw himself at the king's feet and begged for the favor of not being compelled to do any work for him. Likewise he rejected every commission from Mme de Maintenon; in fact, it was with an expression of abhorrence and terror that he refused her request to make a small ring adorned with the attributes of Art, which Racine was to receive from her.

Therefore Mme de Maintenon now said: "I wager that even if I were to send to Cardillac merely to learn for whom he designed this jewelry, he'd refuse to come, because he might fear receiving a commission though he absolutely refuses to do any work for me. And yet he has seemed recently to relax his rigid obstinacy, because I hear he's now working more diligently than ever and delivers his work on the spot, though still with profound annoyance, with his face turned away."

Mlle de Scudéry, who was also greatly interested in getting that jewelry back in its rightful owner's hands quickly, if it was still possible, thought they could have Master Loony informed right at the outset that they didn't want him to do a job, but just appraise some gems. The marquise consented. Cardillac was sent for and, as if he had already been on the way there, he entered the room very shortly thereafter.

When he caught sight of Mlle de Scudéry, he looked embarrassed; like a man who, suddenly confronted with the unexpected, forgets the claims of propriety that the moment calls for, he first made a low, respectful bow to that honorable lady and only then turned to the marquise. She asked him hastily, pointing to the jewelry that was sparkling on the dark-green tablecloth, whether it was his handiwork. Cardillac scarcely cast a glance at it and, staring the marquise in the face, quickly packed away the bracelets and the necklace in the little box, which stood next to them, and which he violently shoved away from himself.

Now, an ugly smile playing over his ruddy face, he said: "Indeed, marquise, one would have to be unfamiliar with René Cardillac's work to believe for even a moment that any other goldsmith in the world could have created pieces like these. Of course it's my work."

«So sagt denn», fuhr die Marquise fort, «für wen Ihr diesen Schmuck gefertigt habt?»

«Für mich ganz allein», erwiderte Cardillac, «ja, Ihr möget», fuhr er fort, als beide, die Maintenon und die Scuderi, ihn ganz verwundert anblickten, jene voll Mißtrauen, diese voll banger Erwartung, wie sich nun die Sache wenden würde, «ja, Ihr möget das nun seltsam finden, Frau Marquise, aber es ist dem so. Bloß der schönen Arbeit willen suchte ich meine besten Steine zusammen und arbeitete aus Freude daran fleißiger und sorgfältiger als jemals. Vor weniger Zeit verschwand der Schmuck aus meiner Werkstatt auf unbegreifliche Weise.»

«Dem Himmel sei es gedankt», rief die Scuderi, indem ihr die Augen vor Freude funkelten, und sie rasch und behende wie ein junges Mädchen von ihrem Lehnsessel aufsprang, auf den Cardillac losschritt und beide Hände auf seine Schultern legte, «empfangt», sprach sie dann, «empfangt, Meister René, das Eigentum, das Euch verruchte Spitzbuben raubten, wieder zurück.» Nun erzählte sie ausführlich, wie sie zu dem Schmuck gekommen.

Cardillac hörte alles schweigend mit niedergeschlagenen Augen an. Nur mitunter stieß er ein unvernehmliches «Hm! – So! – Ei! – Hoho!» – aus und warf bald die Hände auf den Rücken, bald streichelte er leise Kinn und Wange. Als nun die Scuderi geendet, war es, als kämpfe Cardillac mit ganz besondern Gedanken, die währenddessen ihm gekommen, und als wolle irgendein Entschluß sich nicht fügen und fördern. Er rieb sich die Stirne, er seufzte, er fuhr mit der Hand über die Augen, wohl gar um hervorbrechenden Tränen zu steuern.

Endlich ergriff er das Kästchen, das ihm die Scuderi darbot, ließ sich auf ein Knie langsam nieder und sprach: «Euch, edles, würdiges Fräulein, hat das Verhängnis diesen Schmuck bestimmt. Ja, nun weiß ich es erst, daß ich während der Arbeit an Euch dachte, ja für Euch arbeitete. Verschmäht es nicht, diesen Schmuck als das Beste, was ich wohl seit langer Zeit gemacht, von mir anzunehmen und zu tragen.»

«Ei, ei», erwiderte die Scuderi, anmutig scherzend, «wo denkt Ihr hin, Meister René, steht es mir denn an, in meinen Jahren mich noch so herauszuputzen mit blanken Steinen? – Und wie kommt Ihr denn dazu, mich so überreich zu beschenken? Geht, geht, Meister René, wär ich so schön wie die Marquise de Fontange und reich, in der Tat, ich ließe den Schmuck nicht aus den Händen, aber was soll diesen welken Armen die eitle Pracht, was soll diesem verhüllten Hals der glänzende Putz?»

"Then tell us," the marquise continued, "for whom you made this jewelry."

"For myself alone," Cardillac replied. "Yes," he went on, when both Mme de Maintenon and Mlle de Scudéry gazed at him in complete amazement, the former filled with distrust and the latter with fearful expectancy as to what turn things would now take, "yes, you may find that odd, marquise, but it's true. Purely for the sake of fine craftsmanship I assembled my best stones and, from joy, worked at it more diligently and carefully than ever before. Not long ago the jewelry disappeared from my workshop in an incomprehensible way."

"Thank heaven!" cried Mlle de Scudéry, her eyes sparkling with joy, as she quickly and nimbly jumped up from her armchair like a young girl, strode over to Cardillac, and placed both hands on his shoulders. She then said: "Master René, take back the property which wicked thieves stole from you." Then she told him in detail how she had received the jewelry.

Cardillac heard it all in silence, with eyes cast down. Only occasionally did he utter an imperceptible "Hmm," "So," "Well," or "Ho, ho!" At times he put his hands behind his back, at times he gently stroked his chin and cheek. When Mlle de Scudéry was done, Cardillac seemed to be struggling with very particular ideas that had come to him in the meanwhile, as if some decision refused to fit in neatly with his plans. He rubbed his brow, he sighed, and he passed his hand over his eyes, presumably to check gushing tears.

Finally he seized the box that Mlle de Scudéry presented to him, slowly dropped onto one knee, and said: "Fate has destined this jewelry for you, my noble, worthy lady. Yes, it has just become clear to me that I was thinking of you while working on it, and that I meant it for you. Don't disdain to accept from me, and to wear, this jewelry, which is surely the best I've made in some time."

"My, my," Mlle de Scudéry replied with charming banter, "what are you thinking of, Master René? Is it proper for me, at my age, to go on adorning myself with bright gems? And how do you come to give me such an extremely costly present? Come, come, Master René, if I were as beautiful as the Marquise de Fontanges, and wealthy, then I really wouldn't let this jewelry out of my hands, but what do these withered arms want with vain splendor, what does this closely wrapped throat want with gleaming adornment?"

Cardillac hatte sich indessen erhoben und sprach, wie außer sich, mit verwildertem Blick, indem er fortwährend das Kästchen der Scuderi hinhielt: «Tut mir die Barmherzigkeit, Fräulein, und nehmt den Schmuck. Ihr glaubt es nicht, welche tiefe Verehrung ich für Eure Tugend, für Eure hohen Verdienste im Herzen trage! Nehmt doch mein geringes Geschenk nur für das Bestreben an, Euch recht meine innerste Gesinnung zu beweisen.»

Als nun die Scuderi immer noch zögerte, nahm die Maintenon das Kästchen aus Cardillacs Händen, sprechend: «Nun beim Himmel, Fräulein, immer redet Ihr von Euern hohen Jahren, was haben wir, ich und Ihr, mit den Jahren zu schaffen und ihrer Last! – Und tut Ihr denn nicht eben wie ein junges verschämtes Ding, das gern zulangen möchte nach der dargebotnen süßen Frucht, könnte das nur geschehen ohne Hand und ohne Finger. – Schlagt dem wackern Meister René nicht ab, das freiwillig als Geschenk zu empfangen, was tausend andere nicht erhalten können, alles Goldes, alles Bittens und Flehens unerachtet. –»

Die Maintenon hatte der Scuderi das Kästchen währenddessen aufgedrungen, und nun stürzte Cardillac nieder auf die Knie – küßte der Scuderi den Rock – die Hände – stöhnte – seufzte – weinte – schluchzte – sprang auf – rannte wie unsinnig, Sessel – Tische um- stürzend, daß Porzellan, Gläser zusammenklirrten, in toller Hast von dannen. –

Ganz erschrocken rief die Scuderi: «Um aller Heiligen willen, was widerfährt dem Menschen!»

Doch die Marquise, in besonderer heiterer Laune bis zu sonst ihr ganz fremdem Mutwillen, schlug eine helle Lache auf und sprach: «Da haben wir's, Fräulein, Meister René ist in Euch sterblich ver- liebt und beginnt nach richtigem Brauch und bewährter Sitte echter Galanterie Euer Herz zu bestürmen mit reichen Geschenken.» Die Maintenon führte diesen Scherz weiter aus, indem sie die Scuderi er- mahnte, nicht zu grausam zu sein gegen den verzweifelten Liebhaber, und diese wurde, Raum gebend angeborner Laune, hin- gerissen in den sprudelnden Strom tausend lustiger Einfälle. Sie meinte, daß sie, stünden die Sachen nun einmal so, endlich besiegt, wohl nicht werde umhin können, der Welt das unerhörte Beispiel einer dreiundsiebzigjährigen Goldschmiedsbraut von untadeligem Adel aufzustellen. Die Maintenon erbot sich, die Brautkrone zu flechten und sie über die Pflichten einer guten Hausfrau zu belehren, wovon freilich so ein kleiner Kiekindiewelt von Mädchen nicht viel wissen könne.

Meanwhile Cardillac had risen, and now said, as if beside himself, with a savage gaze, while he constantly held out the box to Mlle de Scudéry: "Be merciful to me, lady, and take the jewelry. You wouldn't believe what great reverence I have in my heart for your virtue, for your great merits! Please consider my insignificant present merely as an attempt to prove to you my heartfelt attachment."

When Mlle de Scudéry continued to hesitate, Mme de Maintenon took the box out of Cardillac's hands, saying: "Now by heaven, my lady, you keep on talking about your advanced years. What do we, you and I, have to do with the years and their burden? And aren't you acting just like a bashful young girl who'd gladly reach out for the sweet fruit being offered, if she could only do it without using her hands and fingers? Don't refuse honest Master René, but accept voluntarily as a gift something that thousands of others couldn't obtain in spite of all their wealth, begging, and imploring!"

Meanwhile Mme de Maintenon had thrust the box upon Mlle de Scudéry, and now Cardillac knelt hastily, kissed Mlle de Scudéry's skirt and hands, groaned, sighed, wept, sobbed, jumped to his feet, and ran off at full speed like a madman, overturning chairs and tables and making china and glassware clink together.

In great alarm Mlle de Scudéry exclaimed: "By all the saints, what's going on with that man?"

But the marquise, whose especially good mood bordered on playfulness, which was usually quite alien to her, burst into loud laughter and said: "There we have it, my lady, Master René is mortally in love with you and, in line with the proper customs and traditional manners of true gallantry, he's beginning to besiege your heart with expensive presents." Mme de Maintenon expanded on that joke by admonishing Mlle de Scudéry not to treat her despairing lover too cruelly, and the mademoiselle, indulging her inborn temperament, got carried away in the effervescent current of a thousand humorous notions. If things stood that way, she said, and she was finally conquered, she wouldn't be able to avoid giving society the unheard-of example of a seventy-three-year-old woman of unimpeachable nobility becoming a goldsmith's fiancée. Mme de Maintenon offered her services for weaving the bridal wreath and instructing her in the duties of a good housewife, which such a young novice like her surely couldn't know much about.

Da nun endlich die Scuderi aufstand, um die Marquise zu verlassen, wurde sie, alles lachenden Scherzes ungeachtet, doch wieder sehr ernst, als ihr das Schmuckkästchen zur Hand kam. Sie sprach: «Doch, Frau Marquise, werde ich mich dieses Schmuckes niemals bedienen können. Er ist, mag es sich nun zugetragen haben wie es will, einmal in den Händen jener höllischen Gesellen gewesen, die mit der Frechheit des Teufels, ja wohl gar in verdammtem Bündnis mit ihm rauben und morden. Mir graust vor dem Blute, das an dem funkelnden Geschmeide zu kleben scheint. – Und nun hat selbst Cardillacs Betragen, ich muß es gestehen, für mich etwas sonderbar Ängstliches und Unheimliches. Nicht erwehren kann ich mich einer dunklen Ahnung, daß hinter diesem allem irgendein grauenvolles, entsetzliches Geheimnis verborgen, und bringe ich mir die ganze Sache recht deutlich vor Augen mit jedem Umstande, so kann ich doch wieder gar nicht auch nur ahnen, worin das Geheimnis bestehe, und wie überhaupt der ehrliche, wackere Meister René, das Vorbild eines guten, frommen Bürgers, mit irgend etwas Bösem, Verdammlichem zu tun haben soll. So viel ist aber gewiß, daß ich niemals mich unterstehen werde, den Schmuck anzulegen.»

Die Marquise meinte, das hieße die Skrupel zu weit treiben; als nun aber die Scuderi sie auf ihr Gewissen fragte, was sie in ihrer, der Scuderi, Lage wohl tun würde, antwortete sie ernst und fest: «Weit eher den Schmuck in die Seine werfen, als ihn jemals tragen.»

Den Auftritt mit dem Meister René brachte die Scuderi in gar anmutige Verse, die sie den folgenden Abend in den Gemächern der Maintenon dem Könige vorlas. Wohl mag es sein, daß sie auf Kosten Meister Renés, alle Schauer unheimlicher Ahnung besiegend, das ergötzliche Bild der dreiundsiebzigjährigen Goldschmiedsbraut von uraltem Adel mit lebendigen Farben darzustellen gewußt. Genug, der König lachte bis ins Innerste hinein und schwur, daß Boileau Despréaux seinen Meister gefunden, weshalb der Scuderi Gedicht für das Witzigste galt, das jemals geschrieben.

Mehrere Monate waren vergangen, als der Zufall es wollte, daß die Scuderi in der Glaskutsche der Herzogin von Montansier über den Pontneuf fuhr. Noch war die Erfindung der zierlichen Glaskutschen so neu, daß das neugierige Volk sich zudrängte, wenn ein Fuhrwerk der Art auf den Straßen erschien. So kam es denn auch, daß der gaffende Pöbel auf dem Pontneuf die Kutsche der Montansier umringte, beinahe den Schritt der Pferde hemmend. Da vernahm die Scuderi plötzlich ein Geschimpfe und Gefluche und gewahrte, wie ein Mensch mit Faustschlägen und Rippenstößen sich Platz machte

After Mlle de Scudéry finally rose to take leave of the marquise, despite all their laughing and joking she became very serious again when she had to take the jewel box. She said: "And yet, marquise, I'll never be able to wear this jewelry. No matter what actually occurred, it was once in the hands of those hellish fellows who steal and kill with the impudence of the Devil, perhaps even in accursed league with him. I shudder at the blood that seems to adhere to the sparkling gems. And now, I must confess, even Cardillac's behavior has in it something strangely frightening and uncanny to me. I can't get over an obscure foreboding that some ghastly, terrible mystery is hidden in all this, and when I recall every circumstance of the whole matter very clearly, still I can't even imagine where the mystery lies or how that honest, upright Master René, the model of a good, God-fearing citizen, can have anything at all to do with something evil and reprehensible. But this much is certain: I'll never bring myself to put on the jewelry."

The marquise said that she was carrying her scruples too far, but when Mlle de Scudéry then asked her, on her conscience, what she would do in her place, she replied with firm gravity: "I'd much sooner throw the jewelry into the Seine than ever wear it."

Mlle de Scudéry wrote a very charming poem about the scene with Master René, and read it to the king the following evening in Mme de Maintenon's apartment. It may very well be that, at Master René's expense, she was able to overcome all the dread of her uneasy foreboding and to project in lively colors the entertaining picture of the goldsmith's seventy-three-year-old fiancée of an ancient noble line. At any rate, the king laughed heartily and swore that Boileau-Despréaux had found his master, and therefore Mlle de Scudéry's poem was considered the funniest thing ever written.

Several months had gone by when it so chanced that Mlle de Scudéry was riding across the Pont Neuf in the Duchesse de Montansier's glass coach. Those pretty glass coaches were still such a recent invention that the curious populace formed a crowd whenever a vehicle of that sort appeared in the street. And so it was that the gawking commoners surrounded the Montansier coach on the Pont Neuf, almost blocking the horses' path. Then Mlle de Scudéry suddenly heard scolding and cursing, and noticed that a man was making his way through the

durch die dickste Masse. Und wie er näher kam, trafen sie die
durchbohrenden Blicke eines todbleichen, gramverstörten Jünglings-
antlitzes.

Unverwandt schaute der junge Mensch sie an, während er mit
Ellbogen und Fäusten rüstig vor sich wegarbeitete, bis er an den
Schlag des Wagens kam, den er mit stürmender Hastigkeit aufriß, der
Scuderi einen Zettel in den Schoß warf und, Stöße, Faustschläge
austeilend und empfangend, verschwand, wie er gekommen.

Mit einem Schrei des Entsetzens war, sowie der Mensch am
Kutschenschlage erschien, die Martiniere, die sich bei der Scuderi
befand, entseelt in die Wagenkissen zurückgesunken. Vergebens riß
die Scuderi an der Schnur, rief dem Kutscher zu; der, wie vom bösen
Geiste getrieben, peitschte auf die Pferde los, die den Schaum von
den Mäulern wegspritzend, um sich schlugen, sich bäumten, endlich
in scharfem Trab fortdonnerten über die Brücke. Die Scuderi goß ihr
Riechfläschchen über die ohnmächtige Frau aus, die endlich die
Augen aufschlug und, zitternd und bebend, sich krampfhaft festklam-
mernd an die Herrschaft, Angst und Entsetzen im bleichen Antlitz,
mühsam stöhnte: «Um der heiligen Jungfrau willen! was wollte der
fürchterliche Mensch? – Ach! er war es ja, er war es, derselbe, der
Euch in jener schauervollen Nacht das Kästchen brachte!»

Die Scuderi beruhigte die Arme, indem sie ihr vorstellte, daß ja
durchaus nichts Böses geschehen, und daß es nur darauf ankomme,
zu wissen, was der Zettel enthalte. Sie schlug das Blättchen auseinander und fand die Worte:

«Ein böses Verhängnis, das Ihr abwenden konntet, stößt mich in
den Abgrund! – Ich beschwöre Euch, wie der Sohn die Mutter,
von der er nicht lassen kann, in der vollsten Glut kindlicher
Liebe, den Halsschmuck und die Armbänder, die Ihr durch mich
erhieltet, unter irgendeinem Vorwand – um irgend etwas daran
bessern – ändern zu lassen, zum Meister René Cardillac zu
schaffen; Euer Wohl, Euer Leben hängt davon ab. Tut Ihr es
nicht bis übermorgen, so dringe ich in Eure Wohnung und er-
morde mich vor Euern Augen!»

«Nun ist es gewiß», sprach die Scuderi, als sie dies gelesen, «daß,
mag der geheimnisvolle Mensch auch wirklich zu der Bande verruchter Diebe und Mörder gehören, er doch gegen mich nichts Böses
im Schilde führt. Wäre es ihm gelungen, mich in jener Nacht zu
sprechen, wer weiß, welches sonderbare Ereignis, welch dunkles
Verhältnis der Dinge mir klar geworden, von dem ich jetzt auch nur

thickest of the throng with blows of his fist and pokes in people's ribs. As he got closer, she was pierced by the penetrating gaze from the face of a deathly pale young man, distraught with grief.

The young fellow stared at her unswervingly while energetically making his way forward with elbows and fists, until he reached the coach door, which he pulled open in hot haste. Tossing a note into Mlle de Scudéry's lap, he vanished as he had come, dealing and receiving shoves and punches.

The moment that the fellow appeared at the coach door, Martinière, who was with Mlle de Scudéry, had uttered a cry of terror and had fallen back onto the coach cushions in a faint. It was in vain that Mlle de Scudéry pulled the signal cord and shouted to the coachman; as if spurred by an evil spirit, he lashed the horses, which, shaking the foam off their muzzles, jerked to and fro, reared, and finally thundered away over the bridge at a quick trot. Mlle de Scudéry poured her bottle of smelling salts over the unconscious woman, who finally opened her eyes and, trembling and shaking, clinging convulsively to her mistress, fear and terror on her pallid face, groaned out with difficulty: "By the Holy Virgin, what did that awful man want? Oh! It was he, it was he, the one who brought you the box that dreadful night!"

Mlle de Scudéry calmed the poor woman by assuring her that nothing at all bad had happened, and that all they now had to do was to learn what the note said. She unfolded the sheet and found these words:

"An evil destiny, which you might have averted, is thrusting me into the abyss! I implore you, as a son implores his mother, from whom he can't tear himself away, in the full warmth of a child's love, to send the necklace and bracelets you received through me to Master René Cardillac on some pretext or other, to improve or alter something. Your well being, your life depends on this. If you don't do it by the day after tomorrow, I shall break into your home and kill myself right before your eyes!"

"Now it's beyond doubt," said Mlle de Scudéry after reading this, "that, even if the mysterious man really belongs to that gang of wicked thieves and murderers, he nevertheless has no evil designs against me. If he had succeeded in speaking with me that night, who knows what strange occurrence or what obscure connection of events might have become clear to me, whereas now

die leiseste Ahnung vergebens in meiner Seele suche. Mag aber auch
die Sache sich nun verhalten wie sie will, das, was mir in diesem Blatt
geboten wird, werde ich tun, und geschähe es auch nur, um den un-
seligen Schmuck los zu werden, der mir ein höllischer Talisman des
Bösen selbst dünkt. Cardillac wird ihn doch wohl nun, seiner alten
Sitte getreu, nicht so leicht wieder aus den Händen geben wollen.»

Schon andern Tages gedachte die Scuderi, sich mit dem Schmuck
zu dem Goldschmied zu begeben. Doch war es, als hätten alle schönen Geister von ganz Paris sich verabredet, gerade an dem Morgen
das Fräulein mit Versen, Schauspielen, Anekdoten zu bestürmen.
Kaum hatte la Chapelle die Szene eines Trauerspiels geendet und
schlau versichert, daß er nun wohl Racine zu schlagen gedenke, als
dieser selbst eintrat und ihn mit irgendeines Königs pathetischer
Rede zu Boden schlug, bis Boileau seine Leuchtkugeln in den
schwarzen tragischen Himmel steigen ließ, um nur nicht ewig von der
Kolonnade des Louvre schwatzen zu hören, in die ihn der architekti-
sche Doktor Perrault hineingeengt.

Hoher Mittag war geworden, die Scuderi mußte zur Herzogin
Montansier, und so blieb der Besuch bei Meister René Cardillac bis
zum andern Morgen verschoben.

Die Scuderi fühlte sich von einer besondern Unruhe gepeinigt.
Beständig vor Augen stand ihr der Jüngling, und aus dem tiefsten
Innern wollte sich eine dunkle Erinnerung aufregen, als habe sie dies
Antlitz, diese Züge schon gesehen. Den leisesten Schlummer störten
ängstliche Träume, es war ihr, als habe sie leichtsinnig, ja strafwürdig
versäumt, die Hand hilfreich zu erfassen, die der Unglückliche, in den
Abgrund versinkend, nach ihr emporgestreckt, ja, als sei es an ihr
gewesen, irgendeinem verderblichen Ereignis, einem heillosen
Verbrechen zu steuern! – Sowie es nur hoher Morgen, ließ sie sich
ankleiden und fuhr, mit dem Schmuckkästchen versehen, zu dem
Goldschmied hin.

Nach der Straße Nicaise, dorthin, wo Cardillac wohnte, strömte das
Volk, sammelte sich vor der Haustüre – schrie, lärmte, tobte – wollte
stürmend hinein, mit Mühe abgehalten von der Marechaussee, die
das Haus umstellt. Im wilden, verwirrten Getöse riefen zornige
Stimmen: «Zerreißt, zermalmt den verfluchten Mörder!» – Endlich
erscheint Desgrais mit zahlreicher Mannschaft, *die* bildet durch den
dicksten Haufen eine Gasse. Die Haustüre springt auf, ein Mensch,
mit Ketten belastet, wird hinausgebracht und unter den greulichsten

I can't even imagine them in the slightest in my mind! But whatever the truth of the matter may be, I will do what he asks of me in this note, even if all I achieve is to get rid of that unholy jewelry, which appears to me like an infernal talisman of the Evil One himself. If Cardillac is true to his old habits, he won't let it out of his hands again so soon."

Mlle de Scudéry intended to take the jewelry to the goldsmith the very next day. But all the intellectual lights in Paris seemed to have conspired to besiege the lady with poems, plays, and anecdotes on that very morning. Scarcely had La Chapelle finished reading a scene from a tragedy, slyly assuring his listeners that he now expected to outdo Racine, when the latter entered and crushed him with some king's emotional speech, until Boileau sent up his fireworks into the dark skies of tragedy in order to avoid the unending chatter about the colonnade of the Louvre, into which the architect Doctor Perrault[5] had cramped him.

It was now high noon, and Mlle de Scudéry had to attend the Duchesse de Montansier, so that her visit to Master René Cardillac was postponed until the following morning.

Mlle de Scudéry felt tormented by a decided restlessness. The image of the young man was constantly before her eyes, and from the depths of her consciousness an obscure recollection was beginning to arise, as if she had already seen that face and those features. Her very light sleep was disturbed by frightening dreams; she felt as if she had carelessly, even criminally, neglected to grasp the hand which the unfortunate man, sinking into the abyss, had held out to her for help; as if, indeed, it had been up to her to counteract some catastrophic event, some irremediable crime! As soon as the sun was bright, she had herself dressed and, provided with the jewel box, she drove to the goldsmith's home.

People were swarming toward the rue Nicaise, where Cardillac lived; they were gathering in front of the door, yelling, carrying on, raging; they wanted to break in but were restrained with difficulty by the *maréchaussée,* which had formed a cordon around the house. From the wild, confused racket issued the angry cries: "Tear apart the damned killer! Crush him!" Finally Desgrais showed up with numerous men, who forced a path through the midst of the mob. The front door flew open, and a

5. Claude Perrault, brother of fairy-tale author Charles, was traditionally (but incorrectly) credited with the design for the Louvre colonnade; this design dated to 1667–70, and was no longer news in 1680.

Verwünschungen des wütenden Pöbels fortgeschleppt. – In dem
Augenblick, als die Scuderi, halb entseelt vor Schreck und furchtbarer
Ahnung, dies gewahrt, dringt ein gellendes Jammergeschrei ihr in die
Ohren. «Vor! – weiter vor!» ruft sie ganz außer sich dem Kutscher zu,
der mit einer geschickten, raschen Wendung den dicken Haufen
auseinanderstäubt und dicht vor Cardillacs Haustüre hält.

Da sieht die Scuderi Desgrais und zu seinen Füßen ein junges
Mädchen, schön wie der Tag, mit aufgelösten Haaren, halb entklei-
det, wilde Angst, trostlose Verzweiflung im Antlitz, die hält seine Knie
umschlungen und ruft mit dem Ton des entsetzlichsten, schneidendsten Todesschmerzes: «Er ist ja unschuldig! – er ist unschuldig!»
Vergebens sind Desgrais', vergebens seiner Leute Bemühungen, sie
loszureißen, sie vom Boden aufzurichten. Ein starker, ungeschlachter
Kerl ergreift endlich mit plumpen Fäusten die Arme, zerrt sie mit
Gewalt weg von Desgrais, strauchelt ungeschickt, läßt das Mädchen
fahren, die hinabschlägt die steinernen Stufen und lautlos – tot auf
der Straße liegen bleibt.

Länger kann die Scuderi sich nicht halten. «In Christus' Namen,
was ist geschehen, was geht hier vor?» ruft sie, öffnet rasch den
Schlag, steigt aus. – Ehrerbietig weicht das Volk der würdigen Dame,
die, als sie sieht, wie ein paar mitleidige Weiber das Mädchen aufgehoben, auf die Stufen gesetzt haben, ihr die Stirne mit starkem
Wasser reiben, sich dem Desgrais nähert und mit Heftigkeit ihre
Frage wiederholt.

«Es ist das Entsetzliche geschehen», spricht Desgrais, «René
Cardillac wurde heute morgen durch einen Dolchstich ermordet gefunden. Sein Geselle Olivier Brusson ist der Mörder. Eben wurde er
fortgeführt ins Gefängnis.»

«Und das Mädchen?» ruft die Scuderi, – «ist», fällt Desgrais ein, «ist
Madelon, Cardillacs Tochter. Der verruchte Mensch war ihr
Geliebter. Nun weint und heult sie und schreit ein Mal übers andere,
daß Olivier unschuldig sei, ganz unschuldig. Am Ende weiß sie von
der Tat, und ich muß sie auch nach der Conciergerie bringen lassen.»
Desgrais warf, als er dies sprach, einen tückischen, schadenfrohen
Blick auf das Mädchen, vor dem die Scuderi erbebte.

Eben begann das Mädchen leise zu atmen, doch keines Lauts,
keiner Bewegung mächtig, mit geschlossenen Augen lag sie da, und
man wußte nicht, was zu tun, sie ins Haus bringen oder ihr noch
länger beistehen bis zum Erwachen. Tief bewegt, Tränen in den
Augen, blickte die Scuderi den unschuldsvollen Engel an, ihr graute
vor Desgrais und seinen Gesellen. Da polterte es dumpf die Treppe

man loaded with chains was led out and dragged away amid the most horrible curses from the frenzied populace. At the moment when Mlle de Scudéry, half-swooning with fright and terrible foreboding, noticed this, a shrill outcry of sorrow penetrated her ears. "Move on! Move on!" she shouted, completely beside herself, to the coachman, who with a quick, skillful turn dispersed the dense throng and halted right in front of Cardillac's door.

There Mlle de Scudéry saw Desgrais and, at his feet, a young woman as beautiful as the day, her hair undone, half undressed, wild fear and comfortless despair on her face; she was clasping his knees and calling in a tone of the most terrible and chilling deathly sorrow: "But he's innocent! He's innocent!" In vain were Desgrais's efforts and those of his men to pull her away and raise her from the ground. Finally a strong, uncouth fellow gripped the poor girl in his coarse fists, tore her away from Desgrais by force, and stumbled awkwardly, letting go of the girl, who tumbled down the stone steps and lay on the street without a sound, as if dead.

Mlle de Scudéry could contain herself no longer. "In the name of Christ, what has happened? What's going on here?" she cried, quickly opening the coach door and getting out. The people moved aside from the dignified lady respectfully; when she saw that a couple of sympathetic women had picked the girl up and had sat her on the steps, and were rubbing her brow with alcohol, she approached Desgrais and repeated her question emphatically.

"The most terrible thing has happened," said Desgrais. "René Cardillac was found this morning stabbed to death. His journeyman Olivier Brusson is the killer. He has just been taken away to prison."

"And the girl?" Mlle de Scudéry exclaimed. "Is Madelon," Desgrais interjected, "Cardillac's daughter. That wicked fellow was her sweetheart. Now she's weeping, wailing, and yelling time and again that Olivier is innocent, completely innocent. Anyway, she knows about the deed, and I must have her taken to the Conciergerie as well." As he was saying this, Desgrais cast a sly, malicious glance at the girl which made Mlle de Scudéry shudder.

The girl was just beginning to breathe softly, but she lay there with her eyes shut, unable to speak or move, and no one knew what to do, whether to carry her into the house or keep watch over her until she awoke. Deeply moved, tears in her eyes, Mlle de Scudéry looked at that innocent angel, and she felt a horror of Desgrais and his men. Then there was a hollow rumble down

herab, man brachte Cardillacs Leichnam. Schnell entschlossen rief die Scuderi laut: «Ich nehme das Mädchen mit mir, Ihr möget für das übrige sorgen, Desgrais!» Ein dumpfes Murmeln des Beifalls lief durch das Volk. Die Weiber hoben das Mädchen in die Höhe, alles drängte sich hinzu, hundert Hände mühten sich, ihnen beizustehen, und, wie in den Lüften schwebend, wurde das Mädchen in die Kutsche getragen, indem Segnungen der würdigen Dame, die die Unschuld dem Blutgericht entrissen, von allen Lippen strömten.

Serons, des berühmtesten Arztes in Paris, Bemühungen gelang es endlich, Madelon, die stundenlang in starrer Bewußtlosigkeit gelegen, wieder zu sich selbst zu bringen. Die Scuderi vollendete, was der Arzt begonnen, indem sie manchen milden Hoffnungsstrahl leuchten ließ in des Mädchens Seele, bis ein heftiger Tränenstrom, der ihr aus den Augen stürzte, ihr Luft machte. Sie vermochte, indem nur dann und wann die Übermacht des durchbohrendsten Schmerzes die Worte in tiefem Schluchzen erstickte, zu erzählen, wie sich alles begeben.

Um Mitternacht war sie durch leises Klopfen an ihrer Stubentür geweckt worden und hatte Oliviers Stimme vernommen, der sie beschworen, doch nur gleich aufzustehen, weil der Vater im Sterben liege. Entsetzt sei sie aufgesprungen und habe die Tür geöffnet. Olivier, bleich und entstellt, von Schweiß triefend, sei, das Licht in der Hand, mit wankenden Schritten nach der Werkstatt gegangen, sie ihm gefolgt. Da habe der Vater gelegen mit starren Augen und geröchelt im Todeskampfe. Jammernd habe sie sich auf ihn gestürzt und nun erst sein blutiges Hemde bemerkt. Olivier habe sie sanft weggezogen und sich dann bemüht, eine Wunde auf der linken Brust des Vaters mit Wundbalsam zu waschen und zu verbinden.

Währenddessen sei des Vaters Besinnung zurückgekehrt, er habe zu röcheln aufgehört und sie, dann aber Olivier mit seelenvollem Blick angeschaut, ihre Hand ergriffen, sie in Oliviers Hand gelegt und beide heftig gedrückt. Beide, Olivier und sie, wären bei dem Lager des Vaters auf die Knie gefallen, er habe sich mit einem schneidenden Laut in die Höhe gerichtet, sei aber gleich wieder zurückgesunken und mit einem tiefen Seufzer verschieden. Nun hätten sie beide laut gejammert und geklagt.

Olivier habe erzählt, wie der Meister auf einem Gange, den er mit ihm auf sein Geheiß in der Nacht habe machen müssen, in seiner Gegenwart ermordet worden, und wie er mit der größten Anstrengung den schweren Mann, den er nicht auf den Tod verwundet gehalten, nach Hause getragen. Sowie der Morgen angebrochen, wären die

the steps; Cardillac's body was being carried out. With a rapid decision Mlle de Scudéry shouted loudly: "I'm taking the girl with me. You can take care of the rest, Desgrais!" A subdued murmur of approval circulated among the crowd. The woman lifted the girl up, everyone pressed forward, a hundred hands strove to be of assistance, and, as if she were floating in the air, the girl was carried into the coach, while blessings on the worthy lady, who had rescued the innocent from savage judgment, flowed from all lips.

The efforts of Seron, the most celebrated doctor in Paris, finally succeeded in reviving Madelon, who had lain rigid and unconscious for hours. Mlle de Scudéry ended what the doctor had begun, making many a gentle ray of hope shine into the girl's soul, until a violet flood of tears burst from her eyes and gave her air. With the mighty force of the most piercing sorrow only now and then stifling her words with heavy sobs, she was able to tell how it all happened.

Around midnight she had been awakened by gentle rapping at the door to her room; she had heard Olivier's voice beseeching her to get up right away because her father was dying. She had jumped up in horror and had opened the door. Olivier, pale, his features distorted, dripping with sweat, had gone to the workshop, candle in hand, with shaky steps, and she had followed him. There her father lay with staring eyes, emiting a rattle in his struggle against death. She had thrown herself upon him, lamenting, and only then had noticed his bloody shirt. Olivier had pulled her away gently and had then occupied himself with washing a wound on the left side of her father's chest with balm, and binding it.

Meanwhile her father had regained consciousness, his death rattle had ceased, he had looked soulfully at her and then at Olivier, he had seized her hand, placed it in Olivier's, and squeezed both of them hard. The two, she and Olivier, had knelt down at her father's bed, he had sat up with a heartrending cry, but had fallen back again immediately and died with a deep sigh. Then they had both sorrowed and lamented loudly.

Olivier had told her that, during a walk which he had had to take with him by night at his orders, he had been stabbed in his presence, and that, by the greatest exertions, he had carried home the heavy man, who he didn't think had been fatally wounded. As soon as day broke, the tenants, who had heard the noise and the loud

Hausleute, denen das Gepolter, das laute Weinen und Jammern in der Nacht aufgefallen, heraufgekommen und hätten sie noch ganz trostlos bei der Leiche des Vaters kniend gefunden. Nun sei Lärm entstanden, die Marechaussee eingedrungen und Olivier als Mörder seines Meisters ins Gefängnis geschleppt worden.

Madelon fügte nun die rührendste Schilderung von der Tugend, der Frömmigkeit, der Treue ihres geliebten Oliviers hinzu. Wie er den Meister, als sei er sein eigener Vater, hoch in Ehren gehalten, wie dieser seine Liebe in vollem Maß erwidert, wie er ihn trotz seiner Armut zum Eidam erkoren, weil seine Geschicklichkeit seiner Treue, seinem edlen Gemüt gleichgekommen. Das alles erzählte Madelon aus dem innersten Herzen heraus und schloß damit, daß, wenn Olivier in ihrem Beisein dem Vater den Dolch in die Brust gestoßen hätte, sie dies eher für ein Blendwerk des Satans halten, als daran glauben würde, daß Olivier eines solchen entsetzlichen, grauenvollen Verbrechens fähig sein könne.

Die Scuderi, von Madelons namenlosen Leiden auf das tiefste gerührt und ganz geneigt, den armen Olivier für unschuldig zu halten, zog Erkundigungen ein und fand alles bestätigt, was Madelon über das häusliche Verhältnis des Meisters mit seinem Gesellen erzählt hatte. Die Hausleute, die Nachbarn rühmten einstimmig den Olivier als das Muster eines sittigen, frommen, treuen, fleißigen Betragens, niemand wußte Böses von ihm, und doch, war von der gräßlichen Tat die Rede, zuckte jeder die Achseln und meinte, darin liege etwas Unbegreifliches.

Olivier, vor die Chambre ardente gestellt, leugnete, wie die Scuderi vernahm, mit der größten Standhaftigkeit, mit dem hellsten Freimut die ihm angeschuldigte Tat und behauptete, daß sein Meister in seiner Gegenwart auf der Straße angefallen und niedergestoßen worden, daß er ihn aber noch lebendig nach Hause geschleppt, wo er sehr bald verschieden sei. Auch dies stimmte also mit Madelons Erzählung überein.

Immer und immer wieder ließ sich die Scuderi die kleinsten Umstände des schrecklichen Ereignisses wiederholen. Sie forschte genau, ob jemals ein Streit zwischen Meister und Gesellen vorgefallen, ob vielleicht Olivier nicht ganz frei von jenem Jähzorn sei, der oft wie ein blinder Wahnsinn die gutmütigsten Menschen überfällt und zu Taten verleitet, die alle Willkür des Handelns auszuschließen scheinen. Doch je begeisterter Madelon von dem ruhigen häuslichen Glück sprach, in dem die drei Menschen in innigster Liebe verbunden lebten, desto mehr verschwand jeder Schatten des Verdachts wider den auf den Tod angeklagten Olivier.

weeping and wailing during the night, had come upstairs and found them still kneeling by her father's body in inconsolable grief. Then a hubbub had begun, the *maréchaussée* had burst in, and Olivier had been hauled away to jail as the murderer of his master.

Then Madelon added the most touching description of her beloved Olivier's virtue, piety, and fidelity: how he had respected his master deeply, like his own father; how the older man had loved him in full measure in return, and had chosen him as a son-in-law despite his poverty, because his skill was equal to his fidelity and his noble mind. Madelon told all this in the most heartfelt manner, stating in conclusion that, even if Olivier had thrust the dagger into her father's breast in her presence, she would sooner have taken it to be an illusion of Satan's than have believed Olivier capable of such a terrible, grisly crime.

Mlle de Scudéry, deeply touched by Madelon's unspeakable sorrow, and fully inclined to consider Olivier innocent, made inquiries and found complete confirmation of all that Madelon had told her about the domestic relations between master and journeyman. The tenants and neighbors unanimously praised Olivier as the model of a well-behaved, pious, loyal, and diligent man; no one connected him with any wrongdoing; and yet, whenever the conversation turned to that awful deed, they all shrugged their shoulders and said that there was an incomprehensible mystery involved.

When Olivier was brought before the *chambre ardente,* he denied his guilt, as Mlle de Scudéry heard, with the greatest staunchness and the most open candor, claiming that his master had been attacked and stabbed in the street in his presence, but was still alive when he dragged him home, where he died very soon. This, too, agreed with Madelon's story.

Again and again Mlle de Scudéry asked to hear a repetition of the slightest details of the fearful occurrence. She made close inquiries as to whether there had ever been a quarrel between master and journeyman, whether Olivier wasn't completely free of that sudden anger which often assails the most good-natured people like a fit of unthinking madness, and seduces them into deeds that appear to cancel all the free will of their actions. But the more enthusiastically Madelon spoke of the calm domestic happiness in which those three people lived, joined in the warmest affection, the more every shadow of doubt disappeared concerning Olivier, who had been accused of that capital crime.

Genau alles prüfend, davon ausgehend, daß Olivier unerachtet alles dessen, was laut für seine Unschuld spräche, dennoch Cardillacs Mörder gewesen, fand die Scuderi im Reich der Möglichkeit keinen Beweggrund zu der entsetzlichen Tat, die in jedem Fall Oliviers Glück zerstören mußte. – «Er ist arm, aber geschickt. – Es gelingt ihm, die Zuneigung des berühmtesten Meisters zu gewinnen, er liebt die Tochter, der Meister begünstigt seine Liebe, Glück, Wohlstand für sein ganzes Leben wird ihm erschlossen! – Sei es aber nun, daß, Gott weiß, auf welche Weise gereizt, Olivier vom Zorn übermannt, seinen Wohltäter, seinen Vater mörderisch anfiel, welche teuflische Heuchelei gehört dazu, nach der Tat sich so zu betragen, als es wirklich geschah!» – Mit der festen Überzeugung von Oliviers Unschuld faßte die Scuderi den Entschluß, den unschuldigen Jüngling zu retten, koste es, was es wolle.

Es schien ihr, ehe sie die Huld des Königs selbst vielleicht anrufe, am geratensten, sich an den Präsidenten la Regnie zu wenden, ihn auf alle Umstände, die für Oliviers Unschuld sprechen mußten, aufmerksam zu machen und so vielleicht in des Präsidenten Seele eine innere, dem Angeklagten günstige Überzeugung zu erwecken, die sich wohltätig den Richtern mitteilen sollte.

La Regnie empfing die Scuderi mit der hohen Achtung, auf die die würdige Dame, von dem Könige selbst hoch geehrt, gerechten Anspruch machen konnte. Er hörte ruhig alles an, was sie über die entsetzliche Tat, über Oliviers Verhältnisse, über seinen Charakter vorbrachte. Ein feines, beinahe hämisches Lächeln war indessen alles, womit er bewies, daß die Beteuerungen, die von häufigen Tränen begleiteten Ermahnungen, wie jeder Richter nicht der Feind des Angeklagten sein, sondern auch auf alles achten müsse, was zu seinen Gunsten spräche, nicht an gänzlich tauben Ohren vorüberglitten. Als das Fräulein nun endlich ganz erschöpft, die Tränen von den Augen wegtrocknend, schwieg, fing la Regnie an:

«Es ist ganz Eures vortrefflichen Herzens würdig, mein Fräulein, daß Ihr, gerührt von den Tränen eines jungen, verliebten Mädchens, alles glaubt, was sie vorbringt, ja, daß Ihr nicht fähig seid, den Gedanken einer entsetzlichen Untat zu fassen; aber anders ist es mit dem Richter, der gewohnt ist, frecher Heuchelei die Larve abzureißen. Wohl mag es nicht meines Amts sein, jedem, der mich frägt, den Gang eines Kriminalprozesses zu entwickeln. Fräulein! ich tue meine Pflicht, wenig kümmert mich das Urteil der Welt. Zittern sollen die Bösewichter vor der Chambre ardente, die keine Strafe kennt als Blut und Feuer. Aber vor Euch, mein würdiges Fräulein, möcht ich nicht

As she weighed all the details, starting out from the premise that, despite everything that spoke loudly for his innocence, Olivier was Cardillac's murderer after all, Mlle de Scudéry found no motive within the realm of possibility for the horrible deed, which in any case had to destroy Olivier's happiness. "He's poor, but skilled. He succeeds in winning the affections of the most celebrated artisan; he loves his daughter; his master favors his love; happiness and lifelong prosperity await him! But if it's the case that Olivier, irritated only God knows how, and overcome by anger, attacked his benefactor, his father, with intent to kill, how diabolically hypocritical he would have to be to behave after the fact as he actually did!" Firmly convinced that Olivier was innocent, Mlle de Scudéry determined to save the guiltless young man at any cost.

Before perhaps appealing to the mercy of the king himself, it seemed most advisable to her to apply to chief judge La Reynie, to alert him to all the circumstances that had to proclaim Olivier's innocence, and thus perhaps arouse an inward conviction favorable to the accused in the judge's mind, which would communicate itself to the other judges in a beneficial way.

La Reynie received Mlle de Scudéry with the highest esteem, to which the worthy lady, highly honored by the king himself, could lay just claim. Calmly he listened to everything she stated about the horrible deed, about Olivier's situation in life, and about his character. A shrewd, almost spiteful smile was the only way in which he indicated that her asseverations, her admonitions, accompanied by frequent tears, to the effect that a judge shouldn't be the enemy of an accused man, but should pay attention to anything that spoke in his favor, hadn't fallen on totally deaf ears. When the lady, completely exhausted and wiping the tears from her eyes, finally ended, La Reynie began:

"It is altogether becoming to your excellent heart, my lady, that, touched by the tears of a young girl in love, you believe everything she tells you, and aren't even capable of comprehending the idea of a monstrous crime; but it isn't that way with a judge, who is accustomed to tear away the mask of insolent hypocrisy. It surely isn't part of my job to reveal the details of an ongoing criminal investigation to anyone who asks about it. Mademoiselle, I do my duty, and I don't care much about other people's opinion of me. Let the criminals tremble at the *chambre ardente,* which inflicts no penalty except blood and fire! But

für ein Ungeheuer gehalten werden an Härte und Grausamkeit,
darum vergönnt mir, daß ich Euch mit wenigen Worten die
Blutschuld des jungen Bösewichts, der, dem Himmel sei es gedankt!
der Rache verfallen ist, klar vor Augen lege. Euer scharfsinniger Geist
wird dann selbst die Gutmütigkeit verschmähen, die Euch Ehre
macht, mir aber gar nicht anstehen würde. – Also! – Am Morgen wird
René Cardillac durch einen Dolchstoß ermordet gefunden. Niemand
ist bei ihm, als sein Geselle Olivier Brusson und die Tochter. In
Oliviers Kammer, unter andern, findet man einen Dolch von frischem
Blute gefärbt, der genau in die Wunde paßt. ‹Cardillac ist›, spricht
Olivier, ‹in der Nacht vor meinen Augen niedergestoßen worden.› –
‹Man wollte ihn berauben?› ‹Das weiß ich nicht!› – ‹Du gingst mit ihm,
und es war dir nicht möglich, dem Mörder zu wehren? – ihn
festzuhalten? um Hilfe zu rufen?› ‹Fünfzehn, wohl zwanzig Schritte
vor mir ging der Meister, ich folgte ihm.› ‹Warum in aller Welt so entfernt?› – ‹Der Meister wollt es so.› ‹Was hatte überhaupt Meister
Cardillac so spät auf der Straße zu tun?› – ‹Das kann ich nicht sagen.›
‹Sonst ist er aber doch niemals nach neun Uhr abends aus dem Hause
gekommen?› – Hier stockt Olivier, er ist bestürzt, er seufzt, er
vergießt Tränen, er beteuert bei allem, was heilig, daß Cardillac wirklich in jener Nacht ausgegangen sei, und seinen Tod gefunden habe.
Nun merkt aber wohl auf, mein Fräulein. Erwiesen ist es bis zur voll-
kommensten Gewißheit, daß Cardillac in jener Nacht das Haus nicht
verließ, mithin ist Oliviers Behauptung, er sei mit ihm wirklich ausgegangen, eine freche Lüge. Die Haustüre ist mit einem schweren
Schloß versehen, welches bei dem Auf- und Zuschließen ein durch-
dringendes Geräusch macht, dann aber bewegt sich der Türflügel,
widrig knarrend und heulend, in den Angeln, so daß, wie es
angestellte Versuche bewährt haben, selbst im obersten Stock des
Hauses das Getöse widerhallt. Nun wohnt in dem untersten Stock,
also dicht neben der Haustüre, der alte Meister Claude Patru mit
seiner Aufwärterin, einer Person von beinahe achtzig Jahren, aber
noch munter und rührig. Diese beiden Personen hörten, wie
Cardillac nach seiner gewöhnlichen Weise an jenem Abend Punkt
neun Uhr die Treppe hinabkam, die Türe mit vielem Geräusch verschloß und verrammelte, dann wieder hinaufstieg, den Abendsegen
laut las und dann, wie man es an dem Zuschlagen der Türe
vernehmen konnte, in sein Schlafzimmer ging. Meister Claude leidet
an Schlaflosigkeit, wie es alten Leuten wohl zu gehen pflegt. Auch in
jener Nacht konnte er kein Auge zutun. Die Aufwärterin schlug
daher, es mochte halb zehn Uhr sein, in der Küche, in die sie, über

in your eyes, my worthy lady, I don't wish to be considered a
monster of severity and cruelty, and so allow me to present to
you clearly and concisely the guilt of the young criminal who
has fallen prey to our vengeance, heaven be praised! Then your
penetrating mind will of its own accord disdain that kindliness
which does you honor but would be quite out of place in my position. Well, then! In the morning René Cardillac is found
stabbed to death. No one is with him except his journeyman
Olivier Brusson and his daughter. In Olivier's room, among
other things, we find a dagger, stained with freshly shed blood,
which fits the wound exactly. 'Cardillac,' says Olivier, 'was
stabbed right before my eyes last night.' 'Was someone trying to
rob him?' 'I don't know!' 'You were walking with him, and you
were unable to ward off the killer, hold onto him, or call for
help?' 'My master was walking fifteen, maybe twenty paces
ahead of me, and I was following him.' 'Why in God's name
were you so far away?' 'My master wanted it that way.' 'What
was Master Cardillac doing in the street that late in the first
place?' 'I couldn't say.' 'And yet, before that, he never left his
house at night after nine?' At that point Olivier faltered; he was
confused, he sighed, he shed tears, he swore by all that's holy
that Cardillac really did go out that night and met with his
death. Now pay close attention, mademoiselle! It has been
proved to the greatest degree of certainty that Cardillac did not
leave his house that night, and so Olivier's claim to have really
gone out with him is an insolent lie. The front door is provided
with a heavy lock, which makes a piercing noise when opened
and closed; and then the door makes a repellent, wailing sound
on its hinges when it opens, so that, as tests we've made have
proved, the noise echoes even through the highest story of the
house. Now, on the lowest floor, and so, right next to the front
door, lives old Master Claude Patru with his attendant, a
woman of almost eighty but still alert and nimble. These two
people heard Cardillac come downstairs that evening at exactly
nine, as his custom was, lock and bar the door with a lot of
noise, then go back upstairs, read evening prayers aloud, and
then, as they could tell by the slamming of the door, enter his
bedroom. Master Claude suffers from insomnia, as many elderly people do. That night, too, he was unable to close an eye.
Therefore, about nine-thirty his attendant crossed the vestibule
into the kitchen, lit a candle there, and sat down at the table

den Hausflur gehend, gelangt, Licht an und setzte sich zum Meister Claude an den Tisch mit einer alten Chronik, in der sie las, während der Alte, seinen Gedanken nachhängend, bald sich in den Lehnstuhl setzte, bald wieder aufstand und, um Müdigkeit und Schlaf zu gewinnen, im Zimmer leise und langsam auf und ab schritt. Es blieb alles still und ruhig bis nach Mitternacht. Da hörte sie über sich scharfe Tritte, einen harten Fall, als stürze eine schwere Last zu Boden und gleich darauf ein dumpfes Stöhnen. In beide kam eine seltsame Angst und Beklommenheit. Die Schauer der entsetzlichen Tat, die eben begangen, gingen bei ihnen vorüber. – Mit dem hellen Morgen trat dann ans Licht, was in der Finsternis begonnen.»

«Aber», fiel die Scuderi ein, «aber um aller Heiligen willen, könnt Ihr bei allen Umständen, die ich erst weitläufig erzählte, Euch denn irgendeinen Anlaß zu dieser Tat der Hölle denken?»

«Hm», erwiderte la Regnie, «Cardillac war nicht arm – im Besitz vortrefflicher Steine.»

«Bekam», fuhr die Scuderi fort, «bekam denn nicht alles die Tochter? – Ihr vergeßt, daß Olivier Cardillacs Schwiegersohn werden sollte.»

«Er mußte vielleicht teilen oder gar nur für andere morden», sprach la Regnie.

«Teilen, für andere morden?» fragte die Scuderi in vollem Erstaunen.

«Wißt», fuhr der Präsident fort, «wißt, mein Fräulein, daß Olivier schon längst geblutet hätte auf dem Greveplatz, stünde seine Tat nicht in Beziehung mit dem dicht verschleierten Geheimnis, das bisher so bedrohlich über ganz Paris waltete. Olivier gehört offenbar zu jener verruchten Bande, die, alle Aufmerksamkeit, alle Mühe, alles Forschen der Gerichtshöfe verspottend, ihre Streiche sicher und ungestraft zu führen wußte. Durch ihn wird – muß alles klar werden. Die Wunde Cardillacs ist denen ganz ähnlich, die alle auf der Straße, in den Häusern Ermordete und Beraubte trugen. Dann aber das Entscheidendste, seit der Zeit, daß Olivier Brusson verhaftet ist, haben alle Mordtaten, alle Beraubungen aufgehört. Sicher sind die Straßen zur Nachtzeit wie am Tage. Beweis genug, daß Olivier vielleicht an der Spitze jener Mordbande stand. Noch will er nicht bekennen, aber es gibt Mittel, ihn sprechen zu machen wider seinen Willen.»

«Und Madelon», rief die Scuderi, «und Madelon, die treue, unschuldige Taube.»

«Ei», sprach la Regnie mit einem giftigen Lächeln, «ei, wer steht

beside Master Claude with an old chronicle from which she read while the old man, lost in thought, at times sat down in an easy chair, at times stood up again and, in order to get tired and sleepy, paced back and forth in the room quietly and slowly. Everything remained silent and calm until after midnight. Then they heard rapid steps overhead, a loud thud, as if a heavy object had fallen on the floor, and, immediately afterward, a low groaning. Both of them were seized by a strange fear and anguish. The horror of the awful deed that had just been committed communicated itself to them. With broad daylight, that which was undertaken in darkness came to light."

"But," Mlle de Scudéry interrupted, "but, by all the saints, in view of all the circumstances I have just stated in great detail, can you imagine any motive for such an infernal deed?"

"Hm," La Reynie replied, "Cardillac wasn't poor, but in the possession of excellent gems."

Mlle de Scudéry continued: "But wasn't everything left to his daughter? You're forgetting that Olivier was to become Cardillac's son-in-law."

"Maybe he had to share in the loot, or even do the killing altogether for the sake of others," La Reynie said.

"Share? Kill for others?" asked Mlle de Scudéry, completely astonished.

"I'll have you know, my lady," the chief judge went on, "that Olivier would have been executed on the Place de Grève long before now if his deed hadn't been connected with the closely veiled mystery that has reigned until today as a threat to all of Paris. Olivier obviously belongs to that wicked gang which, scorning all the alertness, efforts, and searches of the courts, have been able to carry out their operations in safety and with impunity. Through him everything will—must—become clear. Cardillac's wound is just like those borne by all the people killed and robbed on the street or in houses. But what is most conclusive: since Olivier Brusson was arrested, all the murders and robberies have ceased. The streets are as safe by night as by day: proof enough that Olivier may have been the leader of that murderous gang. He still refuses to confess, but there are ways to make him talk against his will."

"And Madelon," Mlle de Scudéry exclaimed, "Madelon, the faithful, innocent dove?"

"Well," said La Reynie with a poisonous smile, "well, who'll

mir dafür, daß sie nicht mit im Komplott ist. Was ist ihr an dem Vater gelegen, nur dem Mordbuben gelten ihre Tränen.»

«Was sagt Ihr», schrie die Scuderi, «es ist nicht möglich; den Vater! dieses Mädchen!»

«O!» fuhr la Regnie fort, «o! denkt doch nur an die Brinvillier! Ihr möget es mir verzeihen, wenn ich mich vielleicht bald genötigt sehe, Euch Euern Schützling zu entreißen und in die Conciergerie werfen zu lassen.»

Der Scuderi ging ein Grausen an bei diesem entsetzlichen Verdacht. Es war ihr, als könne vor diesem schrecklichen Manne keine Treue, keine Tugend bestehen, als spähe er in den tiefsten, geheimsten Gedanken Mord und Blutschuld. Sie stand auf. «Seid menschlich», das war alles, was sie beklommen, mühsam atmend hervorbringen konnte. Schon im Begriff, die Treppe hinabzusteigen, bis zu der der Präsident sie mit zeremoniöser Artigkeit begleitet hatte, kam ihr, selbst wußte sie nicht wie, ein seltsamer Gedanke. «Würd es mir wohl erlaubt sein, den unglücklichen Olivier Brusson zu sehen?» So fragte sie den Präsidenten, sich rasch umwendend.

Dieser schaute sie mit bedenklicher Miene an, dann verzog sich sein Gesicht in jenes widrige Lächeln, das ihm eigen. «Gewiß», sprach er, «gewiß wollt Ihr nun, mein würdiges Fräulein, Euerm Gefühl, der innern Stimme mehr vertrauend, als dem, was vor unsern Augen geschehen, selbst Oliviers Schuld oder Unschuld prüfen. Scheut Ihr nicht den düstern Aufenthalt des Verbrechens, ist es Euch nicht gehässig, die Bilder der Verworfenheit in allen Abstufungen zu sehen, so sollen für Euch in zwei Stunden die Tore der Conciergerie offen sein. Man wird Euch diesen Olivier, dessen Schicksal Eure Teilnahme erregt, vorstellen.»

In der Tat konnte sich die Scuderi von der Schuld des jungen Menschen nicht überzeugen. Alles sprach wider ihn, ja, kein Richter in der Welt hätte anders gehandelt wie la Regnie bei solch entscheidenden Tatsachen. Aber das Bild häuslichen Glücks, wie es Madelon mit den lebendigsten Zügen der Scuderi vor Augen gestellt, überstrahlte jeden bösen Verdacht, und so mochte sie lieber ein unerklärliches Geheimnis annehmen, als daran glauben, wogegen ihr ganzes Inneres sich empörte.

Sie gedachte, sich von Olivier noch einmal alles, wie es sich in jener verhängnisvollen Nacht begeben, erzählen zu lassen und soviel möglich in ein Geheimnis zu dringen, das vielleicht den Richtern verschlossen geblieben, weil es wertlos schien, sich weiter darum zu bekümmern.

vouch to me that she isn't in on the plot? What did she care about her father? Her tears are only for the killer."

"What are you saying?" Mlle de Scudéry cried. "It isn't possible! Her father! That girl!"

"Oh," La Reynie continued, "oh, just think about Mme de Brinvilliers! You must forgive me if I soon find myself compelled to tear your protégée from you and have her thrown into the Conciergerie."

When she heard that horrible suspicion, Mlle de Scudéry shuddered. She felt as if no loyalty, no virtue meant anything to this frightening man, as if he read murder and bloody guilt in one's deepest, most secret thoughts. She stood up. "Be humane," was all that she could say, she was so oppressed, breathing with difficulty. Already on the point of descending the stairs, to which the chief judge had escorted her with ceremonious politeness, a strange thought occurred to her, she herself didn't know how. "Would I be permitted to see the unfortunate Olivier Brusson?" she asked the chief judge, turning around brusquely.

He gazed at her with a dubious expression, then his face was distorted into that abhorrent smile which was characteristic of him. "Surely," he said, "surely you now wish to test Olivier's guilt or innocence yourself, my worthy lady, putting greater trust in your emotions and your inner voice than in what occurred before our very eyes. If you have no fear of that dismal abode of crime, if you don't loathe to look upon the images of depravity in all its gradations, the gates of the Conciergerie will be open to you in two hours. You will meet this Olivier, whose fate arouses your sympathy."

Indeed, Mlle de Scudéry couldn't be convinced that the young man was guilty. Everything spoke against him, and surely no judge in the world would have acted differently from La Reynie in the face of such conclusive facts. But the picture of domestic happiness that Madelon had painted to Mlle de Scudéry's view in the liveliest brushstrokes outshone all suspicions of evil, and so she preferred to accept the presence of an insoluble mystery rather than believe something her whole being rebelled against.

She intended to hear again from Olivier everything that had happened on that fateful night, and thus penetrate as far as possible a secret that might have remained hidden to the judges because they had considered it pointless to concern themselves with it further.

In der Conciergerie angekommen, führte man die Scuderi in ein großes, helles Gemach. Nicht lange darauf vernahm sie Kettengerassel. Olivier Brusson wurde gebracht. Doch sowie er in die Türe trat, sank auch die Scuderi ohnmächtig nieder. Als sie sich erholt hatte, war Olivier verschwunden. Sie verlangte mit Heftigkeit, daß man sie nach dem Wagen bringe, fort, augenblicklich fort wollte sie aus den Gemächern der frevelnden Verruchtheit. Ach! – auf den ersten Blick hatte sie in Olivier Brusson den jungen Menschen erkannt, der auf dem Pontneuf jenes Blatt ihr in den Wagen geworfen, der ihr das Kästchen mit den Juwelen gebracht hatte.

Nun war ja jeder Zweifel gehoben, la Regnies schreckliche Vermutung ganz bestätigt. Olivier Brusson gehört zu der fürchterlichen Mordbande, gewiß ermordete er auch den Meister! – Und Madelon? – So bitter noch nie vom innern Gefühl getäuscht, auf den Tod angepackt von der höllischen Macht auf Erden, an deren Dasein sie nicht geglaubt, verzweifelte die Scuderi an aller Wahrheit. Sie gab Raum dem entsetzlichen Verdacht, daß Madelon mitverschworen sein und teilhaben könne an der gräßlichen Blutschuld.

Wie es denn geschieht, daß der menschliche Geist, ist ihm ein Bild aufgegangen, emsig Farben sucht und findet, es greller und greller auszumalen, so fand auch die Scuderi, jeden Umstand der Tat, Madelons Betragen in den kleinsten Zügen erwägend, gar vieles, jenen Verdacht zu nähren. So wurde manches, was ihr bisher als Beweis der Unschuld und Reinheit gegolten, sicheres Merkmal freveliger Bosheit, studierter Heuchelei. Jener herzzerreißende Jammer, die blutigen Tränen konnten wohl erpreßt sein von der Todesangst, nicht den Geliebten bluten zu sehen, nein – selbst zu fallen unter der Hand des Henkers.

Gleich sich die Schlange, die sie im Busen nähre, vom Halse zu schaffen; mit diesem Entschluß stieg die Scuderi aus dem Wagen. In ihr Gemach eingetreten, warf Madelon sich ihr zu Füßen. Die Himmelsaugen, ein Engel Gottes hat sie nicht treuer, zu ihr emporgerichtet, die Hände vor der wallenden Brust zusammengefaltet, jammerte und flehte sie laut um Hilfe und Trost. Die Scuderi, sich mühsam zusammenfassend, sprach, indem sie dem Ton ihrer Stimme so viel Ernst und Ruhe zu geben suchte, als ihr möglich: «Geh – geh – tröste dich nur über den Mörder, den die gerechte Strafe seiner Schandtaten erwartet. – Die heilige Jungfrau möge verhüten, daß nicht auf dir selbst eine Blutschuld schwer laste.»

After Mlle de Scudéry arrived in the Conciergerie, she was led to a large, bright room. Shortly thereafter she heard the rattling of chains. Olivier Brusson was being brought in. But the moment he appeared in the doorway, Mlle de Scudéry fell down in a faint. When she came to, Olivier was gone. She made an urgent request to be taken to her coach; away, she wanted to get away at once from that abode of wicked criminals! Alas, at first glance she had recognized Olivier Brusson as the young man who had tossed that note into her coach on the Pont Neuf, and who had brought her the box of jewels.

Now there was no more room for doubt; La Reynie's terrible assumption was fully confirmed. Olivier Brusson belonged to that frightful gang of murderers, surely he had also killed his master! And Madelon? Never yet so bitterly betrayed by her innermost feelings, in the fatal grip of hell's power on earth, the existence of which she hadn't believed in, Mlle de Scudéry despaired of finding any truth. She allowed herself the awful suspicion that Madelon might be a conspirator and participant in that gruesome homicide.

Just as the human mind, when presented with an image, is accustomed to seek diligently until it finds more and more lurid colors with which to deck it out, so Mlle de Scudéry, too, weighing every circumstance of the deed and Madelon's behavior in the greatest detail, found a great deal to nourish that suspicion. And so, many elements that she had taken hitherto as proof of her innocence and purity now became the sure sign of criminal malice and studied hypocrisy. That heartrending sorrow, those tears of blood could have been forced from her by her deathly fear—not of seeing her lover executed, no, but of falling into the hangman's hands herself.

She must immediately rid herself of the serpent she was nurturing in her bosom! With that determination Mlle de Scudéry descended from her coach. When she entered her room, Madelon threw herself at her feet. Her heavenly eyes (an angel of God doesn't have truer ones) lifted toward the lady, her hands clasped over her heaving breast, she lamented and wept loudly for aid and comfort. Mlle de Scudéry, composing herself with difficulty, and trying to lend her voice as much gravity and calmness as possible, said: "Go! Go! Console yourself about the murderer, whom the just punishment of his shameful deeds awaits. May the Holy Virgin forbid that a blood guilt should weigh heavily upon you as well!"

«Ach, nun ist alles verloren!» – Mit diesem gellenden Ausruf stürzte Madelon ohnmächtig zu Boden. Die Scuderi überließ die Sorge um das Mädchen der Martiniere und entfernte sich in ein anderes Gemach. –

Ganz zerrissen im Innern, entzweit mit allem Irdischen, wünschte die Scuderi, nicht mehr in einer Welt voll höllischen Truges zu leben. Sie klagte das Verhängnis an, das in bitterm Hohn ihr so viele Jahre vergönnt, ihren Glauben an Tugend und Treue zu stärken, und nun in ihrem Alter das schöne Bild vernichte, welches ihr im Leben geleuchtet.

Sie vernahm, wie die Martiniere Madelon fortbrachte, die leise seufzte und jammerte: «Ach! – auch *sie* – auch *sie* haben die Grausamen betört. – Ich Elende, – armer, unglücklicher Olivier!» – Die Töne drangen der Scuderi ins Herz, und aufs neue regte sich aus dem tiefsten Innern heraus die Ahnung eines Geheimnisses, der Glaube an Oliviers Unschuld. Bedrängt von den widersprechendsten Gefühlen, ganz außer sich rief die Scuderi: «Welcher Geist der Hölle hat mich in die entsetzliche Geschichte verwickelt, die mir das Leben kosten wird!»

In dem Augenblick trat Baptiste hinein, bleich und erschrocken, mit der Nachricht, daß Desgrais draußen sei. Seit dem abscheulichen Prozeß der la Voisin war Desgrais' Erscheinung in einem Hause der gewisse Vorbote irgendeiner peinlichen Anklage, daher kam Baptistes Schreck, deshalb fragte ihn das Fräulein mit mildem Lächeln: «Was ist dir, Baptiste? – Nicht wahr! – der Name Scuderi befand sich auf der Liste der la Voisin?»

«Ach, um Christus' willen», erwiderte Baptiste, am ganzen Leibe zitternd, «wie möget Ihr nur so etwas aussprechen, aber Desgrais – der entsetzliche Desgrais, tut so geheimnisvoll, so dringend, er scheint es gar nicht erwarten zu können, Euch zu sehen!»

«Nun», sprach die Scuderi, «nun, Baptiste, so führt ihn nur gleich herein, den Menschen, der Euch so fürchterlich ist und der *mir* wenigstens keine Besorgnis erregen kann.»

«Der Präsident», sprach Desgrais, als er ins Gemach getreten, «der Präsident la Regnie schickt mich zu Euch, mein Fräulein, mit einer Bitte, auf deren Erfüllung er gar nicht hoffen würde, kennte er nicht Eure Tugend, Euern Mut, läge nicht das letzte Mittel, eine böse Blutschuld an den Tag zu bringen, in Euern Händen, hättet Ihr nicht selbst schon teilgenommen an dem bösen Prozeß, der die Chambre ardente, uns alle in Atem hält. Olivier Brusson, seitdem er Euch gesehen hat, ist halb rasend. So sehr er schon zum Bekenntnis sich zu

"Ah, now all is lost!" With that shrill cry Madelon fell to the floor in a faint. Mlle de Scudéry let Martinière take care of the girl, while she herself went to another room.

Her mind at war with itself, estranged from all earthly doings, Mlle de Scudéry wished she might no longer live in this world full of infernal deception. She accused that destiny which, with bitter mockery, had granted her so many years in which to strengthen her belief in virtue and loyalty, and now in her old age was destroying the beautiful image that had brightened her life.

She heard Martinière leading away Madelon, who was softly sighing and lamenting: "Alas! Those cruel men have misled her, too—her, too. How wretched I am! Poor, unhappy Olivier!" Her tones pierced Mlle de Scudéry's heart, and once again there stirred deep in her mind the premonition of some mystery and the belief in Olivier's innocence. Oppressed by the most contradictory emotions, and quite beside herself, Mlle de Scudéry exclaimed: "What demon from hell has entangled me in this horrible affair, which will cost me my life?"

At that moment Baptiste came in, pale and frightened, with the news that Desgrais was just outside the door. Ever since the Voisin woman's abhorrent trial, Desgrais's appearance at a house had been the sure harbinger of some serious accusation; hence Baptiste's terror; and so his lady asked him with a gentle smile: "What's wrong with you, Baptiste? The name of Scudéry was on Voisin's list, right?"

"Oh, in the name of Christ," Baptiste replied, trembling all over, "how can you even say such a thing? But Desgrais, that terrible Desgrais, is acting so mysteriously and asking for you so urgently! He looks as if he just can't wait to see you!"

"Well," said Mlle de Scudéry, "well, Baptiste, show him right in then, that man who frightens you so, but can't arouse any worries in me, at least."

"Chief judge La Reynie," said Desgrais after entering the room, "has sent me to you, my lady, with a request he wouldn't hope to see granted, if he didn't know your virtue and courage, if the last means of disclosing an evil homicide didn't lie in your hands, if you yourself hadn't already participated in that criminal investigation which is keeping the *chambre ardente* and all of us in suspense. Since Olivier Brusson saw you, he's been half-crazy. As close as he seemed to confessing before that, now he

neigen schien, so schwört er doch jetzt aufs neue bei Christus und allen Heiligen, daß er an dem Morde Cardillacs ganz unschuldig sei, wiewohl er den Tod gern leiden wolle, den er verdient habe. Bemerkt, mein Fräulein, daß der letzte Zusatz offenbar auf andere Verbrechen deutet, die auf ihm lasten. Doch vergebens ist alle Mühe, nur ein Wort weiter herauszubringen, selbst die Drohung mit der Tortur hat nichts gefruchtet. Er fleht, er beschwört uns, ihm eine Unterredung mit Euch zu verschaffen, *Euch* nur, *Euch* allein will er alles gestehen. Laßt Euch herab, mein Fräulein, Brussons Bekenntnis zu hören.»

«Wie!» rief die Scuderi ganz entrüstet, «soll ich dem Blutgericht zum Organ dienen, soll ich das Vertrauen des unglücklichen Menschen mißbrauchen, ihn aufs Blutgerüst zu bringen? – Nein, Desgrais! mag Brusson auch ein verruchter Mörder sein, nie wär es mir doch möglich, ihn so spitzbübisch zu hintergehen. Nichts mag ich von seinen Geheimnissen erfahren, die wie eine heilige Beichte in meiner Brust verschlossen bleiben würden.»

«Vielleicht», versetzte Desgrais mit einem feinen Lächeln, «vielleicht, mein Fräulein, ändert sich Eure Gesinnung, wenn Ihr Brusson gehört habt. Batet Ihr den Präsident nicht selbst, er solle menschlich sein? Er tut es, indem er dem törichten Verlangen Brussons nachgibt und so das letzte Mittel versucht, ehe er die Tortur verhängt, zu der Brusson längst reif ist.»

Die Scuderi schrak unwillkürlich zusammen. «Seht», fuhr Desgrais fort, «seht, würdige Dame, man wird Euch keineswegs zumuten, noch einmal in jene finsteren Gemächer zu treten, die Euch mit Grausen und Abscheu erfüllen. In der Stille der Nacht, ohne alles Aufsehen bringt man Olivier Brusson wie einen freien Menschen zu Euch in Euer Haus. Nicht einmal belauscht, doch wohl bewacht, mag er Euch dann zwanglos alles bekennen. Daß Ihr für Euch selbst nichts von dem Elenden zu fürchten habt, dafür stehe ich Euch mit meinem Leben ein. Er spricht von Euch mit inbrünstiger Verehrung. Er schwört, daß nur das düstre Verhängnis, welches ihm verwehrt habe, Euch früher zu sehen, ihn in den Tod gestürzt. Und dann steht es ja bei Euch, von dem, was Euch Brusson entdeckt, so viel zu sagen, als Euch beliebt. Kann man Euch zu mehrerem zwingen?»

Die Scuderi sah tief sinnend vor sich nieder. Es war ihr, als müsse sie der höheren Macht gehorchen, die den Aufschluß irgendeines entsetzlichen Geheimnisses von ihr verlange, als könne sie sich nicht mehr den wunderbaren Verschlingungen entziehen, in die sie willenlos geraten. Plötzlich entschlossen, sprach sie mit Würde: «Gott wird

once again swears by Christ and all the saints that he's completely innocent of the murder of Cardillac, although he'd gladly suffer the death that he does deserve. Observe, my lady, that this last addendum obviously refers to other crimes that are on his conscience. But all our efforts to get one word more out of him are in vain; even the threat of torture was totally fruitless. He beseeches and implores us to arrange an interview with you; only to you, to you alone, is he willing to confess everything. Condescend, my lady, to hear Brusson's confession."

"What!" Mlle de Scudéry exclaimed in great indignation. "I am to be a tool of the bloody assizes? I am to abuse the confidence of that unfortunate man, in order to lead him to the scaffold? No, Desgrais, even if Brusson is a wicked killer, I would never be able to deceive him so criminally. I don't want to learn any of his secrets, which would remain locked in my heart like a holy Church confession!"

"Perhaps," Desgrais replied with a subtle smile, "perhaps, my lady, you'll change your mind after listening to Brusson. Didn't you yourself ask the chief judge to be humane? He's obeying you by yielding to Brusson's foolish request and trying the last remaining recourse before ordering torture, which Brusson should have undergone long ago."

Mlle de Scudéry involuntarily started. "Look," Desgrais continued, "look, worthy lady, we don't at all expect you to set foot again in those dark rooms which fill you with horror and repulsion. In the still of the night, without attracting any attention, we'll bring Olivier Brusson to you in your house as a free man. Without our listening in, though we *will* stand guard, he can then make a full confession to you without constraint. I guarantee with my life that you will have nothing to fear personally from that wretch. He speaks of you with ardent reverence. He swears that it was only the dismal fate which prevented him from seeing you earlier that plunged him into his death. Afterwards, it will be left to you to report just as much as you like of what Brusson reveals to you. Can you be forced to do more?"

Mlle de Scudéry looked down at the floor, lost in thought. She felt she had to obey the higher power that was commanding her to clear up some terrible mystery; she felt as if she could no longer escape from the remarkable snare into which she had fallen through no doing of her own. With sudden determination

mir Fassung und Standhaftigkeit geben; führt den Brusson her, ich will ihn sprechen.»

So wie damals, als Brusson das Kästchen brachte, wurde um Mitternacht an die Haustüre der Scuderi gepocht. Baptiste, von dem nächtlichen Besuch unterrichtet, öffnete. Eiskalter Schauer überlief die Scuderi, als sie an den leisen Tritten, an dem dumpfen Gemurmel wahrnahm, daß die Wächter, die den Brusson gebracht, sich in den Gängen des Hauses verteilten.

Endlich ging leise die Türe des Gemachs auf. Desgrais trat herein, hinter ihm Olivier Brusson, fesselfrei, in anständigen Kleidern. «Hier ist», sprach Desgrais, sich ehrerbietig verneigend, «hier ist Brusson, mein würdiges Fräulein!» und verließ das Zimmer.

Brusson sank vor der Scuderi nieder auf beide Knie, flehend erhob er die gefalteten Hände, indem häufige Tränen ihm aus den Augen rannen.

Die Scuderi schaute erblaßt, keines Wortes mächtig, auf ihn herab. Selbst bei den entstellten, ja durch Gram, durch grimmen Schmerz verzerrten Zügen strahlte der reine Ausdruck des treusten Gemüts aus dem Jünglingsantlitz. Je länger die Scuderi ihre Augen auf Brussons Gesicht ruhen ließ, desto lebhafter trat die Erinnerung an irgendeine geliebte Person hervor, auf die sie sich nur nicht deutlich zu besinnen vermochte. Alle Schauer wichen von ihr, sie vergaß, daß Cardillacs Mörder vor ihr kniee, sie sprach mit dem anmutigen Tone des ruhigen Wohlwollens, der ihr eigen: «Nun, Brusson, was habt Ihr mir zu sagen?»

Dieser, noch immer kniend, seufzte auf vor tiefer, inbrünstiger Wehmut und sprach dann: «O mein würdiges, mein hochverehrtes Fräulein, ist denn jede Spur der Erinnerung an mich verflogen?»

Die Scuderi, ihn noch aufmerksamer betrachtend, erwiderte, daß sie allerdings in seinen Zügen die Ähnlichkeit mit einer von ihr geliebten Person gefunden, und daß er nur dieser Ähnlichkeit es verdanke, wenn sie den tiefen Abscheu vor dem Mörder überwinde und ihn ruhig anhöre.

Brusson, schwer verletzt durch diese Worte, erhob sich schnell und trat, den finstern Blick zu Boden gesenkt, einen Schritt zurück. Dann sprach er mit dumpfer Stimme: «Habt Ihr denn Anne Guiot ganz vergessen? – ihr Sohn Olivier – der Knabe, den Ihr oft auf Euern Knien schaukeltet, ist es, der vor Euch steht.»

«O um aller Heiligen willen!» rief die Scuderi, indem sie, mit beiden Händen das Gesicht bedeckend, in die Polster zurücksank. Das Fräulein hatte wohl Ursache genug, sich auf diese Weise zu entsetzen.

she said, in a dignified tone: "God will grant me composure and steadfastness; bring Brusson here, and I'll speak with him."

As on the night when Brusson delivered the box, it was around midnight when there came a knocking at Mlle de Scudéry's front door. Baptiste, who had been informed about the nocturnal visit, opened it. Mlle de Scudéry was chilled to the bone when quiet steps and a low murmur told her that the guards who had brought Brusson had taken up positions in every corridor of the house.

Finally the door to the room opened quietly. In walked Desgrais, and behind him Olivier Brusson, liberated from his shackles and wearing respectable clothes. "Here," said Desgrais, bowing deferentially, "here is Brusson, my worthy lady!" Then he left the room.

Brusson fell on both knees in front of Mlle de Scudéry; he held up his clasped hands in supplication, while frequent tears flowed from his eyes.

Mlle de Scudéry, pale, unable to speak, looked down at him. Even though his features were distorted, even twisted, by sorrow and cruel pain, the pure expression of a most loyal nature beamed from the young man's face. The longer Mlle de Scudéry let her eyes rest on Brusson's face, the livelier became her recollection of some well-loved person, whom she just couldn't call to mind distinctly. Her shuddering ceased; she forgot that it was the murderer of Cardillac kneeling before her; and, with the gracious tone of calm benevolence that was natural to her, she said: "Well, Brusson, what have you got to tell me?"

He, still kneeling, heaved a sigh of deep, ardent melancholy, and then said: "Oh, my worthy, deeply revered lady, has every trace of your recollection of me really vanished?"

Mlle de Scudéry, observing him even more attentively, replied that she *had* found in his features a resemblance to a person she had loved, and that it was only thanks to that resemblance that she was overcoming her profound abhorrence of a murderer and listening to him calmly.

Brusson, deeply hurt by those words, stood up quickly and, his gloomy gaze directed at the floor, moved back one pace. Then he said in a hollow voice: "So you've forgotten Anne Guiot entirely? Her son Olivier, the boy you often cradled on your knees, is the man standing before you."

"Oh, by all the saints!" Mlle de Scudéry cried as she sank back into the cushions with her hands over her face. The lady had sufficient reason for that dismay. Anne Guiot, the daughter of an

Anne Guiot, die Tochter eines verarmten Bürgers, war von klein auf bei der Scuderi, die sie, wie die Mutter das liebe Kind, erzog mit aller Treue und Sorgfalt. Als sie nun herangewachsen, fand sich ein hübscher sittiger Jüngling, Claude Brusson geheißen, ein, der um das Mädchen warb. Da er nun ein grundgeschickter Uhrmacher war, der sein reichliches Brot in Paris finden mußte, Anne ihn auch herzlich liebgewonnen hatte, so trug die Scuderi gar kein Bedenken, in die Heirat ihrer Pflegetochter zu willigen. Die jungen Leute richteten sich ein, lebten in stiller, glücklicher Häuslichkeit, und was den Liebesbund noch fester knüpfte, war die Geburt eines wunderschönen Knaben, der holden Mutter treues Ebenbild.

Einen Abgott machte die Scuderi aus dem kleinen Olivier, den sie stunden-, tagelang der Mutter entriß, um ihn zu liebkosen, zu hätscheln. Daher kam es, daß der Junge sich ganz an sie gewöhnte und ebenso gern bei ihr war als bei der Mutter. Drei Jahre waren vorüber, als der Brotneid der Kunstgenossen Brussons es dahin brachte, daß seine Arbeit mit jedem Tage abnahm, so daß er zuletzt kaum sich kümmerlich ernähren konnte. Dazu kam die Sehnsucht nach seinem schönen heimatlichen Genf, und so geschah es, daß die kleine Familie dorthin zog, des Widerstrebens der Scuderi, die alle nur mögliche Unterstützung versprach, unerachtet. Noch ein paarmal schrieb Anne an ihre Pflegemutter, dann schwieg sie, und diese mußte glauben, daß das glückliche Leben in Brussons Heimat das Andenken an die früher verlebten Tage nicht mehr aufkommen lasse.

Es waren jetzt gerade dreiundzwanzig Jahre her, als Brusson mit seinem Weibe und Kinde Paris verlassen und nach Genf gezogen.

«O entsetzlich», rief die Scuderi, als sie sich einigermaßen wieder erholt hatte, «o entsetzlich! – Olivier bist du? – der Sohn meiner Anne! – Und jetzt!»

«Wohl», versetzte Olivier ruhig und gefaßt, «wohl, mein würdiges Fräulein, hättet Ihr nimmermehr ahnen können, daß der Knabe, den Ihr wie die zärtlichste Mutter hätscheltet, dem Ihr, auf Euerm Schoß ihn schaukelnd, Näscherei auf Näscherei in den Mund stecktet, dem Ihr die süßesten Namen gabt, zum Jünglinge gereift, dereinst vor Euch stehen würde, gräßlicher Blutschuld angeklagt! – Ich bin nicht vorwurfsfrei, die Chambre ardente kann mich mit Recht eines Verbrechens zeihen; aber, so wahr ich selig zu sterben hoffe, sei es auch durch des Henkers Hand, rein bin ich von jeder Blutschuld, nicht durch mich, nicht durch mein Verschulden fiel der unglückliche Cardillac!» – Olivier geriet bei diesen Worten in ein Zittern und

impoverished bourgeois, had lived since childhood with Mlle de Scudéry, who raised her faithfully and tenderly, as a mother raises a beloved child. When she had grown up, a handsome, well-mannered young man named Claude Brusson had appeared on the scene and had courted the girl. Since he was a highly skilled watchmaker who was bound to make a good living in Paris, and Anne had fallen deeply in love with him as well, Mlle de Scudéry had had no qualms about consenting to her foster daughter's marriage. The young couple set up housekeeping, and lived in quiet, happy domesticity, and their loving bond was made even firmer by the birth of a remarkably handsome boy, the very image of his lovely mother.

Mlle de Scudéry idolized little Olivier, whom she stole from his mother for hours and days at a time to caress and pamper him. And so the boy became completely accustomed to her and enjoyed her company as much as his mother's. After three years passed by, the professional jealousy of Brusson's colleagues caused his custom to diminish daily, so that finally he was barely able to earn a meager living. Besides, he was homesick for his beautiful native Geneva, and so it came about that the little family moved there, despite the resistance of Mlle de Scudéry, who promised them all possible support. Anne wrote to her foster mother a few times, then fell silent, and the older woman was compelled to believe that their happy life in Brusson's native city had extinguished the remembrance of earlier days.

It was now exactly twenty-three years since Brusson had left Paris for Geneva with his wife and child.

"How horrible!" Mlle de Scudéry exclaimed when she had recovered from her shock somewhat. "How horrible! You're Olivier? The son of my Anne! And now!"

"Surely," Olivier replied with calm composure, "surely, my worthy lady, you would never have been able to guess that the boy you pampered like the most adoring mother, whom you cradled on your knees, popping sweet after sweet into his mouth, on whom you lavished the most endearing names, would once stand before you, when grown into a young man, accused of a gruesome homicide! I'm not without fault, and the *chambre ardente* can rightfully accuse me of a crime, but, as I hope to die as a good Christian, even if it be at the hangman's hands, I am guiltless of any bloodshed; it was not by my hand, or through any fault of mine, that the unhappy Cardillac died!" As he said this, Olivier

Schwanken. Stillschweigend wies die Scuderi auf einen kleinen Sessel, der Olivier zur Seite stand. Er ließ sich langsam nieder.

«Ich hatte Zeit genug», fing er an, «mich auf die Unterredung mit Euch, die ich als die letzte Gunst des versöhnten Himmels betrachte, vorzubereiten und so viel Ruhe und Fassung zu gewinnen als nötig, Euch die Geschichte meines entsetzlichen, unerhörten Mißgeschicks zu erzählen. Erzeigt mir die Barmherzigkeit, mich ruhig anzuhören, so sehr Euch auch die Entdeckung eines Geheimnisses, das Ihr gewiß nicht geahnet, überraschen, ja mit Grausen erfüllen mag. – Hätte mein armer Vater Paris doch niemals verlassen! – Soweit meine Erinnerung an Genf reicht, finde ich mich wieder, von den trostlosen Eltern mit Tränen benetzt, von ihren Klagen, die ich nicht verstand, selbst zu Tränen gebracht. Später kam mir das deutliche Gefühl, das volle Bewußtsein des drückendsten Mangels, des tiefen Elends, in dem meine Eltern lebten. Mein Vater fand sich in allen seinen Hoffnungen getäuscht. Von tiefem Gram niedergebeugt, erdrückt, starb er in dem Augenblick, als es ihm gelungen war, mich bei einem Goldschmied als Lehrjunge unterzubringen. Meine Mutter sprach viel von Euch, sie wollte Euch alles klagen, aber dann überfiel sie die Mutlosigkeit, welche vom Elend erzeugt wird. *Das* und auch wohl falsche Scham, die oft an dem todwunden Gemüte nagt, hielt sie von ihrem Entschluß zurück. Wenige Monden nach dem Tode meines Vaters folgte ihm meine Mutter ins Grab.»

«Arme Anne! arme Anne!» rief die Scuderi, von Schmerz überwältigt.

«Dank und Preis der ewigen Macht des Himmels, daß sie hinüber ist und nicht fallen sieht den geliebten Sohn unter der Hand des Henkers, mit Schande gebrandmarkt.» So schrie Olivier laut auf, indem er einen wilden entsetzlichen Blick in die Höhe warf. Es wurde draußen unruhig, man ging hin and her.

«Ho ho», sprach Olivier mit einem bittern Lächeln, «Desgrais weckt seine Spießgesellen, als ob ich *hier* entfliehen könnte. – Doch weiter! – Ich wurde von meinem Meister hart gehalten, unerachtet ich bald am besten arbeitete, ja wohl endlich den Meister weit übertraf. Es begab sich, daß einst ein Fremder in unsere Werkstatt kam, um einiges Geschmeide zu kaufen. Als der nun einen schönen Halsschmuck sah, den ich gearbeitet, klopfte er mir mit freundlicher Miene auf die Schultern, indem er, den Schmuck beäugelnd, sprach: ‹Ei, ei! mein junger Freund, das ist ja ganz vortreffliche Arbeit. Ich wüßte in der Tat nicht, wer Euch noch anders übertreffen sollte, als René Cardillac, der freilich der erste Goldschmied ist, den es auf der

began to tremble and stagger. Mlle de Scudéry silently directed him to a small chair that stood next to him. He sat down slowly.

"I had enough time," he began, "to prepare myself for this interview with you, which I look on as the last favor granted by reconciled heaven, and to gain as much calm and composure as I'd need to tell you the story of my terrible, extraordinary misfortune. Show me the mercy of hearing me out calmly, however much the discovery of a secret you surely have no notion of may surprise you, or even fill you with horror. If only my poor father had never left Paris! As far as I can remember Geneva, I see myself again wet with the tears of my inconsolable parents, and reduced to tears myself by their laments, which I couldn't understand. Later on I acquired the distinct realization and the full consciousness of that most oppressive want and that profound poverty in which my parents lived. My father was disappointed in all his hopes. Bowed down and crushed by tremendous grief, he died at the very moment when he had succeeded in placing me as apprentice to a goldsmith. My mother spoke about you a great deal, she wanted to let you know about all her troubles; but then she fell prey to the discouragement that poverty breeds. That, and probably that false sense of shame which often gnaws at a mortally wounded mind, kept her from acting on her determination. A few months after my father's death my mother followed him to the grave."

"Poor Anne! Poor Anne!" Mlle de Scudéry exclaimed, overcome with grief.

"Thanks and praise to the eternal power of heaven that she's gone and won't see her beloved son fall beneath the hangman's hands branded with disgrace!" Olivier shouted those words loudly, casting a wild, terrible glance upward. Outside the room the guards became restless and paced to and fro.

"Ho, ho!" said Olivier with a bitter smile, "Desgrais is waking up his confederates, as if I could escape from *here*. But let me go on! I was harshly treated by my master, even though I soon was doing the finest work, and eventually perhaps surpassed my master by far. It came about once that a stranger visited our workshop to buy some jewelry. When he saw a beautiful necklace that I had crafted, he put on a friendly expression and patted me on the shoulder, then said, staring at the jewelry: 'Well, well, my young friend, this is truly excellent work. Actually I don't know who could surpass you except René Cardillac, who of

Welt gibt. Zu dem solltet Ihr hingehen; mit Freuden nimmt er Euch in seine Werkstatt, denn nur *Ihr* könnt ihm beistehen in seiner kunstvollen Arbeit, und nur von ihm allein könnt Ihr dagegen noch lernen.›

Die Worte des Fremden waren tief in meine Seele gefallen. Ich hatte keine Ruhe mehr in Genf, mich zog es fort mit Gewalt. Endlich gelang es mir, mich von meinem Meister loszumachen. Ich kam nach Paris. René Cardillac empfing mich kalt und barsch. Ich ließ nicht nach, er mußte mir Arbeit geben, so geringfügig sie auch sein mochte. Ich sollte einen kleinen Ring fertigen. Als ich ihm die Arbeit brachte, sah er mich starr an mit seinen funkelnden Augen, als wollt er hinein-schauen in mein Innerstes. Dann sprach er: ‹Du bist ein tüchtiger, wackerer Geselle, du kannst zu mir ziehen und mir helfen in der Werkstatt. Ich zahle dir gut, du wirst mit mir zufrieden sein.›

Cardillac hielt Wort. Schon mehrere Wochen war ich bei ihm, ohne Madelon gesehen zu haben, die, irr ich nicht, auf dem Lande bei ir-gendeiner Muhme Cardillacs damals sich aufhielt. Endlich kam sie. O du ewige Macht des Himmels, wie geschah mir, als ich das Engelsbild sah! – Hat je ein Mensch so geliebt als ich! Und nun! – O Madelon!»

Olivier konnte vor Wehmut nicht weiter sprechen. Er hielt beide Hände vors Gesicht und schluchzte heftig. Endlich mit Gewalt den wilden Schmerz, der ihn erfaßt, niederkämpfend, sprach er weiter:

«Madelon blickte mich an mit freundlichen Augen. Sie kam öfter und öfter in die Werkstatt. Mit Entzücken gewahrte ich ihre Liebe. So streng der Vater uns bewachte, mancher verstohlne Händedruck galt als Zeichen des geschlossenen Bundes. Cardillac schien nichts zu merken. Ich gedachte, hätte ich erst seine Gunst gewonnen, und konnte ich die Meisterschaft erlangen, um Madelon zu werben. Eines Morgens, als ich meine Arbeit beginnen wollte, trat Cardillac vor mich hin, Zorn und Verachtung im finstern Blick. ‹Ich bedarf deiner Arbeit nicht mehr›, fing er an, ‹fort aus dem Hause noch in dieser Stunde, und laß dich nie mehr vor meinen Augen sehen. Warum ich dich hier nicht mehr dulden kann, brauche ich dir nicht zu sagen. Für dich armen Schlucker hängt die süße Frucht zu hoch, nach der du trachtest!› Ich wollte reden, er packte mich aber mit starker Faust und warf mich zur Türe hinaus, daß ich niederstürzte und mich hart ver-wundete an Kopf und Arm.

Empört, zerrissen vom grimmen Schmerz, verließ ich das Haus und fand endlich am äußersten Ende der Vorstadt St. Martin einen gutmütigen Bekannten, der mich aufnahm in seine Bodenkammer. Ich hatte keine Ruhe, keine Rast. Zur Nachtzeit umschlich ich

course is the foremost goldsmith in the world. You ought to go and work for him; he'll be glad to take you into his shop, because you alone can assist him in his artistic labors, and, on the other hand, he's the only man who could still teach you something.'

"The stranger's words had affected me deeply. I knew no more repose in Geneva; I felt drawn away forcefully. I finally managed to release myself from my master's employ. I came to Paris. René Cardillac received me coldly and gruffly. I persisted, saying he had to give me an assignment, no matter how trivial. He gave me a little ring to make. When I brought the job to him, he stared at me with his blazing eyes as if he wanted to see inside me. Then he said: 'You're a competent, honest journeyman; you can move in with me and help me in my studio. I'll give you a good salary, and you'll be satisfied with me.'

"Cardillac kept his word. I had already been with him for several weeks without seeing Madelon, who, if I'm not mistaken, was staying in the country at the time with some female cousin of Cardillac's. She finally arrived. Oh, you eternal power of heaven, how I felt when I saw that angelic image! Has ever a man loved as I do? And now! Oh, Madelon!"

In his melancholy Olivier was unable to continue. He covered his face with his hands and sobbed violently. Finally, conquering with an effort the wild grief that had him in its grip, he went on:

"Madelon looked on me kindly. She visited the workshop more and more frequently. With delight I became aware that she loved me. No matter how strictly her father kept watch over us, many a stolen clasp of hands betokened the union between us. Cardillac seemed not to notice a thing. I intended to ask for Madelon's hand once I had won his favor and could become a master myself. One morning, when I was about to start working, Cardillac came up to me with anger and contempt in his dark gaze. 'I have no further use for your help,' he began. 'Out of my house within the hour, and don't let me see your face again! I don't need to tell you why I can no longer abide your presence here. The sweet fruit you're longing for is hanging too high on the tree for a poor devil like you!' I wanted to say something, but he seized me in his powerful fist and threw me out the door, so that I fell and hurt my head and arm badly.

"Furious and devoured by fierce sorrow, I left the house and finally found a good-natured acquaintance at the farthest end of the faubourg St-Martin, who took me into his garret. I had no

Cardillacs Haus, wähnend, daß Madelon meine Seufzer, meine Klage vernehmen, daß es ihr vielleicht gelingen werde, mich vom Fenster herab unbelauscht zu sprechen. Allerlei verwogene Pläne kreuzten in meinem Gehirn, zu deren Ausführung ich sie zu bereden hoffte. An Cardillacs Haus in der Straße Nicaise schließt sich eine hohe Mauer mit Blenden und alten, halb zerstückelten Steinbildern darin. Dicht bei einem solchen Steinbilde stehe ich in einer Nacht und sehe hinauf nach den Fenstern des Hauses, die in den Hof gehen, den die Mauer einschließt. Da gewahre ich plötzlich Licht in Cardillacs Werkstatt. Es ist Mitternacht, nie war sonst Cardillac zu dieser Stunde wach, er pflegte sich auf den Schlag neun Uhr zur Ruhe zu begeben. Mir pocht das Herz vor banger Ahnung, ich denke an irgendein Ereignis, das mir vielleicht den Eingang bahnt. Doch gleich verschwindet das Licht wieder.

Ich drücke mich an das Steinbild, in die Blende hinein, doch entsetzt pralle ich zurück, als ich einen Gegendruck fühle, als sei das Bild lebendig geworden. In dem dämmernden Schimmer der Nacht gewahre ich nun, daß der Stein sich langsam dreht und hinter demselben eine finstere Gestalt hervorschlüpft, die leisen Trittes die Straße hinabgeht. Ich springe an das Steinbild hinan, es steht wie zuvor dicht an der Mauer. Unwillkürlich, wie von einer innern Macht getrieben, schleiche ich hinter der Gestalt her. Gerade bei einem Marienbilde schaut die Gestalt sich um, der volle Schein der hellen Lampe, die vor dem Bilde brennt, fällt ihr ins Antlitz. Es ist Cardillac!

Eine unbegreifliche Angst, ein unheimliches Grauen überfällt mich. Wie durch Zauber festgebannt, muß ich fort – nach – dem gespenstischen Nachtwanderer. Dafür halte ich den Meister, unerachtet nicht die Zeit des Vollmonds ist, in der solcher Spuk die Schlafenden betört. Endlich verschwindet Cardillac seitwärts in den tiefen Schatten. An einem kleinen, wiewohl bekannten Räuspern gewahre ich indessen, daß er in die Einfahrt eines Hauses getreten ist. ‹Was bedeutet das, was wird er beginnen?› – So frage ich mich selbst voll Erstaunen und drücke mich dicht an die Häuser.

Nicht lange dauert's, so kommt singend und trillerierend ein Mann daher mit leuchtendem Federbusch und klirrenden Sporen. Wie ein Tiger auf seinen Raub, stürzt sich Cardillac aus seinem Schlupfwinkel auf den Mann, der in demselben Augenblick röchelnd zu Boden sinkt. Mit einem Schrei des Entsetzens springe ich heran, Cardillac ist über den Mann, der zu Boden liegt, her. ‹Meister Cardillac, was tut Ihr?› rufe ich laut.

repose, no rest. At night I'd skulk around Cardillac's house, imagining that Madelon would hear my sighs and laments, that she might perhaps manage to speak to me through her window without being detected. All sorts of reckless plans crisscrossed in my brain; I hoped I could persuade her to carry them out. Abutting Cardillac's house in the rue Nicaise is a high wall with niches containing old stone statues that are half-crumbled away. Right by one such statue I was standing one night gazing up at the house windows that overlook the courtyard which that wall encloses. I suddenly noticed a light in Cardillac's workshop. It was midnight, and Cardillac was never before up at that hour; he used to go to bed at the stroke of nine. My heart was pounding with a fearful foreboding, and I pictured some occurrence which might make my entry possible. But the light was gone again immediately.

"I pressed up against the statue, backing into the niche, but I recoiled in terror when I felt a counterpressure, as if the statue had come to life. Then I noticed in the dusky glimmer of the night that the stone was slowly turning; from behind it there slipped a dark form, which proceeded down the street with quiet steps. I leapt over to the statue: just as before, it was right up against the wall. Involuntarily, as if driven by some force inside me, I slinked after the figure in the street. Precisely alongside a statue of the Virgin, the figure looked back, and the full light of the bright lamp burning in front of the image fell right on his face. It was Cardillac!

"An incomprehensible fear, an uncanny terror, came over me. As if spellbound, I had to walk on, following the spectral somnambulist. That's what I considered the master to be, even though it wasn't the time of the full moon, when such visitations disturb sleepers. Finally Cardillac vanished off to the side into the deep darkness. Meanwhile I could tell, by a slight clearing of his throat which was very familiar to me, that he had stepped into the gateway of a house. 'What does this mean? What is he up to?' I asked myself in amazement, as I pressed up close against the houses.

"Before very long, a man with a bright plume and clinking spurs came by singing and warbling. Like a tiger upon its prey, Cardillac dashed out of his hiding place at the man, who at the same moment fell to the ground with a death rattle. I ran over with a cry of terror; Cardillac was stooped over the man on the ground. 'Master Cardillac, what are you doing?' I loudly cried.

‹Vermaledeiter!› brüllt Cardillac, rennt mit Blitzesschnelle bei mir
vorbei und verschwindet. Ganz außer mir, kaum der Schritte mächtig,
nähere ich mich dem Niedergeworfenen. Ich knie bei ihm nieder,
vielleicht, denk ich, ist er noch zu retten, aber keine Spur des Lebens
ist mehr in ihm. In meiner Todesangst gewahre ich kaum, daß mich
die Marechaussee umringt hat. ‹Schon wieder einer von den Teufeln
niedergestreckt – he he junger Mensch, was machst du da – bist einer
von der Bande? – fort mit dir!› So schrien sie durcheinander und
packen mich an.

Kaum vermag ich zu stammeln, daß ich solche gräßliche Untat ja
gar nicht hätte begehen können, und daß sie mich im Frieden ziehen
lassen möchten. Da leuchtet mir einer ins Gesicht und ruft lachend:
‹Das ist Olivier Brusson, der Goldschmiedsgeselle, der bei unserm
ehrlichen, braven Meister Cardillac arbeitet! – ja – *der* wird die Leute
auf der Straße morden! – sieht mir recht darnach aus – ist recht nach
der Art der Mordbuben, daß sie beim Leichnam lamentieren und sich
fangen lassen werden. Wie war's, Junge? – erzähle dreist.›

‹Dicht vor mir›, sprach ich, ‹sprang ein Mensch auf den dort los,
stieß ihn nieder und rannte blitzschnell davon, als ich laut aufschrie.
Ich wollt doch sehen, ob der Niedergeworfene noch zu retten wäre.›

‹Nein, mein Sohn›, ruft einer von denen, die den Leichnam aufgehoben, ‹der ist hin, durchs Herz, wie gewöhnlich, geht der Dolchstich.›

‹Teufel›, spricht ein anderer, ‹kamen wir doch wieder zu spät wie
vorgestern›; damit entfernen sie sich mit dem Leichnam.

Wie mir zumute war, kann ich gar nicht sagen; ich fühlte mich an,
ob nicht ein böser Traum mich necke, es war mir, als müßt ich nun
gleich erwachen und mich wundern über das tolle Trugbild. –
Cardillac – der Vater meiner Madelon, ein verruchter Mörder! – Ich
war kraftlos auf die steinernen Stufen eines Hauses gesunken. Immer
mehr und mehr dämmerte der Morgen herauf, ein Offiziershut, reich
mit Federn geschmückt, lag vor mir auf dem Pflaster. Cardillacs
blutige Tat, auf der Stelle begangen, wo ich saß, ging vor mir hell auf.
Entsetzt rannte ich von dannen.

Ganz verwirrt, beinahe besinnungslos sitze ich in meiner Dach-
kammer, da geht die Tür auf, und René Cardillac tritt herein. ‹Um
Christus' willen! was wollt Ihr?› schrie ich ihm entgegen. Er, das gar
nicht achtend, kommt auf mich zu und lächelt mich an mit einer Ruhe
und Leutseligkeit, die meinen innern Abscheu vermehrt. Er rückt
einen alten, gebrechlichen Schemel heran und setzt sich zu mir, der

"'Damn you!' Cardillac roared; then as fast as lightning he ran past me and disappeared. Completely beside myself and barely able to walk, I approached the felled man. I knelt down beside him, thinking he might still be saved, but there was no sign of life left in him. In my deathly fear I was scarcely aware that the *maréchaussée* had encircled me. 'Another one of those poor fellows brought down!' 'Say, young man, what are you doing here?' 'Are you one of the gang?' 'Come away with us!' That's what they were yelling in confusion as they apprehended me.

"I was barely able to stammer that I could never have committed such a gruesome crime, and that they should let me go in peace. Then someone shone a light in my face and called with a laugh: 'It's Olivier Brusson, the journeyman goldsmith who works for our honest, upright Master Cardillac! Sure! *He'd* murder people in the street! Looks just like a killer, doesn't he? It's the regular practice of assassins to wail over the body and let themselves get caught! How did it happen, boy? Tell us without fear!'

"'Right in front of me,' I said, 'a person pounced on this man, felled him, and ran away as fast as lightning when I gave a loud yell. I just wanted to see if the wounded man could still be saved.'

"'No, son,' called one of the men who had picked up the body, 'he's a goner. The dagger wound is right through the heart, as usual.'

"'Damn!' another man said. 'We got here too late again, just like the day before yesterday.' Then they went away with the body.

"I can't tell you how I felt; I touched myself to see whether some bad dream wasn't mocking me; it seemed as if I had to awaken at once and marvel at that crazy vision. Cardillac, my Madelon's father, a wicked killer! I had sat down on the stone steps of a house, my strength gone. The sky was growing increasingly bright. An officer's hat with abundant feather decoration lay on the pavement in front of me. Cardillac's bloody deed, performed on the spot where I was sitting, appeared clearly before me. In terror I dashed away from there.

"Completely confused, and almost insensible, I was seated in my garret room when the door opened and René Cardillac walked in. 'In the name of Christ, what do you want?' I shouted to him. Paying no mind, he came up to me and smiled at me with a calm and affability that increased my inner repulsion. He pulled over a rickety old stool and sat down beside me, while I

ich nicht vermag, mich von dem Strohlager zu erheben, auf das ich mich geworfen.

‹Nun, Olivier›, fängt er an, ‹wie geht es dir, armer Junge? Ich habe mich in der Tat garstig übereilt, als ich dich aus dem Hause stieß, du fehlst mir an allen Ecken und Enden. Eben jetzt habe ich ein Werk vor, das ich ohne deine Hilfe gar nicht vollenden kann. Wie wär's, wenn du wieder in meiner Werkstatt arbeitetest? – Du schweigst? – Ja, ich weiß, ich habe dich beleidigt. Nicht verhehlen wollt ich's dir, daß ich auf dich zornig war wegen der Liebelei mit meiner Madelon. Doch recht überlegt habe ich mir das Ding nachher und gefunden, daß bei deiner Geschicklichkeit, deinem Fleiß, deiner Treue ich mir keinen bessern Eidam wünschen kann als eben dich. Komm also mit mir und siehe zu, wie du Madelon zur Frau gewinnen magst.›

Cardillacs Worte durchschnitten mir das Herz, ich erbebte vor seiner Bosheit, ich konnte kein Wort hervorbringen. ‹Du zauderst›, fuhr er nun fort mit scharfem Ton, indem seine funkelnden Augen mich durchbohren, ‹du zauderst? – du kannst vielleicht heute noch nicht mit mir kommen, du hast andere Dinge vor! – du willst vielleicht Desgrais besuchen oder dich gar einführen lassen bei d'Argenson oder la Regnie. Nimm dich in acht, Bursche, daß die Krallen, die du hervorlocken willst zu anderer Leute Verderben, dich nicht selbst fassen und zerreißen.›

Da macht sich mein tief empörtes Gemüt plötzlich Luft. ‹Mögen die›, rufe ich, ‹mögen die, die sich gräßlicher Untat bewußt sind, jene Namen fühlen, die Ihr eben nanntet, ich darf das nicht – ich habe nichts mit ihnen zu schaffen.›

‹Eigentlich›, spricht Cardillac weiter, ‹eigentlich, Olivier, macht es dir Ehre, wenn du bei mir arbeitest, bei mir, dem berühmtesten Meister seiner Zeit, überall hochgeachtet wegen seiner Treue und Rechtschaffenheit, so daß jede böse Verleumdung schwer zurückfallen würde auf das Haupt des Verleumders. – Was nun Madelon betrifft, so muß ich dir nur gestehen, daß du meine Nachgiebigkeit ihr allein verdankest. Sie liebt dich mit einer Heftigkeit, die ich dem zarten Kinde gar nicht zutrauen konnte. Gleich als du fort warst, fiel sie mir zu Füßen, umschlang meine Knie und gestand unter tausend Tränen, daß sie ohne dich nicht leben könne. Ich dachte, sie bilde sich das nur ein, wie es denn bei jungen verliebten Dingern zu geschehen pflegt, daß sie gleich sterben wollen, wenn das erste Milchgesicht sie freundlich angeblickt. Aber in der Tat, meine Madelon wurde siech und krank, und wie ich ihr denn das tolle Zeug ausreden wollte, rief sie hundertmal deinen Namen. Was konnt ich endlich tun, wollt ich sie nicht

was unable to rise from the straw pallet onto which I had dropped.

"'Well, Olivier,' he began, 'how are you doing, poor boy? I was really terribly hasty when I drove you out of my house; I miss you everywhere I turn. I just now have a job in mind that I can't complete without your assistance. How about working in my atelier again? You say nothing? Yes, I know I insulted you. I wouldn't want to conceal from you that I was angry with you over your infatuation with my Madelon. But later I considered the matter carefully, and I decided that, given your skill, diligence, and loyalty, I can't hope for a better son-in-law than you. So come with me and set your mind on obtaining Madelon as your wife.'

"Cardillac's words ripped my heart apart; I trembled at his malice; I couldn't utter one word. 'You're hesitating?' he then continued in a biting tone, while his blazing eyes bored through me. 'You're hesitating? Maybe you can't come with me today because you have other business to attend to! Maybe you'll visit Desgrais or even seek admission to D'Argenson or La Reynie. Watch out, my lad, lest the talons you wish to entice forth for the destruction of others seize you yourself and tear you to bits!'

"Then I suddenly gave vent to my deep indignation. I cried: 'Let those who are conscious of having committed a gruesome crime be affected by those names you have just mentioned; I don't need to—I have no business with them.'

"'Actually,' Cardillac went on, 'it does you honor, Olivier, to work for me, the most celebrated master of our day, esteemed universally for his loyalty and uprightness, so that any malicious defamation would rebound heavily on the head of the defamer. As for Madelon, I must admit to you that you have her alone to thank for my indulgence toward you. She loves you with a passion I couldn't believe the gentle child capable of. Right after you left, she knelt at my feet, clasped my knees, and confessed with a thousand tears that she couldn't live without you. I thought it was only her imagination, just as a young girl in love always says she's going to die as soon as the first whey-faced boy gives her a friendly glance. But really and truly, my Madelon became sick and ill, and when I tried to talk her out of her foolish notion, she called your name a hundred times. What could I do finally if I didn't want to drive her to despair? Last night I told

verzweifeln lassen? Gestern abend sagt ich ihr, ich willige in alles und
werde dich heute holen. Da ist sie über Nacht aufgeblüht wie eine
Rose und harrt nun auf dich, ganz außer sich vor Liebessehnsucht.›
Mag es mir die ewige Macht des Himmels verzeihen, aber selbst
weiß ich nicht, wie es geschah, daß ich plötzlich in Cardillacs Hause
stand, daß Madelon, laut aufjauchzend: ‹Olivier – mein Olivier – mein
Geliebter – mein Gatte!› auf mich gestürzt, mich mit beiden Armen
umschlang, mich fest an ihre Brust drückte, daß ich im Übermaß des
höchsten Entzückens bei der Jungfrau und allen Heiligen schwor, sie
nimmer, nimmer zu verlassen!»
Erschüttert von dem Andenken an diesen entscheidenden
Augenblick, mußte Olivier innehalten. Die Scuderi, von Grausen erfüllt über die Untat eines Mannes, den sie für die Tugend, die Rechtschaffenheit selbst gehalten, rief: «Entsetzlich! – René Cardillac
gehört zu der Mordbande, die unsere gute Stadt so lange zur
Räuberhöhle machte?»
«Was sagt Ihr, mein Fräulein», sprach Olivier, «zur *Bande*? Nie hat
es eine solche Bande gegeben. Cardillac *allein* war es, der mit verruchter Tätigkeit in der ganzen Stadt seine Schlachtopfer suchte und
fand. Daß er es *allein* war, darin liegt die Sicherheit, womit er seine
Streiche führte, die unüberwundene Schwierigkeit, dem Mörder auf
die Spur zu kommen. – Doch laßt mich fortfahren, der Verfolg wird
Euch die Geheimnisse des verruchtesten und zugleich unglücklich-
sten aller Menschen aufklären.
Die Lage, in der ich mich nun bei dem Meister befand, jeder mag
die sich leicht denken. Der Schritt war geschehen, ich konnte nicht
mehr zurück. Zuweilen war es mir, als sei ich selbst Cardillacs
Mordgehilfe geworden, nur in Madelons Liebe vergaß ich die innere
Pein, die mich quälte, nur bei ihr konnt es mir gelingen, jede äußere
Spur namenlosen Grams wegzutilgen. Arbeitete ich mit dem Alten in
der Werkstatt, nicht ins Antlitz vermochte ich ihm zu schauen, kaum
ein Wort zu reden vor dem Grausen, das mich durchbebte in der
Nähe des entsetzlichen Menschen, der alle Tugenden des treuen,
zärtlichen Vaters, des guten Bürgers erfüllte, während die Nacht
seine Untaten verschleierte.
Madelon, das fromme, engelreine Kind, hing an ihm mit abgötti-
scher Liebe. Das Herz durchbohrt es mir, wenn ich daran dachte,
daß, träfe einmal die Rache den verlarvten Bösewicht, sie ja, mit aller
höllischen List des Satans getäuscht, der gräßlichsten Verzweiflung
unterliegen müsse. Schon das verschloß mir den Mund, und hätt ich
den Tod des Verbrechers darum dulden müssen. Unerachtet ich aus

her that I consented to everything and that I'd come to get you today. She blossomed out like a rose overnight, and she's now waiting for you, completely beside herself with yearning.'

"May the eternal might of heaven forgive me, but I myself don't know how it happened that I was suddenly standing in Cardillac's house, while Madelon, with the jubilant cry 'Olivier! My Olivier! My beloved! My husband!' dashed over to me, threw her arms around me, and pressed me close to her breast, so that in the excess of my highest rapture I swore by the Virgin and all the saints never, never to forsake her!"

Shaken by the recollection of that decisive moment, Olivier had to pause. Mlle de Scudéry, filled with horror at the crime of a man she had considered virtue and uprightness itself, cried: "How terrible! René Cardillac belonged to the gang of assassins that made our city a den of thieves for so long?"

"What are you saying, my lady?" Olivier said. "To the gang? No such gang ever existed. It was Cardillac alone who, with criminal diligence, sought and found his victims throughout the city. His doing it all alone was the reason for the impunity with which he executed his deeds, and the insurmountable difficulty of tracking down the killer. But let me continue; what I go on to say will explain to you the secrets of the most villainous, and at the same time most unfortunate, of all men.

"Anyone may easily imagine the situation in which I now found myself at the master's place. The step had been taken, I couldn't pull out again. At times I felt as if I had become Cardillac's accomplice in murder; only Madelon's love helped me forget the inward torment that assailed me; only in her presence could I manage to eliminate all outward signs of unspeakable sorrow. When I worked in the studio with the old man, I was unable to look him in the face and could scarcely speak a word, because of the horror that made me shudder all over in the proximity of that terrifying person, who fulfilled every virtuous duty of a loyal, loving father and good citizen while the night veiled his crimes.

"Madelon, the pious, angelically pure child, was devoted to him with idolatrous love. It pierced me to the heart when I reflected that, should vengeance ever overtake the unmasked scoundrel, she, deceived by all the infernal cunning of Satan, must succumb to the most dreadful despair. That alone was enough to seal my lips, even if I had to suffer a criminal's death

den Reden der Marechaussee genug entnehmen konnte, waren mir
Cardillacs Untaten, ihr Motiv, die Art, sie auszuführen, ein Rätsel; die
Aufklärung blieb nicht lange aus.

Eines Tages war Cardillac, der sonst, meinen Abscheu erregend,
bei der Arbeit in der heitersten Laune, scherzte und lachte, sehr ernst
und in sich gekehrt. Plötzlich warf er das Geschmeide, woran er eben
arbeitete, beiseite, daß Stein und Perlen auseinander rollten, stand
heftig auf und sprach: ‹Olivier! – es kann zwischen uns beiden nicht
so bleiben, dies Verhältnis ist mir unerträglich. – Was der feinsten
Schlauigkeit Desgrais' und seiner Spießgesellen nicht gelang zu entdecken, das spielte dir der Zufall in die Hände. Du hast mich
geschaut in der nächtlichen Arbeit, zu der mich mein böser Stern
treibt, kein Widerstand ist möglich. – Auch dein böser Stern war es,
der dich mir folgen ließ, der dich in undurchdringliche Schleier
hüllte, der deinem Fußtritt die Leichtigkeit gab, daß du unhörbar
wandeltest wie das kleinste Tier, so daß ich, der ich in der tiefsten
Nacht klar schaue wie der Tiger, der ich straßenweit das kleinste
Geräusch, das Sumsen der Mücke vernehme, dich nicht bemerkte.
Dein böser Stern hat dich, meinen Gefährten, mir zugeführt. An
Verrat ist, so wie du jetzt stehst, nicht mehr zu denken. Darum magst
du alles wissen.›

‹Nimmermehr werd ich dein Gefährte sein, heuchlerischer
Bösewicht.› So wollt ich aufschreien, aber das innere Entsetzen, das
mich bei Cardillacs Worten erfaßt, schnürte mir die Kehle zu. Statt
der Worte vermochte ich nur einen unverständigen Laut auszustoßen. Cardillac setzte sich wieder in seinen Arbeitsstuhl. Er trock-
nete sich den Schweiß von der Stirne. Er schien, von der Erinnerung
des Vergangenen hart berührt, sich mühsam zu fassen. Endlich fing
er an:

‹Weise Männer sprechen viel von den seltsamen Eindrücken, deren
Frauen in guter Hoffnung fähig sind, von dem wunderbaren Einfluß
solch lebhaften, willenlosen Eindrucks von außen her auf das Kind.
Von meiner Mutter erzählte man mir eine wunderliche Geschichte.
Als *die* mit mir im ersten Monat schwanger ging, schaute sie mit andern Weibern einem glänzenden Hoffest zu, das in Trianon gegeben
wurde. Da fiel ihr Blick auf einen Kavalier in spanischer Kleidung mit
einer blitzenden Juwelenkette um den Hals, von der sie die Augen gar
nicht mehr abwenden konnte. Ihr ganzes Wesen war Begierde nach
den funkelnden Steinen, die ihr ein überirdisches Gut dünkten.

for it. Even though I could understand a great deal on the basis
of the *maréchaussée*'s reports, Cardillac's misdeeds, their motive, and his mode of performing them were a puzzle to me; I
didn't have to wait long for elucidation.

"One day Cardillac, who was usually in the brightest spirits
while at work, joking and laughing (which I found abhorrent),
was very grave and introspective. Suddenly he threw aside the
piece of jewelry he was working on, so that the gems and pearls
were scattered; he stood up impetuously and said: 'Olivier!
Things can't remain this way between us; this situation is unbearable to me. That which the subtlest cunning of Desgrais and
his cohorts failed to discover, chance played right into your
hands. You observed me at my nocturnal labors, to which my evil
star drives me, with no possibility of resistance. It was your evil
star, too, which led you to follow me, which enveloped you in
impenetrable veils, which lent your steps such lightness that you
walked as inaudibly as the smallest animal, so that I, I who see
as clearly as a tiger in the darkest night, I who can hear the
slightest sound, the buzzing of a mosquito, for blocks around,
failed to notice you. Your evil star led you to me, my accomplice.
In your present situation you can no longer think of betraying
me. And so it's all right for you to know everything.'

"'I'll never be your accomplice, you hypocritical scoundrel!'
That's what I wanted to shout, but the inward terror that gripped
me at Cardillac's words tightened my throat. Instead of words I
could only utter a meaningless sound. Cardillac sat back down
on his work chair. He wiped the sweat from his brow. He
seemed to be collecting himself with difficulty, strongly agitated
by the remembrance of the past. Finally he began:

"'Wise men speak a great deal about the odd impressions that
pregnant women can have, about the miraculous external influence that such a strong, involuntary impression can have on the
child. I was told a strange story about my own mother. When she
was in her first month of pregnancy with me, she and other
women were spectators at brilliant court festivities being held in
the Trianon.[6] Her glance fell on a cavalier in Spanish attire wearing a flashing jeweled chain around his neck, from which she
couldn't tear her eyes away. Her whole being was filled with a
craving for those sparkling stones, which she looked on as a

---

6. An anachronism: the (Grand) Trianon wasn't built until 1687.

Derselbe Kavalier hatte vor mehreren Jahren, als meine Mutter noch nicht verheiratet, ihrer Tugend nachgestellt, war aber mit Abscheu zurückgewiesen worden. Meine Mutter erkannte ihn wieder, aber jetzt war es ihr, als sei er im Glanz der strahlenden Diamanten ein Wesen höherer Art, der Inbegriff aller Schönheit. Der Kavalier bemerkte die sehnsuchtsvollen, feurigen Blicke meiner Mutter. Er glaubte jetzt glücklicher zu sein als vormals. Er wußte sich ihr zu nähern, noch mehr, sie von ihren Bekannten fort an einen einsamen Ort zu locken. Dort schloß er sie brünstig in seine Arme, meine Mutter faßte nach der schönen Kette, aber in demselben Augenblick sank er nieder und riß meine Mutter mit sich zu Boden. Sei es, daß ihn der Schlag plötzlich getroffen, oder aus einer andern Ursache: genug, er war tot. Vergebens war das Mühen meiner Mutter, sich den im Todeskrampf erstarrten Armen des Leichnams zu entwinden. Die hohlen Augen, deren Sehkraft erloschen, auf sie gerichtet, wälzte der Tote sich mit ihr auf dem Boden. Ihr gellendes Hilfsgeschrei drang endlich bis zu in der Ferne Vorübergehenden, die herbeieilten und sie retteten aus den Armen des grausigen Liebhabers. Das Entsetzen warf meine Mutter auf ein schweres Krankenlager. Man gab sie, mich verloren, doch sie gesundete, und die Entbindung war glücklicher, als man je hatte hoffen können. Aber die Schrecken jenes fürchterlichen Augenblicks hatten *mich* getroffen. Mein böser Stern war aufgegangen und hatte den Funken hinabgeschossen, der in mir eine der seltsamsten und verderblichsten Leidenschaften entzündet. Schon in der frühesten Kindheit gingen mir glänzende Diamanten, goldenes Geschmeide über alles. Man hielt das für gewöhnliche kindische Neigung. Aber es zeigte sich anders, denn als Knabe stahl ich Gold und Juwelen, wo ich sie habhaft werden konnte. Wie der geübteste Kenner unterschied ich aus Instinkt unechtes Geschmeide von echtem. Nur dieses lockte mich, unechtes sowie geprägtes Gold ließ ich unbeachtet liegen. Den grausamsten Züchtigungen des Vaters mußte die angeborne Begierde weichen. Um nur mit Gold und edlen Steinen hantieren zu können, wandte ich mich zur Goldschmiedsprofession. Ich arbeitete mit Leidenschaft und wurde bald der erste Meister dieser Art. Nun begann eine Periode, in der der angeborne Trieb, so lange niedergedrückt, mit Gewalt empordrang und mit Macht wuchs, alles um sich her wegzehrend. Sowie ich ein Geschmeide gefertigt und abgeliefert, fiel ich in eine Unruhe, in eine Trostlosigkeit, die mir Schlaf, Gesundheit – Lebensmut raubte. – Wie ein Gespenst stand Tag und Nacht die Person, für die ich gearbeitet, mir vor Augen, geschmückt mit meinem Geschmeide, und eine

celestial prize. Several years earlier, before my mother was married, the same cavalier had had designs on her virtue, but had been rejected with abhorrence. My mother recognized him, but now, in the glow of those radiant diamonds, he seemed to her like a being of a higher nature, the paragon of handsomeness. The cavalier noticed my mother's fiery, longing glances. He thought that now he'd be more fortunate than in the past. He contrived to approach her and, what's more, to lure her away from her acquaintances to a secluded spot. There he threw his arms around her in hot desire, and my mother reached for the beautiful chain, but at that moment he fell and pulled my mother to the floor with him. Whether it was a sudden stroke or there was some other cause: he was dead. My mother's efforts to free herself from the arms of the corpse, which had become rigid in his mortal agony, were fruitless. His hollow eyes, whose sight was extinguished, staring at her, the dead man rolled on the floor with her. Finally her shrill cries for help reached distant passersby, who hastened over and rescued her from the arms of her grisly lover. Her terror sent my mother to bed, seriously ill. She and I were both considered lost, but she recovered and the delivery was smoother than anyone could have hoped. But the terrors of that fearful moment had affected *me*. My evil star had ascended and had emitted the spark that kindled one of the strangest and most pernicious passions in me. In my earliest childhood bright diamonds and gold jewelry already meant more to me than anything else. That was judged to be a normal childish propensity. But it proved to be otherwise, because as a boy I stole gold and jewels wherever I could lay my hands on them. Like the most experienced connoisseur I instinctively distinguished fake jewelry from the real thing. Only genuine items enticed me; fakes and gold plating I paid no attention to. My inborn desire had to yield to my father's extremely cruel castigations. In order to be involved with gold and precious stones I turned to the profession of goldsmith. I worked passionately and soon became the foremost master of that kind. Now a period began in which my inborn urge, so long repressed, returned forcefully and increased mightily, consuming everything around it. Whenever I completed and delivered a piece of jewelry, I lapsed into an unrest, a disconsolate state, that robbed me of sleep, health—and joy in life. Day and night the person who had commissioned the job was before my eyes like a ghost, adorned with my jewelry, and a voice murmured in my

Stimme raunte mir in die Ohren: ‹Es ist ja dein – es ist ja dein – nimm
es doch – was sollen die Diamanten dem Toten!› – Da legt ich mich
endlich auf Diebeskünste. Ich hatte Zutritt in den Häusern der
Großen, ich nützte schnell jede Gelegenheit, kein Schloß widerstand
meinem Geschick, und bald war der Schmuck, den ich gearbeitet,
wieder in meinen Händen. – Aber nun vertrieb selbst das nicht meine
Unruhe. Jene unheimliche Stimme ließ sich dennoch vernehmen und
höhnte mich und rief: ‹Ho ho, dein Geschmeide trägt ein Toter!› –
Selbst wußte ich nicht, wie es kam, daß ich einen unaussprechlichen
Haß auf die warf, denen ich Schmuck gefertigt. Ja! im tiefsten Innern
regte sich eine Mordlust gegen sie, vor der ich selbst erbebte. – In
dieser Zeit kaufte ich dieses Haus. Ich war mit dem Besitzer handelseinig geworden, hier in diesem Gemach saßen wir, erfreut über das
geschlossene Geschäft, beisammen und tranken eine Flasche Wein.
Es war Nacht geworden, ich wollte aufbrechen, da sprach mein
Verkäufer: ‹Hört, Meister René, ehe Ihr fortgeht, muß ich Euch mit
einem Geheimnis dieses Hauses bekannt machen.› Darauf schloß er
jenen in die Mauer eingeführten Schrank auf, schob die Hinterwand
fort, trat in ein kleines Gemach, bückte sich nieder, hob eine Falltür
auf. Eine steile, schmale Treppe stiegen wir hinab, kamen an ein
schmales Pförtchen, das er aufschloß, traten hinaus in den freien Hof.
Nun schritt der alte Herr, mein Verkäufer, hinan an die Mauer, schob
an einem nur wenig hervorragenden Eisen, und alsbald drehte sich
ein Stück Mauer los, so daß ein Mensch bequem durch die Öffnung
schlüpfen und auf die Straße gelangen konnte. Du magst einmal das
Kunststück sehen, Olivier, das wahrscheinlich schlaue Mönche des
Klosters, welches ehemals hier lag, fertigen ließen, um heimlich aus-
und einschlüpfen zu können. Es ist ein Stück Holz, nur von außen
gemörtelt und getüncht, in das von außenher eine Bildsäule, auch nur
von Holz, doch ganz wie Stein, eingefügt ist, welches sich mitsamt der
Bildsäule auf verborgenen Angeln dreht. – Dunkle Gedanken stiegen
in mir auf, als ich diese Einrichtung sah, es war mir, als sei vorgear-
beitet solchen Taten, die mir selbst noch Geheimnis blieben. Eben
hatt ich einem Herrn vom Hofe einen reichen Schmuck abgeliefert,
der, ich weiß es, einer Operntänzerin bestimmt war. Die Todesfolter
blieb nicht aus – das Gespenst hing sich an meine Schritte – der
lispelnde Satan an mein Ohr! – Ich zog ein in das Haus. In blutigem
Angstschweiß gebadet, wälzte ich mich schlaflos auf dem Lager! Ich
seh im Geiste den Menschen zu der Tänzerin schleichen mit meinem

ears: "But it's yours! It's yours! Take it! What does a dead man need with diamonds?" Then I finally turned toward thievery. I had access to the homes of grandees; I quickly used every opportunity, no lock withstood my skill, and soon the piece that I had crafted was back in my hands. But now even that didn't dispel my unrest. That uncanny voice made itself heard all the same; it mocked me and called: "Ho, ho, a dead man is wearing your jewelry!" I myself didn't know how it happened that I developed an inexpressible hatred for those who had commissioned my work. Yes, deep inside me an urge to kill them was stirring, an urge that frightened me. Around that time I bought this house. I had agreed with the owner on the price, we were sitting together here in this room drinking a bottle of wine, happy over the conclusion of the deal. Night had fallen and I wanted to leave, when the seller said: "Listen, Master René, before you go I must acquaint you with a secret of this house." Then he opened that wall closet, slid aside its back wall, stepped into a little room, bent over, and lifted a trapdoor. We descended a steep, narrow flight of stairs, reached a narrow little gate, which we opened, and stepped outdoors into the courtyard. Now the old gentleman, the seller, walked up to the enclosing wall and pushed aside a slightly protruding iron bar; immediately a section of the wall turned, so that a man could easily slip through the opening and reach the street. You ought to see that device sometime, Olivier; it was probably designed for some crafty monks in the monastery that used to be located here, so they could slip out and back in clandestinely. It's a piece of wood, plastered and whitewashed only outside, into which a statue, also merely of wood, though it looks just like stone, is inserted from outside; the whole piece, including the statue, turns on hidden hinges. Dark thoughts came to my mind when I saw that device; I felt as if it were the preparation for deeds that were still a secret even to me. I had just delivered an expensive piece of jewelry to a gentleman of the court, which I knew was intended for a ballerina of the opera.[7] My horrible torture didn't fail to attack me, the ghost attached itself to my steps, and whispering Satan to my ear! I moved into the house. Soaked in the bloody sweat of fear, I tossed back and forth in bed sleeplessly! In my mind I saw the fellow sneaking off to the ballerina's with my jewelry. Enraged, I jumped up, threw on my

---

7. There were few, if any, professional ballerinas in 1680.

Schmuck. Voller Wut springe ich auf – werfe den Mantel um – steige herab die geheime Treppe – fort durch die Mauer nach der Straße Nicaise. – Er kommt, ich falle über ihn her, er schreit auf, doch von hinten festgepackt stoße ich ihm den Dolch ins Herz – der Schmuck ist mein! – Dies getan, fühlte ich eine Ruhe, eine Zufriedenheit in meiner Seele, wie sonst niemals. Das Gespenst war verschwunden, die Stimme des Satans schwieg. Nun wußte ich, was mein böser Stern wollte, ich mußt ihm nachgeben oder untergehen! – Du begreifst jetzt mein ganzes Tun und Treiben, Olivier! – Glaube nicht, daß ich darum, weil ich tun muß, was ich nicht lassen kann, jenem Gefühl des Mitleids, des Erbarmens, was in der Natur des Menschen bedingt sein soll, rein entsagt habe. Du weißt, wie schwer es mir wird, einen Schmuck abzuliefern; wie ich für manche, deren Tod ich nicht will, gar nicht arbeite, ja wie ich sogar, weiß ich, daß am morgenden Tage Blut mein Gespenst verbannen wird, heute es bei einem tüchtigen Faustschlage bewenden lasse, der den Besitzer meines Kleinods zu Boden streckt und mir dieses in die Hand liefert.›

Dies alles gesprochen, führte mich Cardillac in das geheime Gewölbe und gönnte mir den Anblick seines Juwelenkabinetts. Der König besitzt es nicht reicher. Bei jedem Schmuck war auf einem kleinen daran gehängten Zettel genau bemerkt, für wen es gearbeitet, wann es durch Diebstahl, Raub oder Mord genommen worden. ‹An deinem Hochzeitstage›, sprach Cardillac dumpf und feierlich, ‹an deinem Hochzeitstage, Olivier, wirst du mir, die Hand gelegt auf des gekreuzigten Christus Bild, einen heiligen Eid schwören, sowie ich gestorben, alle diese Reichtümer in Staub zu vernichten durch Mittel, die ich dir dann bekannt machen werde. Ich will nicht, daß irgendein menschlich Wesen, und am wenigsten Madelon und du, in den Besitz des mit Blut erkauften Horts komme.›

Gefangen in diesem Labyrinth des Verbrechens, zerrissen von Liebe und Abscheu, von Wonne und Entsetzen, war ich dem Verdammten zu vergleichen, dem ein holder Engel mild lächelnd hinaufwinkt, aber mit glühenden Krallen festgepackt hält ihn der Satan, und des frommen Engels Liebeslächeln, in dem sich alle Seligkeit des hohen Himmels abspiegelt, wird ihm zur grimmigsten seiner Qualen. – Ich dachte an Flucht – ja, an Selbstmord – aber Madelon! – Tadelt mich, tadelt mich, mein würdiges Fräulein, daß ich zu schwach war, mit Gewalt eine Leidenschaft niederzukämpfen, die mich an das Verbrechen fesselte; aber büße ich nicht dafür mit schmachvollem Tode?

Eines Tages kam Cardillac nach Hause, ungewöhnlich heiter. Er

cloak, descended the secret stair, and issued through the wall onto the rue Nicaise. He came along, I pounced on him, he cried out, but, gripping him firmly from behind, I plunged my dagger into his heart—the jewelry was mine! After doing that, I felt a repose, a contentment, in my soul as never before. The ghost had vanished, Satan's voice was silent. Now I knew what my evil star wanted of me; I had to yield to it or perish! Now you understand all my activities, Olivier! Don't think that, because I do something I can't avoid, I have altogether renounced that feeling of sympathy and mercy that is said to be integral to human nature. You know how hard it is for me to deliver a piece of jewelry; you know that I refuse to work for many people whose death I don't desire, and that, in fact, though I know that tomorrow blood will banish my ghost, today I content myself with a hefty blow of the fist, which knocks the owner of my jewels to the ground and restores them to my hands.'

"After telling me all this, Cardillac led me to the secret vault and granted me a look into his jewelry collection. The king doesn't possess a finer one. Every piece of jewelry had a small slip of paper attached to it with exact notations on the person for whom it was made and the date on which it was regained by burglary, mugging, or murder. 'On your wedding day, Olivier,' Cardillac said in a hollow, solemn tone, 'on your wedding day, Olivier, you will place your hand on the picture of Christ crucified, and swear a sacred oath that, as soon as I am dead, you will totally annihilate all these riches by the means that I will make known to you on my deathbed. I don't want any human being, least of all Madelon and you, to come into the possession of a hoard purchased with blood.'

"Imprisoned in this labyrinth of crime, torn between love and repulsion, rapture and terror, I could be likened to a man damned, whom a lovely angel beckons from above with a tender smile, while Satan holds him tight in his red-hot talons, so that the pious angel's smile of love, in which all the blessedness of heaven above is reflected, becomes the fiercest of his torments. I thought about running away, even about killing myself. But Madelon? Reproach me, reproach me, my worthy lady, for being too weak to overcome forcefully a passion that shackled me to crime; but am I not atoning for it with an ignominious death?

"One day Cardillac came home in an unusually good mood.

liebkoste Madelon, warf mir die freundlichsten Blicke zu, trank bei
Tische eine Flasche edlen Weins, wie er es nur an hohen Fest- und
Feiertagen zu tun pflegte, sang und jubilierte. Madelon hatte uns verlassen, ich wollte in die Werkstatt: ‹Bleib sitzen, Junge›, rief Cardillac,
‹heut keine Arbeit mehr, laß uns noch eins trinken auf das Wohl der
allerwürdigsten, vortrefflichsten Dame in Paris.› Nachdem ich mit
ihm angestoßen und er ein volles Glas geleert hatte, sprach er: ‹Sag
an, Olivier, wie gefallen dir die Verse:

> Un amant, qui craint les voleurs,
> n'est point digne d'amour.

Er erzählte nun, was sich in den Gemächern der Maintenon mit
Euch und dem Könige begeben, und fügte hinzu, daß er Euch von
jeher verehrt habe, wie sonst kein menschliches Wesen, und daß Ihr,
mit solch hoher Tugend begabt, vor der der böse Stern kraftlos
erbleiche, selbst den schönsten von ihm gefertigten Schmuck tra-
gend, niemals ein böses Gespenst, Mordgedanken in ihm erregen
würdet.

‹Höre, Olivier›, sprach er, ‹wozu ich entschlossen. Vor langer Zeit
sollt ich Halsschmuck und Armbänder fertigen für Henriette von
England und selbst die Steine dazu liefern. Die Arbeit gelang mir wie
keine andere, aber es zerriß mir die Brust, wenn ich daran dachte,
mich von dem Schmuck, der mein Herzenskleinod geworden, trennen zu müssen. Du weißt der Prinzessin unglücklichen Tod durch
Meuchelmord. Ich behielt den Schmuck und will ihn nun als ein
Zeichen meiner Ehrfurcht, meiner Dankbarkeit dem Fräulein von
Scuderi senden im Namen der verfolgten Bande. – Außerdem, daß
die Scuderi das sprechende Zeichen ihres Triumphs erhält, verhöhne
ich auch Desgrais und seine Gesellen, wie sie es verdienen. – Du
sollst ihr den Schmuck hintragen.›

Sowie Cardillac Euern Namen nannte, Fräulein, war es, als würden
schwarze Schleier weggezogen, und das schöne, lichte Bild meiner
glücklichen frühen Kinderzeit ginge wieder auf in bunten, glänzenden Farben. Es kam ein wunderbarer Trost in meine Seele, ein
Hoffnungsstrahl, vor dem die finstern Geister schwanden. Cardillac
mochte den Eindruck, den seine Worte auf mich gemacht,
wahrnehmen und nach seiner Art deuten.

‹Dir scheint›, sprach er, ‹mein Vorhaben zu behagen. Gestehen
kann ich wohl, daß eine tief innere Stimme, sehr verschieden von
der, welche Blutopfer verlangt wie ein gefräßiges Raubtier, mir
befohlen hat, daß ich solches tue. – Manchmal wird mir wunder-

He caressed Madelon, cast the friendliest glances at me, drank a bottle of fine wine at mealtime (something he did only on great occasions and holidays), sang, and made merry. Madelon had left us and I started for the workshop. 'Sit right there, my boy,' Cardillac called; 'no more work today, let's have another drink to toast the health of the most worthy and excellent lady in Paris.' After I clinked glasses with him and he had drained a full glass, he said: 'Tell me, Olivier, how do you like these verses?

> "'A lover who fears thieves
> Is not at all worthy of love.'

"Then he related what had occurred in Mme de Maintenon's apartment with you and the king; he added that he had always revered you more than any other human being, and that you, endowed with such great virtue, in the face of which his evil star lost its force and turned pale, even if you wore the finest piece he ever made, would never arouse an evil ghost or thoughts of murder in him.

"'Listen, Olivier,' he said, 'to what I've determined. Some time ago I was supposed to make a necklace and bracelets for Henrietta of England and even provide the gems for it myself. The work came out better than anything I'd ever done, but it tore my heart out to think about having to part with that piece, which had become my favorite. You know about that princess's unfortunate death by assassination. I kept the jewelry and now, as a token of my respect and gratitude, I want to send it to Mlle de Scudéry as if it came from the gang the police are after. Not only will Mlle de Scudéry receive a striking token of her triumph; in addition, I'll be making fun of Desgrais and his men, as they deserve. You are to bring the jewelry to her.'

"The moment Cardillac mentioned your name, mademoiselle, I felt as if black veils had been drawn aside, and the beautiful, bright image of my happy early childhood were rising up again in variegated, shining colors. A wonderful feeling of comfort entered my soul, a ray of hope before which the dark spirits vanished. Cardillac probably observed the impression his words had made on me, and interpreted them in his own way.

"'You seem,' he said, 'to be pleased with my plan. I must confess that a voice deep inside me, very different from the one that demands bloody victims like a ravenous beast of prey, has commanded me to do this. Sometimes I feel strange in my mind; an

lich im Gemüte –, eine innere Angst, die Furcht vor irgend etwas
Entsetzlichem, dessen Schauer aus einem fernen Jenseits
herüberwehen in die Zeit, ergreift mich gewaltsam. Es ist mir
dann sogar, als ob das, was der böse Stern begonnen durch mich,
meiner unsterblichen Seele, die daran keinen Teil hat, zugerech-
net werden könne. In solcher Stimmung beschloß ich, für die
heilige Jungfrau in der Kirche St. Eustache eine schöne Diaman-
tenkrone zu fertigen. Aber jene unbegreifliche Angst überfiel
mich stärker, so oft ich die Arbeit beginnen wollte, da unterließ
ich's ganz. Jetzt ist es mir, als wenn ich der Tugend und
Frömmigkeit selbst demutsvoll ein Opfer bringe und wirksame
Fürsprache erflehe, indem ich der Scuderi den schönsten
Schmuck sende, den ich jemals gearbeitet.›

Cardillac, mit Eurer ganzen Lebensweise, mein Fräulein, auf das
genaueste bekannt, gab mir nun Art und Weise sowie die Stunde an,
wie und wann ich den Schmuck, den er in ein sauberes Kästchen
schloß, abliefern solle. Mein ganzes Wesen war Entzücken, denn
der Himmel selbst zeigte mir durch den freveligen Cardillac den
Weg, mich zu retten aus der Hölle, in der ich, ein verstoßener
Sünder, schmachte. So dacht ich. Ganz gegen Cardillacs Willen
wollt ich bis zu Euch dringen. Als Anne Brussons Sohn, als Euer
Pflegling gedacht ich, mich Euch zu Füßen zu werfen und Euch
alles – alles zu entdecken. Ihr hättet, gerührt von dem namenlosen
Elend, das der armen, unschuldigen Madelon drohte bei der
Entdeckung, das Geheimnis beachtet, aber Euer hoher, scharfsin-
niger Geist fand gewiß sichre Mittel, ohne jene Entdeckung der ver-
ruchten Bosheit Cardillacs zu steuern. Fragt mich nicht, worin diese
Mittel hätten bestehen sollen, ich weiß es nicht – aber daß Ihr
Madelon und mich retten würdet, davon lag die Überzeugung fest
in meiner Seele wie der Glaube an die trostreiche Hilfe der heiligen
Jungfrau.

Ihr wißt, Fräulein, daß meine Absicht in jener Nacht fehlschlug.
Ich verlor nicht die Hoffnung, ein andermal glücklicher zu sein. Da
geschah es, daß Cardillac plötzlich alle Munterkeit verlor. Er schlich
trübe umher, starrte vor sich hin, murmelte unverständliche Worte,
focht mit den Händen, Feindliches von sich abwehrend, sein Geist
schien gequält von bösen Gedanken. So hatte er es einen ganzen
Morgen getrieben. Endlich setzte er sich an den Werktisch, sprang
unmutig wieder auf, schaute durchs Fenster, sprach ernst und düster:
‹Ich wollte doch, Henriette von England hätte meinen Schmuck getragen!›

inward anxiety, the fear of something terrible, the horrors of which waft into this world from a remote yonder, seizes upon me violently. At such times I even feel as if that which my evil star has undertaken through me, may be reckoned against my immortal soul, which has no part in it. In such a frame of mind I determined to make a beautiful diamond crown for the Holy Virgin in St-Eustache's. But that incomprehensible anxiety came over me more powerfully, every time I tried to begin the work, so I let it go altogether. Now I feel as if I'm humbly making an offering to virtue and piety itself, and gaining an effective advocate, by sending Mlle de Scudéry the most beautiful jewelry I've ever crafted.'

"Cardillac, my lady, who was familiar with every detail of your entire mode of existence, then instructed me as to the manner in which I should deliver to you the jewelry, which he enclosed in a pretty little box, as well as the time when I should do so. I felt nothing but delight, because, by means of the crime-laden Cardillac, heaven itself was showing me the way to escape from the inferno in which I, a cast-off sinner, was languishing. So I thought. Quite contrary to Cardillac's orders, I intended to make my way into your very presence. As Anne Brusson's son, as your protégé, I expected to throw myself at your feet and reveal everything, everything, to you. You would have been touched by the unspeakable misery threatening poor, innocent Madelon should the facts become public, and you would have kept the secret; but your lofty, penetrating mind would surely have found safe ways to counteract Cardillac's wicked malice without exposing anyone. Don't ask me what those ways would have consisted of, I don't know, but that you would save Madelon and me I was firmly convinced in my soul, just as I believe in the comforting aid of the Holy Virgin.

"You know, mademoiselle, that my intentions on that night were thwarted. I didn't lose the hope of being luckier another time. Then it came about that Cardillac suddenly lost his good mood entirely. He skulked around dejectedly, staring into space, mumbling unintelligible words, sparring with his hands, defending himself against a hostile force; his mind seemed tormented by evil thoughts. He had been behaving that way for an entire morning. Finally he sat down at his worktable, jumped up again, out of sorts, looked out the window, and said gravely and somberly: 'I wish after all that Henrietta of England had worn my jewelry!'

Die Worte erfüllten mich mit Entsetzen. Nun wußt ich, daß sein irrer Geist wieder erfaßt war von dem abscheulichen Mordgespenst, daß des Satans Stimme wieder laut geworden vor seinen Ohren. Ich sah Euer Leben bedroht von dem verruchten Mordteufel. Hatte Cardillac nur seinen Schmuck wieder in Händen, so wart Ihr gerettet. Mit jedem Augenblick wuchs die Gefahr. Da begegnete ich Euch auf dem Pontneuf, drängte mich an Eure Kutsche, warf Euch jenen Zettel zu, der Euch beschwor, doch nur gleich den erhaltenen Schmuck in Cardillacs Hände zu bringen. Ihr kamt nicht.

Meine Angst stieg bis zur Verzweiflung, als andern Tages Cardillac von nichts anderm sprach, als von dem köstlichen Schmuck, der ihm in der Nacht vor Augen gekommen. Ich konnte das nur auf Euern Schmuck deuten, und es wurde mir gewiß, daß er über irgendeinen Mordanschlag brüte, den er gewiß schon in der Nacht auszuführen sich vorgenommen. Euch retten mußt ich, und sollt es Cardillacs Leben kosten.

Sowie Cardillac nach dem Abendgebet sich wie gewöhnlich eingeschlossen, stieg ich durch ein Fenster in den Hof, schlüpfte durch die Öffnung in der Mauer und stellte mich unfern in den tiefen Schatten. Nicht lange dauerte es, so kam Cardillac heraus und schlich leise durch die Straße fort. Ich hinter ihm her. Er ging nach der Straße St. Honoré, mir bebte das Herz. Cardillac war mit einemmal mir entschwunden. Ich beschloß, mich an Eure Haustüre zu stellen. Da kommt singend und trillernd, wie damals, als der Zufall mich zum Zuschauer von Cardillacs Mordtat machte, ein Offizier bei mir vorüber, ohne mich zu gewahren. Aber in demselben Augenblick springt eine schwarze Gestalt hervor und fällt über ihn her. Es ist Cardillac. Diesen Mord will ich hindern, mit einem lauten Schrei bin ich in zwei – drei Sätzen zur Stelle.

Nicht der Offizier – Cardillac sinkt, zum Tode getroffen, röchelnd zu Boden. Der Offizier läßt den Dolch fallen, reißt den Degen aus der Scheide, stellt sich, wähnend, ich sei des Mörders Geselle, kampffertig mir entgegen, eilt aber schnell davon, als er gewahrt, daß ich, ohne mich um ihn zu kümmern, nur den Leichnam untersuche. Cardillac lebte noch. Ich lud ihn, nachdem ich den Dolch, den der Offizier hatte fallen lassen, zu mir gesteckt, auf die Schultern und schleppte ihn mühsam fort nach Hause, und durch den geheimen Gang hinauf in die Werkstatt. – Das übrige ist Euch bekannt.

Ihr seht, mein würdiges Fräulein, daß mein einziges Verbrechen nur darin besteht, daß ich Madelons Vater nicht den Gerichten verriet und so seinen Untaten ein Ende machte. Rein bin ich von jeder

"Those words filled me with terror. Now I knew that his sick mind was once again occupied with that repellent, murderous ghost, that Satan's voice was once again speaking loudly in his ears. I saw your life threatened by that wicked, murderous devil. If Cardillac could only regain his jewelry, you were saved. The danger increased with every minute. It was then that I met you on the Pont Neuf, elbowed my way up to your coach, and tossed that note to you, imploring you to return the jewels you had received to Cardillac at once. You didn't come.

"My anxiety became desperation when, on the day following, Cardillac spoke of nothing else but the expensive jewelry that he had seen in a vision that night. I could only interpret that as being your jewelry, and I became certain that he was hatching out some plan of murder, which he had surely determined to carry out that very night. I had to save you, even if it cost Cardillac's life.

"As soon as Cardillac had locked himself in his room as usual after evening prayers, I climbed through a window into the courtyard, slipped through the opening in the wall, and took up a position in the dark not far away. Before very long, Cardillac came out and slinked quietly away down the street. I followed him. He went to the rue St-Honoré; my heart was pounding. Cardillac had suddenly disappeared from my view. I decided to post myself at your front door. Just then an officer walked by me without noticing me; he was singing and warbling just as that other man was on the occasion when chance made me a spectator of Cardillac's murderous attack. But at the same moment a dark figure jumped out of the darkness and pounced on him. It was Cardillac. I wanted to prevent that death; with a loud cry I reached the spot in two or three bounds.

"Not the officer, but Cardillac sank to the ground with a death rattle, mortally wounded. The officer dropped his dagger, rapidly drew his sword from its scabbard, and, imagining that I was the killer's accomplice, stood on his guard against me, but hastened away on observing that, paying no mind to him, I was only examining the body. Cardillac was still alive. After concealing the dagger dropped by the officer on my person, I lifted him onto my shoulders and laboriously carried him home, and into the workshop via the secret passageway. The rest you know.

"You see, my worthy lady, that my only crime consists in failing to betray Madelon's father to the courts, thus putting an end to his atrocities. I am guiltless of any bloodshed. No amount of torture

Blutschuld. – Keine Marter wird mir das Geheimnis von Cardillacs
Untaten abzwingen. Ich will nicht, daß der ewigen Macht, die der tugendhaften Tochter des Vaters gräßliche Blutschuld verschleierte,
zum Trotz das ganze Elend der Vergangenheit, ihres ganzen Seins
noch jetzt tötend auf sie einbreche, daß noch jetzt die weltliche Rache
den Leichnam aufwühle aus der Erde, die ihn deckt, daß noch jetzt
der Henker die vermoderten Gebeine mit Schande brandmarke. –
Nein! – mich wird die Geliebte meiner Seele beweinen als den unschuldig Gefallenen, die Zeit wird ihren Schmerz lindern, aber un-
überwindlich würde der Jammer sein über des geliebten Vaters
entsetzliche Taten der Hölle!» –

Olivier schwieg, aber nun stürzte plötzlich ein Tränenstrom aus
seinen Augen, er warf sich der Scuderi zu Füßen und flehte: «Ihr seid
von meiner Unschuld überzeugt – gewiß, Ihr seid es! – Habt
Erbarmen mit mir, sagt, wie steht es um Madelon?» – Die Scuderi rief
die Martiniere, und nach wenigen Augenblicken flog Madelon an
Oliviers Hals.

«Nun ist alles gut, da du hier bist – ich wußt es ja, daß die edel-
mütigste Dame dich retten würde!» So rief Madelon ein Mal über das
andere, und Olivier vergaß sein Schicksal, alles was ihm drohte, er war
frei und selig. Auf das rührendste klagten beide sich, was sie um
einander gelitten, und umarmten sich dann aufs neue und weinten
vor Entzücken, daß sie sich wiedergefunden.

Wäre die Scuderi nicht von Oliviers Unschuld schon überzeugt
gewesen, der Glaube daran müßte ihr jetzt gekommen sein, da sie die
beiden betrachtete, die in der Seligkeit des innigsten Liebesbünd-
nisses die Welt vergaßen und ihr Elend und ihr namenloses Leiden.
«Nein», rief sie, «solch seliger Vergessenheit ist nur ein reines Herz
fähig.»

Die hellen Strahlen des Morgens brachen durch die Fenster.
Desgrais klopfte leise an die Türe des Gemachs und erinnerte, daß es
Zeit sei, Olivier Brusson fortzuschaffen, da ohne Aufsehen zu erregen
das später nicht geschehen könne. Die Liebenden mußten sich trennen. –

Die dunklen Ahnungen, von denen der Scuderi Gemüt befangen
seit Brussons erstem Eintritt in ihr Haus, hatten sich nun zum Leben
gestaltet auf furchtbare Weise. Den Sohn ihrer geliebten Anne sah sie
schuldlos verstrickt auf eine Art, daß ihn vom schmachvollen Tod zu
retten kaum denkbar schien. Sie ehrte des Jünglings Heldensinn, der
lieber schuldbeladen sterben, als ein Geheimnis verraten wollte, das
seiner Madelon den Tod bringen mußte. Im ganzen Reiche der Mög-

will make me reveal the secret of Cardillac's crimes. The eternal power has so far concealed the father's awful guilt from the virtuous daughter; I don't want to thwart it and have the whole misery of the past, and of her whole existence, break in on her now and kill her. I don't want secular vengeance to dig the corpse even now out of the earth that covers it; I don't want the hangman even now to brand the moldering bones with shame. No! The beloved of my soul shall mourn *me* as one executed though guiltless; time will abate her grief, but her sorrow over her beloved father's terrible, infernal deeds would be insurmountable!"

Olivier fell silent, but now a flood of tears suddenly gushed from his eyes; he threw himself at Mlle de Scudéry's feet and implored her: "You're convinced that I'm innocent; you must be, surely! Have mercy on me; tell me, how is Madelon getting along?" Mlle de Scudéry summoned Martinière, and a few moments later Madelon flung her arms around Olivier.

"Now everything's all right, since you're here! I knew that this most nobleminded lady would save you!" Thus Madelon exclaimed over and over, and Olivier forgot his fate and everything that menaced him; he felt free and blessed. The couple lamented in the most touching way, each one recounting what he had suffered for the other's sake, and then they embraced again and wept in rapture at their reunion.

If Mlle de Scudéry hadn't been convinced already that Olivier was innocent, she would have begun to believe it then, as she observed the couple forget the world, their misery, and their unspeakable suffering in the bliss of the warmest loving bond. "No," she exclaimed, "only a pure heart is capable of such blessed oblivion!"

The bright rays of the morning sun were breaking through the windows. Desgrais tapped lightly at the door to the room, reminding them that it was time to take Olivier Brusson away, since that couldn't be done later without attracting attention. The lovers had to part.

The gloomy forebodings that had occupied Mlle de Scudéry's mind ever since Brusson first entered her house had now come to life in a frightening way. She saw the son of her beloved Anne entangled, though not guilty, in such a manner that it scarcely seemed conceivable to save him from an ignominious death. She honored the young man's heroic intentions of dying laden with guilt rather than betraying a secret that would surely kill his

lichkeit fand sie kein Mittel, den Ärmsten dem grausamen Gerichts-
hofe zu entreißen. Und doch stand es fest in ihrer Seele, daß sie kein
Opfer scheuen müsse, das himmelschreiende Unrecht abzuwenden,
das man zu begehen im Begriffe war.

Sie quälte sich ab mit allerlei Entwürfen und Plänen, die bis an das
Abenteuerliche streiften, und die sie ebenso schnell verwarf als auf-
faßte. Immer mehr verschwand jeder Hoffnungsschimmer, so daß sie
verzweifeln wollte. Aber Madelons unbedingtes, frommes kindliches
Vertrauen, die Verklärung, mit der sie von dem Geliebten sprach, der
nun bald, freigesprochen von jeder Schuld, sie als Gattin umarmen
werde, richtete die Scuderi in eben dem Grad wieder auf, als sie
davon bis tief ins Herz gerührt wurde.

Um nun endlich etwas zu tun, schrieb die Scuderi an la Regnie
einen langen Brief, worin sie ihm sagte, daß Olivier Brusson ihr auf
die glaubwürdigste Weise seine völlige Unschuld an Cardillacs Tode
dargetan habe, und daß nur der heldenmütige Entschluß, ein
Geheimnis in das Grab zu nehmen, dessen Enthüllung die Unschuld
und Tugend selbst verderben würde, ihn zurückhalte, dem Gericht
ein Geständnis abzulegen, das ihn von dem entsetzlichen Verdacht
nicht allein, daß er Cardillac ermordet, sondern daß er auch zur
Bande verruchter Mörder gehöre, befreien müsse. Alles was glühender Eifer, was geistvolle Beredsamkeit vermag, hatte die Scuderi
aufgeboten, la Regnies hartes Herz zu erweichen.

Nach wenigen Stunden antwortete la Regnie, wie es ihn herzlich
freue, wenn Olivier Brusson sich bei seiner hohen, würdigen Gön-
nerin gänzlich gerechtfertigt habe. Was Oliviers heldenmütigen
Entschluß betreffe, ein Geheimnis, das sich auf die Tat beziehe, mit
ins Grab nehmen zu wollen, so tue es ihm leid, daß die Chambre ardente dergleichen Heldenmut nicht ehren könne, denselben
vielmehr durch die kräftigsten Mittel zu brechen suchen müsse. Nach
drei Tagen hoffe er in dem Besitz des seltsamen Geheimnisses zu
sein, das wahrscheinlich geschehene Wunder an den Tag bringen
werde.

Nur zu gut wußte die Scuderi, was der fürchterliche la Regnie mit
jenen Mitteln, die Brussons Heldenmut brechen sollen, meinte. Nun
war es gewiß, daß die Tortur über den Unglücklichen verhängt war. In
der Todesangst fiel der Scuderi endlich ein, daß, um nur Aufschub zu
erlangen, der Rat eines Rechtsverständigen dienlich sein könne.
Pierre Arnaud d'Andilly war damals der berühmteste Advokat in
Paris. Seiner tiefen Wissenschaft, seinem umfassenden Verstande war
seine Rechtschaffenheit, seine Tugend gleich. Zu dem begab sich die

Madelon. In the whole realm of possibility she found no way of snatching the poor fellow from the grasp of the cruel judges. And yet it was clear in her soul that she mustn't avoid any sacrifice in order to avert the outrageous injustice that was about to be committed.

She racked her brain with all sorts of projects and plans, which bordered on the quixotic, and which she rejected as soon as she conceived them. Increasingly every glimmer of hope was vanishing, so that she was nearly in despair. But Madelon's absolute, pious, childlike trust, her transfigured looks when she spoke about the man she loved, who soon now, acquitted of all guilt, would embrace her as his wife, encouraged Mlle de Scudéry to the same degree as it touched her heart deeply.

In order to do something finally, Mlle de Scudéry wrote a long letter to La Reynie in which she told him that Olivier Brusson had demonstrated his total innocence of Cardillac's murder to her in a way most worthy of belief, and that only his heroic decision to take with him to his grave a secret which, if revealed, would destroy innocence and virtue itself was keeping him from making a confession to the judges which would surely free him not merely from the terrible suspicion of having murdered Cardillac, but also from that of belonging to the gang of wicked killers. Mlle de Scudéry had called upon all her powers of ardent zeal and intelligent eloquence in order to soften La Reynie's hard heart.

A few hours later, La Reynie replied that he was sincerely glad that Olivier Brusson had justified himself completely in the eyes of his noble, worthy patroness. As for Olivier's heroic decision to take with him to his grave a secret relating to the crime, he was sorry to state that the *chambre ardente* was unable to honor that kind of heroism, but instead was duty-bound to break it down by the most powerful means. He hoped to be in possession of the strange secret in three days' time; it would probably bring veritable miracles to light.

Mlle de Scudéry knew only too well what the fearsome La Reynie meant by the means that were to break down Brusson's heroism. It was now certain that the unfortunate man was slated for torture. In her deathly fear it finally occurred to Mlle de Scudéry that, merely to gain a delay, a jurist's advice could be helpful. The most famous lawyer in Paris at the time was Pierre Arnauld d'Andilly. His uprightness and virtue were equal to his profound knowledge and comprehensive understanding. Mlle

Scuderi und sagte ihm alles, soweit es möglich war, ohne Brussons
Geheimnis zu verletzen.

Sie glaubte, daß d'Andilly mit Eifer sich des Unschuldigen annehmen werde, ihre Hoffnung wurde aber auf das bitterste getäuscht.
D'Andilly hatte ruhig alles angehört und erwiderte dann lächelnd mit
Boileaus Worten: «Le vrai peut quelque fois n'être pas vraisemblable.» – Er bewies der Scuderi, daß die auffallendsten Verdachts-
gründe wider Brusson sprächen, daß la Regnies Verfahren keineswegs
grausam und übereilt zu nennen, vielmehr ganz gesetzlich sei, ja, daß
er nicht anders handeln könne, ohne die Pflichten des Richters zu
verletzen. Er, d'Andilly, selbst getraue sich nicht durch die geschickteste Verteidigung Brusson von der Tortur zu retten. Nur Brusson
selbst könne das entweder durch aufrichtiges Geständnis oder wenigstens durch die genaueste Erzählung der Umstände bei dem Morde
Cardillacs, die dann vielleicht erst zu neuen Ausmittelungen Anlaß
geben würden.

«So werfe ich mich dem Könige zu Füßen und flehe um Gnade»,
sprach die Scuderi, ganz außer sich mit von Tränen halb erstickter
Stimme.

«Tut das», rief d'Andilly, «tut das um des Himmels willen nicht,
mein Fräulein! – Spart Euch dieses letzte Hilfsmittel auf, das, schlug
es einmal fehl, Euch für immer verloren ist. Der König wird nimmer
einen Verbrecher *der* Art begnadigen, der bitterste Vorwurf des
gefährdeten Volks würde ihn treffen. Möglich ist es, daß Brusson
durch Entdeckung seines Geheimnisses oder sonst Mittel findet, den
wider ihn streitenden Verdacht aufzuheben. Dann ist es Zeit, des
Königs Gnade zu erflehen, der nicht darnach fragen, was vor Gericht
bewiesen ist oder nicht, sondern seine innere Überzeugung zu Rate
ziehen wird.»

Die Scuderi mußte dem tieferfahrnen d'Andilly notgedrungen
beipflichten. – In tiefen Kummer versenkt, sinnend und sinnend, was
um der Jungfrau und aller Heiligen willen sie nun anfangen solle, um
den unglücklichen Brusson zu retten, saß sie am späten Abend in
ihrem Gemach, als die Martinière eintrat und den Grafen von
Miossens, Obristen von der Garde des Königs, meldete, der dringend
wünsche, das Fräulein zu sprechen.

«Verzeiht», sprach Miossens, indem er sich mit soldatischem
Anstande verbeugte, «verzeiht, mein Fräulein, wenn ich Euch so spät,
so zu ungelegener Zeit überlaufe. Wir Soldaten machen es nicht an-

de Scudéry visited him and told him everything, as far as it was possible without violating Brusson's secret.

She thought that D'Andilly would eagerly take the innocent man's case, but her hopes were most bitterly disappointed. D'Andilly had heard her out calmly, then smilingly replied in the words of Boileau: *"Le vrai peut quelquefois n'être pas vraisemblable."*[8] He proved to Mlle de Scudéry that the most conspicuous grounds for suspicion told against Brusson, and that La Reynie's procedure could in no way be called cruel or hasty; rather, it was quite legal; in fact, he couldn't act otherwise without violating his duties as a judge. He, D'Andilly, didn't think he could save Brusson from torture even with the most skillful defense. Only Brusson himself could do so, either by an honest confession or at least by a detailed narration of the circumstances of Cardillac's death, which would then perhaps give rise to new investigations.

"In that case I'll throw myself at the king's feet and beg for a pardon," Mlle de Scudéry said, completely beside herself, in a voice half-choked by tears.

"For heaven's sake, don't do that, mademoiselle," D'Andilly cried. "Keep that ultimate remedy in reserve for the time being; if it fails once, it will never be available to you again. The king will never pardon a criminal of that sort; he'd be the target of the bitterest reproaches from his subjects, whose lives are in danger. Brusson may possibly, by revealing his secret or some other way, find the means to remove the suspicion that is working against him. Then would be the right time to beg for a pardon from the king, who won't ask what is legally proven or not, but will judge by his inner convictions."

Mlle de Scudéry was compelled to agree with the greatly experienced D'Andilly. Plunged into deep cares, constantly thinking of what—by the Holy Virgin and all the saints!—she should now undertake in order to save the unfortunate Brusson, she was sitting in her room late in the evening when Martinière came in and announced the Comte de Miossens, colonel of the king's guard, who urgently wished to speak with the lady.

"Pardon me," said Miossens, bowing with soldierly courtesy, "pardon me, my lady, for breaking in on you so late, at such an inopportune time. That's the way we soldiers are, and, besides,

---

8. "At times what is true may not appear to be so."

ders, und zudem bin ich mit zwei Worten entschuldigt. – Olivier
Brusson führt mich zu Euch.»

Die Scuderi, hochgespannt, was sie jetzt wieder erfahren werde,
rief laut: «Olivier Brusson? der unglücklichste aller Menschen? – was
habt Ihr mit dem?»

«Dacht ich's doch», sprach Miossens lächelnd weiter, «daß Eures
Schützlings Namen hinreichen würde, mir bei Euch ein geneigtes
Ohr zu verschaffen. Die ganze Welt ist von Brussons Schuld überzeugt. Ich weiß, daß Ihr eine andere Meinung hegt, die sich
freilich nur auf die Beteuerungen des Angeklagten stützen soll,
wie man gesagt hat. Mit mir ist es anders. Niemand als ich kann
besser überzeugt sein von Brussons Unschuld an dem Tode
Cardillacs.»

«Redet, o redet», rief die Scuderi, indem ihr die Augen glänzten vor
Entzücken.

«Ich», sprach Miossens mit Nachdruck, «ich war es selbst, der den
alten Goldschmied niederstieß in der Straße St. Honoré unfern
Eurem Hause.»

«Um aller Heiligen willen, Ihr – Ihr!» rief die Scuderi.

«Und», fuhr Miossens fort, «und ich schwöre es Euch, mein
Fräulein, daß ich stolz bin auf meine Tat. Wisset, daß Cardillac der
verruchteste, heuchlerischste Bösewicht, daß er es war, der in der
Nacht heimtückisch mordete und raubte und so lange allen
Schlingen entging. Ich weiß selbst nicht, wie es kam, daß ein innerer
Verdacht sich in mir gegen den alten Bösewicht regte, als er voll
sichtlicher Unruhe den Schmuck brachte, den ich bestellt, als er sich
genau erkundigte, für wen ich den Schmuck bestimmt, und als er auf
recht listige Art meinen Kammerdiener ausgefragt hatte, wann ich
eine gewisse Dame zu besuchen pflege. – Längst war es mir aufgefallen, daß die unglücklichen Schlachtopfer der abscheulichsten
Raubgier alle dieselbe Todeswunde trugen. Es war mir gewiß, daß
der Mörder auf den Stoß, der augenblicklich töten mußte, eingeübt
war und darauf rechnete. Schlug der fehl, so galt es den gleichen
Kampf. Dies ließ mich eine Vorsichtsmaßregel brauchen, die so ein-
fach ist, daß ich nicht begreife, wie andere nicht längst darauf fielen
und sich retteten von dem bedrohlichen Mordwesen. Ich trug einen
leichten Brustharnisch unter der Weste. Cardillac fiel mich von hinten an. Er umfaßte mich mit Riesenkraft, aber der sicher geführte
Stoß glitt ab an dem Eisen. In demselben Augenblick entwand ich
mich ihm und stieß ihm den Dolch, den ich in Bereitschaft hatte, in
die Brust.»

two words will be enough to excuse me. I'm here on Olivier Brusson's account."

Mlle de Scudéry, in great suspense as to what further news she was about to receive, called loudly: "Olivier Brusson? That most unfortunate of men? What's your connection with him?"

"Just as I thought," Miossens went on, smiling. "The name of your protégé was sufficient to obtain a willing ear from you. Everyone is convinced that Brusson is guilty. I know that you have a different opinion, which, as people have said, is of course based entirely on the assertions of the accused. My case is different. No one can be more convinced than I am that Brusson is guiltless of Cardillac's death."

"Speak, oh, speak!" Mlle de Scudéry exclaimed, her eyes shining with delight.

"It was I," Miossens said emphatically, "I myself, who brought the old goldsmith down on the rue St-Honoré, not far from your house."

"By all the saints, you! You!" Mlle de Scudéry cried.

"And," Miossens continued, "I swear to you, mademoiselle, that I'm proud of what I did. I'll have you know that Cardillac was the most wicked and hypocritical scoundrel, that it was he who maliciously killed and robbed at night, eluding all snares for so long. I don't know myself how a suspicion of the old scoundrel happened to formulate itself in my mind, when, filled with visible unrest, he brought the jewelry I had ordered, when he asked in detail to whom I intended to give it, and when he had interrogated my valet in a truly crafty way as to the hour at which I'm accustomed to visit a certain lady. I had been struck much earlier by the fact that all the unlucky victims of that most abhorrent rapacity showed the same fatal wound. I was sure that the killer had trained himself to deliver a blow that would kill at once, and that he relied on this. If that blow were to miss, he'd face an equal combat. This led me to use a precautionary measure that's so simple, I can't understand why it hadn't occurred to others long before, so they could have escaped from that menacing assassin. I wore a light breastplate beneath my waistcoat. Cardillac attacked me from behind. His arms encircled me with the strength of a giant, but his unerringly directed blow glanced off the iron. At the same moment I broke loose from him and plunged into his breast the dagger I had in readiness."

«Und Ihr schwiegt», fragte die Scuderi, «Ihr zeigtet den Gerichten nicht an, was geschehen?»

«Erlaubt», sprach Miossens weiter, «erlaubt, mein Fräulein, zu bemerken, daß eine solche Anzeige mich, wo nicht geradezu ins Verderben, doch in den abscheulichsten Prozeß verwickeln konnte. Hätte la Regnie, überall Verbrechen witternd, mir's denn geradehin geglaubt, wenn *ich* den rechtschaffenen Cardillac, das Muster aller Frömmigkeit und Tugend, des versuchten Mordes angeklagt? Wie, wenn das Schwert der Gerechtigkeit seine Spitze wider mich selbst gewandt?»

«Das war nicht möglich», rief die Scuderi, «Eure Geburt – Euer Stand –»

«O», fuhr Miossens fort, «denkt doch an den Marschall von Luxemburg, den der Einfall, sich von le Sage das Horoskop stellen zu lassen, in den Verdacht des Giftmordes und in die Bastille brachte. Nein, beim St. Dionys, nicht eine Stunde Freiheit, nicht meinen Ohrzipfel geb ich preis dem rasenden la Regnie, der sein Messer gern an unserer aller Kehlen setzte.»

«Aber so bringt Ihr ja den unschuldigen Brusson aufs Schafott?» fiel ihm die Scuderi ins Wort.

«Unschuldig», erwiderte Miossens, «unschuldig, mein Fräulein, nennt Ihr des verruchten Cardillacs Spießgesellen? – der ihm beistand in seinen Taten? der den Tod hundertmal verdient hat? – Nein, in der Tat, *der* blutet mit Recht, und daß ich Euch, mein hochverehrtes Fräulein, den wahren Zusammenhang der Sache entdeckte, geschah in der Voraussetzung, daß Ihr, ohne mich in die Hände der Chambre ardente zu liefern, doch mein Geheimnis auf irgendeine Weise für Euren Schützling zu nützen verstehen würdet.»

Die Scuderi, im Innersten entzückt, ihre Überzeugung von Brussons Unschuld auf solch entscheidende Weise bestätigt zu sehen, nahm gar keinen Anstand, dem Grafen, der Cardillacs Verbrechen ja schon kannte, alles zu entdecken und ihn aufzufordern, sich mit ihr zu d'Andilly zu begeben. *Dem* sollte unter dem Siegel der Verschwiegenheit alles entdeckt werden, *der* solle dann Rat erteilen, was nun zu beginnen.

D'Andilly, nachdem die Scuderi ihm alles auf das genaueste erzählt hatte, erkundigte sich nochmals nach den geringfügigsten Umständen. Insbesondere fragte er den Grafen Miossens, ob er auch die feste Überzeugung habe, daß er von Cardillac angefallen, und ob er Olivier Brusson als denjenigen würde wiedererkennen können, der den Leichnam fortgetragen.

"And you kept silent?" Mlle de Scudéry asked. "You didn't report the event to the judges?"

"Permit me," Miossens continued, "permit me to observe, mademoiselle, that such a declaration, if it didn't lead directly to my ruin, could at least entangle me in the most repugnant investigation and trial. Would La Reynie, who smells crime everywhere, have believed me right off, if *I* had accused the honest Cardillac, the model of all piety and virtue, of attempted murder? What if the sword of Justice had turned its point against *me?*"

"That wasn't possible," Mlle de Scudéry cried. "Your birth, your rank—"

"Oh," Miossens continued, "just think about the Maréchal de Luxembourg, whose whim to have his horoscope cast by Lesage brought him under suspicion of poisoning, and into the Bastille. No, by Saint Denis, I won't sacrifice an hour of freedom, not the tip of my ear, to that rabid La Reynie, who'd like to put his knife to all our throats!"

"But in this way you're leading Brusson, who's innocent, to the scaffold?" Mlle de Scudéry exclaimed, interrupting him.

"Innocent?" Miossens replied. "Mademoiselle, you call the accomplice of the wicked Cardillac innocent? The man who assisted him in his crimes, the man who deserves to die for a hundred reasons? No, indeed, *he* will be executed rightfully and, my greatly revered lady, I revealed the true state of the case to you strictly on the assumption that, without handing me over to the *chambre ardente,* you'd know how to use my secret in some way for the benefit of your protégé."

Mlle de Scudéry, thoroughly delighted to see her opinion that Brusson was innocent confirmed in such a conclusive way, had no hesitation in revealing everything to the comte, who knew about Cardillac's crimes anyway, and in inviting him to visit D'Andilly with her. To *him* everything would now be revealed under the seal of secrecy, and *he* would then offer advice as to what to do next.

After Mlle de Scudéry had told D'Andilly everything in full detail, he asked further questions about the most trivial circumstances. In particular he asked the Comte de Miossens whether he, too, was firmly convinced that he had been attacked by Cardillac, and whether he'd be able to recognize Olivier Brusson as the man who carried away the body.

«Außerdem», ewiderte Miossens, «daß ich in der mondhellen Nacht den Goldschmied recht gut erkannte, habe ich auch bei la Regnie selbst den Dolch gesehen, mit dem Cardillac niedergestoßen wurde. Es ist der meinige, ausgezeichnet durch die zierliche Arbeit des Griffs. Nur einen Schritt von ihm stehend, gewahrte ich alle Züge des Jünglings, dem der Hut vom Kopf gefallen, und würde ihn allerdings wiedererkennen können.»

D'Andilly sah schweigend einige Augenblicke vor sich nieder, dann sprach er: «Auf gewöhnlichem Wege ist Brusson aus den Händen der Justiz nun ganz und gar nicht zu retten. Er will Madelons halber Cardillac nicht als Mordräuber nennen. Das mag er tun, denn selbst, wenn es ihm gelingen müßte, durch Entdeckung des heimlichen Ausgangs, des zusammengeraubten Schatzes dies nachzuweisen, würde ihn doch als Mitverbundenen der Tod treffen. Dasselbe Verhältnis bleibt stehen, wenn der Graf Miossens die Begebenheit mit dem Goldschmied, wie sie wirklich sich zutrug, den Richtern entdecken solle. *Aufschub* ist das einzige, wornach getrachtet werden muß. Graf Miossens begibt sich nach der Conciergerie, läßt sich Olivier Brusson vorstellen und erkennt ihn für den, der den Leichnam Cardillacs fortschaffte. Er eilt zu la Regnie und sagt: ‹In der Straße St. Honoré sah ich einen Menschen niederstoßen, ich stand dicht neben dem Leichnam, als ein anderer hinzusprang, sich zum Leichnam niederbückte, ihn, da er noch Leben spürte, auf die Schultern lud und forttrug. In Olivier Brusson habe ich diesen Menschen erkannt.› Diese Aussage veranlaßt Brussons nochmalige Vernehmung, Zusammenstellung mit dem Grafen Miossens. Genug, die Tortur unterbleibt, und man forscht weiter nach. Dann ist es Zeit, sich an den König selbst zu wenden. Euerm Scharfsinn, mein Fräulein, bleibt es überlassen, dies auf die geschickteste Weise zu tun. Nach meinem Dafürhalten würd es gut sein, dem Könige das ganze Geheimnis zu entdecken. Durch diese Aussage des Grafen Miossens werden Brussons Geständnisse unterstützt. Dasselbe geschieht vielleicht durch geheime Nachforschungen in Cardillacs Hause. Keinen Rechtsspruch, aber des Königs Entscheidung, auf inneres Gefühl, das da, wo der Richter strafen muß, Gnade ausspricht, gestützt, kann das alles begründen. –» Graf Miossens befolgte genau, was d'Andilly geraten, und es geschah wirklich, was dieser vorhergesehen.

Nun kam es darauf an, den König anzugehen, und dies war der

"In addition to the fact," Miossens replied, "that it was a night of bright moonshine and I recognized the goldsmith perfectly, I've also seen in the possession of La Reynie himself the dagger with which Cardillac was cut down. It's mine, as I can tell by the ornamental metalwork on the handle. Standing only one pace away from him, I could observe every feature of the young man, whose hat had fallen off his head, and I'd surely recognize him if I saw him again."

D'Andilly stared down at the floor in silence for a few moments, then said: "As things stand, Brusson can absolutely not be rescued from the hands of justice in the customary way. For Madelon's sake he refuses to name Cardillac as a killer and robber. He isn't wrong, because even though he'd surely succeed in proving it, by revealing the secret exit and the hoard of stolen jewelry, nevertheless he'd be liable to execution as an accessory. The same situation would still hold if the Comte de Miossens were to reveal to the judges the incident with the goldsmith as it really took place. *Delay* is the only thing we should work for. The Comte de Miossens must go to the Conciergerie, where he will request an interview with Olivier Brusson and will recognize him as the man who carried away Cardillac's body. He will then hasten to La Reynie and say: 'I saw a man being stabbed to death on the rue St-Honoré; I was standing right by the body when another man dashed over, stooped down over the body, and, finding signs of life, lifted the wounded man onto his shoulders and carried him away. I have recognized Olivier Brusson as being that man.' This statement will result in a new interrogation of Brusson, who will be brought face to face with the Comte de Miossens. Thereby the torture will be postponed and the investigation will continue. Then it will be time to have recourse to the king himself. I leave it to your intelligence, my lady, to do this in the most skillful way. In my opinion, it would be a good idea to reveal the entire secret to the king. Brusson's confessions will be supported by this statement made by the Comte de Miossens. Perhaps the same result may be achieved by secret searches in Cardillac's house. All this can serve as a basis, not for any legal ruling, but for the king's decision, supported by that inner feeling which pronounces pardon where a judge is compelled to order punishment." The Comte de Miossens followed D'Andilly's advice to the letter, and things turned out exactly as the jurist had foreseen.

Now it was a matter of approaching the king, which was the

schwierigste Punkt, da er gegen Brusson, den er allein für den entsetzlichen Raubmörder hielt, welcher so lange Zeit hindurch ganz
Paris in Angst und Schrecken gesetzt hatte, solchen Abscheu hegte,
daß er, nur leise erinnert an den berüchtigten Prozeß, in den heftig-
sten Zorn geriet. Die Maintenon, ihrem Grundsatz, dem Könige nie
von unangenehmen Dingen zu reden, getreu, verwarf jede
Vermittlung, und so war Brussons Schicksal ganz in die Hand der
Scuderi gelegt. Nach langem Sinnen faßte sie einen Entschluß ebenso
schnell, als sie ihn ausführte.

Sie kleidete sich in eine schwarze Robe von schwerem Seidenzeug,
schmückte sich mit Cardillacs köstlichem Geschmeide, hing einen
langen, schwarzen Schleier über und erschien so in den Gemächern
der Maintenon zur Stunde, da eben der König zugegen. Die edle
Gestalt des ehrwürdigen Fräuleins in diesem feierlichen Anzuge hatte
eine Majestät, die tiefe Ehrfurcht erwecken mußte selbst bei dem
losen Volk, das gewohnt ist, in den Vorzimmern sein leichtsinnig
nichts beachtendes Wesen zu treiben.

Alles wich scheu zur Seite, und als sie nun eintrat, stand selbst der
König ganz verwundert auf und kam ihr entgegen. Da blitzten ihm
die köstlichen Diamanten des Halsbands, der Armbänder ins Auge,
und er rief: «Beim Himmel, das ist Cardillacs Geschmeide!» Und
dann sich zur Maintenon wendend, fügte er mit anmutigem Lächeln
hinzu: «Seht, Frau Marquise, wie unsere schöne Braut um ihren
Bräutigam trauert.»

«Ei, gnädiger Herr», fiel die Scuderi, wie den Scherz fortsetzend,
ein, «wie würd es ziemen einer schmerzerfüllten Braut, sich so
glanzvoll zu schmücken? Nein, ich habe mich ganz losgesagt von
diesem Goldschmied und dächte nicht mehr an ihn, träte mir nicht
manchmal das abscheuliche Bild, wie er ermordet dicht bei mir
vorübergetragen wurde, vor Augen.»

«Wie», fragte der König, «wie! Ihr habt ihn gesehen, den armen
Teufel?»

Die Scuderi erzählte nun mit kurzen Worten, wie sie der Zufall
(noch erwähnte sie nicht der Einmischung Brussons) vor Cardillacs
Haus gebracht, als eben der Mord entdeckt worden. Sie schilderte
Madelons wilden Schmerz, den tiefen Eindruck, den das
Himmelskind auf sie gemacht, die Art, wie sie die Arme unter
Zujauchzen des Volks aus Desgrais' Händen gerettet. Mit immer
steigendem und steigendem Interesse begannen nun die Szenen mit
la Regnie – mit Desgrais – mit Olivier Brusson selbst.

Der König, hingerissen von der Gewalt des lebendigsten

most ticklish point, since he felt such abhorrence of Brusson, whom alone he regarded as the horrible robber and killer that had thrown all of Paris into a fearful panic for such a long time; so that, whenever the slightest mention was made of that notorious investigation, he flew into the most violent rage. Mme de Maintenon, faithful to her principle never to speak to the king about unpleasant matters, refused any intercession, and so Brusson's fate was left completely in Mlle de Scudéry's hands. After lengthy consideration she came to a decision as quickly as she carried it out.

She put on a black dress of heavy silk, adorned herself with Cardillac's costly jewelry, covered her face with a long black veil, and appeared in that array in Mme de Maintenon's apartment at the hour when the king was usually there. The noble form of the venerable lady in that solemn attire possessed a majesty that couldn't fail to instill respect even in those dissolute creatures who are accustomed to hang around antechambers, giddy and thoughtless as they are.

Everyone stood aside timidly, and when she walked in, the king himself stood up in awe and came to meet her. His eye was caught by the flashing of the costly diamonds in the necklace and bracelets, and he cried: "By heaven, Cardillac made that jewelry!" Then, addressing Mme de Maintenon, he added, with a charming smile: "You see, marquise, how our lovely bride is mourning for her bridegroom."

"Oh, gracious lord," interjected Mlle de Scudéry, as if continuing the joke, "how would it look for a sorrowing bride to adorn herself so richly? No, I have broken completely with that goldsmith, and I wouldn't think about him anymore if I didn't sometimes see that awful image of his being carried out right alongside me when he was murdered."

"What?" the king asked. "What? You saw that poor devil?"

Then Mlle de Scudéry told concisely how chance (at this point she still didn't mention Brusson's involvement) had led her to Cardillac's house just after the murder had been discovered. She depicted Madelon's wild sorrow, the deep impression that that angelic child had made on her, and the way she had rescued the poor girl from Desgrais's clutches, to the applause of the crowd. He story became increasingly interesting as she proceeded to the scenes with La Reynie, Desgrais, and Olivier Brusson himself.

The king, fascinated by the force of the pulsating life that

Lebens, das in der Scuderi Rede glühte, gewahrte nicht, daß von dem gehässigen Prozeß des ihm abscheulichen Brussons die Rede war, vermochte nicht ein Wort hervorzubringen, konnte nur dann und wann mit einem Ausruf Luft machen der innern Bewegung. Ehe er sich's versah, ganz außer sich über das Unerhörte, was er erfahren, und noch nicht vermögend, alles zu ordnen, lag die Scuderi schon zu seinen Füßen und flehte um Gnade für Olivier Brusson.

«Was tut Ihr», brach der König los, indem er sie bei beiden Händen faßte und in den Sessel nötigte, «was tut Ihr, mein Fräulein! – Ihr überrascht mich auf seltsame Weise! – Das ist ja eine entsetzliche Geschichte! – Wer bürgt für die Wahrheit der abenteuerlichen Erzählung Brussons?»

Darauf die Scuderi: «Miossens' Aussage – die Untersuchung in Cardillacs Hause – innere Überzeugung – ach! Madelons tugendhaftes Herz, das gleiche Tugend in dem unglücklichen Brusson erkannte!»

Der König, im Begriff, etwas zu erwidern, wandte sich auf ein Geräusch um, das an der Türe entstand. Louvois, der eben im andern Gemach arbeitete, sah hinein mit besorglicher Miene. Der König stand auf und verließ, Louvois folgend, das Zimmer. Beide, die Scuderi, die Maintenon, hielten diese Unterbrechung für gefährlich, denn einmal überrascht, mochte der König sich hüten, in die gestellte Falle zum zweitenmal zu gehen. Doch nach einigen Minuten trat der König wieder hinein, schritt rasch ein paarmal im Zimmer auf und ab, stellte sich dann, die Hände über den Rücken geschlagen, dicht vor der Scuderi hin und sprach, ohne sie anzublicken, halb leise: «Wohl möcht ich Eure Madelon sehen!»

Darauf die Scuderi: «O mein gnädiger Herr, welches hohen – hohen Glücks würdigt Ihr das arme, unglückliche Kind – ach, nur Eures Winks bedurft es ja, die Kleine zu Euren Füßen zu sehen.» Und trippelte dann, so schnell sie es in den schweren Kleidern vermochte, nach der Tür und rief hinaus, der König wolle Madelon Cardillac vor sich lassen, und kam zurück und weinte und schluchzte vor Entzücken und Rührung. Die Scuderi hatte solche Gunst geahnet und daher Madelon mitgenommen, die bei der Marquise Kammerfrau wartete mit einer kurzen Bittschrift in den Händen, die ihr d'Andilly aufgesetzt.

In wenig Augenblicken lag sie sprachlos dem Könige zu Füßen. Angst – Bestürzung – scheue Ehrfurcht – Liebe und Schmerz –

glowed in Mlle de Scudéry's words, temporarily forgot that the subject was the hateful investigation of the Brusson he loathed; he was unable to utter a word, but merely gave vent to his mental excitement with an occasional exclamation. Before he realized it, since he was completely amazed by the extraordinary things he had heard, which he could not yet sort out in his mind, Mlle de Scudéry already lay prostrate at his feet, beseeching him to pardon Olivier Brusson.

"What are you doing?" the king blurted out, seizing her two hands and forcing her onto a chair. "What are you doing, mademoiselle? You surprise me in the strangest way! That is indeed a terrible tale! Who vouches for the truth of Brusson's fantastic story?"

Mlle de Scudéry replied: "Miossens's statement, the search in Cardillac's house, inner convictions—and, oh, Madelon's virtuous heart, which recognized the same virtue in the unfortunate Brusson!"

The king, on the point of making some reply, turned around on hearing a noise at the door. Louvois, who had been working in the adjoining room, was looking in with a worried expression. The king stood up and left the room, with Louvois following. Both Mlle de Scudéry and Mme de Maintenon considered that interruption to be dangerous, because, though he had been taken by surprise once, the king might be on his guard against walking into the trap a second time. But a few minutes later, the king returned, rapidly paced up and down the room a couple of times, and then, his hands behind his back, came to a halt right in front of Mlle de Scudéry, and, without looking at her, said in a moderate tone: "I'd like to see your Madelon!"

To which Mlle de Scudéry replied: "Oh, my gracious lord, what great, great good fortune you are granting to that poor, unhappy child! Oh, only a gesture from you was needed for the girl to appear at your feet." Then, taking small steps, and going as fast as she could in those heavy clothes, she walked to the door and called to those outside that the king was granting audience to Madelon Cardillac; then she returned and wept and sobbed with delight and compassion. Mlle de Scudéry had foreseen the king's graciousness and so she had brought along Madelon, who was waiting in the room of the marquise's lady of the bedchamber, holding a brief petition that had been drawn up for her by D'Andilly.

A few minutes later she had prostrated herself in silence at the king's feet. Fear, confusion, shy respect, love, and sorrow

trieben der Armen rascher und rascher das siedende Blut durch die Adern. Ihre Wangen glühten in hohem Purpur – die Augen glänzten von hellen Tränenperlen, die dann und wann hinabfielen durch die seidenen Wimpern auf den schönen Lilienbusen. Der König schien betroffen über die wunderbare Schönheit des Engelskinds. Er hob das Mädchen sanft auf, dann machte er eine Bewegung, als wolle er ihre Hand, die er gefaßt, küssen. Er ließ sie wieder und schaute das holde Kind an mit tränenfeuchtem Blick, der von der tiefsten innern Rührung zeugte. Leise lispelte die Maintenon der Scuderi zu: «Sieht sie nicht der la Valliere ähnlich auf ein Haar, das kleine Ding? – Der König schwelgt in den süßesten Erinnerungen. Euer Spiel ist gewonnen.»

So leise dies auch die Maintenon sprach, doch schien es der König vernommen zu haben. Eine Röte überflog sein Gesicht, sein Blick streifte bei der Maintenon vorüber, er las die Supplik, die Madelon ihm überreicht, und sprach dann mild und gütig: «Ich will's wohl glauben, daß du, mein liebes Kind, von deines Geliebten Unschuld überzeugt bist, aber hören wir, was die Chambre ardente dazu sagt!» – Eine sanfte Bewegung mit der Hand verabschiedete die Kleine, die in Tränen verschwimmen wollte.

Die Scuderi gewahrte zu ihrem Schreck, daß die Erinnerung an die Valliere, so ersprießlich sie anfangs geschienen, des Königs Sinn geändert hatte, sowie die Maintenon den Namen genannt. Mocht es sein, daß der König sich auf unzarte Weise daran erinnert fühlte, daß er im Begriff stehe, das strenge Recht der Schönheit aufzuopfern, oder vielleicht ging es dem Könige wie dem Träumer, dem, hart angerufen, die schönen Zauberbilder, die er zu umfassen gedachte, schnell verschwinden. Vielleicht sah er nun nicht mehr seine Valliere vor sich, sondern dachte nur an die Sœur Louise de la miséricorde (der Valliere Klostername bei den Karmeliternonnen), die ihn peinigte mit ihrer Frömmigkeit und Buße. – Was war jetzt anders zu tun, als des Königs Beschlüsse ruhig abzuwarten.

Des Grafen Miossens Aussage vor der Chambre ardente war indessen bekannt geworden, und wie es zu geschehen pflegt, daß das Volk leicht getrieben wird von einem Extrem zum andern, so wurde derselbe, den man erst als den verruchtesten Mörder verfluchte und den man zu zerreißen drohte, noch ehe er die Blutbühne bestiegen, als unschuldiges Opfer einer barbarischen Justiz beklagt. Nun erst

made the poor girl's seething blood course ever more swiftly
through her veins. Her cheeks glowed a deep scarlet; her eyes
shone with bright pearly tears, which now and then dropped
through her silken lashes onto her beautiful lily-white bosom.
The king seemed taken aback by the angelic child's miraculous
beauty. He raised the girl up gently, then made a gesture as if he
were about to kiss her hand, which he was holding. He released
it and gazed at the lovely child, his eyes moist with tears and expressive of the deepest emotion. Mme de Maintenon whispered
softly to Mlle de Scudéry: "Doesn't she look exactly like Mme de
La Vallière, the little thing? The king is indulging in the sweetest memories. Your game is won."

As quietly as Mme de Maintenon said that, the king appeared
to have heard it. A blush spread over his face, his glance swept
past Mme de Maintenon, he read the petition that Madelon had
handed him, and then said gently and kindly: "I'm ready to believe, my dear child, that you are convinced of your sweetheart's
innocence, but let's hear what the *chambre ardente* says about
it!" He dismissed the girl with a gentle wave of the hand, and she
was about to dissolve in tears.

To her terror Mlle de Scudéry saw that the memory of Mme
de La Vallière, as beneficial as it seemed at the outset, had made
the king change his mind, as soon as Mme de Maintenon mentioned her name. Maybe it was because the king felt reminded
in an ungentle way that he was on the point of sacrificing strict
justice to beauty, or perhaps he experienced what a dreamer
feels when he is addressed brusquely and the beautiful enchanted images he intended to embrace rapidly vanish. Perhaps
he now no longer saw his La Vallière before him, but was merely
thinking about Sœur Louise de la Miséricorde[9] (La Vallière's
name in religion among the Carmelite nuns), who was torturing
him with her piety and penance. What else could now be done,
except to wait patiently for the king's decisions?

Meanwhile the Comte de Miossens's statement to the *chambre ardente* had become known, and, just as the populace is easily driven from one extreme to the other, so the very man who
was earlier cursed as the most wicked murderer, and whom people threatened to tear apart even before he mounted the block,
was now pitied as the innocent victim of barbaric justice. Now

9. Sister Louise of Mercy.

erinnerten sich die Nachbarsleute seines tugendhaften Wandels, der großen Liebe zu Madelon, der Treue, der Ergebenheit mit Leib und Seele, die er zu dem alten Goldschmied gehegt.

Ganze Züge des Volks erschienen oft auf bedrohliche Weise vor la Regnies Palast und schrien: «Gib uns Olivier Brusson heraus, er ist unschuldig», und warfen wohl gar Steine nach den Fenstern, so daß la Regnie genötigt war, bei der Marechaussee Schutz zu suchen vor dem erzürnten Pöbel.

Mehrere Tage vergingen, ohne daß der Scuderi von Olivier Brussons Prozeß nur das mindeste bekannt wurde. Ganz trostlos begab sie sich zur Maintenon, die aber versicherte, daß der König über die Sache schweige, und es gar nicht geraten scheine, ihn daran zu erinnern. Fragte sie nun noch mit sonderbarem Lächeln, was denn die kleine Valliere mache, so überzeugte sich die Scuderi, daß tief im Innern der stolzen Frau sich ein Verdruß über eine Angelegenheit regte, die den reizbaren König in ein Gebiet locken konnte, auf dessen Zauber sie sich nicht verstand. Von der Maintenon konnte sie daher gar nichts hoffen.

Endlich mit d'Andillys Hilfe gelang es der Scuderi, auszukundschaften, daß der König eine lange geheime Unterredung mit dem Grafen Miossens gehabt. Ferner, daß Bontems, des Königs vertrautester Kammerdiener und Geschäftsträger, in der Conciergerie gewesen und mit Brusson gesprochen, daß endlich in einer Nacht ebenderselbe Bontems mit mehreren Leuten in Cardillacs Hause gewesen und sich lange darin aufgehalten. Claude Patru, der Bewohner des untern Stocks, versicherte, die ganze Nacht habe es über seinem Kopfe gepoltert, und gewiß sei Olivier dabei gewesen, denn er habe seine Stimme genau erkannt. So viel war also gewiß, daß der König selbst dem wahren Zusammenhange der Sache nachforschen ließ, unbegreiflich blieb aber die lange Verzögerung des Beschlusses. La Regnie mochte alles aufbieten, das Opfer, das ihm entrissen werden sollte, zwischen den Zähnen festzuhalten. Das verdarb jede Hoffnung im Aufkeimen.

Beinahe ein Monat war vergangen, da ließ die Maintenon der Scuderi sagen, der König wünsche sie heute abend in ihren, der Maintenon, Gemächern zu sehen.

Das Herz schlug der Scuderi hoch auf, sie wußte, daß Brussons Sache sich nun entscheiden würde. Sie sagte es der armen Madelon, die zur Jungfrau, zu allen Heiligen inbrünstig betete, daß sie doch nur in dem König die Überzeugung von Brussons Unschuld erwecken möchten.

for the first time his neighbors recalled his virtuous way of life, his great love for Madelon, and the fidelity and devotion of body and soul that he had harbored for the old goldsmith.

Whole processions of people often appeared menacingly outside La Reynie's court building, shouting: "Release Olivier Brusson, he's innocent!" Some even threw stones at the windows, so that La Reynie was forced to seek the *maréchaussée's* protection against the enraged mob.

Several days went by without Mlle de Scudéry's learning the least thing about the Olivier Brusson investigation. Entirely disconsolate, she visited Mme de Mainenon, who informed her, however, that the king had said nothing about the matter and it didn't seem at all advisable to remind him of it. When she then asked with a peculiar smile how the little La Vallière was getting along, Mlle de Scudéry was convinced that that proud lady was vexed in her mind by a matter that could lure the easily irritated king into a region whose magic was beyond her own powers. Therefore she couldn't expect any more aid from Mme de Maintenon.

Finally, with D'Andilly's help, Mlle de Scudéry managed to learn that the king had had a long, secret interview with the Comte de Miossens. Furthermore, Bontems, the king's most trusted groom of the chamber and chargé d'affaires, had been in the Conciergerie and spoken with Brusson. Finally, one night the same Bontems had been in Cardillac's house with several followers and had remained there for some time. Claude Patru, who lived on the lower floor, stated that there had been noise overhead all night long, and that Olivier had surely been there, because he had recognized his voice distinctly. Therefore this much was certain: the king himself had instituted an investigation into the true state of affairs; but his long delay in coming to a decision remained incomprehensible. Maybe La Reynie was making every effort to retain in his fangs the victim that they were trying to snatch away from him. That nipped every hope in the bud.

Nearly a month had passed, when Mme de Maintenon sent word to Mlle de Scudéry that the king wished to see her that evening in her, Mme de Maintenon's, apartment.

Mlle de Scudéry's heart leaped up; she knew that Brusson's fate would now be decided. She said as much to poor Madelon, who prayed ardently to the Holy Virgin and all the saints to instill in the king the conviction that Brusson was innocent.

Und doch schien es, als habe der König die ganze Sache vergessen, denn wie sonst weilend in anmutigen Gesprächen mit der Maintenon und der Scuderi, gedachte er nicht mit einer Silbe des armen Brussons. Endlich erschien Bontems, näherte sich dem Könige und sprach einige Worte so leise, daß beide Damen nichts davon verstanden. – Die Scuderi erbebte im Innern. Da stand der König auf, schritt auf die Scuderi zu und sprach mit leuchtenden Blicken: «Ich wünsche Euch Glück, mein Fräulein! – Euer Schützling, Olivier Brusson, ist frei!»

Die Scuderi, der die Tränen aus den Augen stürzten, keines Wortes mächtig, wollte sich dem Könige zu Füßen werfen. *Der* hinderte sie daran, sprechend: «Geht, geht! Fräulein, Ihr solltet Parlamentsadvokat sein und meine Rechtshändel ausfechten, denn, beim heiligen Dionys, Eurer Beredsamkeit widersteht niemand auf Erden. – Doch», fügte er ernster hinzu, «doch, wen die Tugend selbst in Schutz nimmt, mag der nicht sicher sein vor jeder bösen Anklage, vor der Chambre ardente und allen Gerichtshöfen in der Welt!»

Die Scuderi fand nun Worte, die sich in dem glühendsten Dank ergossen. Der König unterbrach sie, ihr ankündigend, daß in ihrem Hause sie selbst viel feurigerer Dank erwarte, als er von ihr fordern könne, denn wahrscheinlich umarme in diesem Augenblick der glückliche Olivier schon seine Madelon. «Bontems», so schloß der König, «Bontems soll Euch tausend Louis auszahlen, die gebt in meinem Namen der Kleinen als Brautschatz. Mag sie ihren Brusson, der solch ein Glück gar nicht verdient, heiraten, aber dann sollen beide fort aus Paris. Das ist mein Wille.»

Die Martiniere kam der Scuderi entgegen mit raschen Schritten, hinter ihr her Baptiste, beide mit vor Freude glänzenden Gesichtern, beide jauchzend, schreiend: «Er ist hier – er ist frei! – o die lieben jungen Leute!»

Das selige Paar stürzte der Scuderi zu Füßen. «Oh, ich habe es ja gewußt, daß Ihr, Ihr allein mir den Gatten retten würdet», rief Madelon.

«Ach, der Glaube an Euch, meine Mutter, stand ja fest in meiner Seele», rief Olivier, und beide küßten der würdigen Dame die Hände und vergossen tausend heiße Tränen. Und dann umarmten sie sich wieder und beteuerten, daß die überirdische Seligkeit dieses Augenblicks alle namenlose Leiden der vergangenen Tage aufwiege, und schworen, nicht voneinander zu lassen bis in den Tod.

✿   ✿   ✿

And yet it seemed as if the king had forgotten the whole affair, because, engrossed in charming conversations with Mme de Maintenon and Mlle de Scudéry, he didn't utter a single syllable about poor Brusson. Finally Bontems arrived, approached the king, and said a few words so quietly that neither lady could make out a thing. Mlle de Scudéry was quaking inside. Then the king rose, walked up to Mlle de Scudéry, and said with a radiant gaze: "I congratulate you, mademoiselle! Your protégé Olivier Brusson is a free man!"

Mlle de Scudéry, tears streaming from her eyes, unable to say a word, was about to throw herself at the king's feet, but he prevented this, saying: "Come, come, mademoiselle! You ought to be a high-court barrister pleading my cases, because, by Saint Denis, no one on earth can resist your eloquence. And yet," he added in a more serious strain, "and yet, when virtue itself takes a man under its wing, won't he be safe against all evil accusations, the *chambre ardente,* and all the lawcourts in the world?"

Now Mlle de Scudéry found words to express her heartfelt gratitude. The king interrupted her, announcing to her that much more ardent thanks were awaiting *her* at home than he could possibly require of her, because at that moment lucky Olivier was probably already embracing his Madelon. "Bontems," the king said in conclusion, "Bontems shall pay you a thousand *louis;* give them to the girl in my name as a dowry. Let her marry her Brusson, who doesn't at all deserve such happiness, but then both of them must leave Paris. That is my command."

Martinière came up to Mlle de Scudéry with rapid steps, Baptiste behind her; both their faces were beaming with joy, both of them called jubilantly: "He's here! He's free! Oh, the darling youngsters!"

The blissful couple fell at Mlle de Scudéry's feet. "Oh, I knew that you, you alone would save my husband!" Madelon exclaimed.

"Ah, my soul trusted firmly in you, my mother!" cried Olivier, and both of them kissed the worthy lady's hands and shed a thousand hot tears. Then they embraced each other again and asserted that the superhuman bliss of that moment made up for all the unspeakable sorrows of the days they had just lived through. They swore to remain united until death.

◦   ◦   ◦

Nach wenigen Tagen wurden sie verbunden durch den Segen des Priesters. Wäre es auch nicht des Königs Wille gewesen, Brusson hätte doch nicht in Paris bleiben können, wo ihn alles an jene entsetzliche Zeit der Untaten Cardillacs erinnerte, wo irgendein Zufall das böse Geheimnis, nun noch mehreren Personen bekannt geworden, feindselig enthüllen und sein friedliches Leben auf immer verstören konnte. Gleich nach der Hochzeit zog er, von den Segnungen der Scuderi begleitet, mit seinem jungen Weibe nach Genf. Reich ausgestattet durch Madelons Brautschatz, begabt mit seltner Geschicklichkeit in seinem Handwerk, mit jeder bürgerlichen Tugend, ward ihm dort ein glückliches, sorgenfreies Leben. Ihm wurden Hoffnungen erfüllt, die den Vater getäuscht hatten bis in das Grab hinein.

Ein Jahr war vergangen seit der Abreise Brussons, als eine öffentliche Bekanntmachung erschien, gezeichnet von Harloy de Chauvalon, Erzbischof von Paris, und von dem Parlamentsadvokaten Pierre Arnaud d'Andilly, des Inhalts, daß ein reuiger Sünder unter dem Siegel der Beichte der Kirche einen reichen geraubten Schatz an Juwelen und Geschmeide übergeben. Jeder, dem etwa bis zum Ende des Jahres 1680, vorzüglich durch mörderischen Anfall auf öffentlicher Straße, ein Schmuck geraubt worden, solle sich bei d'Andilly melden und werde, treffe die Beschreibung des ihm geraubten Schmucks mit irgendeinem vorgefundenen Kleinod genau überein und finde sonst kein Zweifel gegen die Rechtmäßigkeit des Anspruchs statt, den Schmuck wiedererhalten. – Viele, die in Cardillacs Liste als nicht ermordet, sondern bloß durch einen Faustschlag betäubt aufgeführt waren, fanden sich nach und nach bei dem Parlamentsadvokaten ein und erhielten zu ihrem nicht geringen Erstaunen das geraubte Geschmeide zurück. Das übrige fiel dem Schatz der Kirche zu St. Eustache anheim.

A few days later they were joined together by the priest's blessing. Even if it hadn't been the king's command, Brusson still couldn't have remained in Paris, where everything reminded him of that horrible period of Cardillac's crimes, and where some hostile chance might reveal his evil secret, with which several people had now become acquainted, and destroy the peace of his life forever. Right after the wedding he moved to Geneva with his young wife, accompanied by Mlle de Scudéry's blessings. Comfortably set up in business by Madelon's dowry, endowed with rare skill in his trade, and possessing every civic virtue, he soon enjoyed a happy, carefree existence there. He saw those hopes fulfilled which had eluded his father throughout his life.

A year had elapsed since Brusson's departure, when a public notice appeared, signed by Harlay de Champvallon, archbishop of Paris, and the high-court barrister Pierre Arnauld d'Andilly, to the effect that a repentant sinner, under the seal of religious confession, had handed over to the Church a large hoard of stolen gems and jewelry. Anyone from whom jewelry was stolen, particularly in a fatal mugging out on the street, up to about the end of the year 1680, should report to D'Andilly; if his description of the jewelry stolen from him exactly matched any of the pieces on hand, and there was no other doubt about the legitimacy of his claim, he'd get the jewelry back. Many whose names had appeared in Cardillac's list as not having been killed, but merely stunned by a blow of the fist, gradually showed up at the barrister's office and, to their great amazement, received their stolen jewels. The rest was donated to the treasury of St-Eustache's.

Des Vetters Eckfenster

Meinen armen Vetter trifft gleiches Schicksal mit dem bekannten Scarron. So wie dieser hat mein Vetter durch eine hartnäckige Krankheit den Gebrauch seiner Füße gänzlich verloren, und es tut not, daß er sich, mit Hilfe standhafter Krücken und des nervichten Arms eines grämlichen Invaliden, der nach Belieben den Krankenwärter macht, aus dem Bette in den mit Kissen bepackten Lehnstuhl, und aus dem Lehnstuhl in das Bette schrotet.

Aber noch eine Ähnlichkeit trägt mein Vetter mit jenem Franzosen, den eine besondere, aus dem gewöhnlichen Gleise des französischen Witzes ausweichende Art des Humors trotz der Sparsamkeit seiner Erzeugnisse in der französischen Literatur feststellte. So wie Scarron schriftstellert mein Vetter; so wie Scarron ist er mit besonderer lebendiger Laune begabt und treibt wunderlichen humoristischen Scherz auf seine eigne Weise. Doch zum Ruhme des deutschen Schriftstellers sei es bemerkt, daß er niemals für nötig achtete, seine kleinen pikanten Schüsseln mit Asa fötida zu würzen, um die Gaumen seiner deutschen Leser, die dergleichen nicht wohl vertragen, zu kitzeln. Es genügt ihm das edle Gewürz, welches, indem es reizt, auch stärkt. Die Leute lesen gerne, was er schreibt; es soll gut sein und ergötzlich; ich verstehe mich nicht darauf. Mich erlabte sonst des Vetters Unterhaltung, und es schien mir gemütlicher, ihn zu hören, als ihn zu lesen.

Doch eben dieser unbesiegbare Hang zur Schriftstellerei hat schwarzes Unheil über meinen armen Vetter gebracht; die schwerste Krankheit vermochte nicht den raschen Rädergang der Phantasie zu hemmen, der in seinem Innern fortarbeitete, stets Neues und Neues erzeugend. So kam es, daß er mir allerlei anmutige Geschichten

My Cousin's Corner Window

My poor cousin is afflicted with the same destiny as that of the well-known Scarron.[1] Like him, my cousin has completely lost the use of his feet as the result of a stubborn ailment, and he's compelled to seek the aid of sturdy crutches and the sinewy arm of a peevish disabled veteran (who plays the role of his nurse when he feels like it) in order to hobble out of bed and into his easy chair, which is heaped with cushions, and from the easy chair back to bed.

But my cousin has yet another similarity to that Frenchman, whose special brand of humor, which evaded the customary trends of French wit, gave him a firm place in French literary history in spite of the small number of his works. Like Scarron, my cousin is a writer; like Scarron, he's gifted with a particularly vivid sense of fun, and composes eccentrically humorous pieces in a manner all his own. But let it be noted, to the German author's credit, that he has never deemed it necessary to spice his piquant little dishes with asafetida in order to tickle the palate of his German readers, who surely can't abide such things. He's satisfied with noble spices, which fortify you as they stimulate you. People enjoy reading what he writes; they say it's both solid and entertaining; as for me, I don't understand those matters. I used to be charmed by my cousin's conversation, and I thought it was jollier to listen to him than to read him.

But it was precisely that unconquerable penchant for writing that led my poor cousin into grim disaster; even the most serious illness was unable to curb the rapid machinery of his imagination, which kept working within him, generating constantly new product. And so it came about that he'd tell me all sorts of

1. Paul Scarron (1610–1660), French author of travesties, novels, etc.; paralyzed in 1638; first husband of the future Mme de Maintenon, who figures so prominently in "Mademoiselle de Scudéry."

erzählte, die er, des mannigfachen Wehs, das er duldete, unerachtet, ersonnen. Aber den Weg, den der Gedanke verfolgen mußte, um auf dem Papiere gestaltet zu erscheinen, hatte der böse Dämon der Krankheit versperrt. Sowie mein Vetter etwas aufschreiben wollte, versagten ihm nicht allein die Finger den Dienst, sondern der Gedanke selbst war verstoben und verflogen. Darüber verfiel mein Vetter in die schwärzeste Melancholie.

«Vetter!» sprach er eines Tages zu mir, mit einem Ton, der mich erschreckte, «Vetter, mit mir ist es aus! Ich komme mir vor wie jener alte, vom Wahnsinn zerrüttete Maler, der tagelang vor einer in den Rahmen gespannten grundierten Leinewand saß und allen, die zu ihm kamen, die mannigfachen Schönheiten des reichen, herrlichen Gemäldes anpries, das er soeben vollendet; – ich geb's auf, das wirkende, schaffende Leben, welches, zur äußern Form gestaltet, aus mir selbst hinaustritt, sich mit der Welt befreundend! – Mein Geist zieht sich in seine Klause zurück!» Seit der Zeit ließ sich mein Vetter weder vor mir, noch vor irgendeinem andern Menschen sehen. Der alte grämliche Invalide wies uns murrend und keifend von der Türe weg wie ein beißiger Haushund. –

Es ist nötig zu sagen, daß mein Vetter ziemlich hoch in kleinen niedrigen Zimmern wohnt. Das ist nun Schriftsteller- und Dichtersitte. Was tut die niedrige Stubendecke? Die Phantasie fliegt empor und baut sich ein hohes, lustiges Gewölbe bis in den blauen glänzenden Himmel hinein. So ist des Dichters enges Gemach, wie jener zwischen vier Mauern eingeschlossene, zehn Fuß ins Gevierte große Garten, zwar nicht breit und lang, hat aber stets eine schöne Höhe. Dabei liegt aber meines Vetters Logis in dem schönsten Teile der Hauptstadt, nämlich auf dem großen Markte, der von Prachtgebäuden umschlossen ist, und in dessen Mitte das kolossal und genial gedachte Theatergebäude prangt. Es ist ein Eckhaus, das mein Vetter bewohnt, und aus dem Fenster eines kleines Kabinetts übersieht er mit einem Blick das ganze Panorama des grandiosen Platzes.

Es war gerade Markttag, als ich, mich durch das Volksgewühl durchdrängend, die Straße hinab kam, wo man schon aus weiter Ferne meines Vetters Eckfenster erblickt. Nicht wenig erstaunte ich, als mir aus diesem Fenster das wohlbekannte rote Mützchen entgegenleuchtete, welches mein Vetter in guten Tagen zu tragen pflegte. Noch mehr! Als ich näher kam, gewahrte ich, daß mein Vetter seinen

delightful stories he had thought up in spite of the manifold pains he was undergoing. But the evil demon of illness had blocked the path his ideas had to take in order to be formulated on paper. Whenever my cousin wanted to write something down, not only did his fingers refuse to obey him, but his idea itself became scattered, and evaporated. This made my cousin sink into the gloomiest melancholy.

"Cousin!" he said to me one day in a tone that alarmed me. "Cousin, I'm done for! I remind myself of that old painter, troubled by insanity, who'd sit for days on end in front of a primed canvas, stretched on its frame, and who'd praise to all his visitors the manifold beauties of the fine, splendid painting he had just finished.[2] I'm renouncing that operative, creative life which is generated inside me, after it has received an outward form, and which reconciles itself to the world! My mind is withdrawing into its hermitage!" After that, my cousin didn't show his face either to me or to anyone else. The peevish old veteran turned us away from his door, growling and barking like a vicious watchdog.

It's important to add that my cousin lives pretty high up, in small, low-ceilinged rooms. That's usual with authors and poets, after all. What does the low ceiling matter? His imagination soars and builds itself a lofty, cheerful vault that extends into the bright blue sky. And so the poet's cramped quarters, like that ten-foot-square garden, confined within four walls, isn't long or wide, to be sure, but is always beautifully high. Moreover, my cousin's residence is situated in the loveliest part of the capital, facing that large marketplace ringed around by elegant buildings, in the midst of which the colossal, brilliantly conceived theater looms. It's a corner house that my cousin lives in, and from the window of a small room his eyes can take in the whole panorama of the grandiose square.

It was on a market day when I pushed my way through the swarm of people and made my way down the street from which my cousin's corner window can be spotted from a considerable distance. I was not a little astonished when, in that window, I caught the gleam of that familiar little red cap that my cousin used to wear on his good days. Even more! When I got closer, I

---

2. A striking prefiguration (if not a direct inspiration) of Balzac's celebrated story "The Unknown Masterpiece" (1831).

stattlichen Warschauer Schlafrock angelegt und aus der türkischen Sonntagspfeife Tabak rauchte. – Ich winkte ihm zu, ich wehte mit dem Schnupftuch hinauf; es gelang mir, seine Aufmerksamkeit auf mich zu ziehen, er nickte freundlich. Was für Hoffnungen! – Mit Blitzesschnelle eilte ich die Treppe hinauf. Der Invalide öffnete die Türe; sein Gesicht, das sonst, runzlicht und faltig, einem naßgewordenen Handschuh glich, hatte wirklich einiger Sonnenschein zur passablen Fratze ausgeglättet. Er meinte, der Herr säße im Lehnstuhl und sei zu sprechen. Das Zimmer war rein gemacht und an dem Bettschirm ein Bogen Papier befestigt, auf dem mit großen Buchstaben die Worte standen:

Et si male nunc, non olim sic erit.

Alles deutete auf wiedergekehrte Hoffnung, auf neuerweckte Lebenskraft.

«Ei», rief mir der Vetter entgegen, als ich in das Kabinett trat, «ei, kommst du endlich, Vetter; weißt du wohl, daß ich rechte Sehnsucht nach dir empfunden? Denn unerachtet du den Henker was nach meinen unsterblichen Werken frägst, so habe ich dich doch lieb, weil du ein munterer Geist bist und amüsable, wenn auch gerade nicht amüsant.»

Ich fühlte, daß mir bei dem Kompliment meines aufrichtigen Vetters das Blut ins Gesicht stieg.

«Du glaubst», fuhr der Vetter fort, ohne auf meine Bewegung zu achten, «du glaubst mich gewiß in voller Besserung oder gar von meinem Übel hergestellt. Dem ist beileibe nicht so. Meine Beine sind durchaus ungetreue Vasallen, die dem Haupt des Herrschers abtrünnig geworden und mit meinem übrigen werten Leichnam nichts mehr zu schaffen haben wollen. Das heißt, ich kann mich nicht aus der Stelle rühren und karre mich in diesem Räderstuhl hin und her auf anmutige Weise, wozu mein alter Invalide die melodiösesten Märsche aus seinen Kriegsjahren pfeift. Aber dies Fenster ist mein Trost, hier ist mir das bunte Leben aufs neue aufgegangen, und ich fühle mich befreundet mit seinem niemals rastenden Treiben. Komm, Vetter, schau hinaus!»

Ich setzte mich, dem Vetter gegenüber, auf ein kleines Taburett, das gerade noch im Fensterraum Platz hatte. Der Anblick war in der Tat seltsam und überraschend. Der ganze Markt schien eine einzige,

saw that my cousin had put on his elegant Warsaw dressing gown
and was smoking his Sunday Turkish pipe. I beckoned to him, I
waved my handerchief up to him; I succeeded in attracting his
attention, and he gave me a friendly nod. What hopes I had! I
raced up the steps with the speed of lightning. The veteran
opened the door; his wrinkled and lined face, which usually re-
sembled a damp glove, was actually smoothed out by a little sunshine into a passably respectable mug. He said he thought his
master was in his easy chair and was at home to callers. The
room had been cleaned up, and a sheet of paper was fastened to
the bed screen; on it was written in capital letters:

Et si male nunc, non olim sic erit.[3]

All indications pointed to a renewal of hope, a reawakening of
the life force.

"Well!" my cousin called to me as I entered the little room.
"Well, you're finally here, cousin! Do you know that I really
missed you? For, even though you don't give a damn about my
immortal writings, I still like you, because you have an alert
mind and you can be entertained, even if you're not exactly entertaining."

I felt myself blushing at my honest cousin's compliment.

"You must surely think," my cousin continued, paying no attention to my agitation, "that my health is greatly improved, or
that I've even recovered completely from my illness. That's absolutely not the case. My legs are thoroughly disloyal vassals,
which have renounced their allegiance to their overlord's head,
and refuse to have anything more to do with the rest of my worthy body. That is, I can't budge from the spot, and I have myself
charmingly carted to and fro in this wheelchair, while my old
veteran whistles the most melodious marches from his years in
the army. But this window is my consolation; here the colorful
miscellany of life has revealed itself to me again, and I feel reconciled to its never-ending bustle. Come, cousin, take a look
outside!"

I sat down opposite my cousin on a small stool for which there
was just enough room remaining in the window embrasure. The
view was indeed strange and surprising. The whole market was

---

3. "If things are bad now, they won't be in the future." A slightly altered quotation from Ode 10, Book II, of Horace.

dicht zusammengedrängte Volksmasse, so daß man glauben mußte, ein dazwischen geworfener Apfel könne niemals zur Erde gelangen. Die verschiedensten Farben glänzten im Sonnenschein, und zwar in ganz kleinen Flecken, auf mich machte dies den Eindruck eines großen, vom Winde bewegten, hin und her wogenden Tulpenbeets, und ich mußte mir gestehen, daß der Anblick zwar recht artig, aber auf die Länge ermüdend sei, ja wohl gar aufgereizten Personen einen kleinen Schwindel verursachen könne, der dem nicht unangenehmen Delirieren des nahen Traums gliche; darin suchte ich das Vergnügen, das das Eckfenster dem Vetter gewähre, und äußerte ihm dieses ganz unverhohlen.

Der Vetter schlug aber die Hände über dem Kopf zusammen, und es entspann sich zwischen uns folgendes Gespräch.

Der Vetter. Vetter, Vetter! nun sehe ich wohl, daß auch nicht das kleinste Fünkchen von Schriftstellertalent in dir glüht. Das erste Erfordernis fehlt dir dazu, um jemals in die Fußstapfen deines würdigen lahmen Vetters zu treten; nämlich ein Auge, welches wirklich schaut. Jener Markt bietet dir nichts dar als den Anblick eines scheckichten, sinnverwirrenden Gewühls des in bedeutungsloser Tätigkeit bewegten Volks. Hoho, mein Freund, mir entwickelt sich daraus die mannigfachste Szenerie des bürgerlichen Lebens, und mein Geist, ein wackerer Callot oder moderner Chodowiecki, entwirft eine Skizze nach der andern, deren Umrisse oft keck genug sind. Auf, Vetter! ich will sehen, ob ich dir nicht wenigstens die Primizien der Kunst zu schauen beibringen kann. Sieh einmal gerade vor dich herab in die Straße; hier hast du mein Glas, bemerkst du wohl die etwas fremdartig gekleidete Person mit dem großen Marktkorbe am Arm, die, mit einem Bürstenbinder in tiefem Gespräch begriffen, ganz geschwinde andere Domestika abzumachen scheint, als die des Leibes Nahrung betreffen?

Ich. Ich habe sie gefaßt. Sie hat ein grell zitronenfarbiges Tuch nach französcher Art turbanähnlich um den Kopf gewunden, und ihr Gesicht sowie ihr ganzes Wesen zeigt deutlich die Französin. Wahrscheinlich eine Restantin aus dem letzten Kriege, die ihr Schäfchen hier ins trockene gebracht.

Der Vetter. Nicht übel geraten. Ich wette, der Mann verdankt irgendeinem Zweige französischer Industrie ein hübsches Auskom-

like a single, tightly compressed mass of people, so that you would have thought that an apple thrown into their midst would never reach the ground. The most varied colors were shining in the sunlight, and in very small dots; I received the impression of a large bed of tulips ruffled by the breeze and waving to and fro, and I had to admit to myself that the view was really quite attractive, but exhausting after a while; it might even make nervous people a little dizzy, as if in the not unpleasant delirium of an oncoming dream; it was in that aspect of the view that I detected the source of my cousin's delight in the corner window, and I told him so in no uncertain terms.

But my cousin folded his hands on top of his head, and the following dialogue unwound between us.

MY COUSIN: Cousin, cousin! Now I see that not even the tiniest spark of talent as a writer glimmers inside you. You're lacking in the first requirement you'd need if you ever wanted to follow in the footsteps of your worthy, lame cousin; to wit, eyes that really see. That market offers you nothing but the view of a checkered, confusing tangle of people stirring with meaningless activity. Ho, ho, my friend, for me it develops into the most varied stage décor of civic life; and my mind, a hearty Callot[4] or a modern Chodowiecki,[5] conceives of one sketch after another, in contours that are often decidedly bold. Come, cousin, I want to see whether I can't teach you at least the rudiments of the art of seeing. Look straight down into the street; here's my spyglass; can you make out the somewhat singularly clad woman with the big marketing basket on her arm who, conversing wholeheartedly with a brushmaker, seems to be very rapidly transacting other household business than that pertaining to the nourishment of the body?

I: I see her now. She has wound a glaring lemon-yellow cloth around her head like a turban in the French style, and her face, as well as her whole manner, proclaims her to be a Frenchwoman. She's probably a leftover from the latest war who has managed to rescue her fortunes here.

MY COUSIN: Not a bad guess. I'll wager that her husband derives a handsome living from some branch of French commerce,

---

4. Jacques Callot (1592 or 1593–1635), French etcher, whose fantasy and Italian Comedy prints were very dear to Hoffmann.   5. Daniel Chodowiecki (1726–1801), prolific German artist and illustrator who produced many scenes of everyday life.

men, so daß seine Frau ihren Marktkorb mit ganz guten Dingen
reichlich füllen kann. Jetzt stürzt sie sich ins Gewühl. Versuche,
Vetter, ob du ihren Lauf in den verschiedensten Krümmungen verfolgen kannst, ohne sie aus dem Auge zu verlieren; das gelbe Tuch
leuchtet dir vor.

Ich. Ei, wie der brennende gelbe Punkt die Masse durchschneidet.
Jetzt ist sie schon der Kirche nah – jetzt feilscht sie um etwas bei den
Buden – jetzt ist sie fort – o weh! ich habe sie verloren – nein, dort am
Ende duckt sie wieder auf – dort bei dem Geflügel – sie ergreift eine
gerupfte Gans – sie betastet sie mit kennerischen Fingern. –

Der Vetter. Gut, Vetter, das Fixieren des Blicks erzeugt das deutliche Schauen. Doch statt dich auf langweilige Weise in einer Kunst
unterrichten zu wollen, die kaum zu erlernen, laß mich lieber dich auf
allerlei Ergötzliches aufmerksam machen, welches sich vor unsern
Augen auftut. Bemerkst du wohl jenes Frauenzimmer, die sich an der
Ecke dort, unerachtet das Gedränge gar nicht zu groß, mit beiden
spitzen Ellenbogen Platz macht?

Ich. Was für eine tolle Figur – ein seidner Hut, der in kapriziöser
Formlosigkeit stets jeder Mode Trotz geboten, mit bunten, in den
Lüften wehenden Federn – ein kurzer seidner Überwurf, dessen
Farbe in das ursprüngliche Nichts zurückgekehrt – darüber ein ziemlich honetter Shawl – der Florbesatz des gelbkattunenen Kleides
reicht bis an die Knöchel – blaugraue Strümpfe – Schnürstiefeln –
hinter ihr eine stattliche Magd mit zwei Marktkörben, einem
Fischnetz, einem Mehlsack – Gott sei bei uns! was die seidene Person
für wütende Blicke um sich wirft, mit welcher Wut sie eindringt in die
dicksten Haufen – wie sie alles angreift, Gemüse, Obst, Fleisch und
so weiter; wie sie alles beäugelt, betastet, um alles feilscht und nichts
erhandelt. –

Der Vetter. Ich nenne diese Person, die keinen Markttag fehlt, die
rabiate Hausfrau. Es kommt mir vor, als müsse sie die Tochter eines
reichen Bürgers, vielleicht eines wohlhabenden Seifensieders sein,
deren Hand nebst annexis ein kleiner Geheimsekretär nicht ohne
Anstrengung erworben. Mit Schönheit und Grazie hat sie der
Himmel nicht ausgestattet, dagegen galt sie bei allen Nachbaren für
das häuslichste, wirtschaftlichste Mädchen, und in der Tat, sie ist auch
so wirtschaftlich und wirtschaftet jeden Tag vom Morgen bis in den
Abend auf solche entsetzliche Weise, daß dem armen Geheimsekretär
darüber Hören und Sehen vergeht und er sich dorthin wünscht, wo
der Pfeffer wächst. Stets sind alle Pauken- und Trompetenregister der
Einkäufe, der Bestellungen, des Kleinhandels und der mannigfachen

so that his wife can fill her marketing basket abundantly with elegant items. Now she's plunging into the throng. Try and see, cousin, whether you can follow her course through its various windings without losing sight of her; her yellow turban will be a beacon for you.

I: My, how that blazing yellow dot cuts its way through the crowd! Now she's already close to the church. Now she's haggling over something at the booths. Now she's gone. Oh, my, I've lost her! No, she's bobbing up again there, after all—there, by the poultry. She's seizing a plucked goose. She's feeling it with knowledgeable fingers.

MY COUSIN: Good, cousin! The concentration of one's sight produces clear seeing. But, instead of trying to instruct you tediously in an art that can't really be learned, let me rather call your attention to all sorts of amusing things that are happening before our eyes. Do you observe that woman in the corner there who, even though the throng is far from dense, is pushing her way through it with both sharp elbows?

I: What an odd phenomenon! A silk hat whose whimsical shapelessness has always thumbed its nose at every new fashion, with multicolored feathers waving in the breeze. A short silk shoulder wrap, whose color has returned to primeval nothingness. Over that, a fairly respectable shawl. The gauze trim of her yellow calico dress extends to her knuckles. Blue-gray stockings. Laced boots. Behind her, a buxom maid with two marketing baskets, a reticule for fish, and a flour sack. God be with us! What furious glances the person in silk casts all around her! How furiously she pushes her way into the thickest throngs! How she attacks everything, vegetables, fruit, meat, and so forth; how she studies and handles it all, haggling over everything and making no purchases!

MY COUSIN: She doesn't miss a single market day, and I've dubbed her "the rabid housewife." It seems to me that she must be the daughter of some wealthy bourgeois, perhaps a prosperous soap-maker, and that her hand, and concomitant dowry, were won, not without exertions, by some minor confidential clerk. Heaven hasn't bestowed beauty or grace upon her, but, on the other hand, all the neighbors took her to be the most domestic and housewifely girl; and, indeed, she *is* just that housewifely, and she plays the housewife every day from morning to evening in such a horrifying way that the poor confidential clerk is driven out of his senses, and would like to be a million miles away. She constantly pulls out all the drum-and-trumpet stops in an organ rhapsody on the subject of shopping,

Bedürfnisse des Hauswesens gezogen, und so gleicht des Geheim-
sekretärs Wirtschaft einem Gehäuse, in dem ein aufgezogenes
Uhrwerk ewig eine tolle Sinfonie, die der Teufel selbst komponiert
hat, fortspielt; ungefähr jeden vierten Markttag wird sie von einer andern Magd begleitet. –

Sapienti sat! – Bemerkst du wohl – doch nein, nein, diese Gruppe,
die soeben sich bildet, wäre würdig, von dem Krayon eines Hogarths
verewigt zu werden. Schau doch nur hin, Vetter, in die dritte Türöff-
nung des Theaters!

Ich. Ein paar alte Weiber auf niedrigen Stühlen sitzend – ihr ganzer
Kram in einem mäßigen Korbe vor sich ausgebreitet – die eine hält
bunte Tücher feil, sogenannte Vexierware, auf den Effekt für blöde
Augen berechnet, – die andere hält eine Niederlage von blauen und
grauen Strümpfen, Strickwolle und so weiter. Sie haben sich zueinan-
der gebeugt – sie zischeln sich in die Ohren – die eine genießt ein
Schälchen Kaffee; die andere scheint, ganz hingerissen von dem Stoff
der Unterhaltung, das Schnäpschen zu vergessen, das sie eben hinab-
gleiten lassen wollte; in der Tat ein paar auffallende Physiognomien!
Welches dämonische Lächeln – welche Gestikulation mit den dürren
Knochenärmen! –

Der Vetter. Diese beiden Weiber sitzen beständig zusammen,
und unerachtet die Verschiedenheit ihres Handels keine Kollision
und also keinen eigentlichen Brotneid zuläßt, so haben sie sich
doch bis heute stets mit feindseligen Blicken angeschielt und sich,
darf ich meiner geübten Physiognomik trauen, diverse höhnische
Redensarten zugeworfen. Oh, sieh, sieh, Vetter, immer mehr werden sie ein Herz und eine Seele. Die Tuchverkäuferin teilt der
Strumpfhändlerin ein Schälchen Kaffee mit. Was hat das zu bedeuten? Ich weiß es! Vor wenigen Minuten trat ein junges
Mädchen von höchstens sechzehn Jahren, hübsch wie der Tag,
deren ganzem Äußern, deren ganzem Betragen man Sitte und ver-
schämte Dürftigkeit ansah, angelockt von der Vexierware, an den
Korb. Ihr Sinn war auf ein weißes Tuch mit bunter Borde gerichtet,
dessen sie vielleicht eben sehr bedurfte. Sie feilschte darum, die
Alte wandte alle Künste merkantilischer Schlauheit an, indem sie
das Tuch ausbreitete und die grellen Farben im Sonnenschein
schimmern ließ. Sie wurden handelseinig. Als nun aber die Arme
aus dem Schnupftuchzipfel die kleine Kasse entwickelte, reichte

ordering merchandise, retail transactions, and the numerous needs of a household; and so, the confidential clerk's housekeeping resembles a wooden case in which a fully wound clock eternally plays a crazy symphony composed by the Devil himself; approximately every fourth market day she's accompanied by a new maid.

A word to the wise is sufficient! Can you make out—but no, no, that group which is just now forming is worthy of being immortalized by the pencil of a Hogarth.[6] Just look over there, cousin, in the third entrance to the theater!

I: A couple of old women sitting on low chairs. Their entire merchandise spread out in front of them in one moderate-sized basket. One of them is selling brightly colored kerchiefs, so-called novelty goods, calculated to appeal to weak eyes. The other one has a depository of blue and gray stockings, knitting yarn, and the like. They are leaning with their heads together. They're whispering into each other's ears. One of them is drinking a cup of coffee. The other one seems so captivated by the subject they're discussing that she's forgotten about the slug of brandy she was about to send down the hatch. Truly a couple of conspicuous physiognomies! What devilish smiles! What gesticulating with their withered, bony arms!

MY COUSIN: Those two women sit next to each other constantly; and, even though the different nature of their merchandise admits of no conflict of interests, and thus, no real professional jealousy, nevertheless up to this very day they've always given each other hostile squints and, if I can trust my experience in physiognomy, they've flung a number of derisive epithets at each other. Oh, look, look, cousin, they're becoming chummier and chummier. The kerchief vendor is offering a cup of coffee to the dealer in stockings. What does that signify? I know! A few minutes ago a young girl of sixteen at the most, pretty as the daylight, in all of whose looks and behavior one could tell how well-mannered she is, though needy and ashamed of it, stepped up to the basket, enticed by the novelty goods. Her heart was set on a white kerchief with a colorful border, which she perhaps had a pressing need for. She haggled for it, the old woman brought into play every wile of mercantile cunning, spreading out the kerchief and letting the gaudy colors gleam in the sunlight. They agreed on a price. But then, when the poor girl drew her little stock of cash

---

6. William Hogarth (1697–1764), English satirical artist, a favorite of Hoffmann's.

die Barschaft nicht hin zu solcher Ausgabe. Mit hochglühenden
Wangen, helle Tränen in den Augen, entfernte sich das Mädchen,
so schnell sie konnte, während die Alte, höhnisch auflachend, das
Tuch zusammenfaltete und in den Korb zurückwarf. Artige
Redensarten mag es dabei gegeben haben. Aber nun kennt der andere Satan die Kleine und weiß die traurige Geschichte einer verarmten Familie aufzutischen als eine skandalöse Chronik von
Leichtsinn und vielleicht gar Verbrechen, zur Gemütsergötzlichkeit
der getäuschten Krämerin. Mit der Tasse Kaffee wurde gewiß eine
derbe, faustdicke Verleumdung belohnt. –

Ich. Von allem, was du da herauskombinierst, lieber Vetter, mag
kein Wörtchen wahr sein, aber indem ich die Weiber anschaue, ist
mir, Dank sei es deiner lebendigen Darstellung, alles so plausibel, daß
ich daran glauben muß, ich mag wollen oder nicht.

Der Vetter. Ehe wir uns von der Theaterwand abwenden, laß uns
noch einen Blick auf die dicke gemütliche Frau mit vor Gesundheit
strotzenden Wangen werfen, die in stoischer Ruhe und Gelassenheit,
die Hände unter die weiße Schürze gesteckt, auf einem Rohrstuhle
sitzt und vor sich einen reichen Kram von hellpolierten Löffeln,
Messern und Gabeln, Fayence, porzellanen Tellern und Terrinen
von verjährter Form, Teetassen, Kaffeekannen, Strumpfware, und
was weiß ich sonst, auf weißen Tüchern ausgebreitet hat, so daß ihr
Vorrat, wahrscheinlich aus kleinen Auktionen zusammengestümpert,
einen wahren Orbis pictus bildet. Ohne sonderlich eine Miene zu
verziehen, hört sie das Gebot des Feilschenden, sorglos, ob aus dem
Handel was wird oder nicht; schlägt zu, streckt die eine Hand unter
der Schürze hervor, um eben nur das Geld vom Käufer zu empfangen, den sie die erkaufte Ware selbst fortnehmen läßt. Das ist eine
ruhige, besonnene Handelsfrau, die was vor sich bringen wird. Vor
vier Wochen bestand ihr ganzer Kram in ungefähr einem halben
Dutzend feiner baumwollener Strümpfe und ebensoviel Trinkgläsern.
Ihr Handel steigt mit jedem Markt, und da sie keinen bessern Stuhl
mitbringt, die Hände auch noch ebenso unter die Schürze steckt wie
sonst, so zeigt das, daß sie Gleichmut des Geistes besitzt und sich
durch das Glück nicht zu Stolz und Übermut verleiten läßt. Wie
kommt mir doch plötzlich die skurrile Idee zu Sinn! Ich denke mir in
diesem Augenblick ein ganz kleines schadenfrohes Teufelchen, das,
wie auf jenem Hogarthischen Blatt unter den Stuhl der Betschwester,
hier unter den Sessel der Krämerfrau gekrochen ist und, neidisch auf
ihr Glück, heimtückischerweise die Stuhlbeine wegsägt. Plump! fällt

from the corner of her handkerchief, she didn't have enough change for such a large outlay. Her cheeks bright red, tears gleaming in her eyes, the girl walked away as fast as she could, while the old woman, laughing aloud in scorn, folded up the kerchief and tossed it back into the basket. She probably added a few juicy comments. But now, it seems, that other she-devil knows the girl, and is able to dish up the sad story of an impoverished family in the form of a scandalous chronicle of folly, and maybe even crime, for the entertainment of the disappointed vendor. That cup of coffee was surely the reward for a coarse, gross defamation.

I: It may be that not a single word of your entire concoction is true, my dear cousin, but as I look at those women, it's all so plausible, thanks to your vivid presentation, that I have to believe it whether I want to or not.

MY COUSIN: Before we turn away from the theater facade, let's cast a glance at that plump, jolly woman whose cheeks are bursting with good health, the one sitting on a cane chair in stoic calm and composure, her hands beneath her white apron, the one who has, spread out in front of her on white cloths, an abundant lot of brightly polished spoons, knives, and forks, faience, porcelain plates and terrines of an outmoded style, teacups, coffeepots, hosiery, and what have you, so that her merchandise, probably accumulated haphazardly at small auctions, constitutes a veritable picture dictionary. Without putting on any particular facial expression, she's listening to some haggler's offer, not caring whether an actual purchase will result or not; she knocks down the item, takes one hand out from under her apron, merely to receive the money from the purchaser, whom she allows to take away the purchased goods himself. That's a calm and considered businesswoman, who'll make a go of things. Four weeks ago her entire stock consisted of about a half-dozen fine cotton stockings and the same number of tumblers. Her business is increasing with every market, and, since she doesn't bring along a better chair, and is still keeping her hands beneath her apron just as in the past, she obviously possesses equanimity and won't let her good fortune mislead her into pride and haughtiness. What a comical idea just came to me all of a sudden! At this very moment I can picture a very small malicious demon who, like the one underneath the female devotee's chair in that Hogarth print,[7] has crawled under the vendor's seat here

---

7. The engraving "Credulity, Superstition, and Fanaticism."

sie in ihr Glas und Porzellan, und mit dem ganzen Handel ist es aus. Das wäre denn doch ein Fallissement im eigentlichsten Sinne des Wortes. –

Ich. Wahrhaftig, lieber Vetter, du hast mich jetzt schon besser schauen gelehrt. Indem ich meinen Blick in dem bunten Gewühl der wogenden Menge umherschweifen lasse, fallen mir hin und wieder junge Mädchen in die Augen, die, von sauber angezogenen Köchinnen, welche geräumige, glänzende Marktkörbe am Arme tragen, begleitet, den Markt durchstreifen und um Hausbedürfnisse, wie sie der Markt darbietet, feilschen. Der Mädchen modester Anzug, ihr ganzer Anstand läßt nicht daran zweifeln, daß sie wenigstens vornehmen bürgerlichen Standes sind. Wie kommen diese auf den Markt?

Der Vetter. Leicht erklärlich. Seit einigen Jahren ist es Sitte geworden, daß selbst die Töchter höherer Staatsbeamten auf den Markt geschickt werden, um den Teil der Hauswirtschaft, was den Einkauf der Lebensmittel betrifft, praktisch zu erlernen.

Ich. In der Tat eine löbliche Sitte, die nächst dem praktischen Nutzen zu häuslicher Gesinnung führen muß.

Der Vetter. Meinst du, Vetter? Ich für mein Teil glaube das Gegenteil. Was kann der Selbsteinkauf für andere Zwecke haben, als sich von der Güte der Ware und von den wirklichen Marktpreisen zu überzeugen? Die Eigenschaften, das Ansehen, die Kennzeichen eines guten Gemüses, eines guten Fleisches und so weiter, lernt die angehende Hausfrau sehr leicht auf andere Weise erkennen, und das kleine Ersparnis der sogenannten Schwenzelpfennige, das nicht einmal stattfindet, da die begleitende Köchin mit den Verkäufern sich unbedenklich insgeheim versteht, wiegt den Nachteil nicht auf, den der Besuch des Markts sehr leicht herbeiführen kann. Niemals würde ich um den Preis von etlichen Pfennigen meine Tochter der Gefahr aussetzen, eingedrängt in den Kreis des niedrigsten Volks, eine Zote zu hören oder irgendeine lose Rede eines brutalen Weibes oder Kerls einschlucken zu müssen. – Und dann, was gewisse Spekulationen liebeseufzender Jünglinge in blauen Röcken zu Pferde oder in gelben Flauschen mit schwarzen Kragen zu Fuß betrifft, so ist der Markt. – Doch sieh, sieh, Vetter! wie gefällt dir das Mädchen, das soeben dort an der Pumpe, von der ältlichen Köchin begleitet, daherkommt? Nimm mein Glas, nimm mein Glas, Vetter!

and, envious of her good fortune, is insidiously sawing through the chair legs. Boom, she falls onto her glassware and porcelain, and good-bye to her whole business! That would be a *fallissement* in the truest sense of the word.[8]

I: Truly, my dear cousin, you've now taught me how to be a better observer. As I let my eyes roam through the motley tumult of the surging crowd, they now and then alight on young girls accompanied by neatly garbed cooks carrying commodious, shiny marketing baskets; the girls are wandering through the market and haggling for such household necessities as the market has to offer. The girls' modest attire and their entire carriage leaves no room for doubt that they are at least of the upper middle class. What are *they* doing at the market?

My Cousin: Easily explained. In the last few years it's become customary for even the daughters of higher civil servants to be sent to the market for practical lessons in that part of housekeeping which concerns buying foodstuffs.

I: Truly a praiseworthy custom, which, besides its practical usefulness, must surely lead to a housewifely frame of mind.

My Cousin: You think so, cousin? For my part, I believe just the opposite. What other purpose can this personal buying have except familiarization with the quality of merchandise and with actual market prices? The characteristics, the appearance, the fine points of a good vegetable, a good piece of meat, and so forth, can be learned very easily by a novice housewife in a different way, and the slight saving of the so-called "tail-wagging pennies"[9]—a saving that doesn't even occur, because the cook who escorts the girl unquestionably has a secret understanding with the vendors—doesn't outweigh the disadvantages which visiting the market can readily lead to. Never, for the price of a few pennies, would I expose my daughter to the danger, while she's jammed in among the lowest people, of hearing a filthy remark or having to endure the loose talk of some brutal female or fellow. And then, the market is the perfect setting for certain speculations of love-hungry youths, either on horseback and wearing blue jackets, or on foot and wearing yellow frieze coats with black collars. But look, look, cousin! How do you like that girl who's just now walking alongside the pump there, escorted by that elderly cook? Take my spyglass, take my spyglass, cousin!

8. A pun on the French-derived term for bankruptcy (from *faillir,* "to fail") and the German word *Fall* ("a fall, a tumble").   9. Money that the servant sent to the market puts in her own pocket by inflating the bill.

Ich. Ha, was für ein Geschöpf, die Anmut, die Liebenswürdigkeit
selbst, – aber sie schlägt die Augen verschämt nieder – jeder ihrer
Schritte ist furchtsam – wankend – schüchtern hält sie sich an ihre
Begleiterin, die ihr mit forciertem Angriff den Weg ins Gedränge
bahnt – ich verfolge sie – da steht die Köchin still vor den Gemüsekörben – sie feilscht – sie zieht die Kleine heran, die mit halb weggewandtem Gesicht ganz geschwinde, geschwinde Geld aus dem
Beutelchen nimmt und es hinreicht, froh, nur wieder loszukommen –
ich kann sie nicht verlieren, Dank sei es dem roten Shawl – sie
scheinen etwas vergeblich zu suchen – endlich, endlich, dort weilen
sie bei einer Frau, die in zierlichen Körben feines Gemüse feilbietet,
– der holden Kleinen ganze Aufmerksamkeit fesselt ein Korb mit dem
schönsten Blumenkohl – das Mädchen selbst wählt einen Kopf und
legt ihn der Köchin in den Korb, – wie, die Unverschämte! – ohne
weiteres nimmt sie den Kopf aus dem Korbe heraus, legt ihn in den
Korb der Verkäuferin zurück und wählt einen andern, indem ihr
heftiges Schütteln mit dem gewichtigen kantenhaubengeschmückten
Haupte noch dazu bemerken läßt, daß sie die arme Kleine, welche
zum ersten Male selbständig sein wollte, mit Vorwürfen überhäuft.
Der Vetter. Wie denkst du dir die Gefühle dieses Mädchens, der
man eine Häuslichkeit aufdringen will, welche ihrem zarten Sinn
gänzlich widerstrebt? Ich kenne die holde Kleine; es ist die Tochter
eines geheimen Oberfinanzrats, ein natürliches, von jeder Ziererei
entferntes Wesen, von echtem weiblichem Sinn beseelt und mit
jenem jedesmal richtig treffenden Verstande und feinen Takt begabt,
der Weibern dieser Art stets eigen. – Hoho, Vetter! das nenn ich
glückliches Zusammentreffen. Hier um die Ecke kommt das
Gegenstück zu jenem Bilde. Wie gefällt dir *das* Mädchen, Vetter?
Ich. Ei, welch eine niedliche, schlanke Gestalt! – Jung – leichtfüßig
– mit keckem, unbefangenem Blick in die Welt hineinschauend – am
Himmel stets Sonnenglanz – in den Lüften stets lustige Musik – wie
dreist, wie sorglos sie dem dicken Haufen entgegenhüpft – die
Servante, die ihr mit dem Marktkorbe folgt, scheint eben nicht älter
als sie und zwischen beiden eine gewisse Kordialität zu herrschen –
die Mamsell hat gar hübsche Sachen an, der Shawl ist modern – der
Hut passend zur Morgentracht, so wie das Kleid von geschmack-
vollem Muster – alles hübsch und anständig – o weh! was erblicke ich,
die Mamsell trägt weißseidene Schuhe. Ausrangierte Ballchaussure
auf dem Markt! – Überhaupt, je länger ich das Mädchen beobachte,
desto mehr fällt mir eine gewisse Eigentümlichkeit auf, die ich mit
Worten nicht ausdrücken kann. – Es ist wahr, sie macht, so wie es

I: Ha! What a lovely creature! Grace and charm itself! But she has her eyes cast down shamefacedly. Each step she takes is timorous, wavering. She shyly sticks close to her servant, who is cutting a trail for her through the crowd in a violent assault. I'm following her. Now her cook has come to a halt in front of the vegetable baskets. She's haggling. She's pulling over the girl, who, with face half-averted, is rapidly, oh so rapidly, taking money out of her purse and handing it over, glad to get away again. I can't lose sight of her, thanks to her red shawl. They seem to be looking in vain for something. Finally, finally they're lingering by a woman who's selling good vegetables in pretty baskets. The pretty girl's full attention is caught by a basket of the most beautiful cauliflower. The girl is selecting a head of it herself and placing it in her cook's basket. What?! That insolent creature! Without further ado, she's taking the cauliflower out of the basket, putting it back into the vendor's basket, and selecting another one, while the violent shaking of her heavy head, adorned with its lace cap, gives an additional indication that she is heaping reproaches upon the poor girl, who wanted to be independent for the first time.

My Cousin: What do you think that girl's feelings are like? She's having a kind of housewifery forced upon her which is totally repellent to her gentle nature. I know that pretty girl; she's the daughter of a chief clerk of the Treasury; she's an ingenuous person, free of all affectation, endowed with a truly feminine soul, and gifted with that unerring understanding and fine tact which are always characteristic of such women. Ho, ho, cousin, that's what I call a lucky coincidence. Here around the corner is coming the very opposite of that girl. What do you think of *this* girl, cousin?

I: My, what a sweet, slender body! Young, light on her feet, looking at the world through bold, unembarrassed eyes, perpetual sunshine in the sky, perpetual music in the breeze! How daringly, how unconcernedly she skips toward the dense throng! The servant following her with the marketing basket doesn't look older than the girl, and a certain cordiality seems to prevail between them. The young lady is wearing really pretty things; her shawl is modern, her hat is suitable for morning attire, as is her dress with its tasteful pattern—everything pretty and respectable. Oh, no! What's this I see? The young lady is wearing white silk shoes. Discarded dancing slippers in the market! In general, the longer I observe the girl, the more I'm struck by a certain characteristic I can't express in words. It's true that she

scheint, mit sorglicher Emsigkeit ihre Einkäufe, wählt und wählt, feilscht und feilscht, spricht, gestikuliert, alles mit einem lebendigen Wesen, das beinah bis zur Spannung geht; mir ist aber, als wolle sie noch etwas anderes als eben Hausbedürfnisse einkaufen. –

Der Vetter. Bravo, bravo, Vetter! dein Blick schärft sich, wie ich merke. Sieh nur, mein Liebster, trotz der modesten Kleidung hätten die – die Leichtfüßigkeit des ganzen Wesens abgerechnet – schon die weißseidenen Schuhe auf dem Markt verraten müssen, daß die kleine Mamsell dem Ballett oder überhaupt dem Theater angehört. Was sie sonst noch will, dürfte sich vielleicht bald entwickeln – ha getroffen! Schau doch, lieber Vetter, ein wenig rechts die Straße hinauf und sage mir, wen du auf dem Bürgersteig, vor dem Hotel, wo es ziemlich einsam ist, erblickst?

Ich. Ich erblicke einen großen, schlankgewachsenen Jüngling im gelben kurzgeschnittenen Flausch mit schwarzem Kragen und Stahlknöpfen. Er trägt ein kleines rotes, silbergesticktes Mützchen, unter dem schöne schwarze Locken, beinahe zu üppig, hervorquillen. Den Ausdruck des blassen, männlich schön geformten Gesichts erhöht nicht wenig das kleine schwarze Stutzbärtchen auf der Oberlippe. Er hat eine Mappe unter dem Arm – unbedenklich ein Student, der im Begriff stand, ein Kollegium zu besuchen, – aber fest eingewurzelt steht er da, den Blick unverwandt nach dem Markt gerichtet und scheint Kollegium und alles um sich her zu vergessen. –

Der Vetter. So ist es, lieber Vetter. Sein ganzer Sinn ist auf unsere kleine Komödiantin gerichtet. Der Zeitpunkt ist gekommen; er naht sich der großen Obstbude, in der die schönste Ware appetitlich aufgetürmt ist und scheint nach Früchten zu fragen, die eben nicht zur Hand sind. Es ist ganz unmöglich, daß ein guter Mittagstisch ohne Dessert von Obst bestehen kann; unsere kleine Komödiantin muß daher ihre Einkäufe für den Tisch des Hauses an der Obstbude beschließen. Ein runder rotbäckiger Apfel entschlüpft schalkhaft den kleinen Fingern – der Gelbe bückt sich darnach, hebt ihn auf – ein leichter anmutiger Knix der kleinen Theaterfee – das Gespräch ist im Gange – wechselseitiger Rat und Beistand bei einer sattsam schwierigen Apfelsinenwahl vollendet die gewiß bereits früher angeknüpfte Bekanntschaft, indem sich zugleich das anmutige Rendezvous gestaltet, welches gewiß auf mannigfache Weise wiederholt und variiert wird. –

seems to be making her purchases with careful diligence, she se-
lects this and that, she haggles and haggles, she speaks, she ges-
ticulates, and all with a lively quality that almost approaches nervous tension; but I get the feeling that she wants to buy something more than just her household necessities.

MY COUSIN: Bravo, bravo, cousin! Your eyes are getting
sharper, as I see. Just look, my dear fellow: in spite of her modest clothing, you could have told—apart from her all-around
nimbleness—from her white silk shoes alone that the little lady
is a member of the ballet, or some sort of performer.[10] The other
thing she's looking for ought to make itself known before long.
Ha, there we have it! Just look, my dear cousin; up the street, a
little to the right; tell me whom you see on the sidewalk in front
of the hotel, where there are relatively few people?

I: I see a tall, slim young man wearing a short yellow frieze jacket
with a black collar and steel buttons. He has on a small red cap with
silver embroidery, beneath which his beautiful black, almost too lux-
uriant, tresses show. The expression of his pallid, well-shaped, manly
face is heightened not a little by the little black mustache on his
upper lip. He has a briefcase under his arm—without any doubt a
student who was on his way to attend a lecture—but there he stands,
rooted to the spot, his eyes unswervingly fixed on the market, and he
seems to have forgotten the lecture and everything else around him.

MY COUSIN: Quite right, my dear cousin. His mind is entirely
fixed on our little actress. The time has come; he's approaching
the big fruit booth, in which the most beautiful produce is ap-
petizingly piled up, and he seems to be asking for fruit that isn't
available at the moment. It's quite impossible to have a proper
midday meal without fruit for dessert; therefore our little actress
must conclude her marketing for the domestic table at the fruit
booth. A round, red-cheeked apple slyly slips from her little fingers. The man in yellow bends down to get it and picks it up. A
slight, graceful curtsey from the little goddess of the theater.
Their conversation is in full swing. An exchange of advice and assistance in the quite difficult selection of an orange cements the
acquaintance which was surely begun previously, while at the
same time, they have arranged the delightful rendezvous which
will certainly be repeated and varied in many a way.

---

10. At the time, often tantamount to being a prostitute, at least in the opinion of the public.

Ich. Mag der Musensohn liebeln und Apfelsinen wählen, soviel er will; mich interessiert das nicht, und zwar um so weniger, da mir dort an der Ecke der Hauptfronte des Theaters, wo die Blumenverkäuferinnen ihre Ware feilbieten, das Engelskind, die allerliebste Geheimeratstochter, von neuem aufgestoßen ist.

Der Vetter. Nach den Blumen dort schau ich nicht gerne hin, lieber Vetter; es hat damit eine eigne Bewandtnis. Die Verkäuferin, welche der Regel nach den schönsten Blumenflor ausgesuchter Nelken, Rosen und anderer seltenerer Gewächse hält, ist ein ganz hübsches, artiges Mädchen, strebend nach höherer Kultur des Geistes; denn sowie sie der Handel nicht beschäftigt, liest sie emsig in Büchern, deren Uniform zeigt, daß sie zur großen Kralowskischen ästhetischen Hauptarmee gehören, welche bis in die entferntesten Winkel der Residenz siegend das Licht der Geistesbildung verbreitet. Ein lesendes Blumenmädchen ist für einen belletristischen Schriftsteller ein unwiderstehlicher Anblick. So kam es, daß, als vor langer Zeit mich der Weg bei den Blumen vorbeiführte – auch an andern Tagen stehen die Blumen zum Verkauf –, ich, das lesende Blumenmädchen gewahrend, überrascht stehenblieb. Sie saß wie in einer dichten Laube von blühenden Geranien und hatte das Buch aufgeschlagen auf dem Schoße, den Kopf in die Hand gestützt. Der Held mußte gerade in augenscheinlicher Gefahr, oder sonst ein wichtiger Moment der Handlung eingetreten sein; denn höher glühten des Mädchens Wangen, ihre Lippen bebten, sie schien ihrer Umgebung ganz entrückt. Vetter, ich will dir die seltsame Schwäche eines Schriftstellers ganz ohne Rücksicht gestehen. Ich war wie festgebannt an die Stelle – ich trippelte hin und her; was mag das Mädchen lesen? Dieser Gedanke beschäftigte meine ganze Seele. Der Geist der Schriftstellereitelkeit regte sich und kitzelte mich mit der Ahnung, daß es eins meiner eigenen Werke sei, das eben jetzt das Mädchen in die phantastische Welt meiner Träumereien versetze. Endlich faßte ich ein Herz, trat hinan und fragte nach dem Preise eines Nelkenstocks, der in einer entfernten Reihe stand. Während daß das Mädchen den Nelkenstock herbeiholte, nahm ich mit den Worten: «Was lesen Sie denn da, mein schönes Kind?» das geklappte Buch zur Hand. Oh! all ihr Himmel, es war wirklich ein Werklein von mir, und zwar°°°. – Das Mädchen brachte die Blumen herbei und gab zugleich den mäßigen Preis an. Was Blumen, was Nelkenstock; das Mädchen war mir in

I: The son of the Muses may make love and select oranges as
much as he likes; that doesn't interest me, and all the less because
there, at the corner of the theater's principal facade, where the
flowersellers are offering their wares, that angelic girl, the darling
daughter of the chief clerk, has put in a new appearance.

MY COUSIN: I don't like to look in the direction of the flowers
there, my dear cousin; there's a particular reason for my feelings.
The vendor who regularly has the finest assortment of select carnations, roses, and other, more unusual plants, is a very pretty
and well-mannered girl who strives for higher intellectual culture; for, any time she isn't occupied with her trade, she diligently reads books whose uniform shows that they belong to the
great esthetic Kralowsky[11] army corps, which victoriously
spreads the light of education into the remotest corners of the
capital. For a writer of belles lettres, a flower girl who reads is
an irresistible sight. And so, when, a long time ago, my path led
me past the flowers—the flowers are for sale on other days,
too—I came to a halt in surprise upon espying the flower girl
who reads. She was sitting, as it were, in a dense arbor of blossoming geraniums, the book open on her lap, her head resting
on one hand. The hero must have gotten into obvious danger
just at that moment, or else some other important plot element
was just being unfolded, because the girl's cheeks became more
flushed, her lips were trembling, and she seemed altogether remote from her surroundings. Cousin, I shall confess to you quite
unreservedly the odd weakness of an author. I felt as if magically
fixed to the spot—I walked back and forth in short steps—what
could the girl be reading? That thought occupied my mind entirely. The spirit of authorial vanity made itself felt, flattering me
with the presentiment that it was one of my own works which
was just then transporting the girl into the imaginary world of
my reveries. Finally I took heart, walked over, and asked her the
price of a potted carnation that was located in a distant row.
While the girl was fetching the carnations, I picked up the
closed book, saying: "What are you reading there, my lovely
child?" Oh, by all the heavens, it was really one of my little
pieces; to wit: °°°. The girl brought the flowers, at the same time
stating the moderate price. Who cared about flowers or potted

---

11. Friedrich Kralowsky (1765–?1821), proprietor of a lending library.
Hoffmann asked him for research materials for "The Mines at Falun,"
"Mademoiselle de Scudéry," and other stories.

diesem Augenblick ein viel schätzenswerteres Publikum als die ganze
elegante Welt der Residenz. Aufgeregt, ganz entflammt von den
süßesten Autorgefühlen, fragte ich mit anscheinender Gleichgültig-
keit, wie denn dem Mädchen das Buch gefalle.

«I, mein lieber Herr», erwiderte das Mädchen, «das ist ein gar
schnakisches Buch. Anfangs wird einem ein wenig wirrig im Kopfe;
aber dann ist es so, als wenn man mitten darin säße.» Zu meinem
nicht geringen Erstaunen erzählte mir das Mädchen den Inhalt des
kleinen Märchens ganz klar und deutlich, so daß ich wohl einsah, wie
sie es schon mehrmals gelesen haben mußte; sie wiederholte, es sei
ein gar schnakisches Buch, sie habe bald herzlich lachen müssen, bald
sei ihr ganz weinerlich zumute geworden; sie gab mir den Rat, falls
ich das Buch noch nicht gelesen haben sollte, es mir nachmittags von
Herrn Kralowski zu holen, denn sie wechsele eben nachmittags
Bücher.

Nun sollte der große Schlag geschehn. Mit niedergeschlagenen
Augen, mit einer Stimme, die an Süßigkeit dem Honig von Hybla zu
vergleichen, mit dem seligen Lächeln des wonnerfüllten Autors,
lispelte ich: «Hier, mein süßer Engel, hier steht der Autor des Buchs,
welches Sie mit solchem Vergnügen erfüllt hat, vor Ihnen in leib-
haftiger Person.» Das Mädchen starrte mich sprachlos an, mit großen
Augen und offenem Munde. Das galt mir für den Ausdruck der höchsten Verwunderung, ja eines freudigen Schrecks, daß das sublime
Genie, dessen schaffende Kraft solch ein Werk erzeugt, so plötzlich
bei den Geranien erschienen. Vielleicht, dachte ich, als des Mädchens
Miene unverändert blieb, vielleicht glaubt sie auch gar nicht an den
glücklichen Zufall, der den berühmten Verfasser des *** in ihre Nähe
bringt. Ich suchte nun ihr auf alle mögliche Weise meine Identität mit
jenem Verfasser darzutun, aber es war, als sei sie versteinert, und
nichts entschlüpfte ihren Lippen, als: «Hm – so – I das wäre – wie –».
Doch was soll ich dir die tiefe Schmach, welche mich in diesem
Augenblick traf, erst weitläufig beschreiben. Es fand sich, daß das
Mädchen niemals daran gedacht, daß die Bücher, welche sie lese,
vorher gedichtet werden müßten. Der Begriff eines Schriftstellers,
eines Dichters war ihr gänzlich fremd, und ich glaube wahrhaftig, bei
näherer Nachfrage wäre der fromme kindliche Glaube ans Licht
gekommen, daß der liebe Gott die Bücher wachsen ließe wie die
Pilze.

Ganz kleinlaut fragte ich nochmals nach dem Preise des Nelken-

carnations? At that moment the girl was a more highly esteemed public for me than the whole elegant world of the capital. Excited, all on fire with the most delectable authorial emotions, I asked with apparent indifference how the girl liked the book.

"Ooh, my dear sir," the girl replied, "it's a really funny kind of book. At the beginning you get a little mixed up in your head, but later on you feel as if you're right there in the midst of things." To my great astonishment, the girl recounted the contents of the little tale very clearly and distinctly, so that I realized she must have read it several times before; she repeated her comment that it was a very funny kind of book; at times she had had to laugh heartily, at other times she had felt a lot like crying; she advised me that, in case I hadn't read the book yet, I should pick it up at Kralowsky's in the afternoon, because she exchanged books in the afternoon.

Now was the time for my great coup. With lowered eyes, in a tone comparable in sweetness to the honey of Hybla,[12] with the blissful smile of an enraptured author, I whispered: "Here, my sweet angel, here stands the author of the book that has filled you with such delight, in person before your eyes." The girl stared at me, speechless, her eyes wide and her mouth open. I took that as the expression of the greatest amazement, in fact a joyful awe, because the sublime genius whose creative powers had produced such a work had suddenly appeared among the geraniums. "Perhaps," I said to myself, when the girl's expression didn't change, "perhaps she can't even believe in the lucky chance which has brought the famous author of °°° into her presence." Then I tried in every possible way to prove to her that I and the author were one and the same, but she seemed to have been turned to stone, and nothing escaped her lips except: "Hmm—so—oh, you mean—how—." But why should I give you an extended description of the shame that befell me at that moment? It turned out that it had never occurred to the girl that the books she read had to be written first. The concept of an author or poet was completely alien to her, and I truly believe that if I had continued to ask her questions she would have revealed her pious, childlike belief that God made books grow like mushrooms.

Severely humbled, I asked her again how much the potted

12. A mountain in ancient Sicily famous for its bees.

stocks. Unterdessen mußte eine ganz andere dunkle Idee von dem
Verfertigen der Bücher dem Mädchen aufgestiegen sein; denn da ich
das Geld aufzählte, fragte sie ganz naiv und unbefangen, ob ich alle
Bücher beim Herrn Kralowski mache, – pfeilschnell schoß ich mit
meinem Nelkenstock von dannen.

Ich. Vetter, Vetter, das nenne ich gestrafte Autoreitelkeit; doch
während du mir deine tragische Geschichte erzähltest, verwandte ich
kein Auge von meiner Lieblingin. Bei den Blumen allein ließ der
übermütige Küchendämon ihr volle Freiheit. Die grämliche
Küchengouvernante hatte den schweren Marktkorb an die Erde
gesetzt und überließ sich, indem sie die feisten Arme bald über-
einanderschlug, bald, wie es der äußere rhetorische Ausdruck der
Rede zu erfordern schien, in die Seiten stemmte, mit drei
Kolleginnen der unbeschreiblichen Freude des Gesprächs, und ihre
Rede war, der Bibel entgegen, gewiß viel mehr als ja, ja und nein,
nein. Sieh nur, welch einen herrlichen Blumenflor sich der holde
Engel ausgewählt hat und von einem rüstigen Burschen nachtragen
läßt. Wie? Nein, das will mir nicht ganz gefallen, daß sie im Wandeln
Kirschen aus dem kleinen Körbchen nascht; wie wird das feine
Batisttuch, das wahrscheinlich darin befindlich, sich mit dem Obst
befreunden?

Der Vetter. Der jugendliche Appetit des Augenblicks frägt nicht
nach Kirschflecken, für die es Kleesalz und andere probate
Hausmittel gibt. Und das ist eben die wahrhaft kindliche Unbefangenheit, daß die Kleine nun von den Drangsalen des bösen Markts
sich in wiedererlangter Freiheit ganz gehen läßt. – Doch schon lange
ist mir jener Mann aufgefallen und ein unauflösbares Rätsel geblieben, der eben jetzt dort an der zweiten entfernten Pumpe an dem
Wagen steht, auf dem ein Bauernweib aus einem großen Faß, um ein
billiges, Pflaumenmus verspendet. Fürs erste, lieber Vetter, bewun-
dere die Agilität des Weibes, das, mit einem langen hölzernen Löffel
bewaffnet, erst die großen Verkäufe zu viertel, halben und ganzen
Pfunden beseitigt und dann den gierigen Näschern, die ihre
Papierchen, mitunter auch wohl ihre Pelzmütze hinhalten, mit
Blitzesschnelle das gewünschte Dreierkleckschen zuwirft, welches sie
sogleich als stattlichen Morgenimbiß wohlgefällig verzehren – Kaviar
des Volks! Bei dem geschickten Verteilen des Pflaumenmuses mittelst
des geschwenkten Löffels fällt mir ein, daß ich einmal in meiner
Kindheit hörte, es sei auf einer reichen Bauernhochzeit so splendid

carnations cost. Meanwhile, a very different obscure idea about how books were made must have dawned on the girl, because, while I was paying her, she asked quite naïvely and innocently whether I made all the books at Kralowsky's. Swiftly as an arrow I dashed away with my potted carnations.

I: Cousin, cousin, that's what I call punishment for an author's vanity! But while you were telling me your tragic story, I kept my eyes firmly on my sweetheart. That overbearing demon of a cook allowed her complete freedom at the flower stands only. The peevish kitchen manager had set the heavy marketing basket on the ground and, now crossing her pudgy arms and now standing with arms akimbo, in accordance with the demands of the moment for an outward rhetorical expression of her sentiments, she was indulging in the inexpressible pleasure of a conversation with three colleagues; unlike the Bible, she was surely saying much more than "yea, yea" or "nay, nay."[13] Just see what a splendid assortment of flowers that lovely angel has selected and is having carried after her by a sturdy lad! What? No, I'm not altogether pleased to see her nibbling cherries on the sly from that little basket while she walks; how will the fine batiste cloth that's probably inside it get along with the fruit?

MY COUSIN: A momentary youthful appetite doesn't worry about cherry stains, for which there's salt of sorrel and other tried-and-true household remedies. And it's precisely this that shows her truly childlike innocence: after the pressures of the unpleasant market, the girl has regained her liberty and is letting herself go. But for some time now I've noticed that man, and he's remained an insoluble puzzle to me—the one just now standing there by the second, more distant pump alongside the cart on which a farmer's wife is dispensing plum jam at a low price from a big tub. First of all, my dear cousin, admire the agility of the woman, who, armed with a long wooden spoon, first takes care of the big purchases of quarter-, half-, and entire pounds, and then with the speed of lightning flings to the greedy lovers of sweets, who hold out their bits of paper and sometimes even their fur caps, the little threepenny dab they desire, which they at once consume contentedly as if it were a copious breakfast—the caviar of the common people! Watching her skillful distribution of the plum jam by means of the spoon she

---

13. Probably a reference to 2 Corinthians i, 18.

hergegangen, daß der delikate, mit einer dicken Kruste von Zimt, Zucker und Nelken überhäutete Reisbrei mittelst eines Dreschflegels verteilt worden. Jeder der werten Gäste durfte nur ganz gemütlich das Maul aufsperren, um die gehörige Portion zu bekommen, und es ging auf diese Weise recht zu wie im Schlaraffenland. Doch, Vetter, hast du den Mann ins Auge gefaßt?

Ich. Allerdings! – Wes Geistes Kind ist die tolle abenteuerliche Figur? Ein wenigstens sechs Fuß hoher, winddürrer Mann, der noch dazu kerzengrade mit eingebogenem Rücken dasteht! Unter dem kleinen dreieckigen, zusammengequetschten Hütchen starrt hinten die Kokarde eines Haarbeutels hervor, der sich dann in voller Breite dem Rücken sanft anschmiegt. Der graue, nach längst verjährter Sitte zugeschnittene Rock schließt sich, vorne von oben bis unten zugeknöpft, enge an den Leib an, ohne eine einzige Falte zu werfen, und schon erst, als er an den Wagen schritt, konnte ich bemerken, daß er schwarze Beinkleider, schwarze Strümpfe und mächtige zinnerne Schnallen in den Schuhen trägt. Was mag er nur in dem viereckigen Kasten haben, den er so sorglich unter dem linken Arme trägt, und der beinahe dem Kasten eines Tabulettkrämers gleicht? –

Der Vetter. Das wirst du gleich erfahren, schau nur aufmerksam hin.

Ich. Er schlägt den Deckel des Kastens zurück – die Sonne scheint hinein – strahlende Reflexe – der Kasten ist mit Blech gefüttert – er macht der Pflaumenmusfrau, indem er das Hütchen vom Kopfe zieht, eine beinahe ehrfurchtsvolle Verbeugung. – Was für ein originelles, ausdrucksvolles Gesicht – feingeschlossene Lippen – eine Habichtsnase – große, schwarze Augen – hochstehende, starke Augenbrauen – eine hohe Stirn – schwarzes Haar – das Toupet en cœur frisiert, mit kleinen steifen Löckchen über den Ohren. – Er reicht den Kasten der Bauersfrau auf den Wagen, die ihn ohne weiteres mit Pflaumenmus füllt und ihm freundlich nickend wieder zurückreicht. – Mit einer zweiten Verbeugung entfernt sich der Mann – er windet sich hinan an die Heringstonne – er zieht ein Schubfach des Kastens hervor, legt einige erhandelte Salzmänner hinein und schiebt das Fach wieder zu – ein drittes Schubfach ist, wie ich sehe, zu Petersilie und anderem Wurzelwerk bestimmt. – Nun durchschneidet er mit langen, gravitätischen Schritten den Markt in verschiedenen Richtungen, bis ihn der reiche, auf einem Tisch ausgebreitete Vorrat von gerupftem Geflügel festhält. So wie überall, macht er auch hier, ehe er zu

brandishes, I recall that I once heard tell as a child that at an op-
ulent rural wedding things were done with such a liberal hand
that the delicate rice pudding, with its thick coating of cinna-
mon, sugar, and cloves, was distributed by means of a threshing
flail. Each of the honored guests needed only to open his yap
wide, in complete comfort, to receive the proper portion, and in
that way it was just like being in the land of Cockaigne. But,
cousin, have you sighted the man?

I: Yes, indeed! What kind of person is that odd, peculiar figure?
A man at least six feet tall, emaciated, and, on top of that, standing perfectly erect with a bent back! Beneath his squashed little
three-cornered hat, the cockade of a bagwig protrudes in the
back, and the wig then adheres smoothly to his back in its full
breadth. His gray coat, tailored in a long-outmoded fashion, is
buttoned in front from top to bottom and is closely form-fitting
without any creases; and it was only when he walked up to the cart
that I was able to notice he's wearing black trousers, black stockings, and large pewter buckles on his shoes. What can he have in
the square box which he's carrying so carefully under his left arm,
and which almost looks like a hawker's portable display case?

MY COUSIN: You'll soon find out; just observe him attentively.

I: He's opening the cover of the box. The sun shines into it.
Radiant reflections. The box is lined with tin. Taking off his little hat, he makes an almost reverent bow to the woman with
the plum jam. What an unusual, expressive face! Tightly
closed, thin lips. Nose like a hawk. Big, dark eyes. Thick, high
eyebrows. A lofty brow. Black hair. His hair dressed in front *en
coeur*,[14] with small, stiff curls over his ears. He holds out his
box toward the farmwoman's cart, and without further ado she
fills it with plum jam and hands it back to him with a friendly
nod. With a second bow the man walks away. He makes his
winding way up to the herring barrel. He opens a drawer in his
box, places a few purchased salt herrings in it, and shuts the
drawer again. As I see, a third drawer is set aside for parsley
and other herbs. Now with long, solemn strides he traverses
the market in various directions until he's stopped short by the
abundant display of plucked poultry spread out on a table. As
he does everywhere, so here, too, he makes a few low bows before beginning to haggle. He has a long talk with the woman,

14. Heart-shaped.

feilschen beginnt, einige tiefe Verbeugungen – er spricht viel und lange mit der Frau, die ihn mit besonders freundlicher Miene anhört – er setzt den Kasten behutsam auf den Boden nieder und ergreift zwei Enten, die er ganz bequem in die weite Rocktasche schiebt. – Himmel! es folgt noch eine Gans – den Puter schaut er bloß an mit liebäugelnden Blicken – er kann doch nicht unterlassen, ihn wenigstens mit dem Zeige- und Mittelfinger liebkosend zu berühren –; schnell hebt er seinen Kasten auf, verbeugt sich gegen das Weib ungemein verbindlich und schreitet, sich mit Gewalt losreißend von dem verführerischen Gegenstand seiner Begierde, von dannen – er steuert geradezu los auf die Fleischerbuden – ist der Mensch ein Koch, der für ein Gastmahl zu sorgen hat? – er erhandelt eine Kalbskeule, die er noch in eine seiner Riesentaschen gleiten läßt. – Nun ist er fertig mit seinem Einkauf; er geht die Charlottenstraße herauf mit solchem ganz seltsamen Anstand und Wesen, daß er aus irgendeinem fremden Lande hinabgeschneit zu sein scheint.

Der Vetter. Genug habe ich mir schon über diese exotische Figur den Kopf zerbrochen. – Was denkst du, Vetter, zu meiner Hypothese? Dieser Mensch ist ein alter Zeichenmeister, der in mittelmäßigen Schulanstalten sein Wesen getrieben hat und vielleicht noch treibt. Durch allerlei industriöse Unternehmungen hat er viel Geld erworben; er ist geizig, mißtrauisch, Zyniker bis zum Ekelhaften, Hagestolz, – nur einem Gott opfert er – dem Bauche; – seine ganze Lust ist, gut zu essen, versteht sich allein auf seinem Zimmer; – er ist durchaus ohne alle Bedienung, er besorgt alles selbst – an Markttagen holt er, wie du gesehen hast, seine Lebensbedürfnisse für die halbe Woche und bereitet in einer kleinen Küche, die dicht bei seinem armseligen Stübchen belegen, selbst seine Speisen, die er dann, da der Koch es stets dem Gaumen des Herrn zu Dank macht, mit gierigem, ja vielleicht tierischem Appetit verzehrt. Wie geschickt und zweckmäßig er einen alten Malkasten zum Marktkorbe aptiert hat, auch das hast du bemerkt, lieber Vetter.

Ich. Weg von dem widrigen Menschen.

Der Vetter. Warum widrig? Es muß auch solche Käuze geben, sagt ein welterfahrner Mann, und er hat recht, denn die Varietät kann nie bunt genug sein. Doch mißfällt dir der Mann so sehr, lieber Vetter, so kann ich dir darüber, was er ist, tut und treibt, noch eine andere Hypothese aufstellen. Vier Franzosen, und zwar sämtlich Pariser, ein Sprachmeister, ein Fechtmeister, ein Tanzmeister und ein Pastetenbäcker, kamen in ihren Jugendjahren gleichzeitig nach Berlin und fanden, wie es damals (gegen das Ende des vorigen Jahrhunderts) gar

who listens to him with a particularly friendly expression. He carefully sets his box down on the ground and grasps two ducks, which he quite comfortably thrusts into the wide pockets of his coat. Heavens! A goose follows. The turkey he merely looks at with loving glances. But he can't resist at least touching it caressingly with his index and middle fingers. Quickly he picks up his box, bows to the woman uncommonly obligingly, and, tearing himself away by force from the tempting object of his desires, he strides away. He's heading straight for the butchers' booths. Is the fellow a cook preparing a banquet? He buys a shoulder of veal, and this, too, he lets slide into one of his gigantic pockets. Now he's done with his marketing; he walks up Charlottenstrasse with such an extraordinary bearing and manner that he seems to have been wafted here from some foreign land.

MY COUSIN: I've already racked my brains quite enough over that exotic character. Cousin, what do you think about this hypothesis of mine? This fellow is an old drawing teacher who has spent a lot of time working in mediocre schools, and maybe still does. By means of all sorts of industrious enterprises he has earned a lot of money; he's miserly, distrustful, cynical to the point of being repulsive, a confirmed bachelor. He sacrifices to one god alone: his belly. His only pleasure is eating well, and of course alone in his room. He has no servants whatsoever and takes care of everything himself. On market days he buys enough food for half a week, as you've seen, and cooks his own meals in a small kitchen located right next to his miserable little parlor; then, since a cook always does things to his employer's liking, he consumes his food with a greedy, perhaps even a bestial appetite. How skillfully and to the purpose he has adapted an old paintbox for use as a marketing basket, you have observed as well, my dear cousin.

I: Away from the repellent fellow!

MY COUSIN: Why repellent? Eccentrics like that have to exist, too, a worldly-wise man says; and he's right, because we can never have too much variety. But if you dislike the man so much, my dear cousin, I can establish another hypothesis for you on what he is, does, and carries out. Four Frenchmen, all Parisians in fact, a teacher of French, a fencing master, a dancing master, and a pastry chef, came to Berlin at the same time when they were young and, as was inevitable at the time (toward the end of

nicht fehlen konnte, ihr reichliches Brot. Seit dem Augenblick, als die
Diligence sie auf der Reise vereinigte, schlossen sie den engsten
Freundschaftsbund, blieben ein Herz und eine Seele und verlebten
jeden Abend nach vollbrachter Arbeit zusammen, als echte alte
Franzosen, in lebhafter Konversation, bei frugalem Abendessen. Des
Tanzmeisters Beine waren stumpf geworden, des Fechtmeisters
Arme durch das Alter entnervt, dem Sprachmeister Rivale, die sich
der neuesten Pariser Mundart rühmten, über den Kopf gestiegen,
und die schlauen Erfindungen des Pastetenbäckers überboten
jüngere Gaumenkitzler, von den eigensinnigsten Gastronomen in
Paris ausgebildet.

Aber jeder des treu verbundenen Quatuors hatte indessen sein
Schäfchen ins trockne gebracht. Sie zogen zusammen in eine geräumige, ganz artige, jedoch entlegene Wohnung, gaben ihre Geschäfte
auf und lebten zusammen, altfranzösischer Sitte getreu, ganz lustig
und sorgenfrei, da sie selbst den Bekümmernissen und Lasten der
unglücklichen Zeit geschickt zu entgehen wußten. Jeder hat ein
besonderes Geschäft, wodurch der Nutzen und das Vergnügen der
Sozietät befördert wird. Der Tanzmeister und der Fechtmeister besuchen ihre alten Scholaren, ausgediente Offiziers von höherm
Range, Kammerherren, Hofmarschälle und so weiter; denn sie hatten
die vornehmste Praxis, und sammeln die Neuigkeiten des Tages zum
Stoff für ihre Unterhaltung, der nie ausgehen darf. Der Sprachmeister durchwühlt die Läden der Antiquare, um immer mehr
französische Werke auszumitteln, deren Sprache die Akademie
gebilligt hat. Der Pastetenbäcker sorgt für die Küche; er kauft ebensogut selbst ein, als er die Speisen ebenfalls selbst bereitet, worin ihm
ein alter französischer Hausknecht beisteht. Außer diesem besorgt für
jetzt, da eine alte zahnlose Französin, die sich von der französischen
Gouvernante bis zur Aufwaschmagd heruntergedient hatte, gestorben, ein pausbäckiger Junge, den die vier von den Orphelins françois
zu sich genommen, die Bedienung. – Dort geht der kleine Himmel-
blaue, an einem Arm einen Korb mit Mundsemmeln, an dem andern
einen Korb, in dem der Salat hoch aufgetürmt ist. – So habe ich den
widrigen zynischen deutschen Zeichenmeister augenblicklich zum
gemütlichen französischen Pastetenbäcker umgeschaffen, und ich
glaube, daß sein Äußeres, sein ganzes Wesen recht gut dazu paßt.

Ich. Diese Erfindung macht deinem Schriftstellertalent Ehre, lieber
Vetter. Doch mir leuchten schon seit ein paar Minuten dort jene
hohen weißen Schwungfedern in die Augen, die sich aus dem dicksten
Gedränge des Volkes emporheben. Endlich tritt die Gestalt dicht bei

last century), they made a good living here. From the very moment when the stagecoach united them on their journey, they sealed the staunchest covenant of friendship, they remained of one mind, and they spent every evening after work together, the way genuine old Frenchmen do: in lively conversation over a frugal supper. The dancing master's legs had become stiff; the fencing master's arms had lost their sinew from old age; the teacher of French had been left in the shade by rivals who advertised the latest Parisian phraseology; and the clever inventions of the pastry chef had been surpassed by younger palate-ticklers trained by the most capricious gastronomes in Paris.

But in the meantime each of the loyally united foursome had laid aside a nest egg. They moved together into a spacious, quite charming, but out-of-the-way apartment, gave up their trade, and lived under one roof; in accordance with old French customs, they were very merry and carefree, since they themselves had been able to avoid skillfully the worries and burdens of that unfortunate period. Each of them has his own task for the promotion of their mutual benefit and pleasure. The dancing master and the fencing master visit their former pupils, retired officers of higher rank, chamberlains, marshals of the royal court, and the like (because they had the most aristocratic clientèle), and they gather the news of the day for their entertainment, which must never be allowed to run out. The teacher of French rummages through second-hand bookshops to ferret out more and more French works whose diction has been approved by the Académie. The pastry chef takes care of the kitchen; not only does he buy the food himself, he also cooks it himself, with the assistance of an old French servant. In addition to the latter, the housekeeping is in the hands of a chubby-cheeked boy whom the foursome took in from the French orphanage—now that an old, toothless Frenchwoman, who had worked her way down from a French governess to a scullery maid, is dead. There goes the little man, dressed in sky-blue, on one arm a basket of rolls, on the other a basket piled high with lettuce. And so, on the spur of the moment, I've transformed the repellent, cynical German drawing teacher into a congenial French pastry chef, and I think that his appearance and entire manner fit the description very well.

I: This inventiveness does credit to your talent as a writer, my dear cousin. But for a couple of minutes now, those lofty white plumes looming above the densest throng of people have been

der Pumpe hervor – ein großes, schlankgewachsenes Frauenzimmer
von gar nicht üblem Ansehen – der Überrock von rosarotem schwerem
Seidenzeuge ist funkelnagelneu – der Hut von der neuesten Fasson,
der daran befestigte Schleier von schönen Spitzen – weiße
Glacéhandschuhe. – Was nötigte die elegante, wahrscheinlich zu
einem Dejeuner eingeladene Dame, sich durch das Gewühl des
Marktes zu drängen? – Doch wie, auch sie gehört zu den Einkäuferin-
nen? Sie steht still und winkt einem alten, schmutzigen, zerlumpten
Weibe, die ihr, ein lebhaftes Bild der Misere im Hefen des Volks, mit
einem halbzerbrochenen Marktkorbe am Arm mühsam nachhinkt.
Die geputzte Dame winkt an der Ecke des Theatergebäudes, um dem
erblindeten Landwehrmann, der dort an die Mauer gelehnt steht, ein
Almosen zu geben. Sie zieht mit Mühe den Handschuh von der
rechten Hand – hilf Himmel! eine blutrote, noch dazu ziemlich
mannhaft gebaute Faust kommt zum Vorschein. Doch ohne lange zu
suchen und zu wählen, drückt sie dem Blinden rasch ein Stück Geld
in die Hand, läuft rasch bis in die Mitte der Charlottenstraße und setzt
sich dann in einen majestätischen Promenadenschritt, mit dem sie,
ohne sich weiter um ihre zerlumpte Begleiterin zu kümmern, die
Charlottenstraße hinauf nach den Linden wandelt.

Der Vetter. Das Weib hat, um sich auszuruhen, den Korb an die
Erde gesetzt, und du kannst mit einem Blick den ganzen Einkauf der
eleganten Dame übersehen.

Ich. Der ist in der Tat wunderlich genug. – Ein Kohlkopf – viele
Kartoffeln – einige Äpfel – ein kleines Brot – einige Heringe in
Papier gewickelt – ein Schafkäse, nicht von der appetitlichsten Farbe
– eine Hammelleber – ein kleiner Rosenstock – ein Paar Pantoffeln
– ein Stiefelknecht – Was in aller Welt –

Der Vetter. Still, still, Vetter, genug von der Rosenroten! –
Betrachte aufmerksam jenen Blinden, dem das leichtsinnige Kind der
Verderbnis Almosen spendete. Gibt es ein rührenderes Bild unver-
dienten menschlichen Elends und frommer, in Gott und Schicksal ergebener Resignation? Mit dem Rücken an die Mauer des Theaters gelehnt, beide abgedürrte Knochenhände auf einen Stab gestützt, den er einen Schritt vorgeschoben, damit das unvernünftige
Volk ihm nicht über die Füße laufe, das leichenblasse Antlitz empor-
gehoben, das Landwehrmützchen in die Augen gedrückt, steht er
regungslos vom frühen Morgen bis zum Schluß des Markts an derselben Stelle. –

Ich. Er bettelt, und doch ist für die erblindeten Krieger so gut
gesorgt.

flashing in my eyes. Finally their owner is emerging, right by the pump: a tall, slender woman not at all bad-looking. Her skirt of heavy pink silk is brand new. Her hat is in the latest style; the veil attached to it is of excellent lace. White kid gloves. What has compelled that elegant lady, who's probably invited to a luncheon, to push her way through the hubbub of the market? But what's this? Is *she* one of the women buying food, too? She has halted, and she's beckoning to a dirty, ragged old woman, a living image of poverty among the dregs of the populace, who's limping after her painfully with a half-ruined marketing basket on her arm. The well-dressed lady is waving there, at the corner of the theater, where she's about to give alms to the blind ex-militiaman who's leaning against the wall. She laboriously draws the glove from her right hand. Heaven help us! A blood-red fist, pretty much shaped like a man's, emerges. But without searching or choosing for very long, she quickly presses a coin into the blind man's hand, quickly runs to the middle of Charlottenstrasse, and then assumes a majestical promenade pace, with which, paying no more heed to her ragged escort, she walks up Charlottenstrasse to Unter den Linden.

MY COUSIN: In order to take a rest, the woman has put her basket on the ground, and you can take in at a glance everything the elegant lady has purchased.

I: And strange enough it is! A head of cabbage. A lot of potatoes. A few apples. A small loaf of bread. A few herrings wrapped in paper. A sheep's-milk cheese, not of the most appetizing color. A sheep's liver. A small pot of roses. A pair of slippers. A bootjack. What in the world—?

MY COUSIN: Quiet, quiet, cousin, enough about the woman in pink! Pay close attention to the blind man, to whom that frivolous child of corruption gave alms. Is there a more touching picture of undeserved human misery and pious resignation in submission to God and destiny? Resting his back against the theater wall, both of his emaciated, bony hands supported by a stick which he has pushed out one pace in front of him, so that mindless people won't step on his feet, his face, pale as a corpse's, lifted up, his militia cap pulled down over his forehead, he stands on the same spot without moving from early in the morning until the market shuts down.

I: He's begging, and yet society takes such good care of blinded veterans.

254 Des Vetters Eckfenster

Der Vetter. Du bist in gar großem Irrtum, lieber Vetter. Dieser arme Mensch macht den Knecht eines Weibes, welches Gemüse feilhält, und die zu der niedrigeren Klasse dieser Verkäuferinnen gehört, da die vornehmere das Gemüse in auf Wagen gepackten Körben herbeifahren läßt. Dieser Blinde kommt nämlich jeden Morgen, mit vollen Gemüsekörben bepackt, wie ein Lasttier, so daß ihn die Bürde beinahe zu Boden drückt und er sich nur mit Mühe im wankenden Schritt mittelst des Stabes aufrecht erhält, herbei. Eine große, robuste Frau, in deren Dienste er steht, oder die ihn vielleicht nur eben zum Hinschaffen des Gemüses auf den Markt gebraucht, gibt sich, wenn nun seine Kräfte beinahe ganz erschöpft sind, kaum die Mühe, ihn beim Arm zu ergreifen und weiter an Ort und Stelle, nämlich eben an den Platz, den er jetzt einnimmt, hinzuhelfen. Hier nimmt sie ihm die Körbe vom Rücken, die sie selbst hinüberträgt, und läßt ihn stehen, ohne sich im mindesten um ihn eher zu bekümmern, als bis der Markt geendet ist und sie ihm die ganz oder nur zum Teil geleerten Körbe wieder aufpackt.

Ich. Es ist doch merkwürdig, daß man die Blindheit, sollten auch die Augen nicht verschlossen sein, oder sollte auch kein anderer sichtbarer Fehler den Mangel des Gesichts verraten, dennoch an der emporgerichteten Stellung des Hauptes, die den Erblindeten eigentümlich, sogleich erkennt; es scheint darin ein fortwährendes Streben zu liegen, etwas in der Nacht, die den Blinden umschließt, zu erschauen.

Der Vetter. Es gibt für mich keinen rührendern Anblick, als wenn ich einen solchen Blinden sehe, der mit emporgerichtetem Haupt in die weite Ferne zu schauen scheint. Untergegangen ist für den Armen die Abendröte des Lebens, aber sein inneres Auge strebt schon das ewige Licht zu erblicken, das ihm in dem Jenseits voll Trost, Hoffnung und Seligkeit leuchtet. – Doch ich werde zu ernst. – Der blinde Landwehrmann bietet mir jeden Markttag einen Schatz von Bemerkungen dar. Du gewahrst, lieber Vetter, wie sich bei diesem armen Menschen die Mildtätigkeit der Berliner recht lebhaft ausspricht. Oft ziehen ganze Reihen bei ihm vorüber, und keiner daraus verfehlt ihm ein Almosen zu reichen. Aber die Art und Weise, wie dieses Almosen gereicht wird, hierin liegt alles. Schau einmal, lieber Vetter, eine Zeitlang hin und sag mir, was du gewahrst.

Ich. Eben kommen drei, vier, fünf stattliche derbe Hausmägde; die mit zum Teil schwer ins Gewicht fallenden Waren übermäßig vollgepackten Körbe schneiden ihnen beinahe die nervichten, blau aufgelaufenen Arme wund; sie haben Ursache zu eilen, um ihre Last loszuwerden, und doch weilt jede einen Augenblick, greift schnell in

MY COUSIN: You're very, very wrong, my dear cousin. That poor fellow is in the service of a woman who sells vegetables and belongs to the lower sort of such vendors, since the better ones have their vegetables brought over in baskets loaded into carts. You see, that blind man comes here every morning laden down like a beast of burden with filled baskets of vegetables, bent almost to the ground under his load, so that he can stay erect on his wavering way only with difficulty, using his stick. The tall, robust woman who employs him, or perhaps makes use of him merely to carry her vegetables to market, hardly makes an effort to grab his arm, when his strength is nearly exhausted, and to help him reach his goal—that is, the spot he's now standing on. At that point she lifts the baskets off his back and carries them to her area herself, leaving him there without the slightest concern for him until the market is over and she loads him again with the entirely or only partially emptied baskets.

I: It is peculiar, though, how, even if a blind man's eyes aren't shut and no other visible defect reveals his lack of sight, you can still immediately tell he's blind by that upraised position of the head that's characteristic of the blind; it seems to indicate a perpetual attempt to see something in the night that envelops them.

MY COUSIN: For me there's no sight more touching than a blind man of that sort, his head raised as if he were looking into the remote distance. The evening sun of life has set for the poor fellow, but his inward eye is already striving to catch sight of that eternal light which beams at him from heaven, bringing consolation, hope, and bliss. But I'm getting too serious. Every market day the blind militiaman provides me with a treasury of observations. You notice, my dear cousin, how these unfortunate people bring out the charity of Berliners in a very conspicuous way. Often whole lines of people file past him, and none of them fails to hand him some alms. But the manner and fashion in which those alms are given: that tells the whole story. Just observe for a while, my dear cousin, and tell me what you see.

I: Right now three, four, five hefty, coarse housemaids are coming. Their overloaded baskets, some of them containing heavy items, are nearly cutting sores into their sinewy arms, which are swollen and blue. They have every reason to hurry, in order to be rid of their load, but nevertheless each of them

den Marktkorb und drückt dem Blinden ein Stück Geld, ohne ihn einmal anzusehen, in die Hand. Die Ausgabe steht als notwendig und unerläßlich auf dem Etat des Markttages. Das ist recht!

Da kommt eine Frau, deren Anzuge, deren ganzem Wesen man die Behaglichkeit und Wohlhabenheit deutlich anmerkt, – sie bleibt vor dem Invaliden stehen, zieht ein Beutelchen hervor und sucht und sucht, und kein Stück Geld scheint ihr klein genug zum Akt der Wohltätigkeit, den sie zu vollführen gedenkt, – sie ruft ihrer Köchin zu – es findet sich, daß auch dieser die kleine Münze ausgegangen, – sie muß erst bei den Gemüseweibern wechseln – endlich ist der zu verschenkende Dreier herbeigeschafft – nun klopft sie dem Blinden auf die Hand, damit er ja merke, daß er etwas empfangen werde, – er öffnet den Handteller – die wohltätige Dame drückt ihm das Geldstück hinein und schließt ihm die Faust, damit die splendide Gabe ja nicht verloren gehe.

Warum trippelt die kleine niedliche Mamsell so hin und her und nähert sich immer mehr und mehr dem Blinden? Ha, im Vorbeihuschen hat sie schnell, daß es gewiß niemand als ich, der ich sie auf dem Kern meines Glases habe, bemerkte, dem Blinden ein Stück Geld in die Hand gesteckt – das war gewiß kein Dreier.

Der glaue, wohlgemästete Mann im braunen Rocke, der dort so gemütlich dahergeschritten kommt, ist gewiß ein sehr reicher Bürger. Auch er bleibt vor dem Blinden stehen und läßt sich in ein langes Gespräch mit ihm ein, indem er den übrigen Leuten den Weg versperrt und sie hindert, dem Blinden Almosen zu spenden; – endlich, endlich zieht er eine mächtige grüne Geldbörse aus der Tasche, entknüpft sie nicht ohne Mühe und wühlt so entsetzlich im Gelde, daß ich glaube, es bis hieher klappern zu hören. – Parturiunt montes! – Doch will ich wirklich glauben, daß der edle Menschenfreund, vom Bilde des Jammers hingerissen, sich bis zum schlechten Groschen verstieg.

Bei allem dem meine ich doch, daß der Blinde an den Markttagen nach seiner Art keine geringe Einnahme macht, und mich wundert, daß er alles ohne das mindeste Zeichen von Dankbarkeit annimmt; nur eine leise Bewegung der Lippen, die ich wahrzunehmen glaube, zeigt, daß er etwas spricht, was wohl Dank sein mag, – doch auch diese Bewegung bemerke ich nur zuweilen.

Der Vetter. Da hast du den entschiedenen Ausdruck vollkommen

tarries for a moment, quickly reaches into her basket, and presses a coin into the blind man's hand without giving him one look. That expense is a necessary, indispensable entry in their market-day budget. And rightly so!

Here comes a woman whose clothes and whose entire bearing clearly show that she's prosperous and well-off. She halts in front of the disabled veteran, pulls out a little purse, and searches and searches, but none of the coins seems small enough to her for the charitable action she intends to perform. She calls over her cook. It turns out that she, too, is out of small change; she has to break a coin at a vegetable stand first. Finally the threepenny coin that is to be offered has been acquired. Now she taps the blind man's hand so he'll notice that he's going to receive something. He opens his palm. The charitable lady presses the coin into it and closes his fist, so the liberal gift won't get lost.

Why is that small, cute young lady walking to and fro that way with mincing steps, getting closer to the blind man all the time? Ha! As she whizzed by, she put a coin in the blind man's hand so quickly that I'm sure no one noticed it but me (and I have the spyglass focused on her)—and I'm sure it wasn't a threepenny coin!

That keen-eyed, well-fed man in the brown coat, who's striding by so jovially, is certainly a very wealthy bourgeois. He, too, comes to a halt in front of the blind man and begins a long conversation with him, blocking the other people's way and preventing them from giving alms to the blind man. Finally, finally he pulls an enormous green purse out of his pocket, unties it with an effort, and rummages around in the money so noisily that I imagine I hear it clink all the way up here. *Parturiunt montes!*[15] But I'm ready to believe that the noble humanitarian, carried away by that image of misery, has brought himself to donate as much as a bad ten-cent piece!

All that notwithstanding, I think that on market days the blind man takes in a decent amount of money for someone in his position, and I'm surprised that he accepts it all without the least token of gratitude; only a slight movement of his lips, which I think I can perceive, shows that he's saying something, which may be thanks—but even that movement I detect only occasionally.

MY COUSIN: There you have the decided expression of

---

15. The correct quotation is *Parturient montes, [nascetur ridiculus mus]*("Mountains will go into labor, [and a laughable mouse will be born]"). From the *Ars poetica* (Art of Poetry) by Horace.

abgeschlossener Resignation: was ist ihm das Geld, er kann es nicht nutzen; erst in der Hand eines andern, dem er sich rücksichtslos anvertrauen muß, erhält es seinen Wert – ich kann mich sehr irren, aber mir scheint, als wenn das Weib, deren Gemüsekörbe er trägt, eine fatale böse Sieben sei, die den Armen schlecht hält, unerachtet sie höchst wahrscheinlich alles Geld, das er empfängt, in Beschlag nimmt. Jedesmal, wenn sie die Körbe zurückbringt, keift sie mit dem Blinden, und zwar in dem Grade mehr oder weniger, als sie einen bessern oder schlechtern Markt gemacht hat. Schon das leichenblasse Gesicht, die abgehungerte Gestalt, die zerlumpte Kleidung des Blinden läßt vermuten, daß seine Lage schlimm genug ist, und es wäre die Sache eines tätigen Menschenfreundes, diesem Verhältnis näher nachzuforschen.

Ich. Indem ich den ganzen Markt überschaue, bemerke ich, daß die Mehlwagen dort, über die Tücher wie Zelte aufgespannt sind, deshalb einen malerischen Anblick gewähren, weil sie dem Auge ein Stützpunkt sind, um den sich die bunte Masse zu deutlichen Gruppen bildet.

Der Vetter. Von den weißen Mehlwagen und den mehlbestaubten Mühlknappen und Müllermädchen mit rosenroten Wangen, jede eine bella molinara, kenne ich gerade auch etwas Entgegengesetztes. Mit Schmerz vermisse ich nämlich eine Köhlerfamilie, die sonst ihre Ware geradeüber meinem Fenster am Theater feilbot und jetzt hinübergewiesen sein soll auf die andere Seite. Diese Familie besteht aus einem großen robusten Mann mit ausdrucksvollem Gesicht, markichten Zügen, heftig, beinahe gewaltsam in seinen Bewegungen, genug, ganz treues Abbild der Köhler, wie sie in Romanen vorzukommen pflegen. In der Tat, begegnete ich diesem Manne einsam im Walde, es würde mich ein wenig frösteln, und seine freundschaftliche Gesinnung würde mir in dem Augenblicke die liebste auf Erden sein. Diesem Mann steht als zweites Glied der Familie im schneidendsten Kontrast ein kaum vier Fuß hoher, seltsam verwachsener Kerl entgegen, der die Possierlichkeit selbst ist. Du weißt, lieber Vetter, daß es Leute gibt von gar seltsamem Bau; auf den ersten Blick muß man sie für bucklig erkennen, und doch vermag man bei näherer Betrachtung durchaus nicht anzugeben, wo ihnen denn eigentlich der Buckel sitzt.

Ich. Ich erinnere mich hiebei des naiven Ausspruchs eines geistreichen Militärs, der mit einem solchen Naturspiel in Geschäften viel zu

perfectly absolute resignation. What's the money to him? He can't use it. Only in the hands of another, whom he has to trust implicitly, does it acquire its value. I may be very wrong, but it appears to me as if the woman whose vegetable baskets he carries is a terrible shrew, who doesn't look after the poor fellow properly, even though she most probably pockets all the money he gets. Every time she brings back the baskets, she jaws at the blind man, more or less in proportion to her better or poorer earnings at the market that day. The blind man's face, pale as a corpse's, his emaciated body, and his ragged clothing are sufficient indications that his situation is pretty unpleasant, and a real humanitarian would do well to look into their relationship more closely.

I: As I look over the whole market, I notice that the flour carts there, over which cloths are spread out like tents, present a picturesque view because they afford the eye a resting place around which the motley crowd breaks down into distinct groupings.

MY COUSIN: I also know something that is just the opposite of those white flour carts and those flour-dusted miller's lads, and the miller's lasses with their rosy-red cheeks, each one of them a *bella molinara*.[16] You see, I sorely miss a family of charcoal burners who used to sell their wares just opposite my window by the theater but are now said to have been transferred to the other side. That family consists of a tall, robust man with an expressive face and strong features, lively, almost violent, in his movements: in short, a very faithful copy of the charcoal burners you usually come across in novels. Actually, if I ever met that man while walking alone in the woods, I'd feel a slight chill, and his friendly attitude toward me would be the welcomest thing on earth to me just then. A second member of the family is the sharpest contrast to this man: a fellow barely four feet tall, strangely misshapen, and a paragon of comicality. You know, my dear cousin, that there are some very strangely built people; at first glance you have to call them hunchbacked, but when you look more closely, you just can't put your finger on the precise nature of their deformity.

I: On that subject I recall the naïve remark of a witty military man, who transacted a lot of business with just such a freak of

---

16. "Beautiful miller's lass." Possibly a reference to Paisiello's 1788 opera *La molinara*.

tun hatte, und dem das Unergründliche des wunderlichen Baues ein Anstoß war. «Einen Buckel», sagte er, «einen Buckel hat der Mensch; aber wo ihm der Buckel sitzt, das weiß der Teufel!» –

Der Vetter. Die Natur hatte im Sinn, aus meinem kleinen Kohlenbrenner eine riesenhafte Figur von etwa sieben Fuß zu bilden, denn dieses zeigen die kolossalen Hände und Füße, beinahe die größten, die ich in meinem Leben gesehen. Dieser kleine Kerl, mit einem großkragigen Mäntelchen bekleidet, eine wunderliche Pelzmütze auf dem Haupte, ist in steter rastloser Unruhe; mit einer unangenehmen Beweglichkeit hüpft und trippelt er hin und her, ist bald hier, bald dort und müht sich, den Liebenswürdigen, den Scharmanten, den primo amoroso des Markts zu spielen. Kein Frauenzimmer, gehört sie nicht geradehin zum vornehmeren Stande, läßt er vorübergehen, ohne ihm nachzutrippeln und mit ganz unnachahmlichen Stellungen, Gebärden und Grimassen Süßigkeiten auszustoßen, die nun freilich im Geschmack der Kohlenbrenner sein mögen. Zuweilen treibt er die Galanterie so weit, daß er im Gespräch den Arm sanft um die Hüften des Mädchens schlingt und, die Mütze in der Hand, der Schönheit huldigt oder ihr seine Ritterdienste anbietet. Merkwürdig genug, daß die Mädchen sich nicht allein das gefallen lassen, sondern überdem dem kleinen Ungetüm freundlich zunicken und seine Galanterien überhaupt gar gerne zu haben scheinen.

Dieser kleine Kerl ist gewiß mit einer reichen Dosis von natürlichem Mutterwitz, dem entschiedenen Talent fürs Possierliche und der Kraft, es darzustellen, begabt. Er ist der Pagliasso, der Tausendsassa, der Allerweltskerl in der ganzen Gegend, die den Wald umschließt, wo er hauset; ohne ihn kann keine Kindstaufe, kein Hochzeitsschmaus, kein Tanz im Kruge, kein Gelag bestehen; man freuet sich auf seine Späße und belacht sie das ganze Jahr hindurch.

Der Rest der Familie besteht, da die Kinder und etwanigen Mägde zu Hause gelassen werden, nur noch aus zwei Weibern von robustem Bau und finsterm, mürrischem Aussehen, wozu freilich der Kohlenstaub, der sich in den Falten des Gesichts festsetzt, viel beiträgt. Die zärtliche Anhänglichkeit eines großen Spitzes, mit dem die Familie jeden Bissen teilt, den sie während des Marktes selbst genießt, zeigte mir übrigens, daß es in der Köhlerhütte recht ehrlich und patriarchalisch zugehen mag.

Der Kleine hat übrigens Riesenkräfte, weshalb die Familie ihn dazu braucht, die verkauften Kohlensäcke den Käufern ins Haus zu schaffen. Ich sah oft ihn von den Weibern mit wohl zehn großen Körben bepacken, die sie hoch übereinander auf seinen Rücken häuften, und er hüpfte damit fort, als fühle er keine Last. Von hinten

nature, and who was offended by the unfathomability of the man's peculiar physique. He used to say: "The fellow does have a hump, but where it's located only the Devil knows!"

MY COUSIN: Nature intended to make my little charcoal burner a giant some seven feet tall, as shown by his colossal hands and feet, almost the biggest I've ever seen. This little fellow, who wears a short cape with a big collar and has a peculiar fur cap on his head, is in constant, unresting agitation; he hops and trips to and fro with an unpleasant sprightliness—now he's here, now he's there—and makes every effort to play the lovable man, the charmer, the romantic tenor of the market. He doesn't let any female pass by, unless she's clearly of the higher classes, without tripping after her and, with quite inimitable poses, gestures, and grimaces, pouring out sweet nothings, which of course are probably in good taste only to a charcoal burner. Sometimes he carries his gallantry so far that, while they converse, he gently puts one arm around the girl's hips and, cap in hand, pays homage to her beauty or offers her his chivalrous services. Oddly enough, the girls not only put up with it, but in addition give the little monster friendly nods and, in general, seem to like his gallantries quite a bit.

This little fellow is certainly gifted with a healthy dose of natural wit, a decided talent for humor, and the power to express it. He's the pagliaccio, the hell-of-a-fellow, the smart guy of the whole region surrounding the forest he lives in; without him there can't be any christening, wedding feast, alehouse dance, or carousal; people look forward to his jokes and laugh over them the rest of the year.

Since the children and any maids they may have are left at home, the rest of the family consists merely of two women of a robust build and a gloomy, sullen appearance, to which the coal dust that adheres to the creases in their face naturally contributes. The tender devotion of a big spitz dog, with whom the family share every morsel they eat during the market day, showed me, moreover, that life in the charcoal burners' cottage must be truly upright and patriarchal.

In addition, the little fellow is as strong as a giant, so that his family uses him to carry the sacks of charcoal they sell into the purchasers' houses. I often saw the women loading about ten big baskets onto him, stacking them one on top of the other on his back; and he'd hop away with them as if he didn't feel the

sah nun die Figur so toll und abenteuerlich aus, als man nur etwas sehen kann. Natürlicherweise gewahrte man von der werten Figur des Kleinen auch nicht das allermindeste, sondern bloß einen ungeheuren Kohlensack, dem unten ein Paar Füßchen angewachsen waren. Es schien ein fabelhaftes Tier, eine Art märchenhaftes Känguruh über den Markt zu hüpfen.

Ich. Sieh, sieh, Vetter! Dort an der Kirche entsteht Lärm. Zwei Gemüseweiber sind wahrscheinlich über das leidige Meum und Tuum in heftigen Streit geraten und scheinen, die Fäuste in die Seiten gestemmt, sich mit feinen Redensarten zu bedienen. Das Volk läuft zusammen – ein dichter Kreis umschließt die Zankenden – immer stärker und gellender erheben sich die Stimmen – immer heftiger fechten sie mit den Händen durch die Lüfte – immer näher rücken sie sich auf den Leib – gleich wird es zum Faustkampf kommen – die Polizei macht sich Platz – wie? Plötzlich erblicke ich eine Menge Glanzhüte zwischen den Zornigen – im Augenblick gelingt es den Gevatterinnen, die erhitzten Gemüter zu besänftigen – aus ist der Streit – ohne Hilfe der Polizei – ruhig kehren die Weiber zu ihren Gemüsekörben zurück – das Volk, welches nur einigemal, wahrscheinlich bei besonders drastischen Momenten des Streits, durch lautes Aufjauchzen seinen Beifall zu erkennen gab, läuft auseinander.

Der Vetter. Du bemerkst, lieber Vetter, daß dieses während der ganzen langen Zeit, die wir hier am Fenster zugebracht, der einzige Zank war, der sich auf dem Markte entspann und der lediglich durch das Volk selbst beschwichtigt wurde. Selbst ein ernsterer, bedrohlicherer Zank wird gemeinhin von dem Volke selbst auf diese Weise gedämpft, daß sich alles zwischen die Streitenden drängt und sie auseinanderbringt. Am vorigen Markttage stand zwischen den Fleisch- und Obstbuden ein großer, abgelumpter Kerl von frechem, wildem Ansehn, der mit dem vorübergehenden Fleischerknecht plötzlich in Streit geriet; er führte ohne weiteres mit dem furchtbaren Knittel, den er wie ein Gewehr über die Schulter gelehnt trug, einen Schlag gegen den Knecht, der diesen wahrscheinlich auf der Stelle zu Boden gestreckt haben würde, wäre er nicht geschickt ausgewichen und in seine Bude gesprungen. Hier bewaffnete er sich aber mit einer gewaltigen Fleischeraxt und wollte dem Kerl zu Leibe. Alle Aspekten waren dazu da, daß das Ding sich mit Mord und Totschlag endigen

weight. From the rear his figure then looked as odd and peculiar as anything you might see. Naturally, you couldn't make out
the little man's worthy figure in the least, but only an enormous
sack of charcoal with a pair of feet growing out of it underneath.
He looked like a fabulous animal, a sort of fairy-tale kangaroo
hopping across the market.

I: Look, look, cousin! A row is beginning by the church there!
Two vegetable women have probably been led into a violent
quarrel by that accursed affinity for filching,[17] and with their
fists on their hips, they seem to be showering delicate endear-
ments on each other. People are assembling. A dense group surrounds the quarrelers. Their voices are raised more and more
loudly and shrilly. They're sparring in the air with their hands
more and more violently. They're closing in on each other more
and more. It will soon be a fist fight. The police are making their
way through. What's this? I suddenly see a number of oiled hats
between the two irate women. In a moment their colleagues
have managed to calm their heated minds. The quarrel is over.
Without the help of the police. The two women are returning
peacefully to their vegetable baskets. The crowd, which made its
approval known by loud hurrahs only a few times, probably at
especially drastic phases of the quarrel, is dispersing.

MY COUSIN: You observe, my dear cousin, that during this
whole long time we've spent at the window here, this was the only
fight that developed in the market, and it was pacified solely by
the people themselves. Even a more serious and menacing fight
is usually quelled by the people themselves by forcing their way
between the combatants and separating them. Last market day, a
tall, ragged fellow with a rough, insolent appearance was standing
among the meat and fruit booths and suddenly got into a fight
with a butcher's helper who was passing by; without further ado
he aimed a blow at the helper with the terrible cudgel he was carrying over his shoulder like a rifle. That blow would probably have
laid him out on the ground then and there, if he hadn't nimbly
ducked it and dashed into his booth. But, once there, he armed
himself with a huge meat cleaver and tried to get at the fellow
with it. There was every indication that the matter would lead to
homicide or manslaughter, and that there'd be business for the

---

17. Literally, "mine and yours" (in Latin): the inability to differentiate your
neighbor's property from your own.

und das Kriminalgericht in Tätigkeit gesetzt werden würde. Die Obstfrauen, lauter kräftige und wohlgenährte Gestalten, fanden sich aber verpflichtet, den Fleischerknecht so liebreich und fest zu umarmen, daß er sich nicht aus der Stelle zu rühren vermochte; er stand da mit hoch emporgeschwungener Waffe, wie es in jener pathetischen Rede vom rauhen Pyrrhus heißt:

«wie ein gemalter Wütrich, und wie parteilos zwischen Kraft und Willen, tat er nichts.»

Unterdessen hatten andere Weiber, Bürstenbinder, Stiefelknechtverkäufer und so weiter, den Kerl umringend, der Polizei Zeit gegönnt, heranzukommen und sich seiner, der mir ein freigelassener Sträfling schien, zu bemächtigen.

Ich. Also herrscht in der Tat im Volk ein Sinn für die zu erhaltende Ordnung, der nicht anders als für alle sehr ersprießlich wirken kann.

Der Vetter. Überhaupt, mein lieber Vetter, haben mich meine Beobachtungen des Marktes in der Meinung bestärkt, daß mit dem Berliner Volk seit jener Unglücksperiode, als ein frecher, übermütiger Feind das Land überschwemmte und sich vergebens mühte, *den* Geist zu unterdrücken, der bald wie eine gewaltsam zusammengedrückte Spiralfeder mit erneuter Kraft emporsprang, eine merkwürdige Veränderung vorgegangen ist. Mit *einem* Wort: das Volk hat an äußerer Sittlichkeit gewonnen; und wenn du dich einmal an einem schönen Sommertage gleich nachmittags nach den Zelten bemühst und die Gesellschaften beobachtest, welche sich nach Moabit einschiffen lassen, so wirst du selbst unter gemeinen Mägden und Tagelöhnern ein Streben nach einer gewissen Courtoisie bemerken, das ganz ergötzlich ist. Es ist der Masse so gegangen wie dem einzelnen, der viel Neues gesehn, viel Ungewöhnliches erfahren, und der mit dem Nil admirari die Geschmeidigkeit der äußern Sitte gewonnen. Sonst war das Berliner Volk roh und brutal; man durfte zum Beispiel als Fremder kaum nach einer Straße oder nach einem Hause oder sonst nach etwas fragen, ohne eine grobe oder verhöhnende Antwort zu erhalten oder durch falschen Bescheid gefoppt zu werden. Der Berliner Straßenjunge, der den kleinsten Anlaß, einen etwas auffallenden Anzug, einen lächerlichen Unfall, der jemandem geschah, zu dem abscheulichsten Frevel benutzte, existiert nicht mehr. Denn jene

criminal court. But the fruit women, powerful and well-fed characters each and every one, felt obliged to embrace the butcher's
helper so affectionately and so firmly that he couldn't move from
the spot; there he stood, brandishing his weapon high in the air, as
it says in that pathos-filled speech of "rugged" Pyrrhus:

> So as a painted tyrant Pyrrhus stood
> And, like a neutral to his will and matter,
> Did nothing.[18]

Meanwhile, other women, brushmakers, bootjack vendors, and
so on, had surrounded that other fellow, allowing the police time
to arrive and apprehend him (he looked like a released convict
to me).

I: And so the populace actually does possess the notion that
public order must be preserved; that aptitude can only be very
beneficial for everyone.

MY COUSIN: In general, my dear cousin, my observations of the
market have confirmed my opinion that, ever since that disastrous
period when an insolent, haughty foe overran our land and strove
in vain to suppress that spirit which soon leaped up in renewed
strength like a violently compressed metal spring, the people of
Berlin have undergone a remarkable change. In a word: the people have acquired better manners in public; and if, in the early afternoon of some fine summer day, you take a walk to the tents and
observe the parties of excursionists getting onto boats for Moabit,[19]
you'll observe, even among the common housemaids and day la-
borers, a striving for a certain degree of courtesy that is most grat-
ifying. The masses have had the same experience as the individual,
who has seen many new things and learned much that was out of
the ordinary, and who has acquired a suppleness of public behavior along with the motto *nil admirari*.[20] The populace of Berlin
used to be raw and brutal; for instance, an out-of-towner could
scarcely inquire about a street, an address, or the like without receiving a rude or mocking answer, or being fooled by incorrect information. The Berlin street urchin, who once hit upon the least
occasion—somewhat conspicuous clothing, a funny accident happening to somebody—as an excuse for the most abhorrent wan-
tonness, no longer exists. Because those cigar boys just outside of

---

18. From *Hamlet,* Act II, Scene 2.   19. Older name for the district of Berlin
north of the Tiergarten, along the north bank of the river Spree.   20. "Don't be
amazed at anything." From Horace, *Epistles,* I, 6.

Zigarrenjungen vor den Toren, die den «fidelen Hamburger avec du
feu» ausbieten, diese Galgenstricke, welche ihr Leben in Spandau
oder Straußberg oder, wie noch kürzlich einer von ihrer Rasse, auf
dem Schafott endigen, sind keineswegs das, was der eigentliche
Berliner Straßenjunge war, der nicht Vagabund, sondern gewöhnlich
Lehrbursche bei einem Meister, – es ist lächerlich zu sagen – bei aller
Gottlosigkeit und Verderbnis doch ein gewisses Point d'Honneur
besaß, und dem es an gar drolligem Mutterwitz nicht mangelte.

Ich. Oh, lieber Vetter, laß mich dir in aller Geschwindigkeit sagen,
wie neulich mich ein solcher fataler Volkswitz tief beschämt hat. Ich
gehe vors Brandenburger Tor und werde von Charlottenburger
Fuhrleuten verfolgt, die mich zum Aufsitzen einladen; einer von
ihnen, ein höchstens sechzehn-, siebenzehnjähriger Junge, trieb die
Unverschämtheit so weit, daß er mich mit seiner schmutzigen Faust
beim Arm packt. «Will Er mich wohl nicht anfassen!» fahre ich ihn
zornig an. «Nun, Herr», erwiderte der Junge ganz gelassen, indem er
mich mit seinen großen, stieren Augen anglotzte, «nun, Herr, warum
soll ich Ihnen denn nicht anfassen; sind Sie vielleicht nicht ehrlich?»

Der Vetter. Haha! dieser Witz ist wirklich einer, aber recht aus der
stinkenden Grube der tiefsten Depravation gestiegen. – Die Witz-
wörter der Berliner Obstweiber und anderer waren sonst welt-
berühmt, und man tat ihnen sogar die Ehre an, sie Shakespearesch zu
nennen, unerachtet bei näherer Beleuchtung ihre Energie und
Originalität nur vorzüglich in der schamlosen Frechheit bestand,
womit sie den niederträchtigsten Schmutz als bekannte Schüssel
auftischten.

Sonst war der Markt der Tummelplatz des Zanks, der Prügeleien,
des Betrugs, des Diebstahls, und keine honette Frau durfte es wagen,
ihren Einkauf selbst besorgen zu wollen, ohne sich der größten Unbill
auszusetzen. Denn nicht allein daß das Hökervolk gegen sich selbst
und alle Welt zu Felde zog, so gingen noch Menschen ausdrücklich
darauf aus, Unruhe zu erregen, um dabei im trüben zu fischen, wie
zum Beispiel das aus allen Ecken und Enden der Welt zusammenge-
worbene Gesindel, welches damals in den Regimentern steckte.

Sieh, lieber Vetter, wie jetzt dagegen der Markt das anmutige Bild
der Wohlbehaglichkeit und des sittlichen Friedens darbietet. Ich

town who sell "Merry Man of Hamburg cigars, and a light to go with them," those gallows birds who end their lives in Spandau or Strausberg,[21] or (as recently occurred with one of their breed) on the scaffold, are by no means what the real Berlin street urchin used to be: not a vagabond, but usually an apprentice to some master artisan, and, though it may sound comical, with all his impiety and corruptness, nevertheless possessing a certain notion of honor, and not at all lacking in very amusing native wit.

I: Oh, my dear cousin, let me tell you as briefly as I can how I was recently greatly embarrassed by an awful popular joke of that type. I was walking by the Brandenburg Gate when I was followed by some coachmen from Charlottenburg,[22] who invited me to get aboard. One of them, a boy of sixteen or seventeen at the most, went so far in his impudence as to seize my arm with his dirty fist. "Don't touch me, please!" I yelled at him in my rage. "Now, sir," the boy replied quite calmly, goggling at me with his big, vacant eyes. "Now, sir, why shouldn't I touch you? Are you perhaps not respectable?"

MY COUSIN: Ha, ha! Yes, that *is* a real joke, but one that arose from the stinking pit of the deepest depravity. The quips of Berlin fruit women and others used to be world famous,[23] and people even did them the honor of calling them Shakespearean, even though a stronger light revealed that their energy and originality resided, above all, merely in the shameless impudence with which they served up the vilest filth in the form of well-known dishes.

The market used to be the arena of disputes, beatings, cheating, and theft, and no respectable woman would dare to do her own marketing unless she wished to expose herself to the worst insults. Because, not only did the vendors fight among themselves and against everyone else; there were also people intentionally out to stir up trouble, so they could profit by the confusion: for instance, that rabble, recruited from every corner of the world, who were members of the army in those days.

See, my dear cousin, how, on the contrary, the market now offers the pleasant image of comfort and peaceful manners. I

<hr/>

21. Places with prisons. Spandau: a Berlin suburb NW of Charlottenburg (see next footnote). Strausberg: in Brandenburg east of Berlin.   22. The district west of the Tiergarten.   23. Berlin wit has remained famous, at least at the national level.

weiß, enthusiastische Rigoristen, hyperpatriotische Aszetiker eifern
grimmig gegen diesen vermehrten äußern Anstand des Volks, indem
sie meinen, daß mit dieser Abgeschliffenheit der Sitte auch das Volks-
tümliche abgeschliffen werde und verloren gehe. Ich meinesteils bin
der festen, innigsten Überzeugung, daß ein Volk, das sowohl den
Einheimischen als den Fremden nicht mit Grobheit oder höhnischer
Verachtung, sondern mit höflicher Sitte behandelt, dadurch unmöglich seinen Charakter einbüßen kann. Mit einem sehr auffallenden Beispiel, welches die Wahrheit meiner Behauptung dartut,
würde ich bei jenen Rigoristen gar übel wegkommen.

Immer mehr hatte sich das Gedränge vermindert; immer leerer
und leerer war der Markt geworden. Die Gemüseverkäuferinnen
packten ihre Körbe zum Teil auf herbeigekommene Wagen, zum Teil
schleppten sie sie selbst fort – die Mehlwagen fuhren ab – die Gärt-
nerinnen schafften den übriggebliebenen Blumenvorrat auf großen
Schiebkarren fort – geschäftiger zeigte sich die Polizei, alles und
vorzüglich die Wagenreihe in gehöriger Ordnung zu erhalten; diese
Ordnung wäre auch nicht gestört, wenn es nicht hin und wieder
einem schismatischen Bauernjungen eingefallen wäre, quer über den
Platz seine eigne neue Beringsstraße zu entdecken, zu verfolgen und
seinen kühnen Lauf mitten durch die Obstbuden, geradezu nach der
Türe der deutschen Kirche zu richten. Das gab denn viel Geschrei
und viel Ungemach des zu genialen Wagenlenkers.
«Dieser Markt», sprach der Vetter, «ist auch jetzt ein treues Abbild
des ewig wechselnden Lebens. Rege Tätigkeit, das Bedürfnis des
Augenblicks trieb die Menschenmasse zusammen; in wenigen Augenblicken ist alles verödet, die Stimmen, welche im wirren Getöse
durcheinanderströmten, sind verklungen, und jede verlassene Stelle
spricht das schauerliche: ‹Es war!› nur zu lebhaft aus.»
Es schlug ein Uhr, der grämliche Invalide trat ins Kabinett und
meinte mit verzogenem Gesicht: der Herr möge doch nun endlich das
Fenster verlassen und essen, da sonst die aufgetragenen Speisen
wieder kalt würden. «Also hast du doch Appetit, lieber Vetter?» fragte
ich.
«O ja», erwiderte der Vetter mit schmerzlichem Lächeln, «du wirst
es gleich sehen.»
Der Invalide rollte ihn ins Zimmer. Die aufgetragenen Speisen be-
standen in einem mäßigen, mit Fleischbrühe gefüllten Suppenteller,

know that fanatical rigorists and superpatriotic ascetics inveigh rabidly against this improved public decency of the people, opining that this greater polishing of manners means that the national character is being polished away and getting lost. For my part, I am firmly and wholeheartedly convinced that a populace which treats natives and foreigners alike not with rudeness or scornful contempt, but with courtesy and good manners, cannot possibly forfeit its own character by so doing. If I were to offer a very conspicuous example to prove the truth of my assertion, I would come off very badly at the hands of those rigorists.

The crowd had grown progressively thinner; the market had become progressively emptier. Some of their baskets the vegetable vendors loaded onto carts that had pulled up, some they carried away under their own power. The flour carts drove away. The gardeners moved out their remaining supply of flowers on big wheelbarrows. The police were busier keeping everything, and especially the line of carts, in the proper order. That order wouldn't have been disrupted, if it hadn't occasionally occurred to some schismatic farmboy to discover his own new Bering Strait right across the middle of the square, and then to follow its course, directing his mad dash through the midst of the fruit booths, right to the door of the German church.[24] That led to a lot of yelling and a lot of trouble for the excessively brilliant charioteer.

"This market," my cousin said, "is at this hour, too, a faithful image of life's eternal vicissitudes. Bustling activity and the needs of the moment brought the throng of people together; in a few minutes everything is deserted, the voices that flowed together in a confused hubbub have died away, and every abandoned station pronounces the dreadful 'It's over!' all too distinctly."

The clock struck one; the peevish veteran entered the room and, pulling a face, expressed the opinion that his employer should now finally leave the window and eat, or else the food on the table would get cold again. "So, you do have an appetite, my dear cousin?" I asked.

"Oh, yes," my cousin replied with a pinched smile. "You'll see right away."

The veteran rolled him into the big room. The food on the table consisted of a soup plate of moderate size filled with

24. Probably the place now called the Deutscher und Französischer Dom.

einem in Salz aufrecht gestellten, weichgesottenen Ei und einer halben Mundsemmel.

«Ein einziger Bissen mehr», sprach der Vetter leise und wehmütig, indem er meine Hand drückte, «das kleinste Stückchen des verdaulichsten Fleisches verursacht mir die entsetzlichsten Schmerzen und raubt mir allen Lebensmut und das letzte Fünkchen von guter Laune, das noch hin und wieder aufglimmen will.»

Ich wies nach dem am Bettschirm befestigten Blatt, indem ich mich dem Vetter an die Brust warf und ihn heftig an mich drückte.

«Ja, Vetter!» rief er mit einer Stimme, die mein Innerstes durchdrang und es mit herzzerschneidender Wehmut erfüllte, «ja Vetter: Et si male nunc, non olim sic erit!»

Armer Vetter!

meat broth, a soft-boiled egg propped up in salt, and half a roll.

"One bite more than this," my cousin said in a quiet, melancholy tone, squeezing my hand, "or the tiniest morsel of even the most digestible meat, causes me the most horrible pain, and robs me of all my courage to face life and the last little spark of good humor that still tries to glimmer from time to time."

I pointed to the sheet attached to the bed screen, as I flung myself on my cousin's breast and gave him a hard hug.

"Yes, cousin," he cried in a tone that went right to my heart and filled it with the most devastating melancholy. "Yes, cousin: *et si male nunc, non olim sic erit!*"[25]

Poor cousin!

---

25. See footnote 3 on page 225.

A CATALOG OF SELECTED
DOVER BOOKS
IN ALL FIELDS OF INTEREST

A CATALOG OF SELECTED DOVER
BOOKS IN ALL FIELDS OF INTEREST

CONCERNING THE SPIRITUAL IN ART, Wassily Kandinsky. Pioneering work by father of abstract art. Thoughts on color theory, nature of art. Analysis of earlier masters. 12 illustrations. 80pp. of text. 5⅜ x 8½. 23411-8

ANIMALS: 1,419 Copyright-Free Illustrations of Mammals, Birds, Fish, Insects, etc., Jim Harter (ed.). Clear wood engravings present, in extremely lifelike poses, over 1,000 species of animals. One of the most extensive pictorial sourcebooks of its kind. Captions. Index. 284pp. 9 x 12. 23766-4

CELTIC ART: The Methods of Construction, George Bain. Simple geometric techniques for making Celtic interlacements, spirals, Kells-type initials, animals, humans, etc. Over 500 illustrations. 160pp. 9 x 12. (Available in U.S. only.) 22923-8

AN ATLAS OF ANATOMY FOR ARTISTS, Fritz Schider. Most thorough reference work on art anatomy in the world. Hundreds of illustrations, including selections from works by Vesalius, Leonardo, Goya, Ingres, Michelangelo, others. 593 illustrations. 192pp. 7⅛ x 10¼. 20241-0

CELTIC HAND STROKE-BY-STROKE (Irish Half-Uncial from "The Book of Kells"): An Arthur Baker Calligraphy Manual, Arthur Baker. Complete guide to creating each letter of the alphabet in distinctive Celtic manner. Covers hand position, strokes, pens, inks, paper, more. Illustrated. 48pp. 8¼ x 11. 24336-2

EASY ORIGAMI, John Montroll. Charming collection of 32 projects (hat, cup, pelican, piano, swan, many more) specially designed for the novice origami hobbyist. Clearly illustrated easy-to-follow instructions insure that even beginning papercrafters will achieve successful results. 48pp. 8¼ x 11. 27298-2

THE COMPLETE BOOK OF BIRDHOUSE CONSTRUCTION FOR WOODWORKERS, Scott D. Campbell. Detailed instructions, illustrations, tables. Also data on bird habitat and instinct patterns. Bibliography. 3 tables. 63 illustrations in 15 figures. 48pp. 5¼ x 8½. 24407-5

BLOOMINGDALE'S ILLUSTRATED 1886 CATALOG: Fashions, Dry Goods and Housewares, Bloomingdale Brothers. Famed merchants' extremely rare catalog depicting about 1,700 products: clothing, housewares, firearms, dry goods, jewelry, more. Invaluable for dating, identifying vintage items. Also, copyright-free graphics for artists, designers. Co-published with Henry Ford Museum & Greenfield Village. 160pp. 8¼ x 11. 25780-0

HISTORIC COSTUME IN PICTURES, Braun & Schneider. Over 1,450 costumed figures in clearly detailed engravings–from dawn of civilization to end of 19th century. Captions. Many folk costumes. 256pp. 8⅜ x 11¾. 23150-X

CATALOG OF DOVER BOOKS

STICKLEY CRAFTSMAN FURNITURE CATALOGS, Gustav Stickley and L. & J. G. Stickley. Beautiful, functional furniture in two authentic catalogs from 1910. 594 illustrations, including 277 photos, show settles, rockers, armchairs, reclining chairs, bookcases, desks, tables. 183pp. 6½ x 9¼. 23838-5

AMERICAN LOCOMOTIVES IN HISTORIC PHOTOGRAPHS: 1858 to 1949, Ron Ziel (ed.). A rare collection of 126 meticulously detailed official photographs, called "builder portraits," of American locomotives that majestically chronicle the rise of steam locomotive power in America. Introduction. Detailed captions. xi+ 129pp. 9 x 12. 27393-8

AMERICA'S LIGHTHOUSES: An Illustrated History, Francis Ross Holland, Jr. Delightfully written, profusely illustrated fact-filled survey of over 200 American lighthouses since 1716. History, anecdotes, technological advances, more. 240pp. 8 x 10¾. 25576-X

TOWARDS A NEW ARCHITECTURE, Le Corbusier. Pioneering manifesto by founder of "International School." Technical and aesthetic theories, views of industry, economics, relation of form to function, "mass-production split" and much more. Profusely illustrated. 320pp. 6⅛ x 9¼. (Available in U.S. only.) 25023-7

HOW THE OTHER HALF LIVES, Jacob Riis. Famous journalistic record, exposing poverty and degradation of New York slums around 1900, by major social reformer. 100 striking and influential photographs. 233pp. 10 x 7⅞. 22012-5

FRUIT KEY AND TWIG KEY TO TREES AND SHRUBS, William M. Harlow. One of the handiest and most widely used identification aids. Fruit key covers 120 deciduous and evergreen species; twig key 160 deciduous species. Easily used. Over 300 photographs. 126pp. 5⅜ x 8½. 20511-8

COMMON BIRD SONGS, Dr. Donald J. Borror. Songs of 60 most common U.S. birds: robins, sparrows, cardinals, bluejays, finches, more–arranged in order of increasing complexity. Up to 9 variations of songs of each species.
Cassette and manual 99911-4

ORCHIDS AS HOUSE PLANTS, Rebecca Tyson Northen. Grow cattleyas and many other kinds of orchids–in a window, in a case, or under artificial light. 63 illustrations. 148pp. 5⅜ x 8½. 23261-1

MONSTER MAZES, Dave Phillips. Masterful mazes at four levels of difficulty. Avoid deadly perils and evil creatures to find magical treasures. Solutions for all 32 exciting illustrated puzzles. 48pp. 8¼ x 11. 26005-4

MOZART'S DON GIOVANNI (DOVER OPERA LIBRETTO SERIES), Wolfgang Amadeus Mozart. Introduced and translated by Ellen H. Bleiler. Standard Italian libretto, with complete English translation. Convenient and thoroughly portable–an ideal companion for reading along with a recording or the performance itself. Introduction. List of characters. Plot summary. 121pp. 5¼ x 8½. 24944-1

TECHNICAL MANUAL AND DICTIONARY OF CLASSICAL BALLET, Gail Grant. Defines, explains, comments on steps, movements, poses and concepts. 15-page pictorial section. Basic book for student, viewer. 127pp. 5⅜ x 8½. 21843-0

THE CLARINET AND CLARINET PLAYING, David Pino. Lively, comprehensive work features suggestions about technique, musicianship, and musical interpretation, as well as guidelines for teaching, making your own reeds, and preparing for public performance. Includes an intriguing look at clarinet history. "A godsend," *The Clarinet,* Journal of the International Clarinet Society. Appendixes. 7 illus. 320pp. 5⅜ x 8½. 40270-3

HOLLYWOOD GLAMOR PORTRAITS, John Kobal (ed.). 145 photos from 1926-49. Harlow, Gable, Bogart, Bacall; 94 stars in all. Full background on photographers, technical aspects. 160pp. 8⅜ x 11¼. 23352-9

THE ANNOTATED CASEY AT THE BAT: A Collection of Ballads about the Mighty Casey/Third, Revised Edition, Martin Gardner (ed.). Amusing sequels and parodies of one of America's best-loved poems: Casey's Revenge, Why Casey Whiffed, Casey's Sister at the Bat, others. 256pp. 5⅜ x 8½. 28598-7

THE RAVEN AND OTHER FAVORITE POEMS, Edgar Allan Poe. Over 40 of the author's most memorable poems: "The Bells," "Ulalume," "Israfel," "To Helen," "The Conqueror Worm," "Eldorado," "Annabel Lee," many more. Alphabetic lists of titles and first lines. 64pp. 5³⁄₁₆ x 8¼. 26685-0

PERSONAL MEMOIRS OF U. S. GRANT, Ulysses Simpson Grant. Intelligent, deeply moving firsthand account of Civil War campaigns, considered by many the finest military memoirs ever written. Includes letters, historic photographs, maps and more. 528pp. 6⅛ x 9¼. 28587-1

ANCIENT EGYPTIAN MATERIALS AND INDUSTRIES, A. Lucas and J. Harris. Fascinating, comprehensive, thoroughly documented text describes this ancient civilization's vast resources and the processes that incorporated them in daily life, including the use of animal products, building materials, cosmetics, perfumes and incense, fibers, glazed ware, glass and its manufacture, materials used in the mummification process, and much more. 544pp. 6⅛ x 9¼. (Available in U.S. only.) 40446-3

RUSSIAN STORIES/RUSSKIE RASSKAZY: A Dual-Language Book, edited by Gleb Struve. Twelve tales by such masters as Chekhov, Tolstoy, Dostoevsky, Pushkin, others. Excellent word-for-word English translations on facing pages, plus teaching and study aids, Russian/English vocabulary, biographical/critical introductions, more. 416pp. 5⅜ x 8½. 26244-8

PHILADELPHIA THEN AND NOW: 60 Sites Photographed in the Past and Present, Kenneth Finkel and Susan Oyama. Rare photographs of City Hall, Logan Square, Independence Hall, Betsy Ross House, other landmarks juxtaposed with contemporary views. Captures changing face of historic city. Introduction. Captions. 128pp. 8¼ x 11. 25790-8

AIA ARCHITECTURAL GUIDE TO NASSAU AND SUFFOLK COUNTIES, LONG ISLAND, The American Institute of Architects, Long Island Chapter, and the Society for the Preservation of Long Island Antiquities. Comprehensive, well-researched and generously illustrated volume brings to life over three centuries of Long Island's great architectural heritage. More than 240 photographs with authoritative, extensively detailed captions. 176pp. 8¼ x 11. 26946-9

NORTH AMERICAN INDIAN LIFE: Customs and Traditions of 23 Tribes, Elsie Clews Parsons (ed.). 27 fictionalized essays by noted anthropologists examine religion, customs, government, additional facets of life among the Winnebago, Crow, Zuni, Eskimo, other tribes. 480pp. 6⅛ x 9¼. 27377-6

CATALOG OF DOVER BOOKS

FRANK LLOYD WRIGHT'S DANA HOUSE, Donald Hoffmann. Pictorial essay of residential masterpiece with over 160 interior and exterior photos, plans, elevations, sketches and studies. 128pp. 9¼ x 10¾.   29120-0

THE MALE AND FEMALE FIGURE IN MOTION: 60 Classic Photographic Sequences, Eadweard Muybridge. 60 true-action photographs of men and women walking, running, climbing, bending, turning, etc., reproduced from rare 19th-century masterpiece. vi + 121pp. 9 x 12.   24745-7

1001 QUESTIONS ANSWERED ABOUT THE SEASHORE, N. J. Berrill and Jacquelyn Berrill. Queries answered about dolphins, sea snails, sponges, starfish, fishes, shore birds, many others. Covers appearance, breeding, growth, feeding, much more. 305pp. 5¼ x 8¼.   23366-9

ATTRACTING BIRDS TO YOUR YARD, William J. Weber. Easy-to-follow guide offers advice on how to attract the greatest diversity of birds: birdhouses, feeders, water and waterers, much more. 96pp. 5³⁄₁₆ x 8¼.   28927-3

MEDICINAL AND OTHER USES OF NORTH AMERICAN PLANTS: A Historical Survey with Special Reference to the Eastern Indian Tribes, Charlotte Erichsen-Brown. Chronological historical citations document 500 years of usage of plants, trees, shrubs native to eastern Canada, northeastern U.S. Also complete identifying information. 343 illustrations. 544pp. 6½ x 9¼.   25951-X

STORYBOOK MAZES, Dave Phillips. 23 stories and mazes on two-page spreads: Wizard of Oz, Treasure Island, Robin Hood, etc. Solutions. 64pp. 8¼ x 11. 23628-5

AMERICAN NEGRO SONGS: 230 Folk Songs and Spirituals, Religious and Secular, John W. Work. This authoritative study traces the African influences of songs sung and played by black Americans at work, in church, and as entertainment. The author discusses the lyric significance of such songs as "Swing Low, Sweet Chariot," "John Henry," and others and offers the words and music for 230 songs. Bibliography. Index of Song Titles. 272pp. 6½ x 9¼.   40271-1

MOVIE-STAR PORTRAITS OF THE FORTIES, John Kobal (ed.). 163 glamor, studio photos of 106 stars of the 1940s: Rita Hayworth, Ava Gardner, Marlon Brando, Clark Gable, many more. 176pp. 8⅜ x 11¼.   23546-7

BENCHLEY LOST AND FOUND, Robert Benchley. Finest humor from early 30s, about pet peeves, child psychologists, post office and others. Mostly unavailable elsewhere. 73 illustrations by Peter Arno and others. 183pp. 5⅜ x 8½.   22410-4

YEKL and THE IMPORTED BRIDEGROOM AND OTHER STORIES OF YIDDISH NEW YORK, Abraham Cahan. Film Hester Street based on *Yekl* (1896). Novel, other stories among first about Jewish immigrants on N.Y.'s East Side. 240pp. 5⅜ x 8½.   22427-9

SELECTED POEMS, Walt Whitman. Generous sampling from *Leaves of Grass*. Twenty-four poems include "I Hear America Singing," "Song of the Open Road," "I Sing the Body Electric," "When Lilacs Last in the Dooryard Bloom'd," "O Captain! My Captain!"—all reprinted from an authoritative edition. Lists of titles and first lines. 128pp. 5³⁄₁₆ x 8¼.   26878-0

THE BEST TALES OF HOFFMANN, E. T. A. Hoffmann. 10 of Hoffmann's most important stories: "Nutcracker and the King of Mice," "The Golden Flowerpot," etc. 458pp. 5⅜ x 8½. 21793-0

FROM FETISH TO GOD IN ANCIENT EGYPT, E. A. Wallis Budge. Rich detailed survey of Egyptian conception of "God" and gods, magic, cult of animals, Osiris, more. Also, superb English translations of hymns and legends. 240 illustrations. 545pp. 5⅜ x 8½. 25803-3

FRENCH STORIES/CONTES FRANÇAIS: A Dual-Language Book, Wallace Fowlie. Ten stories by French masters, Voltaire to Camus: "Micromegas" by Voltaire; "The Atheist's Mass" by Balzac; "Minuet" by de Maupassant; "The Guest" by Camus, six more. Excellent English translations on facing pages. Also French-English vocabulary list, exercises, more. 352pp. 5⅜ x 8½. 26443-2

CHICAGO AT THE TURN OF THE CENTURY IN PHOTOGRAPHS: 122 Historic Views from the Collections of the Chicago Historical Society, Larry A. Viskochil. Rare large-format prints offer detailed views of City Hall, State Street, the Loop, Hull House, Union Station, many other landmarks, circa 1904-1913. Introduction. Captions. Maps. 144pp. 9⅜ x 12¼. 24656-6

OLD BROOKLYN IN EARLY PHOTOGRAPHS, 1865-1929, William Lee Younger. Luna Park, Gravesend race track, construction of Grand Army Plaza, moving of Hotel Brighton, etc. 157 previously unpublished photographs. 165pp. 8⅞ x 11¾. 23587-4

THE MYTHS OF THE NORTH AMERICAN INDIANS, Lewis Spence. Rich anthology of the myths and legends of the Algonquins, Iroquois, Pawnees and Sioux, prefaced by an extensive historical and ethnological commentary. 36 illustrations. 480pp. 5⅜ x 8½. 25967-6

AN ENCYCLOPEDIA OF BATTLES: Accounts of Over 1,560 Battles from 1479 B.C. to the Present, David Eggenberger. Essential details of every major battle in recorded history from the first battle of Megiddo in 1479 B.C. to Grenada in 1984. List of Battle Maps. New Appendix covering the years 1967-1984. Index. 99 illustrations. 544pp. 6½ x 9¼. 24913-1

SAILING ALONE AROUND THE WORLD, Captain Joshua Slocum. First man to sail around the world, alone, in small boat. One of great feats of seamanship told in delightful manner. 67 illustrations. 294pp. 5⅜ x 8½. 20326-3

ANARCHISM AND OTHER ESSAYS, Emma Goldman. Powerful, penetrating, prophetic essays on direct action, role of minorities, prison reform, puritan hypocrisy, violence, etc. 271pp. 5⅜ x 8½. 22484-8

MYTHS OF THE HINDUS AND BUDDHISTS, Ananda K. Coomaraswamy and Sister Nivedita. Great stories of the epics; deeds of Krishna, Shiva, taken from puranas, Vedas, folk tales; etc. 32 illustrations. 400pp. 5⅜ x 8½. 21759-0

THE TRAUMA OF BIRTH, Otto Rank. Rank's controversial thesis that anxiety neurosis is caused by profound psychological trauma which occurs at birth. 256pp. 5⅜ x 8½. 27974-X

A THEOLOGICO-POLITICAL TREATISE, Benedict Spinoza. Also contains unfinished Political Treatise. Great classic on religious liberty, theory of government on common consent. R. Elwes translation. Total of 421pp. 5⅜ x 8½. 20249-6

CATALOG OF DOVER BOOKS

MY BONDAGE AND MY FREEDOM, Frederick Douglass. Born a slave, Douglass became outspoken force in antislavery movement. The best of Douglass' autobiographies. Graphic description of slave life. 464pp. 5⅜ x 8½. 22457-0

FOLLOWING THE EQUATOR: A Journey Around the World, Mark Twain. Fascinating humorous account of 1897 voyage to Hawaii, Australia, India, New Zealand, etc. Ironic, bemused reports on peoples, customs, climate, flora and fauna, politics, much more. 197 illustrations. 720pp. 5⅜ x 8½. 26113-1

THE PEOPLE CALLED SHAKERS, Edward D. Andrews. Definitive study of Shakers: origins, beliefs, practices, dances, social organization, furniture and crafts, etc. 33 illustrations. 351pp. 5⅜ x 8½. 21081-2

THE MYTHS OF GREECE AND ROME, H. A. Guerber. A classic of mythology, generously illustrated, long prized for its simple, graphic, accurate retelling of the principal myths of Greece and Rome, and for its commentary on their origins and significance. With 64 illustrations by Michelangelo, Raphael, Titian, Rubens, Canova, Bernini and others. 480pp. 5⅜ x 8½. 27584-1

PSYCHOLOGY OF MUSIC, Carl E. Seashore. Classic work discusses music as a medium from psychological viewpoint. Clear treatment of physical acoustics, auditory apparatus, sound perception, development of musical skills, nature of musical feeling, host of other topics. 88 figures. 408pp. 5⅜ x 8½. 21851-1

THE PHILOSOPHY OF HISTORY, Georg W. Hegel. Great classic of Western thought develops concept that history is not chance but rational process, the evolution of freedom. 457pp. 5⅜ x 8½. 20112-0

THE BOOK OF TEA, Kakuzo Okakura. Minor classic of the Orient: entertaining, charming explanation, interpretation of traditional Japanese culture in terms of tea ceremony. 94pp. 5⅜ x 8½. 20070-1

LIFE IN ANCIENT EGYPT, Adolf Erman. Fullest, most thorough, detailed older account with much not in more recent books, domestic life, religion, magic, medicine, commerce, much more. Many illustrations reproduce tomb paintings, carvings, hieroglyphs, etc. 597pp. 5⅜ x 8½. 22632-8

SUNDIALS, Their Theory and Construction, Albert Waugh. Far and away the best, most thorough coverage of ideas, mathematics concerned, types, construction, adjusting anywhere. Simple, nontechnical treatment allows even children to build several of these dials. Over 100 illustrations. 230pp. 5⅜ x 8½. 22947-5

THEORETICAL HYDRODYNAMICS, L. M. Milne-Thomson. Classic exposition of the mathematical theory of fluid motion, applicable to both hydrodynamics and aerodynamics. Over 600 exercises. 768pp. 6⅛ x 9¼. 68970-0

SONGS OF EXPERIENCE: Facsimile Reproduction with 26 Plates in Full Color, William Blake. 26 full-color plates from a rare 1826 edition. Includes "The Tyger," "London," "Holy Thursday," and other poems. Printed text of poems. 48pp. 5¼ x 7. 24636-1

OLD-TIME VIGNETTES IN FULL COLOR, Carol Belanger Grafton (ed.). Over 390 charming, often sentimental illustrations, selected from archives of Victorian graphics—pretty women posing, children playing, food, flowers, kittens and puppies, smiling cherubs, birds and butterflies, much more. All copyright-free. 48pp. 9¼ x 12¼. 27269-9

PERSPECTIVE FOR ARTISTS, Rex Vicat Cole. Depth, perspective of sky and sea, shadows, much more, not usually covered. 391 diagrams, 81 reproductions of drawings and paintings. 279pp. 5⅜ x 8½. 22487-2

DRAWING THE LIVING FIGURE, Joseph Sheppard. Innovative approach to artistic anatomy focuses on specifics of surface anatomy, rather than muscles and bones. Over 170 drawings of live models in front, back and side views, and in widely varying poses. Accompanying diagrams. 177 illustrations. Introduction. Index. 144pp. 8⅜ x11¼. 26723-7

GOTHIC AND OLD ENGLISH ALPHABETS: 100 Complete Fonts, Dan X. Solo. Add power, elegance to posters, signs, other graphics with 100 stunning copyright-free alphabets: Blackstone, Dolbey, Germania, 97 more—including many lower-case, numerals, punctuation marks. 104pp. 8⅛ x 11. 24695-7

HOW TO DO BEADWORK, Mary White. Fundamental book on craft from simple projects to five-bead chains and woven works. 106 illustrations. 142pp. 5⅜ x 8. 20697-1

THE BOOK OF WOOD CARVING, Charles Marshall Sayers. Finest book for beginners discusses fundamentals and offers 34 designs. "Absolutely first rate . . . well thought out and well executed."–E. J. Tangerman. 118pp. 7¾ x 10⅝. 23654-4

ILLUSTRATED CATALOG OF CIVIL WAR MILITARY GOODS: Union Army Weapons, Insignia, Uniform Accessories, and Other Equipment, Schuyler, Hartley, and Graham. Rare, profusely illustrated 1846 catalog includes Union Army uniform and dress regulations, arms and ammunition, coats, insignia, flags, swords, rifles, etc. 226 illustrations. 160pp. 9 x 12. 24939-5

WOMEN'S FASHIONS OF THE EARLY 1900s: An Unabridged Republication of "New York Fashions, 1909," National Cloak & Suit Co. Rare catalog of mail-order fashions documents women's and children's clothing styles shortly after the turn of the century. Captions offer full descriptions, prices. Invaluable resource for fashion, costume historians. Approximately 725 illustrations. 128pp. 8⅜ x 11¼. 27276-1

THE 1912 AND 1915 GUSTAV STICKLEY FURNITURE CATALOGS, Gustav Stickley. With over 200 detailed illustrations and descriptions, these two catalogs are essential reading and reference materials and identification guides for Stickley furniture. Captions cite materials, dimensions and prices. 112pp. 6½ x 9¼. 26676-1

EARLY AMERICAN LOCOMOTIVES, John H. White, Jr. Finest locomotive engravings from early 19th century: historical (1804–74), main-line (after 1870), special, foreign, etc. 147 plates. 142pp. 11⅜ x 8¼. 22772-3

THE TALL SHIPS OF TODAY IN PHOTOGRAPHS, Frank O. Braynard. Lavishly illustrated tribute to nearly 100 majestic contemporary sailing vessels: Amerigo Vespucci, Clearwater, Constitution, Eagle, Mayflower, Sea Cloud, Victory, many more. Authoritative captions provide statistics, background on each ship. 190 black-and-white photographs and illustrations. Introduction. 128pp. 8⅞ x 11¾. 27163-3

LITTLE BOOK OF EARLY AMERICAN CRAFTS AND TRADES, Peter Stockham (ed.). 1807 children's book explains crafts and trades: baker, hatter, cooper, potter, and many others. 23 copperplate illustrations. 140pp. 4⅝ x 6.   23336-7

VICTORIAN FASHIONS AND COSTUMES FROM HARPER'S BAZAR, 1867–1898, Stella Blum (ed.). Day costumes, evening wear, sports clothes, shoes, hats, other accessories in over 1,000 detailed engravings. 320pp. 9⅜ x 12¼.   22990-4

GUSTAV STICKLEY, THE CRAFTSMAN, Mary Ann Smith. Superb study surveys broad scope of Stickley's achievement, especially in architecture. Design philosophy, rise and fall of the Craftsman empire, descriptions and floor plans for many Craftsman houses, more. 86 black-and-white halftones. 31 line illustrations. Introduction 208pp. 6½ x 9¼.   27210-9

THE LONG ISLAND RAIL ROAD IN EARLY PHOTOGRAPHS, Ron Ziel. Over 220 rare photos, informative text document origin (1844) and development of rail service on Long Island. Vintage views of early trains, locomotives, stations, passengers, crews, much more. Captions. 8⅞ x 11¾.   26301-0

VOYAGE OF THE LIBERDADE, Joshua Slocum. Great 19th-century mariner's thrilling, first-hand account of the wreck of his ship off South America, the 35-foot boat he built from the wreckage, and its remarkable voyage home. 128pp. 5⅜ x 8½.
40022-0

TEN BOOKS ON ARCHITECTURE, Vitruvius. The most important book ever written on architecture. Early Roman aesthetics, technology, classical orders, site selection, all other aspects. Morgan translation. 331pp. 5⅜ x 8½.   20645-9

THE HUMAN FIGURE IN MOTION, Eadweard Muybridge. More than 4,500 stopped-action photos, in action series, showing undraped men, women, children jumping, lying down, throwing, sitting, wrestling, carrying, etc. 390pp. 7⅞ x 10⅝.
20204-6 Clothbd.

TREES OF THE EASTERN AND CENTRAL UNITED STATES AND CANADA, William M. Harlow. Best one-volume guide to 140 trees. Full descriptions, woodlore, range, etc. Over 600 illustrations. Handy size. 288pp. 4½ x 6⅜.   20395-6

SONGS OF WESTERN BIRDS, Dr. Donald J. Borror. Complete song and call repertoire of 60 western species, including flycatchers, juncoes, cactus wrens, many more–includes fully illustrated booklet.   Cassette and manual 99913-0

GROWING AND USING HERBS AND SPICES, Milo Miloradovich. Versatile handbook provides all the information needed for cultivation and use of all the herbs and spices available in North America. 4 illustrations. Index. Glossary. 236pp. 5⅜ x 8½.
25058-X

BIG BOOK OF MAZES AND LABYRINTHS, Walter Shepherd. 50 mazes and labyrinths in all–classical, solid, ripple, and more–in one great volume. Perfect inexpensive puzzler for clever youngsters. Full solutions. 112pp. 8⅛ x 11.   22951-3

CATALOG OF DOVER BOOKS

PIANO TUNING, J. Cree Fischer. Clearest, best book for beginner, amateur. Simple repairs, raising dropped notes, tuning by easy method of flattened fifths. No previous skills needed. 4 illustrations. 201pp. 5⅜ x 8½. 23267-0

HINTS TO SINGERS, Lillian Nordica. Selecting the right teacher, developing confidence, overcoming stage fright, and many other important skills receive thoughtful discussion in this indispensible guide, written by a world-famous diva of four decades' experience. 96pp. 5⅜ x 8½. 40094-8

THE COMPLETE NONSENSE OF EDWARD LEAR, Edward Lear. All nonsense limericks, zany alphabets, Owl and Pussycat, songs, nonsense botany, etc., illustrated by Lear. Total of 320pp. 5⅜ x 8½. (Available in U.S. only.) 20167-8

VICTORIAN PARLOUR POETRY: An Annotated Anthology, Michael R. Turner. 117 gems by Longfellow, Tennyson, Browning, many lesser-known poets. "The Village Blacksmith," "Curfew Must Not Ring Tonight," "Only a Baby Small," dozens more, often difficult to find elsewhere. Index of poets, titles, first lines. xxiii + 325pp. 5⅜ x 8¼. 27044-0

DUBLINERS, James Joyce. Fifteen stories offer vivid, tightly focused observations of the lives of Dublin's poorer classes. At least one, "The Dead," is considered a masterpiece. Reprinted complete and unabridged from standard edition. 160pp. 5³⁄₁₆ x 8¼. 26870-5

GREAT WEIRD TALES: 14 Stories by Lovecraft, Blackwood, Machen and Others, S. T. Joshi (ed.). 14 spellbinding tales, including "The Sin Eater," by Fiona McLeod, "The Eye Above the Mantel," by Frank Belknap Long, as well as renowned works by R. H. Barlow, Lord Dunsany, Arthur Machen, W. C. Morrow and eight other masters of the genre. 256pp. 5⅜ x 8½. (Available in U.S. only.) 40436-6

THE BOOK OF THE SACRED MAGIC OF ABRAMELIN THE MAGE, translated by S. MacGregor Mathers. Medieval manuscript of ceremonial magic. Basic document in Aleister Crowley, Golden Dawn groups. 268pp. 5⅜ x 8½. 23211-5

NEW RUSSIAN-ENGLISH AND ENGLISH-RUSSIAN DICTIONARY, M. A. O'Brien. This is a remarkably handy Russian dictionary, containing a surprising amount of information, including over 70,000 entries. 366pp. 4½ x 6⅛. 20208-9

HISTORIC HOMES OF THE AMERICAN PRESIDENTS, Second, Revised Edition, Irvin Haas. A traveler's guide to American Presidential homes, most open to the public, depicting and describing homes occupied by every American President from George Washington to George Bush. With visiting hours, admission charges, travel routes. 175 photographs. Index. 160pp. 8¼ x 11. 26751-2

NEW YORK IN THE FORTIES, Andreas Feininger. 162 brilliant photographs by the well-known photographer, formerly with *Life* magazine. Commuters, shoppers, Times Square at night, much else from city at its peak. Captions by John von Hartz. 181pp. 9¼ x 10¾. 23585-8

INDIAN SIGN LANGUAGE, William Tomkins. Over 525 signs developed by Sioux and other tribes. Written instructions and diagrams. Also 290 pictographs. 111pp. 6⅛ x 9¼. 22029-X

CATALOG OF DOVER BOOKS

ANATOMY: A Complete Guide for Artists, Joseph Sheppard. A master of figure drawing shows artists how to render human anatomy convincingly. Over 460 illustrations. 224pp. 8⅜ x 11¼. 27279-6

MEDIEVAL CALLIGRAPHY: Its History and Technique, Marc Drogin. Spirited history, comprehensive instruction manual covers 13 styles (ca. 4th century through 15th). Excellent photographs; directions for duplicating medieval techniques with modern tools. 224pp. 8⅝ x 11¼. 26142-5

DRIED FLOWERS: How to Prepare Them, Sarah Whitlock and Martha Rankin. Complete instructions on how to use silica gel, meal and borax, perlite aggregate, sand and borax, glycerine and water to create attractive permanent flower arrangements. 12 illustrations. 32pp. 5⅜ x 8½. 21802-3

EASY-TO-MAKE BIRD FEEDERS FOR WOODWORKERS, Scott D. Campbell. Detailed, simple-to-use guide for designing, constructing, caring for and using feeders. Text, illustrations for 12 classic and contemporary designs. 96pp. 5⅜ x 8½.
25847-5

SCOTTISH WONDER TALES FROM MYTH AND LEGEND, Donald A. Mackenzie. 16 lively tales tell of giants rumbling down mountainsides, of a magic wand that turns stone pillars into warriors, of gods and goddesses, evil hags, powerful forces and more. 240pp. 5⅜ x 8½. 29677-6

THE HISTORY OF UNDERCLOTHES, C. Willett Cunnington and Phyllis Cunnington. Fascinating, well-documented survey covering six centuries of English undergarments, enhanced with over 100 illustrations: 12th-century laced-up bodice, footed long drawers (1795), 19th-century bustles, 19th-century corsets for men, Victorian "bust improvers," much more. 272pp. 5⅜ x 8¼. 27124-2

ARTS AND CRAFTS FURNITURE: The Complete Brooks Catalog of 1912, Brooks Manufacturing Co. Photos and detailed descriptions of more than 150 now very collectible furniture designs from the Arts and Crafts movement depict davenports, settees, buffets, desks, tables, chairs, bedsteads, dressers and more, all built of solid, quarter-sawed oak. Invaluable for students and enthusiasts of antiques, Americana and the decorative arts. 80pp. 6½ x 9¼. 27471-3

WILBUR AND ORVILLE: A Biography of the Wright Brothers, Fred Howard. Definitive, crisply written study tells the full story of the brothers' lives and work. A vividly written biography, unparalleled in scope and color, that also captures the spirit of an extraordinary era. 560pp. 6⅛ x 9¼. 40297-5

THE ARTS OF THE SAILOR: Knotting, Splicing and Ropework, Hervey Garrett Smith. Indispensable shipboard reference covers tools, basic knots and useful hitches; handsewing and canvas work, more. Over 100 illustrations. Delightful reading for sea lovers. 256pp. 5⅜ x 8½. 26440-8

FRANK LLOYD WRIGHT'S FALLINGWATER: The House and Its History, Second, Revised Edition, Donald Hoffmann. A total revision—both in text and illustrations—of the standard document on Fallingwater, the boldest, most personal architectural statement of Wright's mature years, updated with valuable new material from the recently opened Frank Lloyd Wright Archives. "Fascinating"–*The New York Times*. 116 illustrations. 128pp. 9¼ x 10¾. 27430-6

PHOTOGRAPHIC SKETCHBOOK OF THE CIVIL WAR, Alexander Gardner. 100 photos taken on field during the Civil War. Famous shots of Manassas Harper's Ferry, Lincoln, Richmond, slave pens, etc. 244pp. 10⅝ x 8¼. 22731-6

FIVE ACRES AND INDEPENDENCE, Maurice G. Kains. Great back-to-the-land classic explains basics of self-sufficient farming. The one book to get. 95 illustrations. 397pp. 5⅜ x 8½. 20974-1

SONGS OF EASTERN BIRDS, Dr. Donald J. Borror. Songs and calls of 60 species most common to eastern U.S.: warblers, woodpeckers, flycatchers, thrushes, larks, many more in high-quality recording. Cassette and manual 99912-2

A MODERN HERBAL, Margaret Grieve. Much the fullest, most exact, most useful compilation of herbal material. Gigantic alphabetical encyclopedia, from aconite to zedoary, gives botanical information, medical properties, folklore, economic uses, much else. Indispensable to serious reader. 161 illustrations. 888pp. 6½ x 9¼. 2-vol. set. (Available in U.S. only.) Vol. I: 22798-7
Vol. II: 22799-5

HIDDEN TREASURE MAZE BOOK, Dave Phillips. Solve 34 challenging mazes accompanied by heroic tales of adventure. Evil dragons, people-eating plants, bloodthirsty giants, many more dangerous adversaries lurk at every twist and turn. 34 mazes, stories, solutions. 48pp. 8¼ x 11. 24566-7

LETTERS OF W. A. MOZART, Wolfgang A. Mozart. Remarkable letters show bawdy wit, humor, imagination, musical insights, contemporary musical world; includes some letters from Leopold Mozart. 276pp. 5⅜ x 8½. 22859-2

BASIC PRINCIPLES OF CLASSICAL BALLET, Agrippina Vaganova. Great Russian theoretician, teacher explains methods for teaching classical ballet. 118 illustrations. 175pp. 5⅜ x 8½. 22036-2

THE JUMPING FROG, Mark Twain. Revenge edition. The original story of The Celebrated Jumping Frog of Calaveras County, a hapless French translation, and Twain's hilarious "retranslation" from the French. 12 illustrations. 66pp. 5⅜ x 8½. 22686-7

BEST REMEMBERED POEMS, Martin Gardner (ed.). The 126 poems in this superb collection of 19th- and 20th-century British and American verse range from Shelley's "To a Skylark" to the impassioned "Renascence" of Edna St. Vincent Millay and to Edward Lear's whimsical "The Owl and the Pussycat." 224pp. 5⅜ x 8½. 27165-X

COMPLETE SONNETS, William Shakespeare. Over 150 exquisite poems deal with love, friendship, the tyranny of time, beauty's evanescence, death and other themes in language of remarkable power, precision and beauty. Glossary of archaic terms. 80pp. 5³⁄₁₆ x 8¼. 26686-9

THE BATTLES THAT CHANGED HISTORY, Fletcher Pratt. Eminent historian profiles 16 crucial conflicts, ancient to modern, that changed the course of civilization. 352pp. 5⅜ x 8½. 41129-X

THE WIT AND HUMOR OF OSCAR WILDE, Alvin Redman (ed.). More than 1,000 ripostes, paradoxes, wisecracks: Work is the curse of the drinking classes; I can resist everything except temptation; etc. 258pp. 5⅜ x 8½. 20602-5

SHAKESPEARE LEXICON AND QUOTATION DICTIONARY, Alexander Schmidt. Full definitions, locations, shades of meaning in every word in plays and poems. More than 50,000 exact quotations. 1,485pp. 6½ x 9¼. 2-vol. set.
Vol. 1: 22726-X
Vol. 2: 22727-8

SELECTED POEMS, Emily Dickinson. Over 100 best-known, best-loved poems by one of America's foremost poets, reprinted from authoritative early editions. No comparable edition at this price. Index of first lines. 64pp. 5³⁄₁₆ x 8¼. 26466-1

THE INSIDIOUS DR. FU-MANCHU, Sax Rohmer. The first of the popular mystery series introduces a pair of English detectives to their archnemesis, the diabolical Dr. Fu-Manchu. Flavorful atmosphere, fast-paced action, and colorful characters enliven this classic of the genre. 208pp. 5³⁄₁₆ x 8¼. 29898-1

THE MALLEUS MALEFICARUM OF KRAMER AND SPRENGER, translated by Montague Summers. Full text of most important witchhunter's "bible," used by both Catholics and Protestants. 278pp. 6⅝ x 10. 22802-9

SPANISH STORIES/CUENTOS ESPAÑOLES: A Dual-Language Book, Angel Flores (ed.). Unique format offers 13 great stories in Spanish by Cervantes, Borges, others. Faithful English translations on facing pages. 352pp. 5⅜ x 8½. 25399-6

GARDEN CITY, LONG ISLAND, IN EARLY PHOTOGRAPHS, 1869–1919, Mildred H. Smith. Handsome treasury of 118 vintage pictures, accompanied by carefully researched captions, document the Garden City Hotel fire (1899), the Vanderbilt Cup Race (1908), the first airmail flight departing from the Nassau Boulevard Aerodrome (1911), and much more. 96pp. 8⅞ x 11¾. 40669-5

OLD QUEENS, N.Y., IN EARLY PHOTOGRAPHS, Vincent F. Seyfried and William Asadorian. Over 160 rare photographs of Maspeth, Jamaica, Jackson Heights, and other areas. Vintage views of DeWitt Clinton mansion, 1939 World's Fair and more. Captions. 192pp. 8⅞ x 11. 26358-4

CAPTURED BY THE INDIANS: 15 Firsthand Accounts, 1750-1870, Frederick Drimmer. Astounding true historical accounts of grisly torture, bloody conflicts, relentless pursuits, miraculous escapes and more, by people who lived to tell the tale. 384pp. 5⅜ x 8½. 24901-8

THE WORLD'S GREAT SPEECHES (Fourth Enlarged Edition), Lewis Copeland, Lawrence W. Lamm, and Stephen J. McKenna. Nearly 300 speeches provide public speakers with a wealth of updated quotes and inspiration—from Pericles' funeral oration and William Jennings Bryan's "Cross of Gold Speech" to Malcolm X's powerful words on the Black Revolution and Earl of Spenser's tribute to his sister, Diana, Princess of Wales. 944pp. 5⅜ x 8⅜. 40903-1

THE BOOK OF THE SWORD, Sir Richard F. Burton. Great Victorian scholar/adventurer's eloquent, erudite history of the "queen of weapons"—from prehistory to early Roman Empire. Evolution and development of early swords, variations (sabre, broadsword, cutlass, scimitar, etc.), much more. 336pp. 6⅛ x 9¼. 25434-8

CATALOG OF DOVER BOOKS

AUTOBIOGRAPHY: The Story of My Experiments with Truth, Mohandas K. Gandhi. Boyhood, legal studies, purification, the growth of the Satyagraha (nonviolent protest) movement. Critical, inspiring work of the man responsible for the freedom of India. 480pp. 5⅜ x 8½. (Available in U.S. only.)　24593-4

CELTIC MYTHS AND LEGENDS, T. W. Rolleston. Masterful retelling of Irish and Welsh stories and tales. Cuchulain, King Arthur, Deirdre, the Grail, many more. First paperback edition. 58 full-page illustrations. 512pp. 5⅜ x 8½.　26507-2

THE PRINCIPLES OF PSYCHOLOGY, William James. Famous long course complete, unabridged. Stream of thought, time perception, memory, experimental methods; great work decades ahead of its time. 94 figures. 1,391pp. 5⅜ x 8½. 2-vol. set.
Vol. I: 20381-6　Vol. II: 20382-4

THE WORLD AS WILL AND REPRESENTATION, Arthur Schopenhauer. Definitive English translation of Schopenhauer's life work, correcting more than 1,000 errors, omissions in earlier translations. Translated by E. F. J. Payne. Total of 1,269pp. 5⅜ x 8½. 2-vol. set.　Vol. 1: 21761-2　Vol. 2: 21762-0

MAGIC AND MYSTERY IN TIBET, Madame Alexandra David-Neel. Experiences among lamas, magicians, sages, sorcerers, Bonpa wizards. A true psychic discovery. 32 illustrations. 321pp. 5⅜ x 8½. (Available in U.S. only.)　22682-4

THE EGYPTIAN BOOK OF THE DEAD, E. A. Wallis Budge. Complete reproduction of Ani's papyrus, finest ever found. Full hieroglyphic text, interlinear transliteration, word-for-word translation, smooth translation. 533pp. 6½ x 9¼.　21866-X

MATHEMATICS FOR THE NONMATHEMATICIAN, Morris Kline. Detailed, college-level treatment of mathematics in cultural and historical context, with numerous exercises. Recommended Reading Lists. Tables. Numerous figures. 641pp. 5⅜ x 8½.　24823-2

PROBABILISTIC METHODS IN THE THEORY OF STRUCTURES, Isaac Elishakoff. Well-written introduction covers the elements of the theory of probability from two or more random variables, the reliability of such multivariable structures, the theory of random function, Monte Carlo methods of treating problems incapable of exact solution, and more. Examples. 502pp. 5⅜ x 8½.　40691-1

THE RIME OF THE ANCIENT MARINER, Gustave Doré, S. T. Coleridge. Doré's finest work; 34 plates capture moods, subtleties of poem. Flawless full-size reproductions printed on facing pages with authoritative text of poem. "Beautiful. Simply beautiful."–Publisher's Weekly. 77pp. 9¼ x 12.　22305-1

NORTH AMERICAN INDIAN DESIGNS FOR ARTISTS AND CRAFTSPEOPLE, Eva Wilson. Over 360 authentic copyright-free designs adapted from Navajo blankets, Hopi pottery, Sioux buffalo hides, more. Geometrics, symbolic figures, plant and animal motifs, etc. 128pp. 8⅜ x 11. (Not for sale in the United Kingdom.)　25341-4

SCULPTURE: Principles and Practice, Louis Slobodkin. Step-by-step approach to clay, plaster, metals, stone; classical and modern. 253 drawings, photos. 255pp. 8⅛ x 11.　22960-2

THE INFLUENCE OF SEA POWER UPON HISTORY, 1660–1783, A. T. Mahan. Influential classic of naval history and tactics still used as text in war colleges. First paperback edition. 4 maps. 24 battle plans. 640pp. 5⅜ x 8½.　25509-3

CATALOG OF DOVER BOOKS

THE STORY OF THE TITANIC AS TOLD BY ITS SURVIVORS, Jack Winocour (ed.). What it was really like. Panic, despair, shocking inefficiency, and a little heroism. More thrilling than any fictional account. 26 illustrations. 320pp. 5⅜ x 8½.
20610-6

FAIRY AND FOLK TALES OF THE IRISH PEASANTRY, William Butler Yeats (ed.). Treasury of 64 tales from the twilight world of Celtic myth and legend: "The Soul Cages," "The Kildare Pooka," "King O'Toole and his Goose," many more. Introduction and Notes by W. B. Yeats. 352pp. 5⅜ x 8½.
26941-8

BUDDHIST MAHAYANA TEXTS, E. B. Cowell and others (eds.). Superb, accurate translations of basic documents in Mahayana Buddhism, highly important in history of religions. The Buddha-karita of Asvaghosha, Larger Sukhavativyuha, more. 448pp. 5⅜ x 8½.
25552-2

ONE TWO THREE . . . INFINITY: Facts and Speculations of Science, George Gamow. Great physicist's fascinating, readable overview of contemporary science: number theory, relativity, fourth dimension, entropy, genes, atomic structure, much more. 128 illustrations. Index. 352pp. 5⅜ x 8½.
25664-2

EXPERIMENTATION AND MEASUREMENT, W. J. Youden. Introductory manual explains laws of measurement in simple terms and offers tips for achieving accuracy and minimizing errors. Mathematics of measurement, use of instruments, experimenting with machines. 1994 edition. Foreword. Preface. Introduction. Epilogue. Selected Readings. Glossary. Index. Tables and figures. 128pp. 5⅜ x 8½.
40451-X

DALÍ ON MODERN ART: The Cuckolds of Antiquated Modern Art, Salvador Dalí. Influential painter skewers modern art and its practitioners. Outrageous evaluations of Picasso, Cézanne, Turner, more. 15 renderings of paintings discussed. 44 calligraphic decorations by Dalí. 96pp. 5⅜ x 8½. (Available in U.S. only.)
29220-7

ANTIQUE PLAYING CARDS: A Pictorial History, Henry René D'Allemagne. Over 900 elaborate, decorative images from rare playing cards (14th–20th centuries): Bacchus, death, dancing dogs, hunting scenes, royal coats of arms, players cheating, much more. 96pp. 9¼ x 12¼.
29265-7

MAKING FURNITURE MASTERPIECES: 30 Projects with Measured Drawings, Franklin H. Gottshall. Step-by-step instructions, illustrations for constructing handsome, useful pieces, among them a Sheraton desk, Chippendale chair, Spanish desk, Queen Anne table and a William and Mary dressing mirror. 224pp. 8⅛ x 11¼.
29338-6

THE FOSSIL BOOK: A Record of Prehistoric Life, Patricia V. Rich et al. Profusely illustrated definitive guide covers everything from single-celled organisms and dinosaurs to birds and mammals and the interplay between climate and man. Over 1,500 illustrations. 760pp. 7½ x 10⅛.
29371-8